Jennifer Armintrout was born in 1980. She has been obsessed with vampires ever since the age of four and her first crush was on Vincent Price. Raised in an enormous Roman Catholic family, Jennifer attributes her interest in the macabre to viewing too many funerals at a formative age. Jennifer lives in Michigan with her husband and children.

Also by
Jennifer Armintrout

BLOOD TIES BOOK ONE:
THE TURNING

BLOOD TIES BOOK TWO:
POSSESSION

BLOOD TIES BOOK THREE:
ASHES TO ASHES

BLOOD TIES BOOK FOUR:
ALL SOULS' NIGHT

BLOOD TIES

POSSESSION

Jennifer Armintrout

MIRA

All the characters in this book have no existence outside the imagination
of the author, and have no relation whatsoever to anyone bearing the
same name or names. They are not even distantly inspired by any
individual known or unknown to the author, and all the incidents are
pure invention.

First published in Great Britain 2010.
MIRA Books, Eton House, 18-24 Paradise Road,
Richmond, Surrey, TW9 1SR

© Jennifer Armintrout 2007

ISBN 978 0 7783 0400 5

58-0410

MIRA's policy is to use papers that are natural, renewable and
recyclable products and made from wood grown in sustainable forests.
The logging and manufacturing processes conform to the legal
environmental regulations of the country of origin.

Printed in Great Britain
by Clays Ltd, St Ives plc

For my family, who encourage me and support everything I do, but especially for Ryerson Louden, who always listened to a child's wild stories and pretended he actually believed them.

ACKNOWLEDGEMENTS

Credit is due:

As always, to my critique group, Mary, Marti, Cheryl, Chris and Michele, even though she swears she'll never read another book by me ever again.

To Sasha Bogin, an editor and a cheerleader, and Kelly Harms, my agent, who I imagine would make a wonderful pirate or hostage negotiator.

To Joe, for listening to me rant about my characters the way some people rant about their co-workers: "Jen, are we talking about a real person now, or someone in your book?"

And to Kevin Park, whom I forgot to mention in the last book, for literally saving my life and not holding the whole disgusting trip to the ER against me. Hopefully, subsequent birthdays have gone much better for you.

Prologue

Welcome Back

He didn't know how long he'd been dead. There was no time, no season, no change, only eternity.

Shadows stumbled around him on the other side of the veil. Two in particular caught his attention. He knew what they were. He'd been one of them.

The life he craved was accessible to them. Now, as in his living death, he wanted to leech it from the mortals who couldn't protect themselves. If he could envy this undead pair, he would, but there was no time. They had no life, so they were none of his concern.

On the other side, they couldn't see him. When he was of the world but not alive, he couldn't see the ones who'd gone before him, either. Despite their sightlessness, they appeared to follow him. He moved away. He wanted life.

It was a fool's errand, his never-ceasing search for that mortal energy. It throbbed in the people and animals he passed every day, but he could not touch it. Thin though the veil was, it separated him from what he craved. He could reach for it, hold it in his hands, but the film of the shadow curtain always kept him from it.

Color, alien to this existence, would have shocked his senses, if he'd had any. The lifeless pair held something between them, shimmering and frightening like the fiery sword the angel held at the gates of Eden. It drew shadows to it like moths to the flame, though he hated such cliché description. He hated more that the thing drew him, as well. The shining rift split wider, and a hand, not full of life but real nonetheless, thrust through.

The other shadows clamored for it, sliding over it. Like water on oil, they rolled off the corporeal skin. As if searching specifically for him, the intruder pushed the others aside and grasped him. He stuck.

He hadn't felt panic since he'd died. Hadn't felt despair since her betrayal. He felt it now as the rough, real fingers pulled him through the rift.

Thick and heavy, feelings he'd almost forgotten happened all at once. Slippery and hot, sensations he remembered being pleasant at one time engulfed him. His formless being squeezed and conformed into a shape at once familiar and hor-rifyingly foreign.

Too bright. Too cold. Too real.

Too loud.

One of the pair laughed like jagged glass. "We fucking did it! I can't believe we fucking did it!"

The light stung his eyes. He blinked, but his vision didn't clear. In his chest, he felt a thump that hadn't been a part of him for centuries—the beating of a human heart.

Alive. He was alive.

He dropped to the floor, screaming and clawing at his mortal prison.

The one who'd done it leaned over him and slapped him on the back. The connection of flesh against flesh drove needles of sensation to the bone.

"Welcome back, Cyrus."

1

Nightmare

"You dreamed about him this morning, Carrie."

At the sound of Nathan's voice, my hands froze on my keyboard. "You're watching me sleep again?"

This worried me. Besides being phenomenally creepy, my sire's habit of spying on my nightmares usually flares up when there's trouble on the horizon. Before our big fight with *him* two months ago, I'd often wake to find Nathan in bed beside me, staring at me as though I'd disappear if he looked away. Just three weeks after that, when our new blood donor had broken in with the intent to stake us in our beds, Nathan had been sitting in my desk chair, watching over me, waiting for something, anything to happen.

Rather than looming in my doorway, he'd come in and sat down on my bed—there really was no place else to go, the room was so small—and settled in as though he'd been invited. Not that I'd been offended. It *was* his apartment, and Ziggy's old room didn't feel quite like home to me.

I studied Nathan as he watched me. I assumed he tried to gauge my mood. He detests arguing with me, and he'd obviously had other hopes for how the conversation would go.

Tough.

"So, I'm worried." At my arched brow, he acceded, "Fine, I'm irrationally angry with you."

Damn him for looking good. Time stops bothering with you when you become a vampire, and Nathan was frozen at thirty-two. Despite the pallor that comes with seventy years of avoiding sunlight, he remained just as young and handsome as he'd appeared in the photographs he'd saved from his prevampire life. More so, actually, because this Nathan was in my bedroom, in living color. Dark hair, gorgeous gray eyes, a body so toned and hard he looked like he'd been a statue of a Greek god in a past life. But it was his eyes that had made me fall for him. Even though he'd been acting tough, and threatening my life the first time we'd met, I'd seen the kindness and sorrow in them. His eyes weren't just windows to his soul. They were doors that let out things he wouldn't have been able to hide from me even without a blood tie between us.

I'd turned back to my computer, where my latest dissertation on vampire physiology had waited with an impatiently flashing cursor. You can take the human out of the doctor, but you can't take the doctor out of the vampire. Or something like that. I'd been working on *A Case Study of Blood Type Compatibility for Metabolic Efficiency* to kill time and distract me from the craziness of the past two months. But it had inevitably caught up with me, so when Nathan had burst in I'd been typing "Crazy Yellow Tube Socks" over and over again. "You said irrationally, not me."

"I can't help it." His embarrassment was evident through the blood tie, but it didn't quell my annoyance. "What's going on?"

"Well, for one, I'm tired of this stupid research project—"

"*You're* tired of it? I was the one drinking AB negative all damn week." Though he chuckled, there was a wearing note to the sound.

"And you've been watching me sleep, which usually means something major is about to happen. Plus, I've been having these nightmares." I covered my face with my hands, massaging my tired skin. "I'm sure it's nothing."

"It didn't sound like 'nothing.'" The bedsprings squeaked as he stood.

I dropped my hands and gave him a withering look. "Oh, he listens as well as watches."

The ghost of a sarcastic smile crossed his face as he knelt beside my chair. "You make it sound so dirty."

I knew he couldn't help the surge of playful lust that reached me through the blood tie, because our brains were on a weird, telepathic party line. Unless he blocked me or vice versa, we heard each other's thoughts and felt each other's emotions. If one of us had even the slightest inclination toward getting physical, the other one knew—and usually acted on—it.

Unfortunately, the blood tie doesn't filter negative emotions out, so I always got a heaping helping of after-sex guilt. Thoughts of Marianne, his dead wife, were never far from his mind, so the punishment game usually kicked in within minutes of *la petit mort*. Once I felt his guilt, I added some of my own over the fact I'd helped cause it, and the resultant snowball effect was a good enough reason to avoid sex with him altogether.

At least, not beyond a few just-to-get-it-out-of-our-system flings. Giving those up would be like kicking heroin cold turkey.

The thought depressed me, so I put it aside. I swiveled my desk chair around and leaned back. "Seriously, why are you watching me?"

"The nightmares."

I shrugged, hoping to pass off my terrifying dreams as a regular occurrence. "I have a lot of nightmares."

"You said *his* name."

Nathan wasn't my first sire. Cyrus, whom I only knew as "John Doe" when he'd attacked me in the hospital morgue, had made me a vampire. He'd also nearly made me dead when I hadn't been willing to satisfy his twisted desires. When I'd turned to Nathan and the Voluntary Vampire Extinction Movement for help, Cyrus had removed one of my two hearts— a strange physiological trait unique to vampires—and left me bleeding to death in the alley behind Nathan's building. When Nathan found me, I'd already died. He'd revived me by giving me his blood, and it'd had the desired effect—I was alive, after all. He just hadn't realized he would "re-sire" me.

He'd already had a deep-seated hatred of Cyrus. Now, as my new sire, he felt it ten times stronger. He hated if I even mentioned my first sire in passing. The evil, antagonistic side of me couldn't help but do it now. "Maybe my dreams about Cyrus are a subconscious thing to rile you."

He raised an eyebrow. "That's the same excuse you use for leaving the cap off the toothpaste."

He was right. He's usually right. *Damned sire's intuition.* I shut off my computer monitor and leaned back in my chair. "I'm guessing you have some sort of theory here."

"Not yet. I was hoping to form it while you tell me—in detail—about these dreams. Then I was going to cut you off with a big, dramatic exclamation, something along the lines of 'aha!' at which point you'd find yourself impressed and slightly aroused by my genius." He shrugged. "But now, I guess I'll just settle for the detail part."

I rolled my eyes and folded my arms across my chest. "I never see his face, but I know it's him."

Nathan nodded, indicating I should continue.

"There aren't any colors except blue." I bit my lip. "The watercolor kind of blue I remember from when I was…dead."

A deep frown creased Nathan's brow, a sure sign I'd piqued his interest with my story. "Are you sure it's not your super-conscious working through that night?"

When I had those dreams, I always saw the same things. The bright orange cat that had passed my splayed body. The thick shapes of the shadow people coming to claim me. I didn't bother Nathan with these memories. My brief death—the second one—had traumatized him enough. "Cut the psych bullshit. You think I'm having these dreams for a reason, don't you?"

He let out a long breath as his mind searched for nonan-swers. "I suppose it could be some residue of your former blood tie to him."

"But why now?" I shook my head. "It's been two months. What could have happened to reactivate the tie now?"

Nathan stood, trying—and failing—to look unconcerned. "It could be anything. I'll have Max do some digging in the Movement files."

The Voluntary Vampire Extinction Movement was a harsh, totalitarian organization demanding the death of vampires who didn't live by their strict code. Nathan had been on probation for seventy years for killing his wife, though it hadn't been entirely his fault, and by siring me he'd broken one of the cardinal rules: preventing the inevitable death of a wounded vampire. Rather than wait until they found out and killed him, Nathan had chosen to go outlaw. But he maintained ties to Max Harrison, the only other vampire who knew the circum-stances surrounding Nathan and me.

I smiled. "I'm sure he'll be thrilled with the assignment."

"He doesn't have a choice," Nathan said cheerfully. He no longer hid the fact he lived to make Max's life hell. "Well, the sun's long down. I'd better get downstairs and earn my keep. Are you going to work tonight? I've got some inventory that needs cataloging."

"As tempting as it sounds, no." I'd clocked enough unpaid hours in Nathan's occult bookshop to last several lifetimes. If I never saw another Book of Shadows or packet of herbs, it would be too soon. I gestured to the computer. "I need to finish this before it drives me insane."

"Likewise." He made a face. "Next time you want to do some crazy experiment, use someone else as your lab rat."

I heard the door shut behind him as he left. Usually, he locked it, but I heard no telltale jingle of keys.

Vampires take the bond between sire and fledgling as seriously as humans do the bond between parent and child. Normally, Nathan was frighteningly overprotective of me. I tried to push aside the feeling that something might be wrong. Those thoughts were like poison ivy. Once you scratch it, the infection spreads and grows. I didn't need to spend the night on pins and needles, jumping at the slightest sound.

I flipped on the monitor, hoping to lose myself in medical jargon, but I couldn't concentrate. My unease grew, my palms began to sweat and my stomach tingled. I ticked off the symptoms in my mind and only then recognized my body's reaction.

Fight or flight.

The primitive response to fear had slowly built in me, but I was in no immediate danger. My heart did a panicky flip-flop in my chest as I stared at my reflection behind the words on the screen. My pupils had dilated. My face began to morph into monster mode. I stood, willing myself to calm down. There was no reason to feel this way.

Unless it was the blood tie.

Nathan.

I ran from my room, knocking over my desk chair as I took off. Our apartment was on the top floor of Nathan's building. The bookstore was in the basement. I tore down the stairs as fast as I could, gripping the rails as my feet tripped gracelessly over themselves. The door at the bottom seemed light-years away. I burst through it and onto the street. The chill air of the early spring night took my breath away.

Then pain took it, and I gave up hope of getting it back.

The blood tie was gone. Not in the way it felt when Nathan simply hid his thoughts from me. That was like a brick wall. This was...void. If the tie were a length of cord stretched between us, one end had simply gone slack.

Nathan was dead.

I clutched the wrought-iron rail as I edged toward the top of the stairs descending below the sidewalk. Moonlight illuminated shattered glass at the bottom. Whatever had gotten to Nathan had broken the window to get in.

Get a weapon. Get help. My heart overrode my rational mind. I needed to get to my sire.

I took the stairs down two at a time. Inside, the light at the back of the store flickered in its death throes. Broken, powdery fluorescent tubes littered the floor. Occasional sparks sputtered like snowflakes from broken wiring overhead.

The tables that usually displayed tasteful arrangements of crystals and tarot cards and other New Age bric-a-brac were utterly destroyed. They lay in splinters on the ground, crushing the merchandise they'd once held. To my right, the glass case in the sales counter had been smashed. I knew Nathan kept an ax in the cupboard behind it. I moved in that direction as quietly as I could with glass crunching beneath my shoes.

Something shuffled in the labyrinth of bookshelves behind me.

The noise froze me for an instant as I weighed the distance to the door against the odds I'd be able to effectively defend myself with the ax. I dismissed the notion of running. I couldn't leave Nathan behind, not if there was even the barest chance he might be saved.

I sprinted the last few steps to the cupboard and retrieved the ax. I tried to force some courage into my stiff fingers as I gripped the handle. Whatever had broken in was still in the shop.

The hair on the back of my neck stood up. The thing hiding in the shadows growled.

The clock behind the counter chimed. I jumped. The creature sprang out at me.

My head bounced off the hard floor as the thing brought me down, and nasty fireworks of pain exploded in my vision. The smell of Nathan's blood, usually a welcome, familiar perfume, filled my nostrils with a sour tang, and I gagged. I squeezed my eyes shut tight and my muscles tensed as I tried not to vomit.

The weight of the thing pressing down on me lifted. I opened my eyes in time to see it leap behind the counter, its noisy respirations nearly drowning out the repeated chimes of the clock.

"Nathan?" I shrieked, barely recognizing my own voice for the panic in it. I screamed his name again. There was no answer.

It became starkly, startlingly clear to me: Nathan couldn't come to my aid. I was alone with this creature, and woefully unequipped to defend myself.

A loud snarl sounded behind the counter. In a split second of sheer terror, I threw the ax that way. It hit the cash register and bounced to the floor, out of my reach.

Alone. Woefully unequipped. And blindingly stupid.

I didn't have long to worry about it. The creature leaped over the countertop and tackled me. My breath escaped in a loud whoosh, and I looked up through a haze of pain at the thing holding me down.

A man. A naked, bleeding man.

The creature hadn't killed Nathan. The creature *was* Nathan.

His face twisted in a feral snarl. His eyes were cold and devoid of recognition. He gripped a shard of blood-drenched glass in his fist. Bloody symbols marred his arms and chest, and I realized with a fresh wave of nausea that he'd carved them into his own flesh.

He bent his head toward me, and I turned my face. He leaned so close his breath stirred the hair at my temple, and he sniffed me. With an audible snarl he raised the glass shard high above his head.

"Nathan, please, don't," I whispered, but I knew he'd never hear. This thing was not Nathan. It was a monster wearing my sire's face.

He brought the shard down, and I flinched as it smashed to the floor beside my head. Warm, fresh blood sprayed across my face from his torn palm, and he gripped my chin and forced me to face him. He rasped in a language I didn't understand, and pushed away from me.

Though I sat up quickly, he was gone before I could see him go. The only evidence that he'd been there were his bloody footprints on the stairs to the street.

Trembling, I lifted my hand as if to reach for him. It was wet with his polluted blood. Usually, the smell of Nathan's blood comforted me. Now, something had tainted it, and the stench made me sick. I covered my nose with the collar of my shirt as I crawled to the door. The broken glass on the floor pricked my arms, but I barely felt it.

Like a zombie, I drifted up the stairs to the apartment, ignoring the blood dripping from my cut hands. My presence of mind returned enough for me to lock the door. Then I went to Nathan's room and sat on the edge of his bed, clutching the cordless phone. I dialed automatically, my gaze fixed on a snag in the carpet near the edge of the runner.

"Harrison." Max sounded chipper on the other end of the line. I wanted to be where he was, with no knowledge of what I'd just seen.

"It's Carrie." I swallowed hard, my tongue too thick for my mouth. "I need you."

2

Familiar Territory

The floor was cold, but the air was hot and too bright. Instinctively, Cyrus flinched from the sunlight touching his flesh.

His naked, human flesh.

How humiliating. He didn't have the energy to rail against the indignation. Fatigue plagued his bones, and hunger gnawed his guts.

As a vampire, he'd equated his need for blood with hunger, but it had been far more than physical desire. Blood hunger was a need for emotional fulfillment, the urge to indulge the most primal drive of his kind. To kill. To control. Human hunger was sadistic in its simplicity. Purely physical agony he hadn't felt in centuries.

What had happened to him?

He winced as he sat up, his muscles screaming in protest, and he collapsed again. Around him, he could make out a cavernous darkness. Above him, a cone of sunlight streamed down, casting a circle of protection, as Dahlia would have called it. *Dahlia.* If she'd had anything to do with this he would rip her pretty little head off her fat shoulders, human or not. As soon as he recovered, he was certain his rage would give him strength enough to take on a whole army of vampire witches.

There were voices in the darkness, but he couldn't see who they belonged to. Though his vision hadn't cleared, it was far better than it had been when he'd been dead.

Dead. Carrie. The pain of her betrayal came back with surprising ferocity. She'd refused his love, refused his blood. Then she'd plunged a knife through his heart without conscience. He could have almost admired that, if he hadn't been on the losing end.

Closing his eyes, he lay on the hard, cold floor. *Marble,* he thought. It was funny how things were coming back to him now, piece by piece. Perhaps that was proof of a soul. Memory of past lives. Dahlia had always insisted her soul had lived several lives as assorted notorious historical figures. No, he wouldn't start believing in a soul now. It would make the whole situation that much more ridiculous.

Like the unpleasant stretched sensation in his lower abdomen. He hadn't felt that in months, but the meaning came back to him effortlessly.

"Hello?" he called to the voices in the darkness, though a crude American "Hey!" might have been more appropriate, considering what they'd done to him. "I need to go to the toilet."

The voices bickered quietly among themselves, growing in intensity until someone shouted and broke the tension. "Well, then you go and get her!"

"Who?" Cyrus cried, but the noise from the darkness swallowed his words. He sincerely hoped the "her" in question wasn't one of the pair of vampires that had pulled him back. One had possessed a voice that would put a banshee to shame, and the other had been so gruff and masculine he'd thought for a moment she was a man.

A door scraped open, then slammed shut. A bloodcurdling scream of terror set off sparks of nostalgia in Cyrus's heart, and the door screeched open again. The *her* in question was apparently terrified. It gave him little satisfaction, as he wasn't terribly safe and secure himself.

"Get moving, bitch," a distorted voice commanded from the shadows.

A shape moved out of the darkness, pale and waifish. As she moved closer, colors swam together. The muted yellow of her dress faded into the plain brown of her hair and her paper-white skin. Blood red splashed across her torso, and ugly purple, black and blue scored her throat and ringed her eye.

She approached warily, halting about two paces from him, and knelt at his side. The sunlight touched her, but she did not burn. *Human.* His relief was palpable. He did not want to be food for the creatures he'd once ruled over.

"I'm here to help you," she said, her voice barely a whisper.

Cyrus looked her over in disdain. He couldn't stand soft-spoken women. They held no interest for him, and he considered anything that didn't amuse him extraneous. He reached a shaking hand to push her hair from her face, and touched the dark bruise marring her eye. "I see you don't listen well."

Her hands clenched to angry fists, earning his respect for a moment. Then she flinched and destroyed the illusion of courage. This wasn't the first black eye she'd received, he knew.

"Hang on to me," she whispered, helping him to his feet. "They said you wouldn't be able to walk."

How humiliating. He'd been deadly and powerful. Now, he was human. The vampires lurking in the shadows knew it. Though they kept their distance, their eagerness was palpable. He knew what he would feel in their place. Desire, curiosity. Not many vampires returned from the dead that he was aware of. That fact alone made him a delicacy.

One of the vampires snarled. Cyrus heard the jingle of chains as the creature approached, and he tensed. At his side, the girl quivered and shrieked. If he could have stood on his own, he would have thrown her to them.

"He's not to be harmed!" another vampire commanded, and the one advancing backed down.

"Where am I?" Cyrus asked, hating himself for relying on this girl.

"St. Anne's," she whispered. "A church."

"I gathered that. There are so few St. Anne's car washes these days." The door scraped open, and he gagged at the stench of death he used to revel in. He looked past the line of gleaming chrome motorcycles parked in the church vestibule, his eyes struggling to focus amid so much detail.

"They said they were going to bury them after the sun went down," the girl said quietly. "They never did."

Cyrus squinted at the tangled forms of two bodies on the carpet. One was dressed in black with a cleric's collar. The other was a woman with white hair, her button-down blouse and matronly cardigan slashed open to reveal the wrinkled skin of her chest. Her skirt tangled around her thighs, showing the tops of her knee-high stockings.

"Father Bart and Sister Helen," the girl whispered tear-fully. "They—"

"I know what they did to her." He turned his head and reached for the wall for support. "Cover her up."

Hello, conscience. We meet again.

When the girl returned to his side, she was trembling. He wanted to strike her for her weakness, as he would have in his former life. Now, he doubted he could lift his arm on his own. Shameful as it was, he relied on her. It wouldn't do much good to put her off helping him.

"The rectory is downstairs." She sniveled pathetically as she opened a door. Shag-carpeted steps led down into darkness.

"I think that's where they'll keep us. It's where they've been keeping me."

His mind raced, trying to piece together the information he remembered from his former life, and how it might apply to his current situation. "And who are 'they'?"

"Monsters." The word came out as less than a whisper.

He wished he could push her down the stairs. Unfortunately, that would send him tumbling, as well. "Yes, vampires. I know. But who are they?"

She shook her head. "I don't know what you're—"

"Who are they? Who are they allies with? Are they the Fangs or the Celts or the Coveners?" He searched his memory for the names of other vampire gangs, and his heart seized in fear. "They're not Movement?"

What a stupid question. Of course they weren't the Movement. It wouldn't make sense for the Voluntary Vampire *Extinction* Movement to bring vampires back from the dead.

Unless his new, human existence was some form of sadistic punishment they'd dreamed up. If it were, he could guess who'd moved his name to the top of that list.

The girl helped him down the stairs to a cinder block apartment with a cot, a reclining chair, a dented aluminum TV tray with a half-eaten microwave dinner and a copy of the TV Guide, turned to the crossword puzzle, atop it. A small bookshelf supported a television and a few books, with a bottle of holy water and a rosary nestled in the corner.

Cyrus gestured to the water. "Hide that."

The girl propped him against the wall before moving to do his bidding. "Why?"

"Because there are a lot of vampires upstairs, and they apparently didn't search this room thoroughly. Any potential weapon we can find would be nice to keep." He frowned at her as she picked up the bottle and walked past him, not sparing him a glance. "What's the matter with you?"

"Nothing." The word was accompanied by a hysterical, terrified hiccup. "Aside from being kidnapped by vampires and watching my two best friends murdered."

He wrinkled his nose at the thought. "If your two best friends were a nun and a priest, I'd say something is definitely the matter with you. But I meant why won't you look at me?"

This forced her to do so, her eyes wide behind a few slashes of mousy-brown hair. "Be-because you're naked."

It had been a long, long while since he'd had a good laugh at another's expense. He thoroughly enjoyed laughing now, though he wobbled precariously against the cinder blocks at his back. "Oh, let me guess. You're a sister, too, Sister?"

She blushed as if the thought was preposterous. "No."

"It's a shame. I always found nuns to be the most fun. They'd all say no at first, but they'd be begging for it by the time I was through." He shrugged and ignored her sob of horror. "I want to use the toilet and have a bath. You'll have to help me. And then you can find some of the preacher's clothes for me."

"What if they come down here?" She clutched his arm, apparently more afraid of their captors than his naked flesh.

"I'd suggest you drop the innocent act quickly. They're more likely to let you live if you're an active participant." He shook her off, then promptly fell to the floor. He couldn't stand the sound of her sharp, pitying gasp, so he tried to crawl.

"Let me help you," she said quietly, kneeling at his side. And, because he was so damn weak, he let her assist him to his feet.

The bathroom was small, nothing like he was used to in his former life. But it had a bathtub, and the hideous orange shag carpet didn't creep past the doorway. If it weren't for the unevenly patterned tile floor, he'd almost say this was his favorite room yet.

He endured the humiliation of another human helping him to use the toilet, then the girl set about turning on the rusted taps to fill the gleaming, porcelain tub.

She helped him into the water, and he hissed at the sting of it on his skin. She didn't seem to care, her thin arms quaking with obvious exhaustion as she lowered him into the tub. "Will you be able to sit up?"

"I am seated in a veritable cauldron of scalding water. I'll endeavor to keep the rest of myself out of it, yes."

She left him alone with his thoughts then, and there were a fair amount of them. Too exhausted to do little more than think, he considered the steps he would take now. First, he'd find out who had done this to him. Then he'd contact his father. *Unless it is Father who has done this.* That wasn't as far-fetched as he'd like to imagine. What didn't make sense was why dear old dad would bring him back as a human.

Of course, it might not have been his father at all. Cyrus prided himself on being a well-known name among vampires. Perhaps a fanatical group had raised him in hopes of fame or a favor.

Or for a sacrifice.

It wasn't unheard of. He'd helped his father sacrifice vampires for centuries. But the key word was *vampire.* Why was he *human?*

He had just gotten comfortable when a soft knock sounded.

"What?" He picked up the nearest object—a bar of soap—and flung it at the door.

The Mouse came in with a pile of neatly folded clothes. "Father Bart was shorter than you. And fatter."

"Pick up the soap." Cyrus watched as she bent to retrieve it. Nothing to write home about, he decided, tilting his head to study her backside.

In the past, he would have fed off her. She had long, slender legs that would have been heaven wrapped around him, and hair just the right length to pull and bare her throat for a bite. But her face was too innocent, her whole manner too timid. Her faded cotton sundress told endless tales of trips to Wal-Mart in Daddy's pickup truck, Garth Brooks blaring over the roar of the road through the open windows.

The vampire Cyrus would have taken his pleasure and her blood in one night, and she wouldn't have lived to see the dawn.

He missed blood more now than when he'd drifted aimlessly on the other side of the veil. He didn't want to think of it anymore.

When she stood and handed him the soap, he snatched it away. "What are those?" he snapped, gesturing to the clothes. "Polyester?"

"I don't know."

"Well, read the bloody tags. Are you completely worthless?" He grabbed the shirt from the top of the pile and scanned the care instructions before flinging it aside in disgust. "I only wear natural fiber."

The girl nodded uncertainly. "I don't think Father Bart had any—"

"The dead priest is not my fucking problem!" He slammed his fists down on the water, sloshing it over the sides of the tub.

The Mouse shrank away, screaming. It lifted Cyrus's spirits considerably to see the girl frightened.

"Get out. If you can't find anything suitable for me, you'll have to ask those morons upstairs." He leaned against the curved back of the tub and closed his eyes, savoring the girl's litany of pleas as she cowered on the floor.

Max arrived five hours later. I was buried beneath the covers on Nathan's bed, clinging to his scent like a life raft and trying to ignore the bedside radio he always kept on. The classic rock station was in the middle of a Fleetwood Mac Rock Block.

"Gypsy" was just finishing up when I heard the front door burst open.

"Carrie?" Something heavy hit the floor in the living room. Probably the duffel bag Max always carried with him. Loud footsteps ran down the hall and I climbed from beneath the blankets in time to see him skid to a stop at the doorway.

"What's going on? Where's Nathan?" Max scanned the room as if he'd see him there.

"Gone." I don't know if it was my relief at finally having an ally in my nightmare or if the reality of the situation had finally set in, but my voice cracked and tears rolled down my face. "He's just gone."

"Oh, God. Carrie." Max dropped to the bed and put his arms around me. His jacket smelled like leather and cigarette smoke where I buried my face against his shoulder. He only held me a moment before he pulled away. Making a motion of a stake going through his heart, he asked quietly, "Gone?"

I shook my head and wiped my eyes. "Not like that. He was here. His body was here. But he wasn't."

"He was possessed?"

"Not exactly." How could I explain it? "There wasn't anything of Nathan left at all. Could you turn off that radio?"

Max nodded and fumbled with the alarm clock until "Go Your Own Way" cut out in the middle. "I hate that song, anyway."

I covered my eyes, and he pulled me into his arms again. No matter how good the physical comfort felt, it did nothing to dull the ache in my heart.

"What happened?" he asked softly.

I didn't let go of him. "I felt it through the blood tie. Something was wrong. So I went downstairs."

When I couldn't finish, he shushed me and patted my back. For all his come-ons and attitude, Max was actually a very understanding man. "Listen, I'm going to go downstairs and look around. You stay up here where you'll be safe." He leaned back and looked me in the eye. "Okay?"

I followed him to the living room and watched him pull some stakes from his bag. "Be careful."

He looked up, the most fake smile I'd ever seen on his face. "I can take care of myself, Doctor."

"No, not that. I mean, if Nathan is down there…"

Max followed my gaze to the stake in his hand. When our eyes met, his expression broke my heart more than it already was. "Give me a little credit, Carrie."

"Sorry." Dangerously close to tears, I turned away and pretended to be interested in something on one of the many bookshelves lining the wall. Only when I heard the door click softly closed behind me did I allow myself to wipe my eyes. When I looked up, the spines of Nathan's ridiculously large collection of books confronted me. When I glanced away, I saw his chair, his shoes. A half-finished mug of blood atop a stack of notebooks. All of the components were there, all of the little parts that made Nathan's life, waiting for him to return to them. It made his absence more real somehow, and mocked my pain. If we never found Nathan, these little reminders of him would remain for me to deal with.

I don't know how long I stood there staring at the photo, but when the rattle of the doorknob heralded Max's return, his speed surprised me.

He shrugged off his jacket and tossed it over the back of the chair. "There's nothing. Just a lot of really nasty-smelling blood. I'm assuming that was his?"

I nodded, not trusting myself to speak.

"There's nothing else we can do tonight." He rubbed the back of his neck and swore. "Tell me what happened."

The symbols.

"There were marks." I scrambled for a notebook and pen I spied on the perpetually cluttered coffee table. "Strange things he'd carved all over his body."

"Carved? As in cut?" Max came around the chair and stood beside me, looming hopefully over my shoulder as I scribbled what I could remember of them.

"I think they were sigils, or something." I closed my eyes, but couldn't get a clear picture. "It all looked like random angles with circles on the end."

When I handed him the paper, he frowned and traced his fingers over the symbols. "You're sure this is right?"

"Well, I didn't take a picture of them, but when a bleeding, naked man with funky writing carved all over his body is pinning you to the ground, you have other things on your mind." I chewed my lip and pointed to the page. "What do you think?"

"He attacked you?" Max's eyes darted over me, looking for signs of injury. "Are you okay?"

"Yeah." I hadn't thought to mention the attack, and the omission seemed ridiculous now. I almost laughed at my stupidity. "He stopped. I think…I think he knew it was me. He smelled me and then he just…stopped."

Max considered the information for a moment, then turned back to the page. "Does Nathan speak any other languages?" He pulled his cell phone from his pocket. "Aramaic, Hindi, Greek? Something with letters that look different from ours?"

I shook my head. "Gaelic, from childhood, but the letters look the same. He slips into it sometimes when he's tired or drunk, but—"

Max chuckled. "I'll file that away for future reference."

The fact he believed Nathan *had* a future reassured me a

little. I sat on the couch while Max punched up a number on his phone. "Who are you calling?"

"Movement," Max said casually as if he wasn't standing in the home of two fugitive vampires.

I lunged for the phone.

He yelped in surprise and jumped back. "Hey, what are you doing?"

"You can't call the Movement," I whispered fiercely as though they could hear me. "They'll kill us."

"They'll want to know something happened to Nathan. Besides, who's going to help us? The oh-so-reliable spell books downstairs?" He turned away to speak into the phone. "*Hola,* baby. It's Harrison. Get me Anne."

My heart pounded in my chest as I stood helplessly by while Nathan's only friend turned Judas.

"Anne, *cómo está?* It's Harrison." He paused, then burst out with a hearty laugh.

How could he do this? I seethed, tuning out his conversation. Nathan had quit the Voluntary Vampire Extinction Movement when he'd sired me. We'd been flying under the radar ever since, and now Max was going to bring us to their attention?

"Gotcha." His smile widened. "We'll be on the plane at sunset."

"Plane?" I barely held the word in until he'd hung up the phone. "Where are you going?"

"*We* are going to Movement headquarters. In Madrid," he added casually as if location would be my prime concern.

"Excuse me? We? You expect me to march into a building full of assassins who've been commanded to kill me on sight?" I shook my head emphatically. "No way."

Max laughed. "You give yourself a lot of credit, you know

that? There are thousands of renegade vampires roaming the earth. You're a two-month-old who killed her sire. Even if you mentioned your name to every person in the place, I bet you wouldn't come across one vampire who recognized it."

"But you told them about Nathan." I gestured to the phone in his hand. "They'll know to look out for him, then."

Max tossed the cell onto the coffee table and sat beside me. "He was a good assassin. They're upset that he's left the fold, but they're not going to put a bounty on him unless he really steps over the line. There are way too many vampires out there doing worse damage to humankind."

I knew it was true. Nathan had told me as much. If they'd wanted us dead, we would have been staked within the week after I'd killed Cyrus. "Over the line?" My heart jumped into my throat. "Like?"

"Like killing someone or making a new vampire." Max tried to maintain a neutral expression, but it grew more serious by degrees. "Listen, I'm not going to tell you this is an ideal situation. Nathan's in grave danger. If I thought we had the resources to help him ourselves, I would never have involved the Movement."

"You won't let them kill him, will you?"

Max shook his head grimly, but a steel band of worry clamped around my heart. "There's something you're not telling me," I murmured.

Max sighed heavily. "We've been monitoring the Soul Eater. There's been…activity."

Of course there had been. Jacob Seymour, Cyrus's father and Nathan's sire, had haunted my nightmares ever since I'd first seen him at Cyrus's Vampire New Year party. He cannibalized other vampires, consuming their blood and their souls to stay alive after years of maniacal acquisition of power had taken their toll on his metabolism. Most of the year he slept safe in his coffin with a full retinue of guards, but a Movement strike team had thrown his feeding schedule off.

"What kind of activity?" My fingernails bit into my palms as I clenched my fists. I wanted to scream, "Just get it over with! Tell me what's going on!" But I couldn't treat Max that way. He was trying to help me by breaking the news gently. He didn't know it was like pulling a Band-Aid off slowly.

"His known fledglings have gone missing. Even Movement guys. Carrie, there's a reason the Soul Eater is so weak. He's made, like, a fledgling a year for five centuries. Now they're all disappearing." Max shrugged helplessly. "And he's getting stronger."

If I'd thought I'd hit bottom before, I'd had no idea. At Max's words, the bottom truly dropped out. "You don't think…" I couldn't say it. There was only one way the Soul Eater grew stronger: consuming a vampire's blood and soul.

"Hey, I only know what they tell me," he said, trying to sound encouraging, I'm sure. "But this thing…listen, there's only one person who's going to be able to tell us what's wrong with Nathan. Unfortunately, she's a little dangerous. That's why the Movement has her." He paused, cursed and ran a hand through his short blond hair. "I don't like the plan, but they think it's the best idea, and frankly, we don't have anything else to go on."

With a shock, I realized my night hadn't started out this way. I'd gotten up, spoken to Nathan, gone for a walk, with no suspicion that another hardship was waiting for us. The unfairness of the situation crushed me. All I wanted was Nathan, to have him with me, to tell me everything was all right. I tried the blood tie, but I felt nothing. Pain, so powerful I couldn't express it with a sound, forced its way from my body, my mouth frozen open in a silent scream. I wrapped my arms around my middle and tried to stand, only to collapse to my knees on the floor.

Max was beside me in a heartbeat, grabbing my upper arms to haul me upright and onto the couch. He put his arms around me, and I collapsed against him. His cotton T-shirt was comforting against my cheek, and for a moment I let myself pretend it was Nathan holding me.

Then I pushed the fantasy away. It would never stop hurting if I didn't face reality. Nathan was gone, maybe forever.

"I don't know what I'm going to do," I sobbed, more to myself than to Max.

His voice was thick as he struggled to keep the emotion out of it. "I know what you're going to do. You're going to get through tonight and probably tomorrow, then we're going to get on that plane to Madrid. We'll meet with the Movement, do some sightseeing, get gloriously drunk and catch a flamenco show. Sound good?"

"How can you joke at a time like this?" I wiped my nose pathetically on the back of my hand, glaring at him. "What if we don't get Nathan back?"

"This isn't the worst thing that's ever happened to Nathan. He'll come out of this." Max hesitated. "I haven't told anyone this…"

I sat up. "Haven't told anyone what?"

He looked away. "I don't know if it will help you if I do tell you."

"It's worth a shot." Nothing he could say would make things worse.

"My sire died." Before I could make any attempt at condolences, he rushed to speak again. "About ten years ago. He wasn't Movement. I wasn't either, at the beginning. I was living with him—nothing gay or anything—and I started talking to this girl. She was an assassin. I didn't know. She used me to get to him, then she gave me a choice. I could join the Movement or die. After I saw what she'd done to Marcus—"

"You don't have to go on," I whispered. The pain in his voice overwhelmed me.

He nodded and smiled as though he was embarrassed to be so emotionally exposed. "I still miss him. Sometimes I think if I could just hear his voice… But for the most part, I've gotten better."

I wanted to say "I can't imagine," or "That must have been awful," but I *could* imagine and it *was* awful. That was why he'd told me. If he could survive losing his sire, I could survive this separation from Nathan. Unfortunately, with that came the implied reassurance I could survive Nathan's death. I didn't want to think about it, so I didn't say anything, and leaned against Max again. Like this, I could rest secure in the familial love that cements good friendships.

"We're going to get him back, Carrie. Nathan's too big a pain in my ass to be gone for long. I'm not that lucky." He gave me a quick squeeze with the arm draped around my shoulders.

Our morose conversation died without a fight as we retreated into ourselves. Max fell asleep, leaning against me on the couch. I'm sure we made a cheerful picture: two wounded souls, both relying on the other to hold them up.

Outside, the sun came up. Wherever Nathan was, I hoped he was okay.

3

Nature of the Beast

Upstairs, a woman screamed over and over. It was a beautiful, delicious sound, and it was going to drive him mad.

Cyrus lay in the dead priest's narrow twin bed. The Mouse slept on the floor, where she'd cried herself to sleep, much to Cyrus's annoyance. But she'd put clean sheets on the bed, so she wasn't the most worthless servant he'd ever had.

The noise upstairs died as he assumed the woman making it had. Next, they would drain her blood and eat her organs. The nostalgia of it parched Cyrus's lips. What he wouldn't do for a taste of blood.

The Mouse had fed him canned soup that was too thin and too salty. Even as a vampire he'd enjoyed various culinary delights—chocolate, expensive cheeses and fine caviar. As blood had been his main source of sustenance, he'd only had to eat for pleasure. The thought of ingesting lowly fare out of necessity was brutally depressing, but it had, fortunately, restored some little bit of strength to his limbs.

"Are you awake?" He sat up and nudged her with his toes. She lay on her side, curled into a ball with the blanket he'd spared her—generously, in his opinion—clutched to her chest. When she didn't move, he gave her a feeble kick. "Get up!"

She didn't budge. For one sick, cheerful moment he wondered if she'd died. Another kick elicited a small shift. A frown creased her brow, and she turned her head. Her dull hair fell back, exposing her neck. The pulse point there leaped with seductive familiarity.

Just one bite.

He was no longer a vampire. He had no fangs, no blood thirst, at least not physically. But his soul still craved it. Craved the rich taste of the blood. The emotional connection from drinking. Canned soup couldn't replace that.

He slid to the ground soundlessly and curved his body around hers, closing his eyes to stop the room from spinning. Though her hips and shoulders were bony, her flesh was warm and welcoming. He remembered this part, the seduction. There had been times when hurting them just to watch them fight had been enjoyable, but he wasn't sure of his strength now, and he didn't want her screaming to alert the vampires upstairs.

Her hair still smelled of shampoo, the cheap, pungent strawberry variety he'd seen in the bathroom. He buried his face against her neck and tasted her skin, salty with perspiration and fear.

His touch didn't wake her. She moaned softly when he traced the shell of her ear with his tongue. Her hips pushed back against his, and he held them there, tight against his growing arousal.

This was how he remembered it. The pure, physical pleasure mingled with overwhelming emotion. There was always a moment where the act made him drunk, made him forget that he'd intended to kill, and overrode his consciousness. For an instant, he'd be tricked into believing it was an expression of love and not a prelude to death. For an instant, he'd be fooled into believing they loved him.

He squeezed his eyes shut tight and slipped his hand into the front of her dress. The warmth of her beating heart echoed his, mocking him.

They never loved him. How could they? He'd never been worthy of love. Not his father's, not his wives' or his companions'. What had he ever done to earn love?

This was where the moment of perfection took an ugly turn. Rage filled him. His hold on her bony hip turned cruel. Even without his vampire strength, he knew he would leave a bruise.

This was what he craved. The pain. The horror. He reveled in it.

She woke with a start. He leaned over her to see the comprehension slowly take her. First confusion at waking from such a sinfully pleasant dream. Then shame when she realized her dream had been reality. Horror, when she saw who held her, and finally, acceptance as she realized what he would do.

Though her body trembled, her limbs were frozen in a pathetic, helpless attempt at pushing him away that never connected with his flesh. He licked his lips and lowered his head, adrenaline fueling his weak body. His blunt, human teeth didn't break the skin. She found her voice to scream as his jaws crushed the tender flesh of her throat, but she didn't fight him. He tried again, and she pummeled his chest with her fists. He ignored her and bit once more, covering her mouth with his hand to quiet her.

She bit him in her struggle, and he cursed. He rolled on top of her to pin her to the cold, bare floor. Her dress rode up her thighs and he wedged himself between her legs. He felt the heat and wetness he'd pulled from her through the thin, damp cotton of her panties, when she'd thought she was dreaming. Her eyes opened wide at the intimate contact. She froze for a mere second before resuming her thrashing and squirming. She thought he would violate her, and she fought harder than when she'd assumed he would kill her.

Her terror was an aphrodisiac. The scent of her fear-tinged sweat filled his nostrils. The feeling of her wriggling for escape against his hard body aroused him further. He twisted one hand in her hair and yanked her head back. Aiming for the angry, red welts he'd left on her neck, he lunged forward and bit.

This time, he didn't release the pressure immediately. He increased it until his jaw ached and his ears rang. She scratched at his back with her nails, dragging slashes of pain across his shoulder blades. Her scream, one long, keening wail, rose in pitch the harder he bore down.

Finally, with a sickening pop, her flesh gave way. She bled, not a gush as from an artery, but a mere trace. If he could have remembered this taste in the afterlife, he would have known he was in hell. To think of ever having been separated from the beautiful violence of drinking blood... He shuddered as he lapped gently at the torn flesh of the wound.

Her scream abated, replaced by silent sobs he only noticed by the heaving of her throat under his mouth. He'd hurt her, made her cry. He had that power again, whether human or not. It excited him.

The taste of her burned an exquisite fire in his groin. He thrust against her thighs and abandoned himself to the horrible pleasure of the blood oozing from her torn neck and the despair emanating from her soul. But it wasn't enough. It wasn't like before.

"Please," she rasped, hauling in breath as though the oxygen weighed a thousand pounds. "Please, don't."

Her desperate whisper pushed him over the edge. He threw his head back and groaned as he came, spilling his seed on the pale flesh of her thighs. Breathing hard, he rolled away from her. She scrambled backward on her elbows then struggled to her feet with unrestrained sobs. The bathroom door slammed shut and the sound of the latch falling dropped a weight of ice in his guts.

He hadn't enjoyed it like he had in the old days. Before, when he'd been a vampire, he wouldn't have given a second thought to what he'd done. Now, his conscience pricked him, a sting he'd trained himself to ignore after he'd been turned. Why had it come back? It was certainly something he could do without.

He'd hurt her. A moment ago it had brought him pleasure. It should have now. He'd done worse to countless other girls, destroyed their innocence and their trust, if not their lives.

It was exactly the same as he'd done to the Mouse.

He sat up, supporting himself on shaking arms, and stared at the closed bathroom door. He couldn't hear her soft sobs, but he imagined them as he listened to the water running in the bathtub. Her spirit had been weak already. She'd seen her friends slaughtered and violated before her eyes. But she hadn't been completely broken. Not until now. Not until the moment he'd abused and terrorized her.

It's what you do. You're a monster.

Though he knew it to be true, he couldn't force himself to believe it. Humanity had been woven back into his frayed soul, for better or for worse. Most likely, for worse.

Climbing to his feet, he went to the bathroom door, gripping objects for support as he went. "Come out of there."

She didn't answer.

"I said come out of there." He had no patience for this game. He should be upstairs, demanding answers of his captors and insisting to be restored to his former state. If he could even make it up the stairs after the energy he'd expended fighting her.

"To hell with you." His words echoed his thoughts. He limped to the small chest of drawers and pulled out some of the dead priest's clothes. The trousers were a bit short and the waist a bit big, but he would worry about proper attire later. He shoved his arms into one of the hideous, button-down, black shirts and headed to the narrow stairs. Halfway there, his legs gave way and he toppled to the floor. Still, he kept going, pulling himself slowly to the foot of the staircase, where he had to catch his breath before he could crawl up the rough steps.

He'd expected the door at the top to be locked somehow, and it was, but only from his side. Apparently, they were less concerned with keeping him in than keeping themselves out. Still, it gave him trouble. He had to stretch to reach the knob, and only after several tries did he manage to turn it. The door opened and his poor balance and awkward position brought him face-first onto the rough carpet of the main floor.

The bodies of the priest and nun had been removed from the vestibule, but they'd been replaced with fresher corpses. Cyrus pulled himself across the floor, the carpet scraping his stomach where his shirt rode up with his motion. He reached for a wheel of one of the motorcycles, thinking to pull himself up. The vehicle tipped, and for a long moment he thought it might topple onto him. With a frustrated sob, he made his way to the wall, pulling himself upright through sheer force of will. He had dealt with these kinds of people before. They had no respect for anyone or anything, but he had a better chance facing them standing than crawling on the ground at their feet.

As he rested, propped against the wall, he glimpsed his surroundings through the dark windows. A badly cracked parking lot in an ocean of desert sand, and beyond that, a barren road. Exactly the sort of place these cretins would imagine when waxing poetic about the open road. His gaze dropped to one of the bikes, and the insignia on the side made his skin crawl.

The Fangs.

A part of him was revolted at the thought of spending another minute with the uncouth gang, but another part was grateful he'd offered them refuge in the days before his untimely death. If they had any decency at all, which he doubted, they would feel indebted to at least explain what was going on.

The large, double doors to the church were shut. Cryptic, occult markings had been drawn on them in chalk. He pulled open the door and stepped inside.

Loud, discordant music, the type Cyrus had been glad to be rid of when they'd ended their extended stay at the mansion, blared from a huge system of stereo equipment hastily arranged on a side altar. A rowdy dice game occupied most of the gang members in the center aisle. A few slept in the pews, obviously not caring what toll their dirty boots and grimy clothes took on the upholstered seats. One Fang used spray paint to draw exaggerated phalluses on the figures in a mural of the Last Supper that graced a side wall. Someone threw a beer bottle and it shattered loudly against the wall. On the whole, they conducted themselves much more respectfully than when they'd been at Cyrus's house, swilling beer and ruining his formal dinner parties. *This must be their church behavior.*

When Cyrus entered, they paused in what they were doing to notice him. All except three of them. They sat in the sanctuary, where he'd been held that morning. Candles marked the perimeter of a circle around them. Their fingertips touched and they chanted in a low drone. He recognized one as the person who'd pulled him from the other side, a tall female with a gravelly voice and an ugly face, even for a vampire. The other two looked as though they'd been younger at the time of their change. One was male, with spiked black hair, the other female, with a similar coif. They all wore their grotesque feeding faces.

Rage so intense it burned in his veins took hold of Cyrus,

but his limbs were so weak that when he ran toward them, he stumbled, falling flat on his face. He looked up blearily as the vampires at the perimeter of the room advanced on him. They tangled their claws in his hair, tore the clothes on his body.

A scream, painfully familiar, rent the air. The monsters holding him froze, and he looked up in time to see the Mouse, her flimsy dress clinging to her wet skin, her sopping hair hanging like a tangled mop around her shoulders. She rushed at the vampires holding him and pushed them away, an action Cyrus might have perceived as fearless if she hadn't been trembling and shrieking hysterically. She'd shocked them, though, and that was enough. They were too stunned to attack or even resist her.

She gripped Cyrus's wrist with her cold, wet hand, pulled him to his feet and supported him with surprising strength. He looked back once at the three vampires in the circle, considered trying again to reach them.

"Please!" The Mouse tugged his arm frantically. "Please!"

She was right to be afraid. The vampires wouldn't stay stunned forever. They would seethe over them like a tide of death, and weak, pathetic, human Cyrus would not be able to stop them. He held tight to the Mouse, his feet twisting beneath him, boneless as she dragged him from the sanctuary.

They made it only as far as the door before the monsters pursued them. The Mouse screamed as one of them caught a handful of her hair, but she tore free, tightening her arm around Cyrus. A few more steps and they would be safe, but those steps seemed like miles due to his deadened legs and her ebbing strength. With a final, heroic burst of energy, the Mouse wrenched the basement door open and pushed him ahead of her. He collapsed and nearly tumbled down the steps. She shoved the door closed and locked it.

The vampires clawed at the door, but the clawing gave way to angry voices, and then the voices faded into heavy footsteps. The Fangs had left them.

Cyrus gasped for breath, his chest aching with the exertion of his actions. "What was that about?"

"Please, don't ever go up there again!" She gripped the front of his torn shirt, catching the long strands of his hair in her fists.

"Do you think I'd go up there again by choice? They'll kill me!" He wanted to take her by the shoulders, dig fingers into her thin flesh as he shook her. But there was no sport in abusing her, he decided. That explained why he'd taken no pleasure in it before.

"If they kill you, they'll kill me!" She clutched at him, her hold impossible to shake.

"What are you talking about?" He lowered his voice. In the past, he would have rather died than show sensitivity to a squalling woman, but she knew more than he did. As loath as he was to admit it, he needed her, and he needed her calm so she could tell him what she knew.

He sank to the second step, and she eased down, too, so they were squeezed side by side between the cinder block walls of the narrow stairwell. She hiccuped pathetically and wiped at her eyes. "If you die, I'm worthless."

I was under the impression you were rather worthless, anyhow. "What do you mean?"

"They only let me live to watch out for you. They don't know how to take care of a...human. They kept me alive so I could take care of you." She seemed suddenly aware that their bodies touched, and she shrank from him. "If you die, they'll kill me. I'm disposable. That's what they told me when they killed Father Bart and Sister Helen."

When she turned her head, he saw the bloody imprint of his

teeth in her flesh. He looked away. "What if I killed myself? What if I went into the kitchen, took a knife and slit my wrists?"

"No!" She grabbed for him again, and he evaded her, though his bones ached with fatigue.

"So, you're charged with watching out for my well-being, at the cost of your life. Yet you've done little to keep me from harming myself. There's a razor in the bathroom, knives in the kitchen drawers. Which tells me you don't care whether you live or die." He studied her face as she absorbed his words.

She looked down, her voice barely a whisper when she spoke. "Would you kill yourself?"

Would he? It would end this miserable human existence. But they'd brought him back once from the realm of the dead, apparently with purpose. They could likely do it again. And it wasn't as though he could lift a razor to slash himself. "No. I don't wish to die." He slipped down the next step, resigned not to look at her again.

"Neither do I," she whispered. "At least, I don't think I do."

That gave him some hope, something to use against her if need be. "Then you'd better keep me alive."

"This is it," Max announced, dropping his duffel bag on the plushly carpeted floor.

Only the faint, hollow sound resulting reminded me we were in an airplane. "Air Fang One?"

"Oh, that was bad." Max flopped onto the cream-colored, silk sofa and kicked his feet up, as if he were on a secondhand couch in a college dorm. "Have a seat. It's a long flight."

I couldn't tear my eyes from the sumptuous decor of the private jet. The walls, carpet and furniture were all in muted, neutral shades. Warm light spilled from recessed fixtures to compliment the dark wood finish of the tabletops and sprawling entertainment center at the end of the cabin. "This is nicer than my apartment."

"There are a lot of places nicer than your apartment." Max flipped open a console on the arm of the couch. A remote control slid up smoothly. He snagged it and turned on the television. "Like my apartment, for one."

I eyed the small, round table and two sturdy-looking wing chairs on either side of it. They were visually appealing, especially with their color-coordinated seat belts, but probably not very comfortable. "Are you just going to hog that sofa the whole time?"

"What?" He pulled his gaze away from what appeared to be a Japanese game show with topless contestants, and sat up. "Oh, no. Sorry. You want the tour?"

"There's more?" I would have been impressed with just this room.

Max rose and gestured to one of the fabric-covered panels in the wall. "Come on."

Sure enough, there was a hidden door handle worked into the ivory molding. Max pulled it open to reveal a small galley, not unlike a commercial airliner's, and beyond that, a cockpit with all manner of flashing buttons and lighted dials. Two pilots in standard uniform conferred with the tower through headsets as they flipped switches and checked instruments. They were perfectly normal. Human, even.

"The Movement has humans working for it?" I asked under my breath when Max led me back to the passenger area.

"Werewolves," Max fairly growled. "You'll see a lot of that at headquarters. They're antivampire, too, so the Movement thinks it's just *great* to have them on board. Wanna see the bedroom?"

"That's subtle." I elbowed him in the ribs. "There'd better be twin beds, or pray the flight doesn't last long."

"The flight probably won't," he admitted. "It's the waiting for sundown on the tarmac that's the real problem."

At the thought of sunup, I panicked. It was one thing to be in the big, sturdy shelter of a house or even Ziggy's old Ford Econoline van when dawn broke, but a plane seemed terribly risky. "We're gonna be in this thing with the sun up?"

"Well, yeah." Max seemed annoyingly unconcerned. "Long flight, short night. Especially since we're flying through it. Why do you think they built this bad boy without windows?"

"Oh, God! What if we crash? Max, we could die!"

"So? You'd die in a crash if you were human, too. If you wanna worry, worry about the pilots offing us for their cause." On that reassuring note, Max led me to the other end of the cabin, where he pulled open a mahogany door with gold fixtures. At the end of a narrow hall there was another equally tasteful, equally neutral room with twin beds.

"Damn." He shook his head as if disappointed. "Unless you want to share?"

"I'll pass. Don't take it personally. It's the whole crushing-emotional-pain thing I'm concentrating on right now." It hadn't gotten any better, but I'd tried my best not think about it. It was something I'd become very good at when my parents had died. If I ignored the grief, I wouldn't be incapacitated by it when there were more important things that needed my attention. Closing my eyes, I sank to the bed. "I left my bag in the other room."

"I'll get it."

When Max returned with the bag, I gave the contents a quick once-over. I'd decided to leave my heart in the wall safe in Nathan's shop. After we'd retrieved it from Cyrus, I'd given my heart to Nathan for safekeeping. He'd really outdone himself in the security department. The box containing my heart was fireproof and welded shut, so nothing short of total apocalypse would harm the contents. Still, I couldn't help the spike of fear when I thought of being separated from it. Though I knew nothing could get to it in the hidden safe—and that leaving it behind was much better than trying to sneak a human heart through customs—it was another thing entirely to convince myself my fear for my life was irrational.

A slender, friendly-looking vampire knocked gently on the doorway to alert us to her presence. A wide grin split Max's face when he saw her. "You're new here."

The young woman flushed, then seemed to remember her duty to be professional. "Yes, I am. My name is Amanda. I'll be your flight attendant."

"I'm Max. Max Harrison. I'll be your passenger." He offered her his hand, and she shook it with a look of mild bewilderment.

She turned her apologetic gaze to me, and I waved dismissively. "He doesn't belong to me."

"The captain says we're cleared for takeoff. You both need to find a seat and buckle your seat belts," she said primly as if clinging to her rehearsed speech would help her resist Max's charms.

"Will do." He winked at her, which sent her scurrying from the room.

"Do you always sexually harass innocent young women?" I rolled my eyes at him before heading down the hall.

He laughed. "I'm sorry, have we met?"

Once we'd taken off and I was reasonably sure we weren't in imminent danger of plunging into the sea while burning to death, I unbuckled and stood. "I'm tired. I didn't sleep well yesterday. Mind if I crash?"

"Not the best terminology to use on a plane, but knock yourself out." Max shook his head, his mouth turned down and his gaze still fixed on the television. "Nine hundred channels. I think I'm good here."

"Great." Truth be told, I was more tired of the Spanish variety show he'd been watching during takeoff than I was actually tired. "Wake me before we land, if I sleep that long."

"Will do."

I briefly heard the staged moans of an over-enthusiastic porn actress blare from the television as I headed to the bedroom. At least he'd have something to occupy his time.

Not that I'd been on a lot of private jets or anything, but the beds were more comfortable than I'd expected. The sheets had a thread count equivalent to Egyptian cotton butter, and the incessant whir of the machinery around me created a womblike environment, or at least what I'd imagine the womb to be like. I should have been able to drop off immediately, but my brain kept replaying the horror of my circumstances. I didn't have a clue where Nathan was or if he was even alive. When I tried to communicate through the blood tie, all I got back was crippling pain. Did that mean he was dead? Just imagining it intensified the agony, so I shielded myself from his thoughts…or the void where they once were. All I wanted was to feel Nathan's arms around me, to hear him tell me that everything would be all right. Instead, I cried, grateful for the mechanical noises that would keep Max from overhearing my sobs.

I wasn't sure when I crossed the line between conscious and asleep, so it was quite a shock when I opened my eyes and found myself in Cyrus's bedroom in his palatial mansion. The mattress beneath me was soft, the linen sheets as cool and crisp as I remembered.

Clarence has really kept the place up.

"You're awake."

I hadn't heard the voice of my former sire, even in dreams, since the night I'd killed him. I'd seen him many times, but always through a murky blue filter. We'd never spoken. Still, I remembered his cloying praise and manipulative words. His gentle tone should have put me on my guard, but I somehow knew I dreamed, so he could do me no harm. I had no reason to resist him. Not that I'd ever been able to in the past.

I rolled onto my side to face him. His long, white-gold hair covered his shoulders and the pillow beneath his head. A smile formed slowly on his beautiful mouth, and I ached to touch him.

"I'm not awake." I couldn't force the sadness from my voice. "I'm on a plane. I'm sleeping."

He nodded and reached for me. His hands weren't the clawed nightmares they'd been after five hundred years of living death. They were smooth and strong when he brushed my hair from my eyes. They slid down my neck to the scar he'd left on the night he'd changed me, and a shudder of longing passed through me at his touch. In reality, Cyrus would have been pleased with that reaction. In my dream, regret softened his usually cruel face. "You're right. You're not awake. But now your eyes are open."

I leaned forward and kissed him. There was none of the need for control or power in it that there had been when he was alive. I surrendered completely, willed him to do the same with my mind. In my dream, I could have him again, the parts of him that I'd loved and not feared. The parts of him that had seduced me into questioning whether my humanity was truly worth keeping.

When I opened my eyes again, I was awake, and a very startled Max was pulling away.

"I was trying to—to wake you up," he stammered, rubbing his chin as though I'd hit him. The look in his eyes was just as accusing. "And you *kissed* me."

"Sorry." I resisted the urge to wipe off my lips. "I was dreaming."

"Must have been a hell of a dream." He slid his hands into

his jeans pockets and rocked back on his heels while looking at anything but me. "There was something on the news I thought you should see."

In the other room, Max had CNN on the television. The picture-in-picture function displayed MSNBC. I dropped onto the couch. "No porn? This must be important."

"Shh, it's on again." He gestured to the screen. "It's been coming on after the 'top of the hour' shit."

The anchorwoman, who'd previously reported a story about a toilet-trained horse, put on a more somber expression. "Police in Grand Rapids, Michigan, are searching for a suspect in a brutal slaying that took place in front of several eyewitnesses Monday night."

"That was last night—" The words stuck in my throat. I grabbed one of the throw pillows and hugged it tight to my chest.

The anchorwoman continued. "The victim, whose name has not been released, was jogging down a public bike path when an unidentified man tackled her to the ground and cut her throat."

A teenager appeared on the screen, her face blotchy and red from crying. "It happened so fast, no one could do anything. His face was all messed up, like it got burned up or something. It was like he just ripped her whole neck out."

"We're following up with witnesses and pairing them with police sketch artists, and we're hoping to get an arrest as soon as possible." I recognized the middle-aged police officer on the screen as the one who'd given me a speeding ticket earlier that year. He looked a lot more forgiving of the psycho killer than he had of my measly eighty in a fifty-five.

Back in the studio, the anchorwoman fixed the camera with a somber gaze. "Police artists have compiled this drawing...."

Though it was hastily sketched in pencil and the jagged

snout of his feeding face had somehow translated to a larger nose and whorled burn scars, there was no denying the man in the picture was meant to be Nathan. The reporter's voice continued. "Police say the suspect is Caucasian, in his midthirties, with facial scars and several tattoos. He should be considered dangerous."

"Tattoos." I pinched the bridge of my nose between my thumb and index finger. "The sigils. Of course."

"Hopefully, the Movement will have more information on this when we land," Max said softly.

"They're going to kill him, aren't they?" I couldn't remember ever feeling so tired. This was where Max was supposed to say something to comfort me. He remained silent.

I covered my face with my hands. "I hope they do kill him. Because if they don't, he'll never forgive himself."

4

A Rabbit Hole

If the dead priest hadn't owned a television, Cyrus might never have known what was happening.

Not that he felt he owed the Father any gratitude. Cyrus hated television. Since its horrible birth, the blasted thing was all humans could talk about. In this wretched captivity, though, Cyrus needed something to occupy his mind, and he wasn't about to take up Bible study.

The Mouse still slept. After she'd finished crying and he'd rested long enough to manage sitting upright again, he'd demanded she bring him a first aid kid to bandage her bruised and bloody neck. He'd let her sleep in the bed. He had no use for it. The care and, God help him, nurturing, he'd displayed had unsettled him. There'd been no chance of sleeping after that.

For the first few hours, he'd busied himself ripping pages from the Bible on the shelf to make paper cranes. He'd worked through the first half of Genesis when he grew bored and flipped on the television. It helped him cover the sounds from upstairs. Though any sensible vampire would have been sleeping by now, the Fangs seemed content to blast pounding, repetitive noise that barely qualified as music.

There were three channels, and only one showed anything of interest. The local news anchorwoman wore too much rouge and her hair looked like one perfectly molded plastic piece. Exactly the kind of woman Cyrus liked to charm, then torture to death. He leaned forward in his chair.

"Authorities in Louden County are calling off their search for three people who were reported missing after a church fire in Hudson." The picture cut to three photos. The dead priest and nun, and a pretty girl with a bright smile wearing a cotton sundress.

The Mouse.

The anchorwoman's nasal voice continued. "Police say Father Bartholomew Straub, Sister Helen Jacobs and Stacey Pickles were working at Saint Anne Catholic Church on Friday when the fire broke out, but the three have not been seen since. Footprints leading away from the building suggest they may have attempted to walk to safety, but with desert temperatures reaching record highs over the weekend, they are presumed dead."

Cyrus eyed the girl on the bed, shaking his head. "Pickles?"

More disturbing than the Mouse's ridiculous name—though barely—was the matter of the fire. Why would the authorities believe the building had burned? And if the weekend had passed…

"Get up." He stood, glad of the little strength sleep had returned to him, and shook her. "What day is it?"

She stared at him in bleary confusion. "Tuesday or Wednesday. I lost track. You're standing."

Tuesday or Wednesday. Which meant he'd been raised on Monday. But they'd been here since Friday. "What happened when people showed up for Mass on Sunday?"

"I don't know. No one came. When Father Bart mentioned it to…" She wet her lips. "That's when they killed him. He tried to tell them people would be coming soon for services. They laughed at him and said no one was coming to help us."

Cyrus turned away from her tears. They might spark that dangerous human guilt in him, and he had no time for it now. "Did they tell you why?"

"No. They just started killing."

"But they kept them for two days before they killed them. Why?" The timeline didn't make sense. If he'd taken hostages, he would have dispensed with the useless ones right away.

When he turned to face the Mouse, her eyes were wide and rimmed with red. "They were doing things. Occult things. Satan worship."

"Impossible. The Fangs think Satanists are pussies." When she flinched at his coarse language, it buoyed his mood. "What, exactly, were they doing?"

She curled her legs beneath her and toyed with the hem of her dress. A perverse memory of the night before came to his mind. He expected guilt, and when it didn't come he found its absence far more disturbing than its presence would have been.

As if sensing the change in him, she wrapped her arms across her chest, hugging herself. "I don't know what they were doing. They didn't tell us. But I heard them say the time had to be right, they had to be sure it was him. And they needed Father Bart's hand."

"He had to take part in the ritual?" It made sense. Though Cyrus didn't believe in all the Catholic tripe he'd been made to swallow as a child, the power of a priest was similar to, if not greater than, that of a practiced magician.

"Not him. Just his hand." The words left her in a whisper. "The rest of the stuff they did to them, that was for fun."

"Why did they spare you?" Cyrus sat beside her on the bed, ignoring the sting of shame he felt when she cringed from him. "Why not use you and feed from you like they did the nun?"

"Because I wasn't as fun." She trembled as she spoke. A tear slid down her cheek. "I didn't scream or pray. That's what they wanted. They wanted her to pray while they did it."

The thought would have amused Cyrus in the past, but it didn't now. Not when this girl was so visibly traumatized by what she'd seen. "Why didn't you?"

For the first time, the Mouse looked him in the eye. He saw no life or hope in those dull brown depths. Her body steadied, and her voice was strong. "Because no one was listening."

She sounded so like him centuries ago. He tried to keep the emotion from his tone as he spoke. "That is the most important thing you'll ever learn. Because no one is listening, and no one is looking out for you."

She broke down then, gulping great lungfuls of air as she sobbed.

He stood and walked to the tiny kitchenette, trying to ignore the trembling in his legs. He would not abide becoming so weak again, so fast. "We're out of milk."

"What's happening?" Her face was swollen and red from crying, contrasting starkly with the white gauze at her neck. "What are they doing?"

"I have no idea." He limped to the refrigerator and opened it, then sniffed a potentially suspicious carton of orange juice. It seemed safe enough. But his balance was not. He slammed the carton on the counter, grabbing the edge for support, but tumbled to the floor. The Mouse was at his side in an instant, helping him to his feet and guiding him to a chair.

"I don't need your help," he sniped, but accepted it anyway.

The Mouse took a glass from the cabinet, then, almost as an afterthought, grabbed another. Her hands shook as she poured the juice.

He considered offering some comfort to her, but dismissed it. He'd already been kind to her, and he didn't want it to become a habit. "On the news, they said they've called off the search for the three of you. And the church has burned down."

"That's impossible." She wiped at her eyes with the back of her hand. "They must have been talking about something else."

"Stacey Pickles?" He watched the recognition flash in her eyes before he continued. "They think you died in the desert."

"They're looking for me?" Hope, then bleak terror crossed her face. "Why do they think this place has burned down?"

"I don't know. There are spells, called glamours, that make a person see what the caster wishes them to see. But to make a whole building disappear, and do it convincingly to fool many people…that takes power I don't believe exists." He shook his head. "Are you going to give me any of that juice?"

She came forward slowly, like a wild animal unaccustomed to humans, and set the glass carefully before him. "They brought you back from the dead. They must know something you don't."

The very notion that she would speak to him so boldly struck him as ridiculous. He laughed and took a long swallow from his glass. The juice was as thick as blood, but cold and with an unpleasant texture. "I can't get used to this."

"To what?" She didn't sound as if she cared.

That alone made him wonder why he'd spoken to her at all. The solitude, he guessed, not only of the last few days, but his long death, as well. It was enough to keep him talking. "Living like a human. It's been so long since I've had to fuel my body with food and liquid. It's unpleasant."

"No. What will be unpleasant is starving to death when the food runs out." Her expression was grim.

"That won't happen. At least, not to me," he said by way of reassurance. "Your life depends on it, remember. You're supposed to be caring for me."

She looked insulted. "I wasn't talking about you. I was talking about me. They're not going to worry about keeping me alive after they're done with you."

He pulled one of the chairs from the flimsy Formica table and sat. "And what, exactly, is it they're going to do with me?"

"I don't know." She chewed her lip. "Something bad."

"Madame, your powers of perception astound me." He closed his eyes, mind working furiously. What he needed was a plan, some currency to bargain with the Fangs for information. What he needed was—

"You talk funny. Where are you from?"

What he needed was for the Mouse to stop talking. "England. But most recently I was confined to a watery blue purgatory. I don't remember the address." He paused. "Were you there? When they did the ritual?"

Her eyes grew hollow and faraway again. Her voice came out in a whisper. "Yes."

"What did they do?" Cyrus pulled another chair from the table and motioned to her to sit. "Were there specific words they said? Did they read them from a book?"

She remained frozen in place, staring blankly at the tabletop. There was a ring from a cup there, and she seemed to have fixated on it. "I don't remember."

He tamped down his impatience. It wouldn't do to frighten her again, not when she'd begun to communicate like a rational human being. "It wasn't that long ago. I'm sure if you take a moment, you'll remember—"

"I don't remember!" She spun toward the counter, where a small stack of dirty dishes and utensils waited to be cleaned, and she swept them to the floor. The shock of her action out-lasted the clatter it created, and she stood, her face a mask of disbelief as she stared at the broken shards on the tile floor.

There were two ways he could react, Cyrus realized. He could lash out at her in anger and impatience, destroying any scrap of trust she might have left and any chance he might have to learn more about his dire situation. Conversely, he could ignore her until she was finished with her tantrum, and reserve his feeble strength for more important matters. He chose the latter, as his actions had caught up with him and he hadn't the stomach nor the energy to do further violence to her.

"Clean it up," he said casually as he rose and headed for the bed. He settled in and pulled the blankets over himself, but found it difficult to sleep with the sun from the small, high window illuminating the room and the sound of the Mouse's pathetic sniffles invading his ears.

As soon as the sun set, Max and I stepped off the private jet and onto the still-warm tarmac.

"I love this time of year. Not too hot at night, not too cold. If you were ever here in July or January, you'd know what I mean," Max said, full of vim and vigor as he carried both our bags toward the sprawling, futuristic building that was the airport.

I hadn't slept well during the day. My dreams had been full of weird symbols I was sure I'd never figure out, the least of which being a weird trip into the woods bearing a pig under each arm. I was in no mood for Max's crap. "We're not here for a pleasure trip. We're here to figure out what's happening with Cyrus."

Max halted and dropped his duffel bag. "With who?"

"With Nathan." I stopped and glared at him. "We don't have time to monkey around. Let's go."

"You said Cyrus. 'We're here to figure out what's happening with Cyrus' is exactly what you said."

My mouth gaped. Had I really said that? My first sire had

certainly been on my mind lately, but I didn't usually make such obvious slips. "I didn't say that."

"Yes, you did. I barely knew the guy. Why would I be mentally inserting his name into your sentences? Carrie, is something going on you're not telling me about?" Max picked up the bag and motioned for me to walk.

Good thing, too, because I was paralyzed with shock at my own stupid mistake. The quadrant in my brain that controls my feet recognized his gesture, and I plodded along beside him. "Not exactly."

Max let out a long, low whistle. "Uh-huh. Are you 'not exactly' telling me what's going on, or is something 'not exactly' going on?"

"A little of both." I stopped again and faced him. "Right before the thing happened to Nathan, he'd confronted me about a dream I'd had. Apparently, I'd said Cyrus's name."

"Nathan was watching you sleep again?" Another whistle. "That's not good."

"I knew something was up, but I couldn't have predicted this." We started walking once more, in silence. After a few steps, I remembered my dream on the plane and the embarrassing consequences of it. "There's something else, too."

"Shoot."

"When we were on the plane, I dreamed about him." I looked at my feet so I wouldn't have to see Max's face. "When I kissed you."

"Well, that's understandable. He's your sire and all." A few more steps, and Max realized what I'd meant. "Wait, you thought I was Cyrus, not Nathan?"

"I was dreaming. I can't control what I do in my dreams." Did I sound defensive? I needed a hot bath and a long time to recover from the monotonous flight.

Luckily, Max dropped the subject once we entered the building. The fluorescent tubes and pale yellow paint of the customs area made it seem less than friendly, and the stern faced police with automatic weapons didn't help much, either. And I couldn't even claim I'd packed my own luggage. I'd been so tired before we'd left, I'd trusted Max to do it for me.

"Where did you bring me? Kazakhstan?" I whispered fiercely to Max as a customs agent rifled through my underwear. "And why did you pack so many thongs?"

Max grinned. "Why do you own so many thongs?"

Once we were cleared to enter the country proper, Max hurried me out of the airport, to a taxi stand.

"Private jet, but no armored car with little flags to pick us up?" I grumbled as I slid into the back of the cramped, European-scale car.

"The Movement doesn't like to attract unnecessary local attention," he said in a low voice. He handed the driver a colorful Spanish bill. *"Plaza del Major, por favor."*

Madrid, what I could see of it from the cab windows, was rather unlike my expectations of a Spanish city. There were no terra-cotta tiles on any of the skyscrapers we passed. Billboards for American products mingled with advertisements for Spanish movies. Except for the enormous aloe plants growing in the median of the boulevard and the signs I couldn't understand, I could have been in Chicago.

Then we passed the modern part of town. The glossy shops and illuminated theater awnings gave way to the terra-cotta and stucco I'd imagined. The streets were less smooth here. Wrought-iron railings surrounded tiny balconies overflowing with geraniums. Laundry hung to dry on lines stretching from one building to another. I figured we'd taken a shortcut until the cab stopped.

The street was so narrow we could open only one door to get out. Max had barely pulled our bags from the backseat when the driver sped off, the taxi bouncing merrily on the cobblestones.

"Are we… Where are we?" I asked, staring up at the sliver of sky between the buildings on either side of us.

"He couldn't drive us to the Plaza del Major." Max pronounced it with a slight lisp, like *platha my-or.* "It's a pedestrians-only kinda place."

I followed him down a maze of alleys, impressed that he could find his way so easily. For the most part, the streets we walked were empty and dark. Vampire or not, if I'd been alone, I would have turned tail and run back the way the cab had brought us.

We emerged from one alley to find a more populated street. People enjoyed drinks on sidewalk tables in front of expensive-looking restaurants, and street performers danced and posed for the tourists. At the end of the street loomed a huge, dark wall with an arched doorway. On the other side was the Plaza del Major.

I'd never seen anything so incredibly beautiful and romantic in my entire life. Buildings the likes of which I'd imagined when I read *Don Quixote* as a child surrounded the square. Cafés and shops proclaimed their wares tastefully for visitors, and a huge sculpture dominated the center. There were many people, but the space felt vast. The ring of voices echoing off the buildings and the stones beneath our feet was swallowed up by the open night air, creating a gentle but unintelligible murmur. Above it all, the clear night sky sparkled with stars that seemed so close I could touch them, and its cold beauty contrasted with the warm life on the ground.

The way Max and I contrasted with the life around us. A pang of longing speared my heart. A group of teens congregated near a vendor's cart, laughing over their ice-cream cones. Near the huge statue of a soldier on horseback, a darkly handsome man lifted a woman in his arms and spun, her blood red, broomstick skirt swirling like a rebellious flag. He set her on her feet and kissed her upturned face, and they melted against each other. It was like a romantic postcard and a cosmic jab at my feelings all at once. I envied these people in a way I hadn't experienced since I'd turned. Oh, I missed my humanity from time to time, but the point of all that had been stolen from me had never been driven home so incredibly hard before.

"This is…"

"Beautiful," Max finished for me. "This is my favorite part of the city. It's so alive, you'd never know it wasn't day."

Miserably, I closed my eyes. "I was going to say 'unbearable.'"

"Carrie, you okay?" He clasped my arm.

I put my hand over his. The romance of the place was getting to me, that was all. "I'm fine. Just worn out from the trip and worried about Nathan. It's nothing, really."

"Well, let's get this over with, then." He pointed to a redbrick building with beautiful white trim around the windows. At street level, patrons spilled out of a bustling café.

"That," Max said with a note of wistfulness in his voice, "is the headquarters of the Voluntary Vampire Extinction Movement."

I rolled my eyes. "I'm not quite sure I follow. Is it the two floors of what appear to be apartments upstairs, or the place with the dinner menu posted on the window?"

"You'll see." He slung my bag across his shoulder and grabbed my hand.

The café was hip with black walls and blue neon recessed lighting. The clientele dined off square plates with barely any food on them—fitting, since they were all thin as rails.

The maître d', a handsome, haughty young man all in black,

looked up from his reservation book. When he saw Max, he grinned. "Ah, Senor Harrison. And this is?"

"Dr. Carrie Ames. She's got a reservation." Max winked at the man, though it was barely perceptible.

The maître d' seemed to catch the meaning behind the expression, and he smiled pleasantly. "Follow me, please."

We wound our way among the tables toward a steel door with a black velvet rope in front of it. A small, black label bearing the letters *V.I.P.* proclaimed its purpose. Diners looked up with interest as we passed, probably trying to figure out how we, in our slept-in clothes, could possibly be VIP's.

The door was an elevator. The black button blended in with the wall. The maître d' pushed it and the panel slid open, allowing us inside.

Once the door closed, the young man turned to us. "First time visiting the Movement, Doctor?"

"First time visiting Spain, as a matter of fact." I tried to keep my tone light. I wasn't sure if I should give away my non-Movement status or not.

"You'll love it here." The man's English was slightly accented, but very good. "After six hundred years, I'm still not sick of it."

Our conversation was cut short by a rude electronic voice. It droned on in several different languages before it reached English. "Voice recognition confirmation required."

The maître d' held a finger to his lips to warn me to silence before stating, "Miguel."

"Voice sample confirmed," the voice informed us after a litany of foreign tongues. "Please enter security clearance code" was the next instruction I could understand.

"Miguel is the front line here at the Movement," Max explained as the vampire flipped open a hidden panel and punched a sequence of numbers on the keypad. "Nobody gets in without his okay. Still, there's plenty of backup."

"The waiter thing is a, how do the spy movies put it, a cover," Miguel said with a wry grin.

"What kind of backup?" I peered over Miguel's arm as the keypad retracted and the panel slid back into place. "What happens if you get it wrong?"

"A debilitating electronic impulse would momentarily paralyze us and the elevator would be sent to a secure floor. Assassins would be waiting to detain and interrogate us until our credentials cleared," Max said with a shrug. "It's not so bad."

"You would know," Miguel said with a laugh, clapping him on the back. "Max is not allowed to take the elevator by himself anymore."

Max was about to snipe back at him when the doors opened on a reception area so bright I had to shield my eyes. The walls, furniture and ceiling were stark white, the overhead fluorescents blinding. Only the floor, covered in low-pile, slate-gray carpet, and a very frightening girl at the front desk, stood out.

"Anne will take care of you from here," Miguel said as we exited the elevator. *"Buenos noches."*

"Buenos noches," Max repeated, though the pleasantry wasn't directed at Miguel.

"Hi, Max," the girl behind the desk said with a smile. Her expression was a startling contrast to the bleakness of her appearance. Her black hair, pale skin and zombie-couture black clothing reminded me of the bored teenagers who worked at the goth shop in the mall back home.

Max leaned casually on the tall counter. "Miss me, baby doll?"

"Oh, yeah. You know I did," the girl quipped with a roll of her eyes.

"This is Dr. Carrie Ames. She should be on the amnesty list."

"Amnesty list?" I asked, looking over the counter with interest.

"The 'do not kill' list," the girl clarified, holding out her hand. "I'm Anne."

I shook it, thinking it best to be polite in case I'd been omitted from the list. After a tense second or two of looking, she found my name. "Okay, you're cleared to meet with General Breton in an hour. Uh, and he is in a *mood* today."

"General?" I snorted. "So, are you guys more like the Salvation Army or the actual army?"

Max cleared his throat with a warning look. "General Breton demands the respect afforded him as an officer of the British Army."

"Oh, so he's, like, a real general." I swallowed. "Great."

Anne patted my arm reassuringly. "Only for, like, a couple years, and only in the War of 1812."

"Carrie is...new," Max said apologetically. "Remember, some of us are not quite as old as you."

Looking at the girl, I had a hard time believing she wasn't a sixteen-year-old human, but I'm a firm believer in never asking a woman her age.

"Sorry," Anne said sheepishly. Then, brightening, she asked, "Do you want the tour while you wait?"

"Sure," I answered for both Max and me. I wasn't about to stroll the halls of the Movement without him there to protect me in case some bored assassin got a hankering to kill.

Anne motioned for us to follow her as she walked to a set of double doors and slid a badge through a card reader. There was a buzz, then the lock popped loudly. She opened the door and ushered us inside.

The inner sanctum of the Movement was decorated similarly to the lobby, but doors with badge readers lined the hallway. Sentries were posted at regular intervals, clad in the same black uniform I'd seen the assassins wear the night they stormed Cyrus's mansion.

"All the rooms with blue labels like these are safe ones in the event of a security breach." She pulled one door open to reveal an office. A woman in a long, flowing caftan and a high turban looked up blandly from a pile of paperwork. "Something I can help you with?"

"Just pointing out the safe rooms to our visitors," Anne said cheerfully before she closed the door again.

"So, what are safe rooms?" I had to admit, the security around Movement headquarters wasn't as impressive as I'd imagined it to be.

"Safe rooms are exactly where you want to be when you hear the security breach countdown announcement," Max interjected. "If someone manages to get in, Anne can pull the alarm. You've got thirty seconds to get into a safe room—they're all unlocked—before the UV lights come on."

"Frying any vampire roaming the halls," she finished for him. "Pretty cool, huh?"

"Pretty cool," I agreed, sounding for all the world like a mom trying to imitate her teen daughter's speech. "But what if it's not a vampire? What if a human gets in?"

"We have a contingency plan for that," Anne replied smugly. "A furry contingency plan."

"Werewolves." Max made a disgusted noise. "They're not affected by UV lights. They do a manual sweep of the halls and kill anything still out there."

The idea that at any time someone could flip a switch and subject us to unnatural, but seriously harmful, daylight unnerved me, and I flinched as the fluorescent bulbs flickered above us.

"Don't worry," Anne said with a laugh. "Only a handful of people have the security breach code. Keeps us safer that way."

The tour continued through a maze of downward sloping halls. Each level had heightened security, like the Pentagon back home. Anne explained what some of the rooms contained, and I nodded politely, but my mind kept wandering to my worries over Nathan.

"And this," she said, sliding her card through a reader and opening a heavy door, "is where our tour ends. General Breton's office."

"Well, thanks," I offered lamely. "This has been…educational."

"You mean boring." Anne sighed dramatically. She might have been hundreds of years old, but she had the sarcastic American teenager act down pat. "Just imagine living here."

"Wah, wah, wah," Max teased cheerfully. "We'll see you on the way out."

Anne left us at the door with a little wave. Before Max could enter the office, I put my hand on his shoulder. "Okay, I get it. High security, superparanoia. Why are we here?"

"We're here because we need to help Nathan." Max put his foot in the door and let it close a bit. "Listen, it's pretty clear that whatever happened to him was a spell someone cast. The Movement can help us find out who."

"How? Do they keep a database of all witches, too? It would be impossible! Do you have any clue how many fifteen-year-old Sabrina wannabes there are out there?" I wanted to kick the wall, I was so frustrated. "Can you just please give me a straight answer? You always have before!"

"Fine!" He scanned the hallway before he spoke. "We're here to see the Oracle."

"The Oracle?" I repeated, a ridiculous image of the magic mirror from *Snow White* popping into my brain.

"She's a vampire, a really old one. She knows things. She knows practically everything, and what she doesn't, she can find out. But she's dangerous." Max blew out a breath, as if he knew the inevitable was about to come. "I was hoping I could convince Breton to let me in to see her."

"Without me, right?" What was it with male vampires that they thought I needed their constant protection? "No way."

"Carrie, you don't understand. She's completely unpredictable, and she's got this telekinesis thing…. She can kill you, Carrie. With her mind. Now, I've got no one depending on me. If I get poofed to dust, fine. But you need to be around for Nathan. I'm not gonna be responsible for getting you killed." His mouth set in a grim line. "And my impassioned speech is not moving you at all."

"Not an inch." I eyed the door. "Do you think this general will go along with your plan?"

Max considered a moment. "I think we have a better chance with him than with some of the others. Just let me do the talking, okay?"

My jaw dropped. "You know I want to help Nathan! Do you think I'd do something to jeopardize our chances?"

"Not intentionally." He opened the door and motioned me inside.

"What do you mean, not intentionally?" I demanded. But he wouldn't say anything more. I sighed and walked in to our meeting with General Breton.

5

Resistance

"What were you like before you died?"

The question startled Cyrus. He'd thought the Mouse asleep. If anyone could sleep through the noise the Fangs made upstairs. It seemed almost as soon as the sun went down, the music started and the engines roared to life, and then there was the inevitable screaming. Usually, the Mouse endeavored to be asleep before then. Having days of experience with them, she knew the Fangs' feeding schedule.

Cyrus would have been asleep himself, if he'd had the testicular fortitude to take the bed from her. He comforted himself by reasoning he liked the sounds of the screaming upstairs. He tugged his thin blanket in a futile attempt to cover his entire body. The hideous, polyester preacher clothes bunched with every movement, but he shuddered to imagine the rough upholstery against his naked skin, so he kept them on.

"What do you mean?" he asked now.

She rolled to face him. She'd stopped cringing from him, at least. Maybe the dark helped. "They brought you back from the dead. What were you like before you died? Were you…the way you are now?"

"Human?" Cyrus sniffed derisively. "No, I wasn't human."

"No." Wrinkles of frustration creased her brow as she sighed. "Did you…hurt people?"

He flinched when her hand strayed to her bandaged throat. He hated himself for regretting he'd hurt her. It was growing tiresome, this feeling of shame at doing something he would have found perfectly natural in the past.

"Of course I did. And far worse than you got." When she didn't respond, a wicked impulse overtook him. The first time he'd killed, he'd been put off by it. But he'd turned it into a game then, to make it engaging. What he'd done to her before had been mindless. How foolish of him. It had always been the chase that satisfied him. "I used to love girls like you."

She leaned up on her elbows, a hint of fear in her eyes. "What do you mean, *like me?*"

Shrugging, he folded the chair's footrest and sat up. "I'm sure you know your type. Starving for affection the way a dog starves for table scraps. Just plain enough that they never get the attention they want, but pretty enough to get noticed by men who are truly desperate. I'll bet you hiked that sundress up for your fair share of please-love-me fucks."

She sat up, hugged her knees. "You're wrong."

"Of course I am." He stood with his hands in his pockets, looking down at her. "You were one of the good girls."

Uncertainty quivered in her watery eyes as she nodded.

"Good girls don't exist." He sat beside her on the bed and placed his hand on her blanket-covered knee. "No matter how they tease, no matter how they insist they want to stay pure, they're burning to know what it's like."

"What…" She closed her eyes, shook her head as if to clear her thoughts. "What what's like?"

Cyrus peeled back the blanket slowly, and she hurried to arrange her skirt over her knees. He reached beneath her legs and cupped the warm, rounded muscle of her calf. "The feeling of completely surrendering yourself to another person."

"I've never—" Her breath hitched, cutting her denial short.

"You have." He moved his hand up, skimming the bend of her knee. She shivered, but didn't draw away.

He stilled his hand. "You don't have to deny it. I've had enough girls like you to know what's happening in your head. You're wondering what I did to them to make them give in. What pleasure I gave them to wear them down so they would surrender to me without hesitation. And you're wondering if I'll do the same to you."

He slid over her in one smooth motion. She gave no resistance, parting her thighs so he could lie between them. It was fear more than desire that made her compliant, he could tell by the look in her eyes. It encouraged him to continue.

"I'd woo them with words they'd never heard from another man, but I never told them I loved them. That was key. They thought if they gave a little more, let me do what I wanted, eventually it would be enough. They thought it would make them special to me, and I would love them." He slipped his hand between their bodies. She'd taken off her panties and washed them in the sink, and they hung over the towel rack to dry. There was nothing to buffer the boldness of his touch as he stroked her, just once, and she gasped and clutched his shoulders even as she tried to push him away.

"See? Even though you know it's a game, and you know what I am, you won't ask me to stop. Oh, you feel guilty and dirty, but you think you can live with the guilt as long as you get what you need." His mind reeled and he closed his eyes to regain control. Her body was wet and ready. He could take her.

He knew she would let him, but then what? He couldn't kill her. He didn't have the strength.

His mind reeled again. He didn't need such a shameful memory hanging around his neck. He had to get under control.

She trembled beneath him, looked up at him with her wide, innocent eyes. He couldn't help himself. He slid his thumb over her slick flesh and leaned close to her face to hear her soft, stifled moan.

"I loved this part," he whispered against her ear, still rubbing her as she rotated her hips against his hand. "But it wasn't the best part."

"What was?" She didn't want to know, that much was evident from her tone, but at the same time he knew her curiosity was too great. It was the same with all of them. Their curiosity was their downfall.

"The best part..." He nipped at her throat, avoiding that horrible, guilt-inducing bandage there, and slipped one finger inside her. "The best part was biting them and listening to them die as I used them."

She tensed. Her body offered too much resistance as he pushed the digit in farther. She was a virgin.

Nausea clawed his guts, and he withdrew, rising to his knees. He'd expected it, of course, but not the shame that paralyzed him. Where had it come from, when he'd been doing so well?

She sat up, a momentary frown crossing her face before she reached for him. Too shocked to resist, he sat motionless as she covered his mouth with hers.

It was as if he twisted helplessly in a powerful storm, relying on a woefully inadequate tether to anchor him to solid ground. He'd had this feeling before, this desperation for human touch that mirrored hers. He'd learned to guard himself against it. The crushing rejection on her face when he pushed her away shot suspicious pain through his chest. It steeled his resolve. "I won't let you whore yourself to me in return for false affection!"

Her hurt boiled over into rage. "Why? You did it for all those other girls! You did it, then you killed them! Why not me?"

"Is that what you want?" Now that he'd touched her skin, heard her soft moans in his ear, the thought repulsed him. Perhaps he had more in common with those needy girls than he'd wanted to admit.

"I want to get it over with!" She flailed her arms and legs like a child having a temper tantrum as she screamed in frustration and despair. "I'm dead already! I just want to get it over with!"

Cyrus paced at the end of the bed, his heart hammering his ribs. How did one deal with humans when they lost control like this? In the first hours after he'd become mortal again, he'd felt panic and terror. He'd prayed for death. He knew her pain. If he could take it from her, he would.

In the weak moonlight that lit the kitchen area, he spied a block of knives on the counter. As soon as the Mouse was dead, he would have peace again, inside and out. No more doubting himself, no more fighting this frightening new humanity.

His anger dried up as her own temper subsided into small, childish sobs, and he felt like a monster again. No, *monster* was too strong a word. *Craven.* That described him better. Craven, to cower before such a formidable opponent as a weeping woman.

"Don't cry." He said it harshly, but he knew it was not a command she would obey. Cursing, he wrapped his arms around her shaking body and pulled her close, as if he could absorb the pain radiating from her.

"I'm just sick of waiting," she sobbed against his shoulder. "I'm so scared, and I'm sick of waiting."

He held her until dawn, though she'd cried herself to sleep

much earlier. As sunlight filtered through the small, basement windows, the stupidity of his actions came crashing down on him.

You're pathetic. It was his father's voice, not his own, that echoed through his head. *Look at you, staying at her side like a whimpering puppy.*

As much as he hated the voice, he knew it was right. There was no room for his conscience in this place.

Still, he couldn't tear himself from the comforting warmth of her body. And that frightened him more than any words his father might use to shame him.

In med school, I dreamed of one day owning my own practice. I'd envisioned exactly the right colors and furnishings to put my patients at ease as they waited to be seen.

The general should have called me for pointers. The waiting room of his office was as stark and white as the rest of the Movement's underground compound. The general, however, took "stark" to a whole new level. Two cold, stainless steel chairs were the only furniture in the room. The fluorescent lights were so bright it seemed the place glowed, and the walls blended seamlessly into the floor, giving one the impression of floating in a void.

Like purgatory, only with folding chairs.

Max sat beside me, drumming his fingers on his thighs. "We weren't supposed to keep him waiting, but he'll keep us waiting?"

My nerves were too fried for me to bother concentrating on Max's sarcasm. I'd anticipated the general would be a hard sell, considering the way Max and Anne had spoken of him, not to mention the fact he'd been the only staff member I'd heard of so far with a military rank before his name.

Of course, Max kept reassuring me things would be fine. I really wished I could believe that, but when the door to the inner office opened, I wanted to run.

My stomach returned to its proper latitude as my eyes bugged out of my head. A woman, tall and slender, dressed from neck to toes in black leather, strode through the door like a Bond girl. Her deep gold gaze slid over us, her slightly upturned eyes deadly serious. Her black hair fell down her back in a perfect, waist-length braid. She growled at us as she passed.

Max's face flashed into feeding mode, his upper and lower jaws elongating to form a vaguely porcine snout with dripping canines. He snarled viciously, then his face returned to normal as quickly as it had changed.

The woman didn't acknowledge him again, and when the outer door clicked shut behind her, he stood and kicked the chair. "Bitch!"

"What was that about? Bad breakup?"

Judging by the look on Max's face, my humor was not appreciated. "That filthy dog? She wishes."

I held up my hands. "Hey, I don't know her, but I should inform you that it greatly offends my sense of sisterhood to hear you call another woman a dog."

"That's what she is." He pointed accusingly to the door. "A stinking werewolf. The day the Movement let them join the ranks, I should have turned in my resignation."

Morbid curiosity forced my gaze toward the closed door she'd exited through. "What is your thing against werewolves?"

"It's not my thing against werewolves that makes me dislike that one. Bella DeCesare. She's a real bitch." He winced at the terminology. "Breton gives her all sorts of prime assignments, flies her all over because she's his only assassin who can travel commercial. He says it's because she's got the best kill record of all the werewolves in the Movement. I say he's boning her."

"Nice." I remembered Cyrus talking about lupins and how they'd distanced themselves from their more primitive cousins, but the way he'd described werewolves had made me picture hairy, half human beasts loping around in the woods, preying on innocent campers. The woman I'd seen had been anything but primitive. "So, they play for this side, as well. There were some lupins at Cyrus's house, but I wasn't sure exactly who they were."

A look of utter disgust crossed Max's face. "Let's limit your use of that name to about zero times a day. But she's not a lupin. She's a werewolf. According to them, they're not interchangeable terms." He sounded as if he didn't care two figs for their differences. "They're not as different as the lupins want you to believe. Werewolves are still tied to the earth and moon. There was some pack council a hundred years ago where they met to discuss controlling their cycles—"

"Wait," I interrupted. "We are talking about their changing-into-dogs cycles and not menstruation, right?"

"Yes. And let's go ahead and put that one on the zero tolerance vocab list, as well." He gave another disgusted look. "Anyway, werewolves have always been really into that hippie-dippy earth magic crap like Nathan's got in his bookstore. Except they know what they're doing, because they're more or less ruled by nature. For centuries, they've dabbled in magic to alter time and skip over the days of the full moon's influence. Then some of them turned to science, came up with an injection that will suppress the change. The resultant rift split the species into two clans, werewolves and lupins.

"The lupins believe they're superior, because they advocate the vaccine that allows them to live as humans. The werewolves think the lupins are traitors for turning away from magic. So a war started, and since lupins have no problem feeding on innocent humans, the Movement sided with the werewolves. They join up and get the chance to kill lupins and vampires. Personally, I wouldn't care if they lost their collective cool and ripped each other to shreds."

"I'll remember that, when it's time to call in a cleaning crew to mop the fur and guts off the walls."

I jumped at the cultured, but very commanding, British voice. So did Max. The man who'd spoken surprised me. I had definitely formed a picture in my head based around Breton's military title. I'd expected a man in his fifties with an iron jaw, deep lines by his eyes and a haircut so precise as to be geometrical. Breton was nothing like that, except for the iron jaw. He'd probably been turned in his late thirties. His long, wheat-colored hair was pulled back in a severe horsetail, accentuating his sharp features and long, straight nose. His lips quirked in an expression that was either annoyance or amusement. It was hard to tell which.

"General Breton, I presume." I hoped I sounded more confident than I felt as I extended my hand and prayed my palms weren't sweaty.

The man didn't take it. "We are not so formal here. You may call me General, Dr. Ames."

"And you can call me..." I hesitated, rolling his words around in my brain. "Doctor?"

He gave me a cool, appraising look. "Come inside."

We followed him through the door, Max showing Breton's back the middle finger the whole time.

The inner office was a bit of a shock, considering the appearance of the waiting area. The walls were dark paneled wood, the carpet a deep, rich print. A huge desk with a carved emblem of a foxhunter dominated the room. Two stiff wing chairs stood before it, where Breton motioned for us to sit. It looked as if we'd entered a bad theme restaurant of British paraphernalia. A coat of arms and crossed swords rested above the mantel over a huge fireplace, and the Union Jack hung from a flag post in the corner. Behind the desk, two large windows—obvious fakes, considering we were below ground—showed a sunny country scene. *Somebody's missing the sunshine.*

Not that I could blame him. I found myself occasionally longing for a lazy day of sunbathing on the beach.

"That's very…pastoral." I tried to sound friendly, but it came off wooden.

Breton's eyes narrowed. They were gray, but nothing like Nathan's. Nathan's eyes were changeable, storm clouds with the occasional silver lining. Breton's eyes were stone-colored, and just as formidable. "York. Lovely hunting there." He settled into his chair, which looked infinitely more comfortable than ours, and placed a manila envelope on the desk. "These may be of interest to you."

Max reached for the envelope. When he lifted it, glossy, black-and-white photographs slid out.

I covered my mouth, but couldn't look away. The horrible pictures showed a woman, her head nearly severed, the column of her throat ripped away to the spine.

"I believe your friend Mr. Galbraith is responsible for this?" Breton asked, as though he needed confirmation.

A wave of sickness crept up my own throat as I nodded slowly. On the news, a witness had mentioned the victim's throat had been torn. In reality, the whole front of her neck had been excised. The ragged edges of the wound were the impressions of teeth.

"Nathan's been possessed by something," Max explained, never looking at the photos. "That's why we're here."

"Yes, that's what Anne tells me. She said he attacked you, Dr. Ames. Tell me what happened." The general leaned back in his chair as though it would fool me into believing his mind hadn't been made up already.

I kept it short. "I went downstairs to our bookstore—"

"You live with Mr. Galbraith?" Breton tapped his lips with his forefinger. "Are you married?"

"No, he's my…" I stopped myself before I could say "sire." Nathan was on probation as it was, and killing this jogger definitely didn't help matters. If they knew he'd saved my life by giving me his blood, instead of just doing away with me as Movement law dictated, he'd definitely be toast.

I tried to think of a way to explain our convoluted relationship and came up with nothing. "He's my…lover?"

A weird expression crossed the general's face, the physical equivalent of the phrase "too much information." "I see. Please, continue."

"I went down to the bookstore. It was messed up, and Nathan attacked me." It hurt just remembering it, phantom pain from the attack, phantom pain where the blood tie should have been.

Breton pushed one of the photos toward me. "He also attacked this young woman. How did you escape when she did not?"

I bit my lip. I assumed the reason Nathan had left me alone was the smell of his blood in me. I couldn't reveal that to Breton. "I talked to him. I asked him not to hurt me."

"I see." The general nodded and reached into the envelope. He pulled a slip of yellow paper from it, and Max took a loud breath.

"What is that?" I looked from the general to Max. "What's going on?"

"It's a kill order." Max's face was grim.

Before I could protest, Breton spoke. "If Mr. Galbraith could be reasoned with at the time he attacked Dr. Ames, he was not possessed."

"What about the symbols?" I stammered. "He had symbols carved into his skin."

"No matter." Breton waved a hand. "Mr. Galbraith was on probation. He's killed again, and he must be dealt with."

"Dealt with?" I stood, knocking the chair back. Max grabbed my arm but I shrugged him off. "I was there. I saw him. Nathan would never do anything like this! Something forced him to act that way."

"And I'm supposed to take your word for that?" Breton's eyes narrowed. "The word of a vampire who has never joined the Movement, standing up for a vampire who turned his back on all we stand for?"

My hands shook with anger. "Fine. I'll join the Movement right now. Where do I sign up? Because once I get my membership card, I'm going to lodge a complaint against you for being…such an asshole!"

"Harrison," Breton barked, though his enraged gaze never left mine. "Kindly keep your visitor under control before drastic measures are taken!"

"Calm down!" Max had never used such a tone with me. That he did it now showed how afraid he was of Breton. "General, there has to be some way to fix this so Nathan doesn't have to die."

"The decision is final." The general scraped the photos into a neat pile.

I turned helplessly to Max. He couldn't look me in the eye. I knew then nothing could be done.

I glared at the slip of yellow paper. For a moment, I imagined grabbing the kill order and shredding it into a hundred pieces, but that wouldn't solve anything. So long as the Movement wished it, Nathan was already dead.

"What about the Oracle?" I asked, hope clutching feebly for purchase in my chest. "What if she—"

Breton's eyes narrowed. "No one has given you permission to speak to the Oracle."

"We were going to ask you, General." Max gave me a frosty glare. "I just hadn't gotten around to it."

"The Oracle is useless. I do not believe she has made an accurate prediction to date. And she is…unpredictable. We cannot risk a civilian in contact with her."

"I think I can handle myself!" It was definitely the wrong tactic to take with him. I realized it too late.

The general shook his head. "We are finished here. See yourselves out, please."

Max put his hand on my arm. "Let's go, Carrie."

Before I knew what I was doing, I reached for the kill order. "Fine. If someone is going to kill him, it might as well be me."

"You're not Movement." Breton offered no further explanation.

"I'm his fledgling!" I pounded my fist on the table. There was no sense keeping it secret if he were going to be killed, anyway.

The general looked to Max, an expression somewhere between anger and mirth crossing his face. "Harrison? You told me she was sired by Simon Seymour."

"I was!" In my anger I'd forgotten the trouble Max would get into for knowing—and not reporting—that Nathan had revived me. "Cyrus tried to kill me. Nathan gave me his blood to revive me. But Max didn't know."

"Is this true, Harrison?" Breton looked at Max the way a venomous snake looks at its next meal.

Max nodded, giving me a terse glance. "I don't doubt it for a minute. Maybe you should let her go after Nathan herself. She'd know best where to find him."

The general shook his head. "We can't trust a non-Movement vampire to carry out this kind of job. Especially not if he is her sire. You know as well as I do the kind of pain that causes. She is not likely to inflict it on herself."

"I'm sorry, Carrie," Max said, taking my hand and squeezing it.

It couldn't end like this. My mind raced. Nathan had given

me some training, but I would be no match in a fight with an assassin. On top of that, I had no idea where I'd find Nathan or if I'd find him in time. For all I knew, another assassin might be headed for him this very moment.

"Let Max do it, then," I blurted.

Max started, as though he'd just woken to find himself in an unfamiliar room. "What?"

"Please, General." I gripped the edge of the desk until my knuckles turned white, silently willing him to bend. "Max and Nathan were friends. I trust him to get the job done. I know he won't let Nathan suffer."

"Your trust in Harrison does not concern me." The comment seemed even colder in Breton's crisp, British accent. He took a deep breath, frowning. When he exhaled, his expression lightened. "Fine. Harrison, tomorrow evening you're on a flight back. But I don't want her within a ten-mile radius of the final kill. Do I make myself clear?"

"Crystal." Max picked up the kill order from the desk and folded it, slipping it into the pocket of his worn leather coat.

"Good. I trust you both know the way out." Breton handed the pictures to Max, but I took them.

We were nearly at the door when the general spoke again. "And, Harrison, if you fail to do your duty by the Movement, I'll send someone who won't."

Numb, I followed Max to the hallway. "Don't do it," I said flatly, once the door had closed behind us.

Max gripped my shoulders and twisted me to face him. His fingers dug painfully into my flesh, and I protested with a loud, "Ow!"

"This is not a game, Carrie." He held his face inches from mine. "I'm going to have to kill Nathan. I don't know what you were thinking in there, but I still have a job to do."

He released me and turned to walk away. I rubbed one sore shoulder. "Yeah, but you don't know where he is yet. You can stall for time while I figure out what's going on."

He laughed, the way someone would laugh at a child's overly simple solution to a serious problem. "And how do you plan on doing that? You've got no resources, no one willing to help you. Even if you can magically cure Nathan of whatever has a hold on him, I'm still under orders to kill on sight. You're on your own here. Nathan is as good as dead, and you're fooling yourself if you think otherwise."

"So that's it then?" I shook my head in disbelief. "You're just giving up?"

"I'm watching my own back!"

I closed my eyes. This was not the Max I knew. This was a complete stranger standing before me. "Max, please trust me. Trust that I'm not going to do anything that would put you in harm's way."

"You're going to do what you need to do for yourself, Carrie." He wiped his sleeve across his forehead. "It's what survivors do."

I looked at the pictures he held. Breton hadn't bothered to put them in an envelope. The cadaver's empty stare bore into me from the glossy surface of the photo.

"I'm not interested in helping myself," I said, choking back tears. "I just want to save Nathan."

"It's too late for that," Max said softly. "The Movement has made their decision, and no matter what happens, they'll just keep coming."

I shook my head. "Not from the Movement. I want to save him from himself."

6

Oracle

Max needed to gather some supplies before we headed out. I had no idea what kind of equipment he needed to kill my sire, but I refused to help him retrieve it. He headed to the armory after giving me strict orders to go directly to the reception area.

Not that I had a choice. As soon as he walked away, a guard came from seemingly nowhere and steered me toward the lobby.

"Nothing personal," he said as he guided me through the doors. "Just can't have non-Movement vampires roaming the halls."

Anne had returned to her post at the desk, and she looked up when the doors closed. Her face brightened. "So, how'd it go with the general?"

"Not well." Normally, I would have resented having to spill to a total stranger, but she wasn't exactly wheedling me for information. In fact, her casual interest made me *want* her to wheedle. I'd never realized I was such an attention whore. "He basically shot me down."

"What a prick." She sounded genuinely sorry. "That's too bad."

I scuffed my toes on the carpet as I went to one of the plush chairs. "He's a very stubborn man, isn't he?"

Anne stood and came around the front of the desk, where she dropped to the floor and sat cross-legged. The shiny buckles on her knee-high combat boots caught the light as she made herself comfortable. "Well, you don't get far in this organization if you're not stubborn."

"I don't know." I watched her toy with the black rubber bracelets that looped her wrist. "You seem to do okay."

With a crooked smile, she rolled her eyes. "Yeah, I'm a great receptionist. Where's Max?"

"Loading up on gadgets and supplies with which to kill my sire." I slumped down in the chair. "I'm insane, to be waiting for him. I should be tearing off to the States."

"Yeah, on a commercial airliner? Good luck." She shook her head. "Max has to look tough and serious about the job. I doubt he'll actually kill him."

"Won't he be penalized?" The Movement seemed to dole out "probation" like candy on Halloween.

"Nah." She made a face to accompany the guttural sound. "Max has shirked assignments before. He'll never come out and actually say, 'No, I'm not going to kill this vampire,' but I can tell when it's going to happen. He'll call to check in and say things like, 'No luck yet, but I'll find the bastard.' You know, things like John Wayne might say in a movie."

"That's how Max usually talks," I reminded her.

She rolled her eyes. "I know, right? But this is different. He puts up a much tougher front if he's reluctant to do the job."

Her assurances made me feel a little better. As much as Max and Nathan bickered, neither of them truly wanted the other dead. Maybe once we were away from the eyes and ears of the Movement, Max would change his mind.

"So," Anne said brightly, grasping the toes of her boots and leaning forward. "What did you think of the place?"

"I thought it was…nice," I offered lamely. "Not at all what I was expecting."

"I know, right? Most people think it's going to be stone walls and torchlight and guys with long beards, in scary robes. I mean, we have the guys with long beards, but they only wear their robes during a ritual." She said this with a shrug, as if it was completely normal to deal with occult forces in the workplace. "Aside from them, there's really nothing that weird here."

"Well, except the Oracle," I began casually. "But I guess I won't be seeing her anytime soon. What's she like?"

"She's like…" Anne pursed her lips as she thought. "She's like a magic eight ball, only she can kill you."

I straightened a little at that. "Like, she can answer your questions?" The "like" popped from my mouth naturally. I could see how Anne had easily adopted modern teenspeak.

"Like, with her mouth? No. But she talks through telepathy all the time." Anne shrugged again. "But she doesn't usually say anything that makes sense. Why, did you have a question?"

I wasn't sure if I should admit it or not. The notion of "personal boundaries" seemed to have escaped this eternal teenager, and while she was nice, I didn't feel like examining my deepest fears with her. I settled on a diplomatic, "Yes."

"That's cool. I've asked her all sorts of questions, but she's never answered. I mean, one time she did give me a freaky vision of my spine snapping in, like, four places, but she never actually did it so I'm not worried." After considering a moment, Anne looked up from her bracelets. "And the general wouldn't clear you to see her?"

"I got the distinct impression the general doesn't care much for the Oracle's knowledge." I picked at the arm of the chair, though there weren't any loose threads or pilled fabric to prompt me to do so.

Anne sighed. "A lot of people here are that way. But you know, any information you could get would probably be helpful, considering your situation. Right?"

"Well, it's not like it matters now. From the way Max made it sound, you need special permission to see her." I sighed loudly in frustration.

There was a long pause. I'd expected an immediate response from Anne, and when I didn't hear one, I looked up. She dangled a key card on a black cord from her fingers, smiling. "Or friends with security clearance."

I hesitated. "You mean, you?"

"Uh-huh. I have clearance to every place in this building. Due to my excellent years of service. And the fact I have to sometimes escort guests around the building." Her naughty grin reached the corners of her eyes now. "So, you wanna?"

I had the uncomfortable feeling I'd gotten in high school when someone would offer me a joint or ask me to skip school. I was pretty good at resisting peer pressure, but she was persuasive, and the situation was certainly different. "Won't you get into trouble?"

She made a plosive sound of denial, as if the answer was obvious. "Only if we get caught. Besides, it's not like they're gonna get rid of me."

She made a compelling argument. Of course, it probably wouldn't have been if our meeting with the general hadn't been so disastrous.

Anne seemed to take the reason for my hesitation as fear. "She hasn't hurt anyone lately. They changed her diet. She was getting too much male blood and the testosterone made her crabby. Now she's pretty mellow."

I felt a fleeting moment of sanity, and seized it. "Max told me to stay here."

"So?" Anne got to her feet and went behind the desk, where she grabbed a pad of sticky notes. "We'll leave him a message. Besides, he's in the armory. He'll be there awhile."

"Men can't resist the lure of shiny new toys," I reluctantly conceded. "He's going to freak out, you know."

"Don't worry, I know how to handle him. He's not so tough." She scrawled something on the paper and stuck it to her computer monitor, then offered to take my bag from me. "It'll be safe back here," she said, stowing it beneath her desk. "You sure didn't bring much."

I followed her to the doors. "Max packed it. Guess he didn't plan on staying long. We leave tomorrow night."

"That's too bad." She shrugged and ran her badge through the reader. "The hotel they've got you staying in is pretty nice."

The fact we were staying in a hotel at all surprised me. "I thought you guys would have underground dormitories or something."

"Oh, we do," Anne assured me. "But only for the staff who are permanently on call. Like me, for instance, or the doctors who take care of the Oracle. The new assassins in training and their mentors stay here, too, but it's not permanent."

A tall, thin man in a frock coat and an Edgar Allen Poe haircut passed us and nodded curtly. Anne gave him a wave and continued on.

"You must be a pretty good receptionist, if they want to keep you on 24/7." I ran my fingers along the wall as we walked, a horrible habit I'd adopted as a human and had to break when I'd learned exactly how many diseases you could pick up that way. Now that germs were no longer a concern, I didn't mind it. It drove Nathan crazy, though.

"Actually, I'm not just a receptionist. I'm more like Miguel," she explained, thankfully taking my mind off my sire.

"Max said Miguel was security. You must have background as an assassin, then?"

She nodded. "Three hundred years. They finally let me retire back in the fifties. Er, the eighteen fifties. Too bad, though. During that whole 'don't exercise or your uterus will fall out' time period, no one would have seen a female assassin coming."

"Three hundred years? Wait…" I stopped her with a hand on her arm. "Nathan told me the Movement was two hundred years old."

"Yeah, but before we started calling ourselves the Movement, because it made a better acronym, we were the Order of the Brethren. Things were a lot tougher back then, let me tell you."

We ventured farther into the building than she'd taken us on our previous tour. This area, I noticed, had fewer safe rooms and more security labels. We reached a large set of double doors with a thick, black-and-yellow-striped line around them. Huge red warning signs, printed in several different languages, plastered the doors. In addition to a key card reader, I noticed there was a palm scan device and a keypad on the wall.

"This is the most secure section of headquarters," Anne explained. "Only high level administrators and security have access. Oh, and the scientists who monitor the Oracle."

"Scientists?" I chewed my lip nervously as I watched her key in the codes. The English language sticker on the door warned an improper access sequence would result in a security breach alert, and I didn't remember where I'd seen the last safe room.

"Yeah. She's got a whole team of doctors and chemists and pharmacists keeping her medicated and fed well and under control." The same computerized voice from the elevator informed us that the access sequence was accepted, and Anne pushed open the door with a flourish.

"If she's drugged up, why is Max so afraid of her?" He's not the kind of guy to be blindly afraid of anything.

Anne made another "pff" sound of dismissal. "He was on the team that moved her to the new facility back in the eighties. Really, he shouldn't have been assigned, he was too young. He's too young now. Anyway, her meds didn't hold, and she twisted one of the team members' heads off."

"Twisted?" My guts mimicked the motion implied by my word. "She's got that kind of power?"

"Oh, yeah. She's got mad telekinesis. It would be cool, if she didn't use it so destructively. But that's why she's constantly doped up. Ah, here we are!"

We turned left and went through thoroughly unintimidating swinging doors, into a room with black walls like an exhibit in a museum. A dark window the size of a movie screen dominated one wall, separated from us by a brass railing.

"Stand there," Anne instructed, moving toward the window, where she turned a dial. The lights dimmed slowly on our side of the glass as the other side illuminated.

"This is like the penguin house at Sea World," I said, my voice sounding way too loud in the quiet room, and Anne snorted in laughter.

Behind the glass, a void of still redness surrounded a murky, suspended shape. It took me a moment to realize what the redness was.

"Is that blood?"

Anne joined me at the rail. "Yup. The Oracle can't feed in the traditional sense anymore. She requires much more blood to support her tissues. Total immersion allows her to draw the blood in through her lungs and pores as well as her digestive system. The blood cycles through purifying and oxygenating filters continually, to provide optimal nourishment for her."

"So, you've got a giant heart-lung machine back there, pumping blood?" I squinted at the tank.

Anne nodded and shrugged. "Pretty much."

As the lights grew brighter, the shape came into focus. A figure, nude and obviously female, floated in the blood. What appeared to be intravenous lines and electrode wires connected to her slender limbs and bald head. Her face was relaxed, eyes closed as if in sleep. She was perfect, except for the three pointed horns protruding from her skull.

I thought back to Cyrus's New Year's party, and the creatures I'd seen there. "Is she part demon?"

"No. The Oracle is pretty old, one of the oldest we know about. The horns are a natural consequence of the aging process. We get twisted when we age." Anne held out her arm and pushed her plastic bracelets aside, revealing the faint beginning of what could only be described as a dew claw. She covered it again with a shrug. "She's also the most psychically gifted vampire we know of."

"You've got that memorized like you work at the Smithsonian," I said, leaning over the rail. "So, she's sealed up in there, or what?"

"Yup. She's been held in various methods of containment since her capture in 1079, Common Era, and was given to the Movement in its first year of inception by King George the II in 1765."

"The Movement is that old?" I asked, my awe diverted for an instant from the Oracle. "I thought back then it was the Order of the Brethren?"

Before Anne could answer, the blood in the tank surged, pounding the glass with a wave that created a thunderous echo.

"Don't worry about that," Anne assured me. "She's responding to your voice because you're new."

Much in the way a big, scary dog is "just playing."

"She has a staff of round-the-clock caregivers who administer sedatives. That's why she's not all vamped out in the face area. The drugs they give her keep her in a light coma. It's safer, and more conducive to her visions. And her specialists monitor her psychic readouts. We can accurately monitor major world events days in advance with the information she supplies us. You know, if she chooses to supply it."

It might have been a trick of the changing light, but I could have sworn the Oracle's eyes opened.

"Weird," Anne whispered. "I'm gonna page them, let them know she's awake."

So, it wasn't just an eerie illusion. Neither, apparently, was the voice in my head. *Carrie,* it called softly. The chill tone paralyzed me. *Carrie, he has come back.*

"Who has?" I asked out loud. But I knew. I knew in my heart who she meant. Two months of horrible nightmares flashed through my mind. *No!* I shouted back at the Oracle through my mind. *Cyrus is dead. No matter what bizarre scenario you try and come up with, nothing can bring him back!*

You doubt me, vampire?

I'm fairly sure that's exactly when things started to go wrong. The Oracle's voice filled my head, and she was angry. *What do you want, vampire? Why do you come to me?*

You told me he's come back, I pressed. *I need to know who you're talking about.*

You're afraid I speak of the one called Simon. But I do not. Another wave of blood rocked the tank and pounded against the glass. Anne, who'd run to the intercom, shrank against the wall. I don't know if she'd called for help or not.

"Simon?" I asked aloud. My thoughts were so scrambled, it took me a moment to remember Cyrus's real name. "I'm not afraid of Cyrus."

You shouldn't be. Though he lives again, he lives. I speak of the one who devours the essence of my blood kin. Another wave rocked the tank.

"The Soul Eater?" But another part of her statement demanded my attention. "What do you mean, Cyrus lives?"

Raised by the toothsome ones in the land of the dead. As the first rises, the second falls. Both will be devoured.

Anne edged closer, keeping to the wall. "We need to go. She's not safe when she's agitated like this."

I couldn't leave yet. Not when I was getting the first real answers I'd received since we'd arrived. "The Soul Eater possessed Nathan?"

The waves of blood came faster and faster now. I felt like a fish in an aquarium someone kept tapping on, and I struggled to keep my mind focused. From the corner of my eye, I saw Anne cover her ears.

You have your answer. Seek the toothsome ones in the land of the dead. The flesh and blood of the destroyer.

Cold fear gripped me. "What if I can't find him? I don't understand!"

The Oracle's eyes snapped open again. In the same instant, Movement guards charged into the room, followed by Max. "Carrie, get away from her!"

The Oracle opened her mouth. Waves of sound rippled through the blood around her as her scream filled the air and my head. *"He will become a god!"*

"No, no, no!" Anne cried, clawing at the wall as if seeking a handhold. A second later, I knew why. As if she were nothing more than a feather in a breeze, her small body flew across the room. Feathers rarely make such a sickening crunch when they collide with walls, though. She crumpled to the floor in a deathly still heap. I tried to run to her, but my feet were immobilized.

"Anne!" Before Max could move, an invisible force pinned him to the wall.

Oddly, my fear fled. The Oracle's voice blocked out the sound of Max's frantic urging for me to run. She insisted I come closer, and I couldn't find a good enough reason not to.

I slid under the brass rail and crossed the space to the tank. Each step reverberated through me like a thunderclap. As I drew nearer to the glass, the Oracle began to move, taking long, lazy steps through the blood. Suspended, she looked as though she walked through air.

The Oracle reached for me. I pressed my palms flat against the tank, expecting the glass to be cool and feeling slightly sickened when I realized the blood behind it was body temperature. I thought she would bring her hands to meet mine on the glass. Instead, she twisted them into claws. At the same time, my throat crushed closed.

I wouldn't die from not breathing, but I was fairly certain I'd die from having my head twisted off my neck.

No! I pleaded in my mind. *I'm not going to die like this. Why would you give me this information only to let it die with me?*

Her hold was broken. The lights flared up in the room and darkened in the tank. Max's arms were suddenly around me, pulling me from the room. Vampires in white coats rushed in to tend Anne.

"What the hell was that?" Max repeated over and over at my side as we raced down the hallway.

I couldn't answer him. The voice of the Oracle echoed in my memory.

He will become a god.

Cyrus jerked awake screaming.

The Mouse sat up beside him and put her arm around his

bare shoulders. Her skin felt too hot and dry, magnifying the slick, cold sweat coating his body.

"You had a nightmare," she said. There was no emotion, just a matter-of-fact statement.

His first instinct was to slap her, but the now-familiar shame washed through him, and he restrained himself. He rose from the narrow bed they'd shared. He'd reveled in the feeling of holding her as she'd slept. It was a sensation he couldn't compare to anything in his vast, lurid experience. Now, in the harsh light of day that streamed weakly through the small basement windows, the night seemed dirty somehow.

He'd been a centuries-old vampire with unlimited financial resources and powerful charm at his disposal. There had never been a time when he could not have what he wanted, and he'd certainly never wanted to comfort a sobbing woman through the dark hours of the night.

You would have for Carrie.

He grabbed his—no, the dead priest's—shirt from the end of the bed and pulled it on, reminding himself to be annoyed with the cheap fabric. He didn't remember taking it off, had only a dim recollection of shrugging out of it and turning over to enfold Mouse in his arms. She called after him as he stalked into the bathroom, but he ignored her and slammed the door, needing space and peace and a way to block the horrible dream from his mind.

But he'd dreamed of *her.* As in all things where Carrie was concerned, he couldn't so easily forget. In the dream, he'd held her. Not a salacious embrace. He'd actually held her. She had let him stroke her hair and kiss her. She had told him she loved him. When Carrie had been his fledgling, she'd always hovered on the edge of revulsion when she'd touched him. In his dream, she'd loved him the way he'd wanted to be loved.

When he'd opened his eyes, he'd held the bleeding, heartless corpse of his beloved Elsbeth. He'd shaken her, as desperate to revive her as he had been the night she'd died. Her auburn curls and delicate features had morphed quickly into Carrie's pale blond hair and strong-boned face. That's when he'd woken, screaming, to find the Mouse beside him, and for a horrible moment, he was certain he'd killed her, too.

I've got to get out of here, he told himself as he turned on the tap and splashed cold water on his face. *I'm losing my mind.*

He shook the thought off. Too much had occurred in his past, too much horror, too much death, to lose his mind over a simple girl like the Mouse. If he was going to lose his mind over anything, it would not be her.

Not if I have anything to say about it, that is. His own voice sounded like his father's in his head, and it pleased him. Finally, he was becoming like his old self again.

Why did that thought sicken him? Why wouldn't he want to reclaim that part of himself his traitorous, human body wanted to erase?

Stupid boy, you never learn. He leaned his forehead against the mirror. Had it been his father or the Soul Eater, the creature who'd evicted Jacob Seymour's sanity, who'd said those words to him time and again? It had been Jacob, at first, after his dear Moll had walked into the sun and burned to ash, and again, one hundred years later, when lovely Francesca had plunged herself into the bathing tub full of holy water. But by the time Elsbeth's blood had cooled and congealed on her marble skin, Jacob Seymour was long dead, and it had been the Soul Eater who'd come to Cyrus. And when Carrie had sunk the stake into his heart, he'd heard Jacob's voice in his head, taunting him with those same words.

Cyrus opened the medicine cabinet. There he found shaving

soap, a razor and scissors. *Morons.* He couldn't help his utter contempt for his captors. They'd been too busy playing at torture with the Mouse and her holy friends to think of removing potential weapons from his cell. The vampires upstairs were either stupid or so out of touch with their humanity, they didn't realize how easy it would be for him to slit his own wrists and end the waiting.

Or would it? Everything about him was so...mortal. Would he really be capable of taking his own life, when the very thought of it, even in the abstract, sent a shudder of revulsion through him? No. He would not go back to that ghost world. Not if he could help it.

He should kill her, he decided. He would prove to himself he had learned something. He would prove to himself he could still be the vampire his father had wanted at his side, and hopefully his father would feel the same.

Cyrus's total dependence on the Mouse for his day-to-day activities would be a hurdle. It was easy enough to overcome. If he learned to live a mortal life, just for a while until his father found him, he could be done with her.

He availed himself of the priest's toiletries, pleased at the thought of returning to his former state. With each stroke of the razor, he hardened his resolve. Though his servants had always taken care of running the modern appliances in the kitchen, he considered himself a smart man and was fairly confident in his ability to figure things out for himself. When he was finished grooming, he would simply go out and kill the Mouse. With his hands, if necessary; with a knife, better. Either way, she would be dead.

Before she can hurt me like the rest of them. See, Father, I have learned something, after all.

He could do it. She made him weak. Killing her would make him strong.

The thought brought on a frown. He didn't like the way it contorted his face, so he forced his features into an impassive mask.

Using the flimsy, plastic comb he'd found in the medicine cabinet, he worked to untangle his long hair. It took only a few painful snarls for him to realize the sad truth. It would have to be cut.

You're making excuses not to kill her.

There were scissors in the medicine cabinet. He could use those to stab her. He'd once cut a man's fingers off with hedge clippers, and that had been a pleasant-enough experience.

The memory turned his stomach, and he focused his attention on cutting.

Cyrus expected the blades to be rusty, but was pleasantly surprised to find they were sharp. A few ragged snips left his hair shoulder length. From there he clipped it shorter, mimicking the generic style he'd seen his former bodyguards wear. It took longer than he'd expected to finish the job, and his arms ached by the time he was done.

Beyond the door, a game show host inquired as to the price of dishwashing liquid, and the Mouse's voice preceded the contestant's answer.

Cyrus wetted his hair and parted it on the side. His own perfectly good eyes stared him down in the mirror. He no longer resembled the monster he once was.

For a frightening moment, he found he liked it. Then he picked up the scissors once more.

He opened the door as quietly as he could. She didn't look away from the television. The sunlight streaming in through the small window above her head surrounded her in a halo of shimmering dust motes. Though she looked tired, the worry had left her face.

A contestant on the game show shouted a number, and the Mouse shook her head. "Way too high."

Cyrus took slow steps, not wanting her to see him until the moment he raised the scissors, the second before they fell. To see her face, serene in recognition, then drawn and pale in the briefest sliver of horror as the deathblow landed. As he imagined the beauty of it, his chest tightened and he sucked in an involuntary gasp of breath.

She turned then, obviously startled.

She knows, his frantic brain shouted. *Do it quick now, she knows.*

The shock on her face melted into a small smile. "You cut your hair."

He'd never seen her smile. She wasn't beautiful, but the unguarded expression transformed her from plain to a simple kind of pretty. It was the meaning behind it, though, that froze his lungs and made the air in the room too thick to breathe. Somewhere in the night, as she nestled against his side, her fear of him had vanished.

If she noticed his distress, she didn't show it. Her smile grew wider. "It looks nice."

Cyrus had never felt self-conscious. It had been easy to be sure of himself when he'd known he was adored. At this moment, he would have done anything to feel so confident again. He reached to touch his shorter strands, realizing too late he still held the scissors in his hand.

Her smile faltered. Though she regained it, the expression was forced. Pained. "What's that for?"

Lying was not something he'd lost in the transition from immortal to dead to mortal. He casually juggled the scissors from one hand to the other. "I thought they'd serve us better in the kitchen."

"Good idea." She rose slowly, and though his back was to her, he knew she followed him.

So, she does still fear me. The thought sickened him. He had actually planned to kill her.

Suddenly, and with shocking clarity, a vision of her slashed throat and bloody dress shot through his mind. The scissors, before a simple, common tool, seemed evil, as though his intent had somehow infused them with malice.

I can't do it. He didn't want to think of why. No matter what the reason, it pointed to the same harsh truth. He was as weak as his father believed him to be.

He slid the scissors into a drawer and closed it, resisting the urge to slam it tight. Was it possible his captors had imagined he would try to kill her, think of killing himself? Was this a planned torture?

Behind him, the Mouse made a small sound of relief. Cyrus turned, not sure if he was angered at her for not trusting him, or ashamed of himself for deserving mistrust. Tears pooled in her eyes, but she smiled. "I knew you wouldn't do it."

"Did you?" He wanted to grab a knife from the block on the counter and prove her wrong, but the rage died in him. Despair took its place, and he sat at the table, cradling his head in his hands. "Because I wasn't sure, myself."

7

Consequences

"How on earth could you be so irresponsible?" Breton paced back and forth behind his desk, reminding me, in his self-righteous anger, of Nathan. I wondered if all Movement vampires were this uptight, or just the ones from the U.K.

"In Max's defense, General, it was Anne who took me to the Oracle," I interjected, only to be met with a steely look from Breton.

"Yes, I know. And for that, she'll be penalized. As for you, you're lucky I don't call a team in here to stake you, or do it myself!" Breton threw down the sheaf of papers he'd been clutching. They hit the desk with a loud smack and skidded toward us. "Your travel information. It's all in order."

"Whoa, what's this?" Max reached for a pink, carbon-copy sheet.

"It's the order removing you from the Galbraith assignment." Breton's lips twitched, and I knew he suppressed a satisfied grin, the smug bastard.

"General, please!" I clenched my hands into fists at my sides. "The Oracle gave me information. 'Seek the toothsome ones in the land of the dead.' That's something we can go on! And it's proof!"

"Proof?" Breton scoffed. "And what, pray, is it proof of?"

"That the Soul Eater is up to something!" I squinted in frustration, the gleam off the polished edge of his desk blurring my vision. How much of what I was saying came from the Oracle's information, and how much was my own mind skewing what I'd heard? "I can't tell you why or how, but you have to believe me. The Soul Eater is behind whatever is going on with Nathan!"

"As far as I can tell, the only problem with Mr. Galbraith is that he has killed. Twice." Breton propped his fingertips together and rested his hands atop his desk. "But rapidly, his friends are becoming my problem. Mr. Harrison, you have been removed from the case. I will assign a more impartial third party."

"You can't do that!" I shot to my feet. "This isn't Max's fault, and it's not Nathan's! He deserves better than this!"

"What Mr. Galbraith deserves," Breton shouted, leaning over his desk, his rage-contorted face inches from my own, "is to die in terror, the way his victims did."

I felt Max's stern presence beside me before he put his hand on my arm. "Let's go. There's nothing we can do about it now."

We were silent on the way to the airport. We'd left too close to sunup, and the lighter the sky got, the more tense we became. By the time we reached the tarmac, we had to race to the plane, the frantic whirring of the jet engines urging us on.

The official reason for our quick dismissal from Movement headquarters was our safety after our run-in with the Oracle. To get us out of her "immediate scope of thought," as they put it. Though I knew it was really because Breton was pissed at me, I was glad we were leaving. We had precious few resources and a seemingly impossible task ahead of us. I would have gone nuts pacing around a hotel room all day, waiting to figure out what was going on, knowing another assassin was out there looking for Nathan.

We made it up the steps to the plane just in time. The hot Spanish sun crested the horizon just as the flight attendant pulled the door shut. A thin line of smoke rose from the back of her hand from the contact with sunlight.

"What the hell were you thinking?" Max gave the woman a sharp look and she took the hint to skip the seat belt demonstration.

"I was thinking I had a way to get some answers, and I should take it!" I sat in one of the chairs, wanting to stand but too tired to fight my own body. "One of us had to!"

"Oh, so this is my fault?" Max gave a sarcastic laugh. "Now there's some other assassin out there looking for him, and we're screwed, Carrie! When it was just me, we could have bought some time!"

"No, we couldn't have!" I covered my face with my hands. "We couldn't have. Cyrus is alive."

Max's eyes narrowed. He raised his hand and rubbed his perpetually stubbled chin as he regarded me with something akin to mistrust. "No way."

I forced back the tears of fatigue that assaulted me. "The Oracle told me. It explains why I've been having these dreams, but, Max…she told me things."

"Did she tell you these things before she started breaking Anne's spine?" Max paced like a caged tiger. "Four places. Four! It's a miracle she wasn't killed."

"It wasn't a miracle." I blew out a frustrated breath. "The Oracle knew exactly what she was doing. Anne said she saw a vision of it years ago. It wasn't an accident."

"Fuckin' A it wasn't an accident!"

"Max, calm down!" My stern tone surprised even me, and for a moment, we stared at each other in shock.

He recovered first, but not much. "Okay."

"What do you mean, okay?" I felt my hysteria rising again. "Cyrus is alive. But I killed him. You were there. We both watched him die. How can he be alive?"

Max shrugged. "It's not unheard of. I know there are ways to do it, but who would want to bring the bastard back?" The Please Fasten Seat Belt light popped on overhead, and Max motioned me over to the couch.

"So, where do we go from here?" I tried to sound brave as I settled myself next to him.

"Carrie," he said softly, as though preparing me for the worst, "you know what will happen if I disobey the Movement."

"And you know, better than I do, what will happen if you obey them and kill my sire." I couldn't take any more of this, though I knew we were only steps into a very long journey. The uncertainty wore me down quickly, cast the shadow of doubt over every thought and action until I just wished this was all over, for better or worse. Because then, at least, I would *know*. I wouldn't have to fear losing Nathan if I'd already lost him, wouldn't have to squash down my hope if it was already fulfilled.

Max's arms were strong around me when he pulled me against his chest. His voice wavered only slightly when he whispered in my ear. "It might not even come to that."

"What's the plan, then? I can't just take this lying down." I sniffled a little, sure it was the recycled air of the cabin wreaking havoc on my respiratory system, not my emotions overwhelming me.

"I know you can't." He paused. "What did the Oracle tell you?"

"She said I should 'seek the toothsome ones in the land of the dead.' All I can think is that she meant the Fangs." I grimaced at the memory of the uncouth vampire gang I'd met at Cyrus's mansion. "Do you think they could raise someone from the dead?"

Max sighed. "Unfortunately, yes. They actually started out as a mystic cabal. They did a lot of ceremonial magic, raising demons and stuff, before the motorcycle thing started getting mixed in. Nowadays there's a pretty healthy blend of both. They've got enough mystics left that the Movement is afraid of them. They devote a huge block of training to learning about them."

"Well, that takes a load off of my mind," I said, sarcasm dripping from each word. "So, would they be able to make the Soul Eater into a god? Because that's the other bomb the Oracle dropped."

"A god?" Max's eyes actually bulged at the suggestion. "I…hope not?"

"Great." I leaned my head back and closed my own eyes, trying to calm my mind. If I decided it was impossible now, how would I feel when we were actually in a position to solve this mess?

"The thing is, they have these witches," Max continued. "They still actively train them. And you know how bad it can be going up against one of them."

Ugh. Witches. The very idea of them made my skin crawl. The granola-crunchy earth worshippers that came into Nathan's shop calling themselves witches had no idea of the true power that existed out there. It was a frightening force, capable of destruction I'd never known. Until I'd met Dahlia.

Dahlia had been Cyrus's most fervent admirer, until he'd made the mistake of trying to serve her as the main course at a dinner party. She'd managed to get herself turned, though I didn't want to imagine the fate the poor vampire who'd supplied her with blood had met. After that, she'd calmed some. She was still out there, though, with the power of a true sorceress and the strength of the undead.

"Could Dahlia have had a hand in this?" I asked.

The mention of her made Max visibly uncomfortable. He'd been thrown on her mercy the night I'd killed Cyrus, but he'd somehow escaped. I didn't want to know what she'd done to him to put that haunted look on his face. "Do you think she would want him back?"

Dahlia hadn't been able to kill Cyrus, but she'd wanted him dead. She'd definitely felt some twisted variation on love for him. But she was as unpredictable as the wind.

"Probably not," I had to admit, answering my own question.

"Well, let's concentrate on 'the land of the dead.' I know the Fangs like it around Barstow down in California, because I've been sent out there a couple of times on assignment. It's pretty dead out there." He made finger quotes around the word *dead*.

I nodded slowly. "Are you suggesting we go and check it out?"

"*I* can't go on a road trip. I think out of the two of us, I'm the best one to find out what happened to Nathan. You, on the other hand…"

I shook my head. "Not by myself."

"Nathan taught you how to take care of yourself," Max reminded me. "He taught you how to fight. You'll run into less trouble looking for Cyrus in the middle of nowhere than you will hanging around your apartment with assassins casing the place."

I was about to point out that Nathan had only taught me self-defense, not imbued me with nonklutziness, but Max was right. It would be no skin off my back to drive out to Barstow. It would definitely be a hell of a lot easier than waiting around for someone to hunt down Nathan and kill him, and I'd never been a good damsel in distress. I was a "hands-on" damsel.

"I just wonder who they're going to send after Nathan."

Max sniffed the air. "Do you smell that?"

For a second I wondered if the flight attendant had quietly burned to death in the galley, but then I caught the scent in question. It wasn't the burning hot dog smell of vampire flesh on fire, but a smell rather like exotic perfume.

Still, it wasn't so distracting we couldn't ignore it. "No, I don't, Scooby."

"Are you sure you don't smell that?" Max got to his feet. "Get up, take a look around."

"What about the seat belt sign?" I asked, hesitant to unbuckle.

"Chance it." There was no humor in his voice. He strode to the door of the galley. I stayed right on his heels. The flight attendant, who was applying a Band-Aid to the back of her burned hand, jumped.

"Is anyone on this plane except for us?" he barked.

She shrugged, her mouth gaping. "Well, the pilots. But other than that—"

Max didn't question her further. We split up to search the other parts of the plane—I don't know what for, but Max was so agitated I didn't bother asking. He took the cockpit and galley, while I searched the bedroom. Though our departure from the Movement was hasty, someone had thought to leave a cellophane-wrapped fruit basket for us.

That would be nice, if we were vampire rabbits like Bunnicula. The reference pulled a bittersweet memory to the surface of my consciousness. I'd mentioned the children's book the night after Nathan had helped me escape Cyrus. That was when Ziggy, Nathan's adopted son, had died. I sank onto the bed, crushed by the weight of my sadness and the heartbreak I'd felt for him that night.

"You think I let him die?" Nathan's accusing voice rang through my head. I'd said cruel, bitter things to him, but in the

end it had been a kind of therapy for both of us. He'd broken down and cried, and I had held him on the floor in the ruins of a breakfast he had destroyed in his anger. We had been out of blood, and had to settle for human food rather than drink the last bag Ziggy had left behind.

I narrowed my eyes at the fruit basket. Human food was a last resort. A vampire would have left a nice, body-temperature bag of O Neg as a housewarming gesture.

Max came in just as I stood and grabbed the basket.

"Son of a bitch! I knew I smelled a dog." He kicked the bed, then sat on the edge as I tore open the cellophane.

"I believe the expression is 'I knew I smelled a rat.'" Inside the basket were apples, cherries, oranges and a cluster of delicate blush blossoms clinging to a slender branch. My face fell. "Oh."

"Dogwood," Max said with a sneer of disgust. He grasped the twig and snapped it, then ground the pale flowers on the carpet with the heel of his boot. I followed him back to the cabin, where we buckled in just in time for takeoff. "She was here. She wanted us to know she was here. And she's already got a head start on us," he said, raising his voice over the whine of the engines as we took to the sky. "I should have known it the second I saw that bitch in Breton's office. He had no intention of letting me go after Nathan, not even when he gave me the kill order! She was already on the fucking job! She hopped another jet and took off while we were still in the building. She even had time to leave us a 'gift.'"

All I could do was lean back in my chair and try to calm myself. The Movement was trying to sabotage us. The Soul Eater was going to become a god. My first sire had risen from the dead. My current sire had two assassins tailing him. And the only thing that could stand in the way of all this chaos was me.

* * *

As night drew closer, Cyrus found himself enjoying Mouse's company. She'd made them as decent a lunch as they could manage, though that wasn't saying much. Still, he'd appreciated her effort.

She'd been good company, too. He'd thought it detrimental that she'd stopped fearing him, but now he found her chatter an excellent way to pass the time. She still grew emotional, and that was a bother, but he trusted that would pass eventually. They'd spoken of it over their lunch. She'd told him of her family, or lack thereof. She was an orphan. Her parents had both died; she didn't give a reason. There was a sister, but she'd moved to Los Angeles to pursue an acting career, and ended up seduced by the easy money to be found in pornographic films. The last Mouse had heard, her sister had escaped from a court-ordered stay at a rehabilitation facility for some kind of drug addiction.

After that, Mouse's only family had been the church. Cyrus had made a face at that, and she'd taken deep offense. Her faith had sustained her this long, she'd admonished, and she wouldn't be mocked for it.

The unfortunate, dead priest had been new to the parish. He'd been set to retire when he'd heard of the struggling church in the small, desert community, and he'd agreed to lead them until a new shepherd could be found. The nun had been with the parish since it had formed twenty-five years earlier. Both of them, Cyrus had reflected, had had awful timing.

Mouse had agreed, looking down at her untouched sandwich. It was only when she sniffled that he realized she'd started to cry.

Cyrus had wanted to take her in his arms and soothe her nerves. She'd seen too much terror at the hands of these monsters. But he'd held back. He hadn't trusted himself not to do something unthinkably cruel to her. And he wouldn't allow himself to be that man now.

It wasn't that he disliked being a vampire. He'd been one for so long he didn't know how to be anything else. He didn't want to accept his seemingly inevitable change on the sole basis of familiarity. Given the chance, he might grow to like humanity. And what was to say he couldn't be as happy with a human life as he'd been as a vampire? The horror of his circumstances had lessened somewhat, and he'd come to enjoy the simple, human sensations he'd learned not to miss. He hungered merely for sustenance, not power and control. He laughed during companionable conversation, not at some cruel action he'd inflicted on another. As a human, he could be kind. He found he rather liked being kind.

So, he'd done the only thing he could do. He hadn't offered bland words of comfort or assurances that things would be all right. He'd simply changed the subject.

"We should have dinner tonight," he'd blurted. When she'd looked up at him, her tear tracks gleaming in the sunlight, he'd continued in the hopes of seeing her expression change. "Make an event of it. I suppose I should celebrate my return to humanity."

"I suppose," she'd said hesitantly. "But we should save some food."

"Don't worry. I know those…people up there. I did some of them a favor once. I'm sure they'll get us more." She'd still looked doubtful, so he'd added, "They won't let me starve to death. They raised me for a reason."

After that, she'd acquiesced, and eagerly discussed lives of the saints and stories of the Bible. He'd tolerated it because it had made her feel better.

Now, she stood over the small stove, making God alone

knew what for them to eat, but she'd bathed and combed her hair, and she hummed while she worked. He knew she watched him as he changed into fresh clothing from the priest's dresser. The damn black, polyester, button-down shirt would serve if he left it unbuttoned over one of the pristine white T-shirts. He turned and held his arms out at his sides. "What do you think?"

Mouse didn't reply. She flushed, embarrassed, and turned back to the stove. He waited at the table while she dished out the food small, rubbery chicken breasts in some suspicious sauce from a frozen dinner; canned carrots; macaroni and cheese—and they were about to eat when the door at the top of the stairs opened.

"I thought that was locked," Cyrus whispered to Mouse, not meaning to sound so accusatory.

Her eyes grew wide with fear, and the pulse in her throat leaped visibly. He wanted to reassure her, but there was no time for that. Heavy footfalls came down the stairs.

"Sorry to interrupt your dinner, folks," a voice raspy from cigarette smoke announced, before its owner came into view. Her face was contorted into its vampire form. Her shoulders were considerably wider than Cyrus's. It took him a moment to realize she was a woman.

Mouse screamed and stood too fast, bumping the table and rattling the dishes. She looked as though she'd run, though there was no place to go except past the monstrous woman at the bottom of the stairs.

"Calm down," he warned Mouse, standing slowly to approach her. "Come to me."

She launched herself at him, winding her arms around his neck. She clutched him tighter as he tried to disentangle himself, but in the end, she had to let go.

"I'm not going to let her hurt you," he said, rubbing his

throat. There would be a bruise there in the morning, he was sure of it. To the vampire, he snapped, "What's the meaning of all this?"

"We need to talk. Get rid of her for a minute." The vampire gestured to the table. "It won't take long."

"Go ahead. Go," he urged Mouse, giving her a push toward the other half of the apartment. He followed her, his eyes never leaving the vampire. What he would do if she tried to attack, he had no clue, but he hoped his warning gaze would make her behave.

Mouse went cautiously to the bed and sat down stiffly, watching. The vampire kicked out the chair Cyrus had been seated in and pulled a pack of cigarettes from her leather vest, tapping them on the table. "Simon Seymour. At last we meet."

"We haven't really met. You haven't told me who you are." He grimaced at the realization he'd answered to his old name. "And it's Cyrus now."

"I've heard." She extended her hand. Her grip was powerful. "Call me Angie. I hear you throw a mean New Year's party. Sit down."

"Some are meaner than others." He nursed his crushed hand discreetly as he sat opposite her. "What's going on?"

She pulled a cigarette from the pack and offered it to him. Though he'd given up smoking before his death—finding tables in restaurants had been an annoying affair in the health-conscious nineties—he accepted it gratefully. His nerves were painfully raw from the ordeal of the last few days. He'd try anything to take the edge off.

Angie leaned back and regarded him a moment, before admitting, "I just came down to make sure you survived this long. I don't really know what I'm supposed to tell you."

"Start with who put you up to this." He mimicked her casual pose and inhaled a lungful of the acrid smoke. Centuries of indulgence hadn't been wiped away by death. He didn't cough or falter, and even produced a perfect smoke ring on the exhale. "Was it my father?"

"Does anyone else have the kind of connections required to bring someone back from the dead?" She raised an eyebrow.

He'd suspected the Soul Eater had done this. Still, icy cold crept up his spine now that his suspicions had been confirmed. "Why?"

She shrugged. "Didn't say. He gave me two-hundred thousand to get the job done. I would have asked for more if I'd known how much work goes into it. But you don't break a promise to the big S.E."

"Address him properly," Cyrus snapped, out of habit more than respect. How could his father have done this to him?

It wasn't as if Jacob Seymour had ever held any faith in his youngest son. The very notion of him needing Cyrus for anything seemed far-fetched. But here that failure of a son was. Alive. Human.

But for how long? "I take it you're going to change me back?" She shook her head. "Nope."

That didn't surprise him. "He probably expects me to earn it. Father always did have a flair for the dramatic. Who's coming to get me?"

"Don't know yet." She took a long draw off her cigarette. "We're waiting for word."

"I can't wait much longer. I'm almost out of food down here." He carefully kept the "we" out of his statement. Though companionable enough, this woman had accepted money to raise the dead. She was dangerous, and definitely not someone he wanted to further expose Mouse to.

Angie nodded. "It'll be taken care of."

"Good." He rose. "I take it we're through here?"

She smiled. The expression was monstrous on her warped face as she stood, as well. "But before I go…"

She pulled an envelope from her leather vest, offering it to him. Frowning, Cyrus lifted the flap and pulled out the contents.

Polaroids. Of him and Mouse lying side by side on the narrow bed the night before. His arm curled protectively around her slender shoulders, his head resting against the curve of her neck.

"Glad to see you're getting on so well down here." Angie's face morphed back to its human form. She looked better as a vampire.

His mouth dry, Cyrus slipped the photographs into his pocket. He said nothing, but he knew what they meant. The Fangs knew he valued Mouse. That knowledge was a formidable weapon, one he hadn't even known the existence of until he saw it with his own eyes. They could hurt her, to test him, to force him to cooperate, for no reason other than because it would be fun to torture him.

"It helps to know what we've got for bargaining material. Don't you think?" Angie stubbed out her cigarette on the plastic tabletop.

His mouth dry, Cyrus nodded. "I suppose it does."

He had to take a few steps toward the door before he could regain some of the confidence she'd shaken from him. When he did, he stopped and faced her. "Remember, I've got bargaining material, as well. I need her. I'm still too weak to care for myself." A lie, but an easy one to tell. "If she dies, I die, and you lose your money."

"Repaying your father's money would be the least of my worries." Angie folded her arms over her chest. "Besides, I could always just raise you again."

Cyrus watched her until she disappeared at the top of the stairs and closed the door behind her. He raced up and locked it, mentally berating himself for not requesting the key or whatever other method Angie had used to get in.

Mouse still perched on the edge of the bed, her thin arms wrapped around her middle. She leaned over her knees, sniffling softly.

"Damn it." Cyrus couldn't help the curse as he hurried down the stairs. "What's the matter?"

She looked up, large eyes red with tears. "What will happen when you're gone? What will they do to me?"

"It will be all right." He hated himself for the empty promise. He had no idea what would happen when his father sent for him. But he sat beside her on the bed, unable to stop the hollow vows tumbling from his lips. "I'll make sure no one hurts you."

You weren't able to save the rest of them, a mean voice in his head taunted. It didn't bother him so much to be reminded of his past failures to save his companions, but that he suddenly thought of Mouse in the same category.

"And what if they…change you?" It seemed as though the words were hard for her to say. "If you become one of them, will you kill me?"

Probably. He thought of what his father had done to Nolen, forcing him to devour the one person he'd wanted to protect with his last human breath. If the Fangs decided to change Cyrus and lock him up with Mouse, the time would come when he would kill from necessity. And if his father did the deed himself, Mouse still might die at his hands.

Cyrus didn't tell her that, though. "No. I won't become some mindless monster. I promise, I will never hurt you."

But he had the distinct impression they were both already dead.

8

Max Harrison had never liked Michigan. Yet somehow, he kept ending up there.

He'd seen Carrie off in Ziggy's old heap of a van with a silent prayer and a dozen false assurances that the vehicle would make it. He didn't like lying, but they didn't have another option. He'd need his car to track down Nathan, and the van's windowless back would at least give Carrie shelter from the sun.

She'd left him the keys to the apartment and told him to make himself at home, but she'd wanted to make it as far as she could before daylight.

As if he could make himself at home in a city where everything shut down at nine o'clock.

He trudged up the stairs to Nathan and Carrie's apartment, shaking his head. The last place he'd stayed for any length of time was Chicago. Blues and booze until the wee hours of the morning. Nothing could beat it. But he couldn't stay there for long. There were too many memories of Marcus. Too much pain.

Now, he wished he could be there. He wished he could be in *Zimbabwe*. Anywhere but here.

He didn't doubt for a minute Carrie's story. Nathan probably *was* possessed. But while she was full of hope and determination, all Max could muster was a lesser level of bone-weary despair.

Demonic possession of a vampire wasn't something that could be cured without drastic measures. Those measures usually involved the sharp end of a wooden stake. Though it was hard to imagine actually killing Nathan, Max knew it would be far better for him to die than be miraculously cured and have to face the death he'd visited on innocent people.

Max dropped his bag at the end of the couch out of habit. The last time he'd stayed in the apartment had been the time he'd helped Nathan and Carrie kill Cyrus. She was a piece of work, running off to face him again after all he'd done to her. Max wasn't sure if, given the same circumstances, he could have managed it.

In the kitchen, he looked guiltily through the refrigerator. No matter how many times someone told him to make himself at home, he always felt as if he was snooping. He grabbed a bag of blood and poured it into the teakettle, praying Carrie hadn't tampered with the contents for one of her experiments.

The hiss of the burner reminded him how quiet it was in the empty apartment, and he went to the stereo. Glancing over the rows of CDs, he found it easy to tell which were Nathan's and which belonged to Carrie. Nathan was all about mellow, moody classic rock. He had a decent selection of Zeppelin and some Floyd. Carrie had a small but respectable jazz collection and some pop albums of questionable taste.

Like oil and water. Max chuckled to himself as he slid a Led Zeppelin album into the CD player. The machine cycled, then the opening notes of "Babe, I'm Gonna Leave You" wafted from the speakers.

"Excellent," Max affirmed to no one in particular. He went

to the kitchen, poured the warmed blood into a mug and seated himself at the cracked Formica dinette table. With no time left to canvass the city, he decided to wait out daylight and start at dusk. Wherever Nathan was, he'd find him. He owed it to his friend to let him die at the hands of a vampire, not some werewolf assassin who reeked of dirt and campfire smoke. The only thing Max hated more than werewolves were hippies, and even he had a hard time telling them apart.

As the tempo of the music slowly picked up, he stood and wandered around the apartment, sipping his dinner. Everywhere he looked were books with creased spines, notebooks and scraps of paper, framed snapshots on the shelves. It was a home. Someone lived here.

He picked up one of the photos. It was a souvenir snapshot people buy at amusement parks, a freeze frame of a moment on a roller coaster, at night, of course. Never in the entire time he'd known Nathan had Max ever seen him look like he was having that much fun.

Carrie was good for him. An ache grew in Max's chest. It would be hell on earth for her when Nathan died. Not just because of the blood tie. Whether or not they admitted it to themselves or each other, Carrie and Nathan were in love.

The constant, fevered wind-up of the song started to grate on Max's nerves. He moved to change the track, and the floorboard creaked. Another creak echoed from the other end of the hall.

He straightened. So, it wasn't the racing tempo of the music that set him on edge. Someone was there, lurking in the dark, empty rooms.

He hoped it was just a garden-variety prowler.

The only weapon at his immediate disposal was a wooden stake. He slipped it into his back pocket, just in case, and retrieved a knife from the kitchen. The plan was to charge in, knife waving, in full monster face. Whoever had broken in would go out the way they'd come and hopefully not break their necks on the way down the fire escape or drainpipe or whatever they'd shimmied up. He changed his face to feeding mode and ran down the hall.

Two steps into Nathan's bedroom, a spike-heeled, leather boot caught Max in the forehead. The wicked thing cut across his face, and he stumbled back, the surprise flashing his vampire face back to human. Two more blows, a punch to the stomach and a knee to his groin forced him against the wall, doubled over, and brought the monster back to his countenance.

When he drew in a gasp of breath through his mouth and nose, he caught the spicy scent of her perfume. Werewolf. *DeCesare.*

With a cry of rage, he launched himself at his assailant. She tumbled backward and he crushed her to the floor. Though he had a good forty pounds on her, she almost wriggled free. She clawed at his face with razor sharp nails, and he leaned back. It was all the space she needed to flip him onto his back and aim a stake at his heart. He froze.

"Nolen Galbraith," she wheezed in a strange accent, "by order of the Voluntary Vampire Extinction Movement, you are sentenced to death for the murder of Marianne Galbraith and Christine Allen. How do you plead?"

"Turn on the light," he said between deep breaths. *You dumb bitch,* he added silently.

She squinted in the darkness. "Nolen Galbraith?"

"No. Nice try, though." Max shoved her off him and stood, brushing at his clothes as though they had been soiled.

In the faint illumination from the mercury light outside, he recognized her. "You met with the general last night. Or should I say, 'your boyfriend, the general'?"

"You turn on the light," she demanded, an exotic lilt adding haughty authority to her words. "I do not have the same quality night vision as you do."

"Could that be because, oh, I don't know, you're not a vampire?" But he turned on the light anyway, because she still had a stake and he was curiously allergic to wooden splinters through the heart. "I always thought dogs could see in the dark. Or is that cats?"

"General Breton sent me. Apparently he was worried about an assassin who is not capable of finishing the assignment." Her last words morphed into a growl.

"That still doesn't explain why you're in my friend's house. Especially when he's running berserk on the streets. What the hell were you thinking, coming here?" The knife was on the floor at his feet. He just had to figure out a way to grab it without getting skewered.

Thankfully, she didn't appear to have noticed his frantic glance downward. "I could ask the same of you. You are walking around, drinking their blood supply, using their appliances. It seems like you might be playing both sides."

"There's only one side, sweetheart. I hate to disappoint you, but Nolen—" Max sketched quotation marks with his fingers "—is on it."

"He has killed."

"Under very extenuating circumstances!"

Bella shook her head. "There are no extenuating circumstances. He has killed, he will be killed."

"Unless I kill you first." Max expected to see some reaction in her eyes, but there was none. Just the cold, calculating stare of a predator who lived only for the hunt.

Moving faster than any mortal creature he'd ever seen, the werewolf threw the stake at him. He ducked it and scooped up the knife. The wooden missile embedded itself in the wall, near where his heart would have been.

She ran for the door, grabbing a handful of clothes from the laundry hamper as she passed.

For the scent, he realized with an inward curse. He admitted with sick fury that she might have the upper hand in this fight. You could train a person to be a hunter, but animals...they were born with it.

He ran after her, nearly catching her at the bottom of the stairs, but when she threw open the door, newborn sunlight flooded the stairwell. He hissed and jumped back.

As she fled down the street, she called, "Stay out of my way, vampire. I will kill you if I must."

I hooked up with I-94 and hauled ass over the state line before the sun rose. After a boring, cramped day in the unbearably stuffy van, I hit the road with a travel mug of cold blood from the cooler I'd brought, and set my sights west.

Just outside of Chicago I caught the junction of 80-90, which would lead me into Iowa, and the landscape flattened almost immediately. With no tape deck and a broken radio, I exhausted my voice—and repertoire of Abba songs—quickly.

With nothing to occupy my mind, my thoughts turned inevitably to Nathan. I knew he wasn't dead. I tried the blood tie vigilantly, though all I ever got in return was the tiniest pull. I filled my mind with as much love and support as I could, and sent it his way, hoping he would get the message. Eventually, memories I would rather have ignored started popping to the surface.

I thought of all our failed attempts to play Risk. The way I'd shouted "Bad omen! Bad omen!" every time he'd rolled the dice. It had driven him mad, but not so mad he couldn't see the humor in it.

I remembered the time we'd tried to repaint The Crypt.

"What the hell is that?" he'd demanded of the botanical border I'd begun sponging around the top of the walls.

I'd squinted at it with what I'd considered a critical eye. "A fig leaf."

Apparently, I'd not been critical enough. He'd looked deeply offended by my artistic skills. "Apparently your idea of a leaf and my idea of a leaf differ greatly."

Frowning, I'd dabbed at the paint protectively. "I think it looks fine."

"All I'm saying is if you were in charge of the Garden of Eden, I'd be glad not to live there." It had been close to dawn and we'd been working since sunset. Nathan's tired voice and his accent, grown thick with exhaustion, had rendered his words barely distinguishable as English.

I'd been unable to resist a guttural "Och!" The ensuing paint fight had splattered the shelves and the ceiling. We would have gotten around to painting over it if we hadn't ended up jumping each other's bones right there on the plastic sheets on the floor.

I pulled all the happiness I could from these memories and gave it over to the blood tie. Maybe it would reassure him we were looking for him, and keep him from despairing.

I wished I could pull the van over and cry, but there was no time. I swallowed my pain and kept my eyes on the road.

What would happen if Max caught up with him? Though Anne had sounded pretty sure he wouldn't finish Nathan off, she'd also seemed certain the Oracle wouldn't hurt anybody, and look where that had gotten her. The thought of Max doing anything to Nathan... I wasn't confident if I would ever be able to face him again should that happen.

Then there was the Cyrus problem. It had been easy to let my grudge against him die when I thought he was dead himself. But how could I possibly endure seeing him again? Would he still have that sick, seductive power over me?

There was very little I feared now that I had become the thing that went bump in the night. Unfortunately, my old sire figured largely in that very little. He'd had a hold over me that had surpassed the power of the blood tie. He'd made me believe he'd needed me, that I could have that power over him. For a person who'd wanted nothing more in life than that kind of control, it had been a dream come true. How would I react to him now that he was human and he really did need me?

Assuming he was still human when I got there. I couldn't imagine him tolerating such a state for long.

Outside the windows, the miles passed by. I never knew why they referred to this landscape as "rolling plains." They didn't roll at all. They just stretched out endlessly into the night, with only the occasional farm or small town to break the illusion of standing still.

As close to dawn as possible, without any clue as to what state I was in, I pulled into a rest stop and climbed behind the heavy canvas curtains to sleep.

Out of loneliness more than hope, I tried the blood tie again.

We're going to fix this, Nathan. I promise, we're going to fix this.

At first, I thought there would be no response at all, not even the strange tug I'd felt when I'd tried to communicate before. This time, though, I heard him.

Help me.

His reply was faint, but I knew it was him and not my frantic imagination. It was definitely Nathan.

And he was in unimaginable pain.

* * *

Cyrus woke at sunup. Mouse lay curled at his side, a rare smile on her sleeping face. Whatever she dreamed of, he hated the thought of waking her.

He rose as carefully as he could to avoid disturbing her, and walked to the bathroom. He closed the door, then thought of the monsters lurking upstairs, and opened it a crack so he could hear them if they came down. Though he was sure his counterthreat had made an impact with the leader, he knew from experience a deal with a vampire was really no deal at all.

He drew a bath, hoping the thunder of water in the tub wouldn't wake Mouse. She deserved to sleep. Every moment she slept was a moment she didn't have to think of their dire situation.

Though he knew she had a name, he couldn't bear to think of her as "Stacey." Certainly not "Stacey Pickles." He made a face at that. She deserved a better name than Mouse, but it fit her, and he couldn't think of a better one.

He slipped into the water and slid down to submerge his head. Though he'd always enjoyed the sensation of being completely enveloped by water, he couldn't stand it now. His mortal lungs cried for air and every faint noise seemed sinister. He sat up, gasping for breath.

He was surprised to see Mouse jump back from the tub. He hadn't heard her come in, and his lack of awareness frightened him. "You scared me."

"I'm sorry," she said softly. She still wore the T-shirt she'd slept in, her skinny legs jutting from beneath the short hem, which afforded her little modesty. "I heard you get up. I didn't want to be alone."

He leaned into the curved end of the tub and let his arm drape over the side. "It's okay."

She took a tentative step forward. "The door was open. I didn't know you were—"

"I don't mind." He liked having her close. At least then he knew she was safe.

Her eyes darted from his naked form beneath the water to the floor as she moved to kneel beside the tub. When he reached out and lazily stroked her hair with his damp hand, she blurted, "Today is my birthday."

"Really?" He didn't know why he was so interested. Captivity was doing strange things to him. "How old are you?"

She nodded earnestly and leaned against the tub as though it were his living flesh. "Nineteen."

"Nineteen, and you're—" He'd meant to comment on her purity, then realized the comment would be crude. It wouldn't have bothered him with anyone else, another dangerous distinction he chose to ignore. "You're nineteen?"

"How old are you?" She looked up at him with terrifyingly earnest eyes.

He knew the look in them, and withdrew his hand. "I don't know. I think I may have been twenty-seven when I became a vampire. I didn't keep track of the years after that. There were seven centuries, if that helps."

"Seven—" She choked on the word. "I thought I was old."

He laughed out loud at the absurdity of her innocent statement. "Hardly."

With a sigh, she dropped her hand over the side of the tub, sliding it gracefully through the water at his side. Her fingers came mere centimeters from his flesh, and for a moment he thought she would touch him. She never did. He stared at her face to try and gauge her intent, but there was no sign of sly seduction or nervous timidity there. She gazed at the cinder block wall, but it was obvious she saw nothing.

"How can you forget how old you are? Don't you look forward to your birthday?" She rested her head on the rolled edge of the bathtub, still twisting her fingers through the water.

One slender digit brushed against his ribs. It took all his will-power not to shudder. "I don't know when my birthday is. My mother died a few days after I was born. From a fever. My father took a new wife, but she didn't know what day I'd been born and my father hadn't kept track."

Mouse turned to him, looking very close to tears. "That's so sad."

"Not really," he assured her. "Birthdays didn't matter much then. There wasn't as much emphasis on them as there is now."

"You could still have one," she offered. "Just keep track from the day they brought you back. Or the day they—"

"Let's not talk about that." He didn't want her to have any knowledge of his vampire world. Didn't want to hear their sordid terminology cross her lips. Forcing a smile, he said, "I have good news."

He could tell she didn't want to believe him. To get her hopes up would only serve to see them dashed again. She couldn't seem to resist temptation, though. "What is it?"

"When I talked to the vampire woman last night, she said they'd bring us more food." He glanced worriedly at his lean stomach. He'd have to watch his intake, or he'd grow fat. That was something he'd never had to think of before.

"Where are they getting it?" Mouse's expression became troubled.

Whatever could be the matter with her? Did she *want* to starve to death? "I don't know. Maybe they have some here. It is a church. Don't they give out alms for the poor?"

"The food pantry is for the low-income families of the parish."

"Yes, and they believe it has burned to the ground." He frowned. "Mouse, we don't have much left."

"Mouse?" A hesitant smile crossed her lips. "Why did you call me that?"

Damn. He'd never addressed her with anything more than "You there," before. "Because you remind me of a mouse."

She looked deeply offended, and he rushed to correct himself. "Not physically. But you're so quiet. If you want me to call you—"

"No. Call me Mouse. I've never had a nickname before." Her smile widened, as if she knew a secret he did not. "It's a good birthday present."

They sat in silence, the only sound the occasional drip of water from the faucet.

"I won't feel right taking that food." She looked him in the eye. Something new sparked there, an inner flame that burned to banish the hopelessness she'd succumbed to before. "But I'll take it, because now it's every man for himself."

"Or herself, as the case may be." Cyrus picked up the soap. "But I'm glad to see you've developed some reason."

She shrugged. "You promised nothing would happen to me. You're the closest thing to a protector I have, so I believe you."

His heart ached with the shameful memories of what he'd done to her, but he wouldn't apologize. Conscience or not, he still had some pride, and he wouldn't live with regret.

He finished his bath and gave Mouse a warning before he stood, so she could modestly turn her back. She went into the other room to change, and when she'd finished she brought him clean clothes, as well. When he emerged from the bathroom, she stood at the bottom of the stairs, looking up with a worried expression.

"What's the matter?" He touched her arm. He wasn't sure why.

She jumped, then nodded with an apologetic look. It hadn't

been him that had startled her. "Are they… I mean, will they come out? If we went up there?"

"They can't go into the light. They'll burn up. If we were in the light, we'd be fine."

She chewed her lip. "So, once we got outside, then…we'd be fine?"

"In theory." What was she insinuating?

Mouse started up the steps, but took them slowly. He caught her arm. "What are you doing?"

She lifted a finger to her lips to signal quiet. He didn't want to follow her, but her single-minded concentration drew him in. He stayed close behind her, one hand on the railing, the other on her wrist. A few times, she stopped. He thought she would change her mind and turn around, but then she moved forward as though she'd screwed up her courage and forced herself on.

Once they entered the vestibule and closed the basement door behind them, her courage deserted her. She stared in terror at the sanctuary doors. A chalk sigil marred the wood. Cyrus could only guess at its purpose.

"They can't come out," he reminded her, pointing to the sunlight slanting across the carpet. How that sight used to terrify him, and now it seemed so harmless. No wonder she doubted its effectiveness in protecting her.

She paused before the exterior doors, bracketed on both sides by long, thin windows. And then he knew why she'd brought him here. Her shoulders, usually slumped in defeat, rose. Her face appeared less tired and sad, and a gleeful smile appeared as she surveyed the bleak landscape outside.

"We can escape." He reached for the handle.

She grabbed his wrist, stopping him. Her shoulders slumped again, and her face regained the sad, haunted look he recognized far better than hope. "We can't."

"Of course we can. Look! We can go out of these doors and go find help." His hands shook as he laid them on the metal push bar. He prayed no alarm would sound. There was a faint click and a screech of hinges, then freedom lay before him in the form of a barren, desert road. His heart fell a little, but he made a desperate attempt to bolster it. "It can't be that far to the nearest town."

She shook her head. "Five miles."

"Five miles? Is that all?" He could easily walk five miles, even as a human. Five miles. He could carry her five miles! "Let's not waste any more time!"

"No." She shook her head sadly.

"Why not?" He felt the old violence rising in him, tempting him to break her neck and save himself.

"We're in Death Valley. You'd never survive. Five miles through burning desert. You'll be dead within half an hour." Her eyes drifted shut; her head drooped on her neck. "It's hopeless."

"No." Panic rose in his chest. They were so close. "What about hitchhiking? What if we…" As he watched the road, he realized that in the entire time they'd stood there, no vehicle had passed. He didn't need to look at her to see her silent denial.

Her eyes filled with tears. "You'd never make it during the day. And at night—"

"At night, they would find us." He ran a hand through his hair. "Well, it was a fine plan, for a moment."

She stood uselessly in place. "If you tried to escape, would you take me with you?"

"Of course I would," he said, and believed it to his bones. The why of it, however, was something he didn't want to admit.

She looked at him for a painfully intense moment. What would her next action be? Would she cry? Would she kiss him? It looked as though she was leaning toward the latter when the doors to the sanctuary rattled, angry voices rising on the other side. Angry voices, and a woman's scream.

Before they could move, the doors burst open and a woman, naked but for a torn scrap of a bra, lunged across the threshold. Bite marks marred every inch of her skin. Her lips were blue, her limbs mottled. These were her dying struggles.

Mouse stiffened at his side, her eyes wide with horror. The woman reached for them, her face twisting in a rictus of pain as she crashed to the floor. From the shadows between the sanctuary doors, the Fangs glared at them.

"They can't come out here," Cyrus reminded Mouse, grabbing her hand and pulling her toward the basement door. He hoped they hadn't found a way to circumvent that law of vampire physiology. If they had, he and Mouse were truly doomed.

A gaunt vampire with hollow eyes and thick stubble on his jaw grabbed the nearly dead woman's ankle and tugged. She raised her head, turning wide, tear-filled eyes upward. Her cracked lips formed a single, soundless "Please," and she dug her fingers into the carpet as the Fang pulled her, screaming, back into the sanctuary.

"Get back downstairs!" another vampire growled at them. Then the doors slammed shut and they were left alone.

"Wh-what—" Mouse stammered, then sagged against Cyrus. She was fainting, he realized, and he was still not strong enough to hold up her weight. He tried for the basement door, but they slipped to the carpet, falling where the dead woman had landed in her ill-fated escape attempt. He glanced at the carpet. Fingernails. They had ripped from her hands, tangled in the fibers as she'd tried desperately to keep the Fangs from pulling her back.

Mouse raised her head, and her gasp told him she saw them, as well. "Were you... When you were..."

"No." Cyrus couldn't look at her, at her horrified face. "No, I was much worse. They looked up to me, even if it affords me no currency with them now."

She pulled away, trembling. "We should go downstairs. Eventually, the sun will go down, and they'll be angry."

Sunlight or not, they were doomed anyway, Cyrus realized as they returned to their basement prison. The Fangs showed a horrible sense of invention, holding them here. Of course they would choose a place like this, where the climate would confine their captives during the daylight, when they themselves were most vulnerable.

Cyrus and Mouse were well and truly trapped. The danger of the situation, which had until now seemed a trivial annoyance, finally dawned on him. Mouse, the flimsy life raft he'd been clinging to, might not live through this. The thought was unfathomable. He, who'd killed with such sadistic pleasure in the past, would be spared out of necessity. Because his father willed it. But she, who'd retained her purity, body and soul, would die as a victim of circumstance.

He wouldn't allow it. Though the realization shocked him, it was, unfortunately, the truth. When he'd told Angie that Mouse's death would be the cause of his own, it had been the truth. And though he realized their situation had greatly influenced and intensified his emotions toward her, he couldn't deny that the thought of losing her terrified him.

And maybe that was more frightening than the Fangs and his father combined.

9

And thou art dead, as young and fair

I pulled into a truck stop on the other side of Cheyenne. It wasn't dawn yet, but I needed a chance to get out of the van and stretch my legs.

The place was small, with diesel pumps behind it and a dusty lot adjacent, where truckers could park for a night's sleep. With more than a little trepidation, I pulled the van to the end of the dirt lot and headed to the tiny restaurant.

Because of the late hour, there weren't many customers at Arlene's Grit Stop and Five Dollar Showers. I assumed most weary travelers stopping at this particular exit would find themselves across the badly patched asphalt road, at the Happy Ending Health Spa.

The cracked pavement of Arlene's parking lot held only two motorcycles and a rusty Cavalier. At least the van wouldn't look out of place.

The restaurant was a narrow room that ran along the front of the building. No tables, just seven or eight plastic booths against each wall. Currently, only one such booth was taken by a grizzled biker with a long, gray beard, and a young man in a leather jacket who looked like he'd just stepped from a Calvin Klein ad.

The latter wore a big smile the moment he spotted me. Considering my limp, greasy hair and bedraggled appearance, his behavior became immediately suspect.

"Come, sit with us," he invited. The bearded one didn't look enthused about it, working the toothpick he gnawed on from one corner of his hairy mouth to the other.

I shook my head as I slid into another booth. "I think I'll let you boys have your privacy."

A waitress, apparently just as pleased with my presence, sighed deeply as she approached my table. I had the distinct feeling there was a neglected Nora Roberts novel behind the counter she'd been leaning on.

"Just coffee," I assured her with a friendly smile.

"Uh-huh." She clicked her pen derisively and put her order pad back in her apron. "This must be my lucky night."

I glanced over at my fellows in late-night dining and saw that they, too, only had coffee. The waitress, Ruby, by her nametag, scratched her backside as she retrieved a brown, ceramic mug and filled it with coffee. She brought it and the pot to my table, setting the mug before me with little ceremony.

"*Another* refill, gentlemen?" she asked in long-suffering sarcasm.

The bearded one said nothing, but put his hand palm down over the rim of his cup. Calvin Klein pushed his mug toward her. "Absolutely. And put the pretty lady's drink on my check, as well."

Ruby rolled her eyes as she left them. "Seventy-five cents. You're a real big spender."

Without invitation or permission, Calvin Klein got up and came to my table. "Don't mind her. She's been a real bitch all night."

I didn't cover my weary annoyance. "I don't use that word when referring to waitresses."

"I've made a bad first impression, haven't I?" His Cheshire Cat grin reminded me of the way Max had looked at the flight attendant. That day seemed so far away now. In solitude I lived in my own time, which functioned with a marked chronological difference from the one everyone else inhabited. An hour felt like a day, a day felt like a lifetime.

Yet, with as long as time seemed, I didn't feel like wasting mine on a cheesy, clean-cut biker in a brokendown rest stop diner. "Better hurry back, before your boyfriend gets lonely."

C.K. seemed amused by this. "If you are insinuating that this gentleman and I are in any way intimate, I'll have you know I am one-hundred-percent heterosexual. And available."

"I'll take note of that." I hadn't noticed his strange accent until I'd heard him speak more than a few words at a time, but now it set off an alarm in my head. "Are you British, by any chance?"

"Guilty as charged," he said with a laugh, this time putting his accent on full display. "I'm a writer. Seeing America for the first time. I hope to find a novel in it somewhere."

"Try Borders. I've seen a few in there from time to time." Still, something about him struck me as odd. "Why do you cover up your accent?"

This question seemed to catch him off guard. In the split second he hesitated before answering, I knew whatever came from his mouth would be a lie. "I suppose I just do it automatically. Probably picked up the Yank accent from him."

I eyed C.K.'s companion, who sat with arms folded across his chest, mirrored sunglasses covering his eyes.

"He doesn't look very talkative," I observed casually. "How long have you been in the country?"

Now he grew visibly suspicious about my line of questioning. "About three weeks."

"Doesn't seem long enough for a Brit to completely drop his

accent." I reached across the table faster than he could move, and grabbed his wrist.

Ice cold.

"You liar," I rasped, dropping his arm. "You're a vampire."

He shot a panicked glance at the waitress. She hadn't looked up from her paperback.

Lowering his voice to a barely audible whisper, he leaned in. "How the hell did you know that?"

I forced my transformation, letting him view my true face for just a second. Before the waitress could notice, I shook it off.

"Holy Christ, you're not Movement, are you?" He reached into his jacket.

"No, I'm not, so leave that stake where it is." I looked up to make sure his friend wasn't prepping for a slaughter, either. "But you should be ashamed of yourself!"

His eyes bugged. "Why?"

"I know what you were doing! You were going to try and charm your way into my pants, and then you were going to eat me. It's disgusting!" I smacked my palm down on the table, and my coffee cup jumped.

This time, the waitress did look up. "Don't let him bother you, honey. He's been trying his same tired act on every gal what come in here tonight. And I do mean all night, Mr. Free Refill."

"Thank you, Ruby," C.K. muttered through clenched teeth. "For your flawless critique of my wooing style."

She cracked her gum. "Whatever."

I grabbed him by the front of his T-shirt and pulled him forward. "So, what's your game? Why are you really out here?"

With a look of pure disgust, he wrenched his clothing from my grasp. "For your information, I wasn't lying. I am a writer."

"Bullshit."

"No, really. Perhaps you've heard of me. George Gordon.

More commonly referred to as Lord Byron?" He puffed up his chest like an ostrich doing a mating dance.

"Bullshit." I leaned back in the booth and gave him the glare I used to reserve for kids in the E.R. who swore they hadn't seen their overdosing friend using recreational drugs.

"No." Guiltily, he held up his hands. "I'm not deliberately seeking trouble to serve as its cause. I'm looking for inspiration."

"Inspiration?" I echoed sarcastically. "I'm supposed to believe Lord Byron has writer's block?"

"You try writing nonstop for centuries and not need a little help getting the creative juices flowing now and then." He reached into his jacket. "I'm just going for my cigarettes."

"I haven't seen any new work from you. Of course, I'm not a big reader." I watched him closely, ready to leap into self-defense mode at the least suspicion.

"Well, of course you haven't. Can't exactly go by George Gordon, can I?" He produced a package covered with dramatic artwork, and pulled a cigarette made with black paper from it. He held the pack toward me. "Clove?"

I shook my head. "Do you have any idea what those do to your lungs? You're better off smoking regular cigarettes. So, what have you been writing?"

"My last release was *Blood Heat*. My pseudonym is Sharon Ekard." He reached into his pocket, slowly again, and withdrew a glossy bookmark. "You can keep this."

I scanned the image. A tall, dark and ridiculously muscled man with badly painted fangs held a woman in a sheer, clinging gown in the crook of his elbow. Her head was thrown back, her eyes closed in ecstasy as he leaned in for a bite. "You write…vampire romance novels?"

"Guilty as charged." He shrugged. "But I'm looking for a change of pace. One can tolerate heaving bosoms and turgid members for only so long. My friend here claims to be heading to Death Valley on some kind of top secret mission. I don't believe a word of it, of course, but a trip like this could easily be parlayed into a humorous travel diary."

The scary biker in the other booth grunted. Byron turned and waved to him. "That is, if he doesn't kill me first. Which is a very real possibility, should I continue to release information so carelessly."

Death Valley. The land of the dead.

The biker flipped the toothpick from one side of his mouth to the other and shifted in the booth, propping his boots up on the seat. The familiar insignia of the Fangs, a single tooth dripping venom, rested on the arm of his leather jacket in the form of a dusty, embroidered patch. I had to bite my tongue to keep from making a crack about the Girl Scouts, but my mouth gaped when I recognized the symbol hastily painted below it.

A dragon curled around a perfect diamond.

The dragon diamond was the Soul Eater's pet emblem. It existed in the form of a large pendant "gifted" to the human who would be sacrificed to the Soul Eater at the vampire New Year's ceremony. Jacob Seymour himself had given the diamond to Nathan's wife, Marianne, and I'd selected Ziggy to be the wearer the night I'd escaped Cyrus's house. Neither sacrifice had gone as planned.

Byron leaned over the table, a grin of pure wickedness curving his lips. "So, are you in town long? Long enough for a day of—"

"I did a paper on you in college." I cocked my head and studied him a bit more closely. He looked more fashionably gaunt than the woodcut in the front of my copy of his collected works made him appear. "What happened?"

He sighed. "Why is it every time vampires meet, they

have to share 'how I was turned' stories? It's not all that interesting."

"Most vampires aren't major figures in literature." I sipped my coffee and stared at him. If he lied to me, I would be able to tell. His face hid nothing, no matter how he might think he was fooling me. I could see the compulsion to lie working across his face as he considered what to say.

Finally, he took on a look of complete hopelessness and held up his hands. "Fine. Since you and the whole bloody world know about me, it was the consumption. I was near dead when one of the physicians attending me did the job. Near enough, anyway, that I made it through the burial convincingly."

"You were buried alive?" A chill went up my spine.

"Undead, actually." He took a draw off his sickly sweet smelling cigarette. "A writer never sneers at experience, Miss—"

"Harrison," I lied quickly. No sense in revealing my real name in front of Grizzly Adams, who never stopped watching us for a moment. "You can call me…Maxine."

"Maxine?" Byron's elegant nose wrinkled in distaste. "But as I was saying, after the burial, the physician dug me up and I've been here ever since."

"I have to give you credit." I leaned back in the seat. "I couldn't have stood it. Claustrophobic."

"That's how it was done in those days. Mozart did it. Hugo did it."

I sat up straighter. "Mozart and Victor Hugo?"

"In the past, if you truly wanted eternal life, you had to work for it," he continued as if he hadn't heard my interruption. "Now a vampire is lucky if he or she even sees the mortician's slab."

"Lucky?" I thought of Cyrus cold and dead on the gurney in the E.R. "I would hardly call it lucky."

"So, since you're bursting to know about *my* change, you must be dying to talk about *yours*. What happened? Dark prince of love sweep you off your feet and then never call?" Byron shook his head and blew a sequence of smoke rings into the air between us. "They always promise eternity, don't they?"

"I was attacked and turned accidentally. It's not the most interesting of stories." I rolled my eyes. "Nothing like *Blood Heat*."

"Well, of course not. It if were, you'd be on the bestseller list, not me." He stubbed out his cigarette. "What are you doing out in the desert, Maxine?"

"What are you doing out in the desert, *George?*" I put the same sarcastic emphasis on his name as he had on my assumed one.

"I already told you mine." He looked over his shoulder at his companion. "I'm writing the great American novel."

"You're British." I took another drink of my quickly cooling coffee.

His gaze, suddenly intense, never wavered. "You're looking for something."

Prickles ran up the back of my neck. The oddest feeling, that he was telling me something I just wasn't picking up on, slowly worked into my hypersensitive brain. I wanted to shrug it off as paranoia, but something in his eyes told me there were parts to this encounter I had missed.

I looked at the biker. The parts I was missing were the parts Byron couldn't tell me.

Hopefully, my distress wasn't obvious to either of them when I looked Byron in the eye and said, "No. I'm not looking for any*thing*."

"*Anybody?*" he mouthed, then looked over his shoulder at the biker, who shifted in his seat.

He knows something is up. Don't say another word, I pleaded inwardly. I had to disentangle myself from this conversation before I revealed too much, or he did. Luckily, the lightening sky gave me the perfect out.

I drained my mug and stood. "Well, I've got to be getting to shelter. What are you guys doing?"

"Painted Pony Motor Lodge. It's on the other side of the highway, but my friend here lives dangerously." Narrowing his eyes suspiciously, Byron took a long drag on his sickly sweet cigarette. "How about you?"

"Still haven't found a place." I certainly didn't want them knocking on my door at sundown, or worse, torching the van with me in it. "I'll probably head up to the next exit."

"You might not make it." Byron pulled a pen from his pocket and swiped my napkin. "If you're still alive at sunset, here's my cell number. Maybe we could get together in a more intimate setting."

He scribbled hastily on the paper and pushed it back to me. Below his number, where he should have written his name, were the words *St. Anne's.*

I looked up sharply, and he gave me a warning glance. I waved at the biker, who lifted two fingers in greeting. "Well, I'll see you gentlemen down the road."

Later, cramped in the hot, confining prison of the van, I groggily punched Byron's number into my cell.

He answered like a man waking after a three-day bender. "What?"

"Are you alone?" I had a fleeting mental image of his hairy traveling companion curled up next to him in bed à la *Planes, Trains & Automobiles,* but it wasn't nearly as funny as it should have been.

"Yes, thank God." There was a long pause, then a noise of disgust. "Did you just call to chat?"

"Why did you write this on the napkin?" I tried, unsuccessfully, to make myself more comfortable on my pallet of sleeping bags.

He gave a lazy yawn. "What? My number? I have no idea. If I'd known you would call in the middle of the day—"

"The other thing. St. Anne's?" I took a deep breath. "What do you know?"

"I know we're going there, and I know any vampire in her right mind wouldn't be traveling through the desert in a van that could break down just for fun. You're looking for someone. I would place a sizable wager on your intended target and my companion's being the same person."

"Are you going to get in my way?" Out of habit, I reached for the ax and stakes tucked beneath my bedding.

"No. I can't promise the same from my associate, however." He paused. "Do you want me to keep our conversation between us?"

"No, I'd like that big, hairy son-of-a-bitch to hunt me down and rip my head right off my neck. What do you think?" I pressed my palm to my forehead. One of the disadvantages of being room temperature was the fact that if the "room" happened to be one-hundred-and-two degrees, you ended up one-hundred-and-two degrees, as well.

The Painted Pony Motor Inn was probably air-conditioned. *Byron, you lucky bastard.*

There was a heavy sigh on the other end of the line. "Sarcasm is terribly overused in your day and age."

"You can gripe about it in your book." I flopped back against the lumpy sleeping bags. "But thanks for the help."

"No problem. I don't know what you're mixed up in, but these vampires are no group to trifle with."

I closed my eyes, praying for strength. "I think I can handle them."

"If you need help, feel free to call. My associate won't room with me. He thinks I am, and I quote, 'a faggot.'" I could hear Byron's wry smile over the phone. "Good luck, milady."

And what great luck I had. I didn't need to worry about finding Cyrus. Like a bookie coming to collect on a gambling debt, Cyrus had found me.

At least, a guy who knew a guy who knew a guy who knew where Cyrus was found me. Since I'd had no idea where to go or what to do when I got there, I would have to take what I could get.

I would just have to follow Byron.

As the policeman poked his flashlight into the hedges, Max thought, *This was an incredibly stupid idea.*

He'd tracked the bitch-dog here, to Ah-Nab-Awen Park. Max hadn't been far from where Nathan had allegedly ripped poor Ms. Allen's throat out when he'd thought the werewolf had picked up his scent. Max's first instinct had been to hide, not because he was afraid of her but because he didn't want her to follow him to Nathan. It had never crossed his mind that the steps coming down the path might have belonged to someone else.

Someone like law enforcement.

It also hadn't occurred to him that lurking in the very same bushes a madman had hidden in before he brutally murdered an innocent pedestrian might look a tad suspicious.

Harrison, you moron.

A loud, resonant howl caused the officer prodding the bushes to jump and drop his light. Max gave silent thanks to the dog.

The officer's shoulder radio crackled, then a long stream of garbled jargon spewed forth.

"Affirmative," the officer responded, groping through the foliage with a clumsy hand. "There's nothing out here, anyway. Everybody seems to be sticking to curfew."

The dog howled again, just as the cop's beefy fingers closed on his flashlight. His steps were brisk as he hurried away.

Max waited until he heard a car door close, then flopped onto his back with much rustling of shrubbery. Cold sweat trickled down his back, and only when he noticed his whole body shaking did he realize he was afraid.

Mortally terrified, more like it. There wasn't much he feared, but the police made that short list. They could cuff you, stick you in the back of their car and drive you off someplace where there was no sun-control.

"You can come out now, coward," a thickly accented voice called.

Max slapped his hands to his face and stretched the skin out of shape. *This is really my night.*

Trying to extricate himself from the bushes as painlessly as possible, he stumbled onto the broken-asphalt path. The werewolf waited for him, standing in the middle of the trail in an all-leather getup that could have come from a bad action movie.

Or a very good porn movie.

"Ever hear the word *inconspicuous?*" He brushed off the torn knees of his jeans.

"Have you ever heard the words 'I do not care'?" She didn't move as he stepped closer.

"You know, lupins are usually easier to intimidate than this." He grinned at her outraged curse. "You're not making my job very easy."

"I am not a lupin. Filthy traitors!" As she crossed herself and spat, her eyes flashed deadly gold. The pupils narrowed to pinpoints, then flared to encompass the irises.

The effect was unnerving, even after all Max had seen. He stepped back.

"Now who is easily intimidated, vampire?"

Was that humor in her voice? If she hadn't been such a stone-cold bitch until now, Max would have found it easier to believe. "You scared off the cop?"

She nodded, just once.

"Why?"

She lifted one shoulder in an elegant shrug as she raised her other arm behind her head. Pulling a heavy, medieval-looking crossbow from her back, she looked it over with a critical eye while she answered. "I hate police."

"We're on the same page there." Max scratched his neck and surveyed the area. "So, you think he's going to revisit the scene of the crime?"

"No." She popped the bolt from the bow and slung the weapon across her back again. Pulling a scrap of white fabric from her pocket, she gave the air a long sniff. She waved the cloth under her nose a few times and lifted her head. "He hasn't been here since he killed her."

Max groaned. "I could have told you that. He's not a psychopath."

"No, he is not." The werewolf frowned and bent to touch the pavement. She lifted her fingers to her nose. "He is not acting as a vampire, either."

"What do you mean?" Max knelt on the path, and the scent of blood caught in his nostrils. It had been days since Nathan had killed the woman, and the air was damp with rain. There must have been an enormous amount of blood for it not to have all been washed away by now. "God almighty."

"When you kill, do you leave this much blood behind?" The werewolf regarded him with a raised eyebrow.

Max couldn't decide if she was being intentionally antagonistic or if her poor manners were due to the fact she was, biologically, a canine. "For your information, I've never killed anyone."

At least, not in the technical sense.

"But no, a vampire wouldn't have left this behind. He would have fed on her." Absently, Max traced the chalk outline of the dead woman's ankle. Rising, he wiped his hands on his jeans as though he'd touched something dirty. "This place gives me the creeps. Let's get out of here."

She looked as surprised as he was sure he did. The words had erupted from him out of habit. They implied a kinship, teamwork, a shared goal. They were certainly not something he would say to a werewolf, of all people.

To his immense relief, she shook her head. Her long black braid slithered across her leather-covered shoulders. "I have a job to do. I will leave you to wallow in the shrubbery."

What a bitch. Still, a wide grin curved his mouth.

He watched her walk away, her braid snapping like a whip behind her. "Bella," he warned through gritted teeth. "If you get in my way again, I will kill you."

Her laughter, low and throaty, floated back to him on a wave of musky perfume in the night air. "No, you will not. If I were you, I would hurry. The police are coming back."

Max looked toward the bridge. No traffic crossed as he stood rooted to the spot, but soon enough the thin, high whine of a siren broke the evening stillness.

When he turned back, Bella was gone.

Cyrus woke in the night in a cold sweat. He wasn't sure, but he thought he might have screamed, because Mouse woke at the same time.

"Cyrus? What's the matter?" Her hand was hot against his shoulder.

He swallowed. His throat was so dry, it was like gulping down razor blades. "Nothing. Go back to sleep."

When he stood, he wrapped the sheet around his waist. Though she slept beside him on the narrow bed, she still possessed a bizarre modesty.

"Tell me, please." She pulled her legs beneath her as she sat up, a waif in her too-large T-shirt.

If he'd been asked at that very moment to describe her in one word, it would have been *fragile*. So how could she expect him to share the details of his nightmare?

"I said go back to sleep."

Two days ago, his sharp tone would have intimidated her. But trapped together in this cinder block hell as they were, the days stretched like weeks, and by now she was accustomed to his moods. "You were screaming. People don't scream if there isn't something wrong."

He went to the wall and leaned his head against it, his forearm over his eyes. The desert heat that had penetrated the basement in the day had escaped into the chilly night, leaving the surface cold against his skin.

"It was just a dream," he said, more to reassure himself than to explain it to her. "I have a history of nightmares."

There was a pause before she answered. "That's terrible."

"It's to be expected, when you've lived a life like mine." He straightened, scrubbing his hands over his face. "I'll be fine in a while. I'm sorry to have disturbed you."

A more refined person would accept his apology and let the matter rest, but Cyrus would never accuse Mouse of being refined. She swung her legs, bare under the hem of the T-shirt, over the edge of the bed, her arms braced against the mattress. A slash of brown hair covered one of her eyes. "What was it about?"

"I couldn't tell you, in good conscience." But a voice in his head mocked him. *You protect her from your deviant nature now?*

"It was just a dream. Telling me about it won't hurt me." Her clearheaded logic was apt to drive him mad.

He sat beside her, not close enough that she could touch him. The last thing he needed or wanted was her pity. "When I became a vampire, my father cut out my heart."

She gasped at his words, from his casual phrasing of the horror, no doubt. But she had asked, so he continued to oblige her. "I don't know how it comes to pass, but after turning, vampires grow a second heart. The first heart, the human one, is the heart to drive the stake through. So my father cut it out of me."

"So you couldn't be killed?" Her innocence was charming.

"So I couldn't betray him. He kept my heart for seven centuries." The familiar, sickening guilt crept over Cyrus. He closed his eyes and breathed in deeply to regain his composure, but all he got was the scent of soap from Mouse's freshly washed skin.

"But you don't have to worry about that now. You're human again," she said, the declaration like a prayer from her lips.

His gaze wandered to the toes on her dainty feet, which rested on the cold, tile floor.

"For the time being." He didn't know why he would say such a thing, when he knew it would bother her. Perhaps he wasn't as changed as he'd imagined in the past few days.

But *she* had changed. Only a day before, she would have trembled at the prospect of his impending transformation. Now, she stood and faced him, her arms folded tightly across her chest. The motion made the hem of the T-shirt hitch up, exposing the fronts of her creamy, white thighs. The sight was painfully arousing, and he closed his eyes in shame as he remembered what he'd done to her on that first night.

"Why would you say something like that to me?" Her lower lip trembled, not in fear, but anger. Seemingly oblivious to his distress, she tightened her arms around herself, lifting the shirt a critical inch higher.

"I don't know," he admitted, unable to face her or look anywhere near her. "I'm sorry."

It was the first time he'd said those words in earnest to anyone. The realization shocked him, almost as much as if he'd been struck by lightning.

He said it again, for the reprehensible way he'd forced himself on her. "I'm sorry," he murmured over and over, for every harsh word she'd had to endure from him. And for the fact that she was caught up in his father's treachery, and it would ultimately cost her her life.

And she would die. There was no way to stop it. He couldn't stand up against the might of his father's adoring cult. Cyrus was nothing, no one, with no power to offer them or riches to seduce them with.

That's when he appreciated the full horror of his humanity. They were at the mercy of fate, he and his Mouse, as he had been at the mercy of his father's whim for centuries.

There was one way he could make what he knew of his father's plan work in his favor. When they turned him, he could turn Mouse.

Cyrus remembered his wives, how he'd loved each of them and lost them to his father, and how they had died hating Cyrus. But then, they'd never really loved him to begin with. Perhaps as humans they had held some affection for him. After he'd changed them, they'd become different. The first had become a mindless harlot, seeking her pleasure wherever she could find it, but never returning to Cyrus's bed. Two had prayed fervently that the Lord would take pity on them and spare their souls. Both had taken their own lives, one by exposure to sunlight, the other by bathing in a basin of holy water. The others, including his beloved Elsbeth, had been lost to his father's appetite for power.

Cyrus couldn't allow Mouse to meet such an end.

Still, his mantra of apology wouldn't stop, nor the stinging tears that rose in his eyes. "I'm sorry."

Kneeling beside him on the bed, she transformed from the demon of lust that had unwittingly tormented him to an angel of compassion as she wrapped her arms around him.

None of them had ever comforted him this way. The closest to come to it had been wretched Carrie, just before her blade had split his heart. He let Mouse stroke his hair, and leaned against her at her gentle urging. It was a disgraceful thing, crying like a woman in front of one. In the past, he would have killed her, when he felt better. Now, her death was the only thing he feared, and it frightened him more than the prospect of his own.

His fear transformed into a landslide of gut-wrenching desperation, and he clung to her, knowing his fingers bruised the fragile skin beneath the T-shirt. She said nothing. The tone of her voice never rose above a gentle murmur as she soothed him with mindless words of reassurance.

Her tenderness only amplified his despair. She didn't deserve this. There were so many people he would love to see die in her place, but it wasn't to be.

He took her face in his hands and looked into her eyes. He needed to see that she understood. "If we survive this, I will give you everything you've ever desired."

Taking his hands in hers, she gently lowered them to his knees. "You won't have to."

She said this to placate him, he knew, because she did not believe him. Or perhaps he'd frightened her. He grasped her shoulders and pulled her forward, trying to communicate the depth of his feeling with an urgent, clumsy kiss.

She didn't resist him. She didn't return his kiss with as much enthusiasm as he'd hoped for, either, but her warm mouth parted beneath his as a sound of surprise reverberated in her throat.

This was exactly what he'd been seeking. Acceptance. Not for what he could give her, but for the intention behind it. He had what he wanted, and he wouldn't need to ask for more.

Mouse looked confused when he pulled away. Cyrus kissed her cheek to reassure her. "Let's go to sleep."

Perhaps if he pretended that the new day on the horizon wouldn't bring them one day closer to the end, he would eventually believe it.

10

March

I was in Cyrus's bed again. Candlelight flickered on the cream-colored walls. Gauzy curtains floated on a cool night breeze. It was a dream, I knew, because I'd gone to sleep in the back of the increasingly unpleasant van. Also, because Nathan lay beside me.

He touched my face, and I leaned into his palm. "You're dead."

That wasn't what I had meant to say. I knew he wasn't dead. His terror and pain assaulted me every moment through the blood tie. It had been so overwhelming I'd had to pull to the side of the highway and concentrate on blocking his voice from my head. Then I'd driven the rest of the night in tears, praying he didn't think I'd abandoned him.

In my dream, he smiled. "I'm not dead. I'm right here."

His voice echoed in my brain, pleading for help. It had a weird, stereo effect, and the sound waves visibly distorted the air around us. "Did you hear that?"

Of course he heard it. He'd said it.

But Nathan just smiled, oblivious to my distress. "Where are you running?"

The tortured screams rent the air again. "I know I'm not dreaming that."

I wasn't sure he'd heard me, so I tried repeating the words, only to find the screams now came from my own mouth.

Nathan pulled me into his arms, and he felt exactly the way he would have in real life, solid and cold.

"You don't have to run," he whispered against my hair. "Please, don't run from me."

A drop of crimson splashed against the pale sheets.

"You're bleeding." I noted the detail with disinterest. The whole scene was boring and loud and annoying. I sat up. Nathan flopped on the mattress, now soaked with red as he bled from the arcane symbols carved into his flesh.

"Carrie, please."

I turned away. Through the magic of dreaming, I was on my feet. A single step carried me far enough from the bed that I couldn't hear Nathan and could barely see him. Cyrus waited for me at the other side of the impossibly long room, and I went to him.

"He needs you," my former sire said without the usual mocking in his tone. "Are you going to go to him?"

I shook my head. "It's out of my hands now."

Cyrus's arms enfolded me, but his hands turned to claws that tore my flesh. I looked into his eyes, and his face transformed grotesquely, then shifted into Nathan's. He screamed, so loudly and long I thought I wouldn't be able to stand it.

When I feared I'd go mad from the sound, I woke. My cell phone rang at my side. Still drunk with sleep, I reached for it.

"We should pull into Nevada tonight."

Byron. "Thank you for the update."

He chuckled. "I thought you might like to know, so you can get a jump on us. Show up before we get your man."

"He's not my man." The denial escaped before I could stop

it. Wincing, I cleared my parched throat. "I mean, I'm looking for him, but—"

"I don't care, either way." Byron sniffed. "Have you fed?"

"No. Some of us sleep in." Truthfully, my blood supply had run so low I'd begun to ration, and my energy had begun to wane. I didn't know what shape I'd find Cyrus in. If they'd turned him, I'd have to keep him alive until we got back to Michigan. With what I'd managed to save, we still might both starve.

"There's a place just over the Nevada border that caters to your kind." The way he stressed the last words of the sentence begged questioning.

Rolling my eyes, I shifted the phone from one ear to the other and groped for my jeans in the tangled sleeping bag. "My kind?"

He chuckled again. "Lady vampires. There's a brothel about twenty miles past the state line. All pretty men, female clientele only."

"It's a donor house," I accused.

"It's a brothel. But if you pay them extra, they'll bare a little neck." He gave a sigh of nostalgia. "Lucky you."

"Sorry, I don't feed from humans." I'd done it twice, once on Dahlia, once with Ziggy, and both times had provided more than adequate doses of guilt.

"Really? Where do you get the blood you drink, then?"

I bristled at the monster logic that was sure to follow, the same rationalizations Cyrus had used to manipulate me. "Where I get my blood is none of your—"

"Hey, I'm not judging. I'm just trying to give you some pointers. Surviving in the harsh, untamed West is a lot different than your posh, midwestern life. At least, that's what Road Dog has been telling me."

"Road Dog?" I remembered his hirsute companion. "For some reason I can't imagine him saying that."

"Well, I read it from his body language. When he was eating a trucker." Byron paused. "So, do you want the address?"

Eyeing the cooler, I sighed. "Can I get it in bulk there?"

"With dry ice."

"Fine. Tell me the directions."

It was almost sunup when I reached the elegant, redbrick manor. Despite the fact it was located on a barren back road in the middle of the desert, the lawn surrounding the house was lush and green. At least, from what I could tell between the slashing bars of the tall iron fence surrounding the place. There wasn't a neighbor for ten miles, but I knew their security concerns didn't extend to simple burglars.

A sleek intercom console was posted at the gate. I pushed the button to ring the buzzer.

A voice crackled over the speaker a second later. "State your business."

I recited the password Byron had given me, feeling dirtier by the second. "Withdrawal."

"Enter." At once, a loud, mechanical whir set the gate in motion. It opened wide, allowing me to drive up the long, cobblestone driveway. I left the van in the care of a bored-looking valet and jogged up the marble steps to the dark wood door.

When Byron had said "brothel," I'd imagined an Old West style whorehouse, with red, flocked wallpaper, old-time lamps with beaded fringe and prostitutes draped over velvet chaise longues. When a uniformed butler opened the door, I was pleasantly surprised. Despite the stodgy English exterior, the inside was decorated like a home from *Architectural Digest.* Long, white runners protected the hardwood floors and sweeping staircase. The walls were painted in very modern white, and track lighting highlighted the hanging artwork.

"The madam will be with you in a moment, madam," the

butler informed me. I almost expected a rim shot to follow his repetitive statement. His face remained humorless, as if he didn't recognize his pun.

I refrained from pointing it out, and walked slowly through the foyer. To my left and to my right, huge double doors blocked me from further exploration, but the hallway that extended behind the curling staircase seemed to be public property. I strolled leisurely, perusing the artwork. A tall, gilded painting in an ostentatious frame stopped me in my tracks.

"Klimt."

The rough voice startled me. I turned toward the source of it, a short, generously curved woman with long, springy gray curls cascading over her shoulders.

"Yes, I know," I said, recovering quickly from my fright. "It's not the original, is it?"

"You're damn straight it is." I couldn't tell if she was upset by my question or enthusiastic about her property.

Smiling, I sought to correct my faux pas. "My old sire owned a lot of art, but it was all fake, so I find pretty much anything suspect."

"Oh, shit, honey, I don't care." The woman came to stand beside me, pulling a pack of cigarettes from the sleeve of her flowing caftan. "If it was fake, I'd tell you."

"I didn't want to offend." Though my apology probably did offend her. Something in her body language suggested she lived within a "no bullshit" zone.

The woman's eyes lit up with a spark of amusement. "Did I hear you right? Did you say, 'old sire'?"

That was a stupid mistake. "I didn't catch your name."

A knowing smile crinkled the corners of her eyes. "Because I didn't give it. I'm March. I'm what you'd call the 'pimp' around here, but we say 'madam' because it's more genteel sounding. Don't worry about your little slip. I like secrets, so long as they don't drag trouble onto my property."

I cleared my throat and glanced at the high, arched ceiling. "Your house is beautiful."

"Thank you. But you didn't come here to look at the house." She crooked her finger as she backed to the doors. "Are we on liquid lunch today, or just here for some fun?"

"I need blood." I spread my hands helplessly. "Whatever you'd call that."

"I'd call it your lucky day." With a goofy flourish, March pushed open the doors to my left.

I might have envisioned the decor wrong, but I'd been right on the money about the prostitutes. Everywhere I looked, gorgeous men draped themselves over ultramasculine leather furniture. My eyes boggled at the variety. Dark, fair, long-haired or neatly trimmed, some with androgynous bodies, some overly muscled.

"Take your pick," March said proudly. "These are the feeders."

"Um…" I gestured to the foyer, where the butler stood with my bag. One of Nathan's many, stringent rules was "always be prepared." In my bag I had all the necessities for harvesting blood from a willing donor. I don't know how I'd planned to find one in case I needed to, but I was definitely prepared.

"I'm not what you would call…traditional," I told March. Chewing my lip, I scanned each of the men.

The madam laughed. "There's nothing you can do to shock them."

"No, I mean, I don't bite." I stepped forward and cleared my throat. Many pairs of curious male eyes turned to me. "I'm looking for someone who's not afraid of needles."

There was a noticeable shift in the energy of the room. Some of the men looked away, as if they'd become suddenly interested in the walls. The rest looked worried or amused, or a combination of both.

"Nothing kinky," I assured them. "I just need blood."

"Why not bite us?" a tall, thin man with model looks asked.

"Excuse me?" March placed her hands on her hips and raked an angry glare over the men. "Do I pay you to question my customers?"

A few of them offered a grudging, "No."

"I can't hear you," March insisted, raising her hand to her ear.

One voice rose above the chorus of resulting answers. "I'll do it."

When I found the source of the voice, my stomach leaped into my throat. When I'd said, "Nothing kinky," I may have lied. The guy was gorgeous, with long blond hair and a tan that would make Icarus weep with jealousy. He was shirtless, and his faded jeans rode low on his hips.

My mouth suddenly dry, I gestured for him to come closer. "What's your blood type?"

He laughed. "You're kidding, right?"

"No. I've been doing some research," I explained, feeling like a hopeless dork. Then I wondered why I cared if some random male prostitute thought I was a nerd. Wiping my suddenly damp palms on my jeans, I continued. "Vampires are able to metabolize the blood they drink more efficiently if the donor's type matches their own, prevampire type. By metabolize, I mean—"

"I know what metabolize means," he said with a kneecap-melting smile. "I'm O positive. Universal donor."

"I think you two will get along just fine," March announced, stepping forward to loop an arm around the man's broad shoulders, despite the fact there was a good foot difference in their heights. "Unfortunately, we need to discuss the vagaries of payment and restrictions. Shall we do that in private?"

"Why not?" I followed March and the demigod into the foyer, where I stopped. "I just need my bag."

The butler was disinclined to release it. "After I search it, madam. Then I will bring it to your room posthaste."

March winked at me. "It's a technicality. We've had some interesting guests here, haven't we, Evan?"

"Yes, ma'am."

Evan? He looked more like a...Tarzan, to me.

I followed them up the stairs. March took her time, filling me in on the history of the place. "This house was left to me by my late husband, Edgar, God rest his soul. I lived in it from the time we were married until I moved it here in 1973."

At the top of the landing, she touched the wall lovingly. "I had it shipped from Massachusetts in bricks and reassembled here, then did some updating and remodeling. Of course, Edgar would roll in his grave if he knew what I was doing with it. Bless him, he never did have much enthusiasm for heterosexual sex." She sighed and indicated a hallway to the right. "I'll put you down here."

Even Cyrus's mansion, grand as it had been, didn't rival the sprawling splendor of this house. We stopped at the seventh door on the left—at least I thought it was seven, I might have lost count—and March pulled a tiny gold key from her sleeve.

"There are twenty-nine legal, licensed brothels in Nevada, and we're the only one that caters to vampires. There are automatic steel shutters in every room, and I do mean every room, of this house, to keep the sun out. There's also an on-duty physician, in case your session gets a little out of hand."

"I am a physician," I said, feeling the familiar sting to my pride as an inner voice taunted, *You mean you used to be.*

March seemed impressed with this declaration, and I felt we

were somehow kindred spirits. We were both professional women, struggling to get by in a man's world.

Then again, prostitution was pretty much a girls' club.

The spark of admiration left her eyes and she waved her hand. "In any case, I don't want it to go that far. You seem like a nice girl. I don't want to have to put you on my shit list, you hear?"

"Don't worry about it." I gave Evan a once-over. Vampires might be stronger than humans, but I was betting Evan had a good fifty pounds of rock-hard muscle on me. He looked as though he could easily snap my neck, and she was concerned for *his* safety? "What about money? You said we needed to cover payment."

"I can get it from you at dusk. The standard room rate is two hundred dollars a day. You have to work out the service prices with Evan." March pushed open the door, revealing a room so stunning it could have been on the cover of a furniture catalog. In the center, on a raised dais, sat an ultramodern four-poster bed enameled in sleek black. The bedding matched the spotless white of the carpet, which was broken at intervals by black leather armchairs and gleaming ebony end tables. The only color in the room was supplied by a vase of bright pink tulips on the nightstand.

Good thing I've got some wiggle room in my budget.

"And one last thing," she said as Evan and I stepped across the threshold. "You might be immortal, but they're not. All my guys have to use protection, no if, ands or buts. Got it?"

"Oh, we won't be having—" The gentle, yet oddly pointed closing of the door cut me off.

"We won't?" The demigod—Evan—actually sounded disappointed. His body heat crept into me as he stepped forward, his hard chest brushing against my back.

I turned to face him. "Don't you ever want a night off?"

A deliciously wicked smile crossed his face. "Not usually, no."

In that heart-stopping moment, he reminded me so much of Cyrus, I couldn't breathe. Oh, he was much more powerfully built than my former sire had been, and definitely more tan. Cyrus had been lean and pale, his hair lighter than Evan's, nearly white. But the vibe from him was identical: dangerous sensuality coupled with desperation so keen it struck pain in my own heart.

I'd have to have been blind to miss that part: like my first sire, Evan obviously smothered his loneliness in the surety of physical gratification. Unfortunately for him, he didn't wield as much power over my libido as he thought he did.

A soft knock at the door brought me out of my silent reverie. My face flamed at the realization I'd been staring intently at the man before me, and he'd clearly misinterpreted quiet contemplation for dumbstruck passion. I was relieved to have a reason to turn away from him.

"Your bag, madam," the butler intoned with a dry note of disapproval as he opened the door.

I wondered how such a stuffy old guy ended up working in a brothel. "Thanks. Just set it down."

When I was once again alone with my hulking he-man of a donor, I took a deep, fortifying breath.

"Sit in that chair and…" I paused, taking in his shirtless state. "Well, I was going to say 'roll up your sleeve' out of habit, but I guess it won't be necessary."

"I could take off something else," he offered, flashing his predatory grin.

"No, that's fine. You're about as naked as I can handle right now." I reached into my bag and pulled out a coiled length of tubing and a collection bag, as well as a butterfly-shaped needle and some antiseptic swabs. I laid my supplies out like a torture chamber cache, expecting his cocky demeanor to waver.

It never did. He leaned against the back of the chair and aligned his arm perfectly with the armrest to display the crease of his elbow. "This is my good arm."

I eyed the fat, blue vein there with clinical interest, but my rumbling stomach betrayed my intent. "Have your blood drawn a lot?"

"Have to, in my line of work." He reached for one of the antiseptic pads and tore the wrapper. Sponging a wide circle of alcohol over his arm, he shrugged. "We have to get tested for STDs often, or we lose our licenses."

"So, what's up with your friends that they're so afraid? I mean, they'd rather be bitten by a vampire than get poked by a tiny little needle?" I busied myself connecting the tube to the collection bag.

"That's probably not it." He stretched his legs out, and I couldn't help but notice how long they were. "We get a lot of customers here, and they're not all pillars of the vampire community. Or maybe they are, and that's their problem. But after a while, we've all learned our respective lessons, and we don't generally trust vamps who bring props."

I made a noise of understanding as I stretched a strip of latex around his biceps. I didn't want to think about what kind of depraved torture these guys had been exposed to. "So, why did you trust me?"

Evan chuckled, a rich, velvety sound that reverberated down my spine. "Because you look harmless. And damn good."

"Right." I could barely contain my exhausted laughter. "I'm driving cross-country without a shower, rationing my clean underwear. I've been sleeping in a van for the past couple days now. You're going to have to do a damn sight better than that before I shell out my hard-earned cash on your compliments."

"I'm not lying," he said with an earnestness that didn't sound quite rehearsed enough to not seem genuine. "You're not caked in weird makeup or wearing all black like the rest of our customers. I'd let you bite me for free."

It was certainly a tantalizing prospect, at least to my monster side. A brief, vivid image of being crushed beneath his hard body as I sank my teeth into his neck flashed through my mind, and I closed my eyes, shaking my head to get rid of the picture.

"So, how much do you charge?" I asked, turning my mind from impure thoughts.

"For what? The sex or the blood?"

"There will be no sex," I insisted, a little to myself, a little to him.

"Come on," he pressed, sliding his hand up my arm. "You can't tell me you're not bored, day after day in the back of a van."

There was a note of neediness in his voice. This man wanted something from me. And there was only one thing humans wanted from vampires. To be turned.

"No," I said quietly. "I haven't been bored."

I'd been kept awake all day by nightmares. As soon as the sun came up, my head filled with Nathan's screams. Cyrus was out in the desert somewhere and I had to find him before his father got his hands on him. No way was I bored.

With an exasperated sigh, I stabbed the needle into Evan's vein while he was still planning his next tactic. "And no amount of pretty talk will get you turned tonight."

My head throbbed. Physical and mental fatigue overwhelmed me. "Is there a bathroom? I really need to get the road dirt off of me."

Evan pointed the way.

I stepped into the spacious, marble bathroom and turned the taps to fill the tub. I'd collect what I needed from Evan, then pay him and kick him the hell out and take a nice, hot bath.

I leaned my forehead against the cool glass of the mirror above the sink and took a deep breath, preparing to let my guard down and open the blood tie. As soon as I did, Nathan was there, angry and screaming as he had been for the last few days. But there was another presence, too, one I hadn't felt since the night Nathan had poured his blood down my throat while I was unconscious.

This has to be a mistake.

The steam from the running water became horrendously oppressive, and I struggled to drag in breath out of habit. I wiped my damp hair from my forehead with a trembling hand. If it wasn't a mistake, it had been a punishment meted out by the cruelest of fates.

The sound of *him,* a single heart beating in his human chest, almost drowned out the sound of Nathan's agony as my two sires fought for dominance in my mind.

I gripped the edge of the marble countertop so hard I expected to leave gouges in the stone. When I exhaled, a single word exploded from my mouth.

"Cyrus."

Then, I was falling, and I didn't feel it when I hit the ground.

11

Connections

This time, when he woke, he was careful not to disturb Mouse. He didn't want to have to explain to her about Carrie, and why he could still feel her.

Because he didn't have the answer himself.

Trembling, he went to stand beneath the small, high window. The moon was full, filling the basement with an eerie slash of light. Upstairs, the heavy footsteps he'd learned not to hear shook the floor.

In the past few days, he'd almost forgotten he'd been like them. Carrie's voice in his dream had reminded him. He'd heard her in his water-colored memories in the shadow world. They'd inspired a feeling as close to anger as he'd been capable of then. It had really been more of a passing annoyance. When he'd been pulled back, he'd been enraged at the thought of her. "The one who got away," some would say, though it wasn't with fond nostalgia in his case.

But now, he couldn't conjure even a speck of hatred for her. It was too tiring to be consumed so fully by an emotion, and he was finished wasting time.

Maybe that's why he'd heard her calling his name. Perhaps

his subconscious had been giving him some sort of signal. After all, the school of dream interpretation couldn't be complete bullshit.

Things were never that simple. In all his life, never once had something turned out to his advantage, and he was sure this would be no different. The dream was a warning. He would meet her again.

The thought of Carrie, who could not love him when he'd been at the height of his power and influence, seeing him in his human shell didn't rankle the way it should have. Humanity had a few advantages. One being companionship. As a vampire, he wouldn't have tolerated the company of someone like Mouse. He'd wanted ones who would do anything to be with him. Though timid, Mouse had a quiet dignity. She wasn't as outspoken and abrasive as Carrie had been—qualities Cyrus had truly admired at the time. Mouse had settled into their bizarre circumstances gradually, and every day a little more of what he assumed was her original personality surfaced.

He was going to have to stop calling her Mouse. But he certainly wasn't going to start calling her Stacey.

She'd gone to sleep with wet hair, much to his annoyance, but now it curled softly around her face. The fact that she slept so soundly in his presence gave him a little hope for himself. She trusted him to protect her from the monsters. From himself.

Let Carrie haunt me, he thought bitterly. If her memory reminded him of his shameful past, he would bear it. Shame seemed integral to humanity, and if it made him more human, so much the better.

With a shock, he realized he intended to stay this way. Perhaps he hadn't thought of it before. Perhaps he'd only felt removal from his former species, and just this moment had learned of his intent to distance himself permanently. More likely he'd known, somewhere in the most distant, inaccessible reaches of his soul, since the moment he'd drawn human breath.

Mouse stirred. He went to her side, easing onto the narrow bed as she lifted her head and peered at him with sleepy eyes.

"Did you have a nightmare?"

He straightened the bedclothes to cover both of them and pulled her close. "No."

She leaned her head against his shoulder. "Are you lying?"

"No, little Mouse. I'm not lying."

In fact, when he closed his eyes, Cyrus drifted into the first dreamless sleep he'd encountered in seven hundred years.

When I woke, my head throbbed. The room was dim, thanks in part to the metal shutters, the other part to the dial-controlled recessed lighting. Two bags of blood rested in a well-stocked ice bucket on the nightstand.

Evan was gone.

I sat up, wincing at the soreness in my skull. There was a slender vial nestled in the ice bucket between the two bags, and a note attached. I had to squint to read it.

> The doctor caught Evan with this. I'd keep a close eye on it, if you weren't looking to be a sire.
>
> March

I snatched up the vial, my face flaming with anger. How close had I been to having yet another open channel in my head? I glared down at my arm. He'd put a Band-Aid over the bend of my elbow. I didn't need it, and anyone who'd done any research—such as reading *The Sanguinarius,* the most well-known and widely respected book in the vampire community—would have known that. It might be the med school in me, but

I think anyone who's about to make a life-changing choice about their physiology ought to know at least the basics of what they're getting into.

My head buzzed and my vision jarred. It definitely felt as if I was about to have my head filled with voices, so I took a deep breath and imagined a brick wall, the way Nathan had taught me. Of course, when he'd explained it, it had been a shield of white light, but a brick wall with some nice, climbing ivy seemed a bit stronger than that New Age, hippie claptrap. It would block other minds—Nathan's and now, apparently, Cyrus's—from entering my own and sapping my strength.

I lifted the vial of my own blood, popped the top off and downed it, trying to ignore the taste. To my vampire tongue, human blood is amazing. Thick and warm and rich with a coppery bite, it's like no food a human could experience. Vampire blood—at least Nathan's and Cyrus's, on the few times I've tasted it—was the same, but with an emptiness to it, as though my senses could tell I would not receive the kind of sustenance I needed from it. Plus it was the equivalent of deep-fried, sugar-loaded food for a human. It could screw up your metabolism permanently, like the Soul Eater's, and for a vampire, permanently was an awfully long time. My own blood, however, tasted just like regular old blood, like I'd gotten a paper cut and licked it clean. It wasn't pleasant, and I forced my uncooperative gag reflex away in order to swallow. Still, it was better than leaving it out for one of March's boys to find.

My stomach growled at the reminder of the blood I'd been denied earlier, and I reached into the ice bucket for a bag. Under ordinary circumstances, the blood would be suspect, but I was too hungry and weak to argue myself out of drinking it. My hands brushed something definitely not ice buried under the bag. It was a note, this one folded tightly, the ink beginning to run from the moisture of the ice.

I've left some Tylenol in the bedside table drawer. Take it easy until sundown. And then, if you know what's good for you, get as far away from here as possible.
Evan

I reread the note and stuffed it back into the ice bucket. No way was I taking any pills Evan had left behind. I knew better than to take candy from strangers, especially when they'd already tried to steal my blood. Besides, my headache was nothing a little food and rest couldn't cure.

Feeling good and lazy, I skipped a glass and slid my fangs through the thin plastic of the bag. I hadn't fed enough on the trip, and I had a hard time sleeping in the back of the van, let alone in a strange bed in a bordello. All this left me with too much time to think, and of the two people on my mind most lately, the one I didn't want to dwell on kept forcing his way into my thoughts.

Probably because Evan had almost put me into the same situation Cyrus had been forced into. I'd always imagined Cyrus had some sinister motive for making me a vampire, though he'd insisted it was an accident, and what I could remember of the evening—aside from crawling on my hands and knees through formaldehyde and harvested human livers—didn't suggest otherwise. As much as I hated the thought he might have been a victim of circumstance like I was, it seemed as though it was true.

What if Evan had taken my blood? When I'd become Nathan's first fledgling, he'd been incapacitated by fear of losing me. More precisely, the fear of the pain he would feel if he'd lost me. Cyrus had tried everything short of physical re-straints to keep me by his side. I knew I was stronger than Cyrus. I must have been, to look him in the eye as I stabbed a knife through his heart. I'd assumed I was stronger than Nathan, but that assertion seemed unfair now. Nathan had lost his son and gained yet another emotional burden, right along with his blood tie to me. All of this, on top of the lifetime of guilt he'd endured for the murder of his wife. How could I measure my untested strength against a man who'd been put through an unending gauntlet of emotional pain?

At times I felt Nathan had overlooked a key component of our blood bond, though. While he ached with loneliness for his wife and son, he had me. We could laugh and joke and fuck, but God forbid he ever share any emotion with me.

I hadn't considered the possibility Nathan might hear my thoughts until a shattering pain nearly tore the bones of my skull apart. There were no words across the blood tie, only crushing regret.

Now you want to be a part of my life. I knew Nathan was locked in some unimaginable, hellish prison now, but I couldn't stand a second more of the physical and emotional pain I felt being tied to him. I blocked off the blood tie and wiped tears of shame from my eyes.

I had been so tired, I almost overlooked Evan's warning. "Get as far away as possible." Was I in danger here? Would someone burst in and kill me the second I fell asleep? Snapping fully awake, I clicked on the lamp on the bedside table and flopped back on the pillows. I looked at the door. There had to be a way to secure it from the inside, even if it wasn't immediately visible. After all, March had used a key to unlock it. I rallied what little strength I had left and wobbled to the door. There weren't any latches immediately obvious in the vicinity of the doorknob, and there wasn't a dead bolt. But then, why had March needed a key? I tried to turn the knob.

It didn't budge. I'd been locked in.

Regardless of how much I needed it, I didn't think I'd be getting much sleep, after all.

12

It's a Small World

The werewolf waited for someone.

Max watched her from the safety of his rental car as she sat in the small coffee shop. The Trans-Am, though badass, would have tipped her off to his presence, so he'd had to leave it behind.

He'd add that to his list of "Reasons to Extremely Dislike the Were-bitch."

To the untrained eye, Bella would have appeared as one of those überconfident women who went to coffee shops alone. No book, no laptop, not even a newspaper to distract her from her solitude. Framed as she was in the sole window of the tiny, brick establishment, she drew the attention of anyone who passed on the sidewalk outside. One man walked into a mailbox, totally oblivious to the world around him as he stared at Bella.

She appeared to be absorbed in thought, but Max saw the way her golden eyes surreptitiously scanned the passersby, and the coffee she'd been nursing had long since gone cold. In the sky above, the moon was full. She wouldn't assume her animal form. Few of them ever did, though they frowned on the use of science to stop it. No, they did spells, probably with gross ingredients like baby tongues and eye of newt. And they thought a little prick of a needle once a month was a sin worth killing over.

The warm light of the coffee shop's interior spilled onto the street, illuminating her from behind like an unnatural sun. Supernaturally motionless, she seemed a figure in a painting. Her admirers had no inkling how deadly and dark this mysterious beauty really was.

Shaking his head, Max groaned. She was *not* beautiful. He was just horny. He'd find a way to make that her fault—not in the obvious way, because bestiality wasn't his thing—later.

A shadowy figure, dressed far too warmly for the weather, in a heavy black coat, entered through the shop's narrow door. In the window, Bella straightened and sniffed the air.

The motion accentuated the slender column of her neck and the tracery of blue veins that seemed visible even from across the street. *Bullshit, you're imagining things.* Still, Max's stomach growled and his dick hardened. He could take care of only one problem without getting arrested, so he fumbled in the backseat for his thermos of blood.

"You're a fucking pervert, Harrison," he growled to himself as he unscrewed the lid. B positive. Best blood type, hands down.

The shadowy figure sat across from Bella. It was a woman with a shiny black bob and generous cleavage. Something about her seemed oddly familiar, but then, Max could have been confusing her with a chick from the movies.

The two conferred briefly. Though he couldn't read the werewolf's facial expression, and the curvy woman's face was obscured by the shadow of a hanging lamp, he could tell from their body language things were all-business at that table.

"What I wouldn't pay to hear what's going on in that messed up little head of yours, wolf." He lifted the thermos to his mouth, wanting to finish off the blood quickly. He'd never cared for clots.

He'd no sooner taken a swallow than he'd noticed Bella was no longer in the window. Max's gaze shot from the door to the sidewalk, where she was striding briskly and purposefully away.

He counted to ten before he exited the car and headed for the coffee shop. Seconds later, the werewolf's associate exited. Max was ready for her.

He clamped his hand over the woman's mouth as he hauled her into the alley between the shop and an optometrist's office that had closed for the night. "Don't make a fucking sound, or so help me I'll—"

She bit him.

Reflexively, he released her, then cursed himself for doing it.

She laughed, loud and half-crazy. "You'll what?"

The familiarity he'd sensed at first sight crawled up his spine, and he forced away the resultant shiver. "Who are you?"

"What, you don't remember me?" She laughed again and grabbed a handful of her black hair. The wig slipped from her head in a smooth motion, and a riot of red curls, which seemed too voluminous to have been hidden beneath, tumbled onto her shoulders.

"How could I forget?" Max stepped forward, backing her up to the damp brick. "Though your name escapes me. Begonia?"

She made a face. "Dahlia. But I'm glad to see I made an impression."

Max groaned as she slid her hand across the front of his jeans and the substantial bulge there. The night he'd gone with Nathan to help Carrie take out Cyrus, he'd been thrown on the mercy of this insatiable vampire. He'd never really been attracted to ladies with such generous figures, but he'd always said he'd try anything once, especially if it might save his neck.

It had been the best twenty minutes of his life.

Still, that was the past, and Max never looked back. "Darlin'—"

"Dahlia."

"I didn't forget." He extricated himself from her greedy hands. "Listen, I'd never say that I didn't have a good time with you, but—"

"But you've got it bad for Jo Jo the Dog-Faced Girl." She sniffed. "I guess there's no accounting for taste."

He made a face he hoped conveyed pure disgust. "I'm not into the flea scene."

"Whatever. It's not like I can read your mind." Dahlia arched a dramatically shaped brow. "Or can I?"

Damn, she was fun. Or would have been, if he wasn't in a hurry to catch up with Bella before she gave his best friend a fatal case of splinters. "What did you tell her?"

"Five thousand dollars." Dahlia held out her plump hand and wiggled her fingers.

"You're shitting me." The first tentacles of hopelessness wound around his ribs.

Negative thinking will get you nowhere, he scolded himself. "Come on, baby. You know I don't have that kind of cash."

She sighed theatrically. "That's too bad, then."

"Come on, cut me a break." He grinned, slowly leaning into her. "I'll make it worth your while."

"That's more like it." She crooked her pinkie finger and led him farther down the alley.

He held up his hands. "Whoa, I was thinking more like a hotel or something. At least, let me take you back to the car like a real gentleman."

She shoved him against the wall so hard he thought the bricks would shatter.

"What the fuck—"

"Shut up," she hissed, grabbing a handful of his hair and forcing his head back with a resounding thud. "You think I would tell you shit? Just for a little touch?"

"Hey, I thought you were just that kind of girl," he snarled. "You sold out your ex pretty fast once I slipped it to you."

Keep up the hard-ass comments. Her voice invaded his head like a bolt of lightning, and he almost shouted at the pain. He squinted at her face, but her lips never moved as the voice continued. *I'm gonna keep throwing out generic threats, just respond appropriately and listen to me.*

"Shut the fuck up, bitch," he managed to reply, though his face had gone numb and the insult wasn't up to par. His head felt as if it was going to split apart. It had been a long time since he'd communicated through a blood tie, but he remembered what it felt like, and it sure wasn't this. He tried to respond to her, focusing his thoughts through the haze of pain reverberating in his skull. *What are you doing to me?*

Simple mind invasion. Bella didn't go far. She'd hear every damn word we'd say. This is the only way to communicate without her listening.

Dahlia kneed him in the groin and he doubled over with a groan.

We need to make it look like we're fighting, so she doesn't get suspicious. But that was for forgetting my name.

"Fuck you," he wheezed out loud. *How did she know where to find you? And what did she want?*

I don't know. Maybe she looked up all area vampires who aren't aligned with your stupid club. I'm sure you all keep a record somewhere. Dahlia didn't roll her eyes, but Max imagined it to go along with her tone. *She wanted to know where your bookstore friend went. I don't have a clue. I told her to try the cemeteries, but I suggest you follow her because I might not have been far off.*

Dahlia leaned her face dangerously close to his and transformed into a snarling, angry vampire. It might have intimidated him if she wasn't idly stroking the hair at the back of his neck with her fingernails.

"Listen up, bitch. You tell me what's going on or I'll slit your throat from ear to ear." He pushed his hand into her coat and found the buttons of her blouse, deftly popping a few to reach inside.

She shifted her face back and leaned in to trace his ear with her tongue. God, how great she'd been with that wicked tongue. "I'd like to see you try, once I rip your fat head right off your shoulders."

Fat head? he shot back mentally, though the strain of responding sent up a buzz of feedback in his ears.

Don't take it personally. She punctuated the telepathic message with a physical shrug. *I heard Cyrus is in Nevada.*

Who'd you hear that from? "Get your hands off me," he growled aloud, but as her hands had found the zipper of his fly, he shook his head vehemently to signal she should disregard that instruction as play-acting.

"Make me," she snarled back at him, simultaneously explaining, *The pictures in my head showed me.* She made it sound so matter-of-fact he couldn't bring himself to doubt her sources. *All I'm seeing is Louden and Hudson and Nevada. And for some reason, the Virgin Mary. Don't ask me where that all came from. Now, seriously, shove me. That's all I've got, and she's starting to think something's up.*

As if on cue, Bella stepped into the alley. Her cold gaze fixed on Dahlia. "That was a truly pathetic display. Did you think you would fool me?"

Dahlia raised her hands and shouted arcane words. A glowing ball of blue grew between her fingers. Before she could release it, Bella whipped her arm out and an arc of red light split the sphere in two, knocking Dahlia back violently.

Then the werewolf leveled a crossbow at Max's chest. The bolt was metal-tipped, with a wooden shaft. A coward's long-range weapon.

"I warned you," she reminded him coldly.

He didn't get time to negotiate. She fired.

Max Harrison doesn't die in a dirty alley with his fly unzipped. He dodged, but the bolt caught him in the shoulder. With a roar of pain, he fell to the ground.

Bella bent over him and gripped the end of the arrow. Twisting it cruelly, she wrenched it from his flesh. "One more time, vampire. One more time, and you are dead."

Like a shadow fleeing the light, she was gone.

Dahlia whimpered as she climbed to her feet, though Max suspected her pride hurt more than her body.

"Do you want a ride home?" he offered, though his shoulder leaked like a broken pipe.

She waved him away. "Do what you gotta do. It was good seeing you again...whatever your name is."

"Max."

"Yeah, like I'm going to remember that." She rolled her eyes at him and limped down the alley on a broken boot heel.

Max checked and double-checked the area around the coffee shop before he crossed the street. The last thing he needed was another run-in with Best In Show.

In the car, he retrieved his cell phone and pulled up Carrie's number.

* * *

I drifted in a world of white. No, not white. Light.

Why can I still hear you?

Cyrus's voice threatened to split my head apart. I blinked against the blazing assault. Though the air was bright, it was cold. Everything was cold. "I don't want to be here."

The light flared brighter, and I fell. Before I hit bottom I saw them. Two bodies, tossed carelessly on the floor, like rag dolls. And blood. So much blood.

Then it sucked away, leaving me in a black void. I panicked. Was I dead? Was I dreaming? Why couldn't I wake up, or move, or open my eyes?

Carrie, relax.

I startled at Nathan's voice in my head, calm and coherent for the first time since he'd been taken from me.

I haven't been taken. Not yet. But I'm running out of time.

"Nathan!" I tried to shout out loud, but no sound issued. *What happened? Are you better?*

No. The word sent a wave of despair across the tie between us. *It's sleeping. It has to sleep.*

What has to sleep? I thought of the demon who'd worn his skin, imagined it as a slimy, scaly thing gripping Nathan in its cruel claws.

I don't know. I don't know what it is. There was a note of urgency to his tone. *God, Carrie, I don't what's happening to me.*

His mounting fear turned my throat to dust, and I swallowed. *You're possessed. Max is looking for you, to help you. Where are you?*

I don't know. In the dark. Carrie, please help. The last part came across as a sob wrenched from my own, dry throat. *I'm not possessed. This thing…*

Silence. I'd lost my link to him. I called out to him, my brain trying feverishly to connect with him, like the marrow of a broken bone reaching for a way to rebuild itself.

"Wake up!"

I gasped as I came awake and felt the pressure of a stake at my chest.

March stood over me, her face framed by the fluffy, red marabou lining the edges of her satin dressing gown. Her knuckles were white from gripping the stake. Her body trembled with rage and she twisted the wood hard, grinding the point into my skin. "Who do you work for?"

This is how I die. "I don't work for anyone." I resisted the urge to glance wildly around the room for an escape route. That would give her enough incentive to stab me then and there. "I'm not Movement, I told you."

"I know that! Do you think I'm stupid? I checked you for Movement connections before you even got this room." The pressure of the stake let up a bit. Her reason was returning, though just barely. "But it's not the Movement I'm worried about."

"Then who are you worried about?" I shifted a little, the wooden point still too close for comfort.

March's eyes narrowed. She leaned forward on the stake, worming it into my sternum. I could take her, I realized. She was older than me, and therefore should have been stronger. But she hadn't been at a prime age when she'd been turned. Plus her stance, kneeling on the edge of the bed beside me, wouldn't support her if I kicked her away.

But then I would have a fight on my hands, and something in her expression told me she didn't want that, either. "Who sent you?"

"Byron." I squeezed my eyes shut and prayed it would be

the right answer. When the pressure on my chest abated, I felt a little hope.

March stood and lit a cigarette with shaking hands. She held it out to me, balancing the stake in her other hand. I thought briefly about grabbing it and using it against her, but chances were I was still locked in the room, and she probably had a great security system. I wouldn't make it out of the building.

"No, I've quit." I couldn't remember when. It hadn't exactly been a conscious decision. *Funny, the thoughts that come to you when you're about to die.*

"Evan was there when you collapsed. He said you were babbling about a simultaneous bloodtie." She paused to suck in a lungful of smoke, and continued to speak on the exhale. "Wanna tell me about that?"

I sat up, rubbing my chest. "Why don't you tell me what you're so afraid of?"

She scoffed and rolled her eyes. "Why don't you tell me who your old sire was?"

"Oh, this is fun. I think I would have preferred to be staked rather than argue like thirteen year olds." I sat up and swung my legs over the side of the bed. If she attacked me again, I wanted to meet her on level ground.

"Fine." March held up a hand as if to stop me coming any closer. "I know, anyway."

"You do?" I couldn't keep the surprise from my voice. "How?"

"A lot of forged art. The first person I thought of was Cyrus Seymour." She cracked a shark's grin. "That, and you apparently yelled his named when you collapsed. I put two and two together."

"Very good." I eyed the stake with new terror. I'd been persecuted before for simply being Cyrus's fledgling. I'd thought those days were behind me. "How do you know him?"

In a flash, March was on her feet. Way faster than I would have anticipated. She lunged at me with the stake.

I dodged her easily—one very important thing Nathan had taught me was that being calm in a fight gave you the advantage over an opponent who had completely flipped out—and spun around, ready for her next attack. My bag still rested on the floor beside the armchair. I backed slowly toward it. "March, I'm not working for anyone. I was just on a road trip and Byron told me to look you up."

I was two steps from the bag, but March pursued me slowly, stake raised high over her head like the psycho mom at the end of *Carrie.* "And do you think I don't know what he's up to? Following the Fangs all over the desert, doing whatever they ask of him?"

Byron! Had the little rat sold me out? I should have known not to reveal my intentions for the trip. I should have known not to trust him. How often had men with trendy haircuts and an affinity for overwrought poetry screwed me over?

I bent and scooped up my bag. It was lighter than I remembered it. I didn't even have to look to realize my stakes were gone. I tried to dodge her next lunge, and ended up flat on my back, my head colliding with the floor in a way that made me appreciate the phrase "seeing stars." When my vision cleared, March leaned over me, the stake still in her hand. She took a long drag off the cigarette between her fingers and cracked a sarcastic smile. "From what I understand, we have a connection. At least, your sire and my sire do."

My head was still muzzy. "What?"

She flicked ashes directly onto the floor. A few stinging embers touched my face. "Jacob Seymour. The Soul Eater?"

13

Surrender

They came down the stairs at sunset.

Cyrus's first thought was that he should have locked the door. Then he remembered he *had* locked the door. Then the door, some of the molding still attached to its hinges, flew down the stairway. It landed on the cheap dinette table, which overturned with a crash.

Mouse screamed and sat up beside him, scrambling backward and clutching the sheets to her chest.

There were only three of them, but Cyrus was human. Weak and human. When one grabbed him, he couldn't break free. He could do no more than watch as the other two pinned Mouse to the bed. She screamed his name, begged him to help.

He thought of the reason she hadn't resisted when the nun had been killed, why she hadn't prayed or pleaded with God for help. *Because no one was listening.*

She hadn't made it fun for them. Cyrus knew firsthand the joy of the kill came from breaking the victim. Now, because she had hope, she would be a sweeter plum.

You have to treat her callously. Pretend she is nothing to you, and she will stop struggling. But he couldn't. His arsenal of cruel words, always at the ready, vanished. If they hadn't, he wasn't sure he could have used them, anyway.

He'd promised her safety. He'd lied. He was nothing but an ineffectual boy, playing hero. He could not save this damsel.

The beast on top of her wrenched her head back, baring her throat. At the sight of the healing teeth marks there, the vampire laughed. For a perverse second, Cyrus was relieved her blood was the only prize the monster was after. Then he admonished himself for valuing her chastity above her life. *You are truly your father's son.*

The acknowledgment weighed like lead in his chest. He closed his eyes and prayed it would be quick, that she would not suffer more than she already had.

The pitch of her screams changed to startled disbelief, and the rough hands holding him released their grip. He opened his eyes to see Mouse cowering as the vampire above her burst into flame. He burned quickly, a skeleton of ash hanging suspended for a moment, his ribs disintegrating around the blue, flaming ball of his heart. Then the blazing organ extinguished and the beast fell as a cloud of black dust to the bed. The stake that had pierced his heart dropped with a thud onto the sheets beside Mouse.

The two others scrambled for the stairs. Stakes pierced them in quick succession and they met similar fates.

At the top of the staircase, Angie ground out her cigarette. "Sorry about your door."

Cyrus wanted to rush her with a piece of the broken molding and drive it into her heart. But Mouse was silent, pale and shaking, covered in the remains of a dead vampire. His instincts demanded he go to her more than they urged him to kill Angie.

He helped Mouse stand, and carefully brushed the ashes from her hair, pushing the strands back to examine her neck. There was no fresh puncture. Nevertheless, he asked, "Did he hurt you?"

Mouse shook her head, though if it was a denial or merely the consequence of the tremors racking her body, he wasn't sure.

Angie came down the stairs slowly, surveying the scene in the apartment with cold eyes. Mouse's screams started again when she saw the vampire's face.

Cyrus put himself between Angie and Mouse. "You're terrifying her! For God's sake, take that thing off!"

With a shrug, the vampire shook her head and transformed her features. "They hurt her?"

He turned and pulled Mouse into his arms. Her hysterical tears stung the bare skin of his chest where she buried her face against him.

"We had an agreement," he snarled at Angie. For a moment he heard something of the old Cyrus in his voice. It gave him strength to face her. "What the hell was that?"

"That wasn't my doing. Those morons came down here on their own." She lit another cigarette. "Besides, I took care of it, didn't I?"

She had. But it didn't make him any less angry. They could have killed Mouse. It would have been akin to killing him. What reason did he have to live if she were dead?

No.

Cold, numbing fear shot through his heart.

But there was no denying it. The stealthy way his eyes sought her out during the day. The way his sinful body hardened against her innocent form as he lay awake, watching her, at night. This wasn't only lust. He was achingly familiar with lust, and it was easy to distinguish from what he felt now.

He swallowed, and glared at Angie. "What about the door? How will we keep them out now?"

She laughed, a rough sound around the cigarette she held

in her lips. "Didn't keep 'em out before, did it? But it'll be fixed tonight."

"See that it is." His voice shook as he spoke. Looking down, he saw his hands shook, as well. He willed his body to still. The vampire bitch would assume he feared her, when what he really feared stood clinging to him, her sobs finally dying away.

Angie was halfway up the stairs when she stopped. "Your father's messenger will be here tomorrow night."

Mouse's fingers, sharp in desperation, dug into Cyrus's shoulders as her body tensed in fear.

The vampire didn't pay any heed to her reaction. "I'll have him pick up a spare in town, if you don't want to do her when you've turned."

"Thank you." It was an odd thing to say, but he was truly grateful he wouldn't be tempted to kill Mouse.

At least, not tomorrow.

He led her to the bed, a sick feeling in his gut. Once they turned him, would he be able to see her as something more than food? When he'd been human before, he hadn't held the regard for life the way he did now. Would he be a different vampire, or would the sadist lurking in his worthless soul prove itself stronger than this suspicious humanity?

She stood by, quietly crying as he shook the ashes from the sheets and remade the bed. He looked up from tucking a corner of the blanket in, to see she stood with a dustpan and a broom at the foot of the stairs.

"Let me," he said more gruffly than he'd intended as he took the broom from her hand. He thought it would calm his nerves to focus on the task of cleaning up the monsters' remains, but he only grew more agitated.

They'd been so much stronger than him. If Angie hadn't shown up, he would have had to watch helplessly as Mouse died. The memory of her screams was salt in the wounds to his pride, and he threw aside the broom with a curse.

Mouse jumped, startled out of her lingering terror.

He never shared thoughts of inadequacy with others. Once they knew he doubted himself, they would begin to doubt him, as well. But he couldn't keep these concerns secret from her. Compelled to talk, either from years of bearing his fears alone, or from the fearful emotion tearing at his guts, he muttered, "I couldn't protect you. I can't protect you like this."

"Like what?" Her gaze moved up from his feet. "Naked?"

He would have laughed at that, if he'd been in a better mood. Feeling suddenly vulnerable, exposed, he grabbed his pants from the end of the bed and pulled them on. "I'm not joking. I'm worthless like this."

She wrapped her arms around herself. "You're not worthless."

"I'm human!" He raked a hand through his hair, pulling it away from his forehead. "As long as I'm like this, I can't protect you. And once they turn me, I won't be able to protect you from myself."

"You're scaring me." She climbed backward up a stair, then looked over her shoulder at the looming, open doorway and scrambled back down.

He didn't want to scare her. He liked it so much better when she gave shy smiles and fell into stilted conversation with him. But he wanted more. He wanted her at his side willingly. He wanted to know she was safe, and wanted her to know it.

"I don't want you to die." He went to the bed and dropped down, covering his face in his hands. The words, once he began to speak, were surprisingly easy and terrifying. "I want you to be alive, with me. I want to leave this place, and I want you to follow me. For once, I want someone to follow me. Because I want you. I love you, and…"

She knelt at his side and laid her hand on his knee, but she didn't speak.

God, what had he said? What would he say when he opened his mouth next?

Words he couldn't stop poured from him like the hot tears that welled in the corners of his eyes. He lifted his head to look at her. Her expression was kind and concerned, as though he were a child who'd scraped his knees.

Her kindness was a high ledge on a tall building, one he couldn't help but test by stepping onto it. "Could you ever love me?"

She didn't answer right away. What fearful iron door would slam closed to him if she said no? Would he bury his hurt in cruelty, the way he'd always done when someone rejected him? That wasn't the kind of person he wanted to be. His tongue felt thick in his mouth as he tried to repeat himself. "Could you—"

"You can't love me," she interrupted quietly. Her palm was warm against his face, but not as shockingly hot as it would have been if he were a vampire. No, now human touch wasn't severe. Her eyes sad, she stroked his cheek. "You've only known me for three days."

He laughed at his own stupidity. "It feels…"

"Real," she finished for him. After a moment's hesitation, she took his hand and laced their fingers together. "I know. And I know it can't be real. But I've always prayed for something to happen. Something to make me happy. I know I'm going to die. Maybe you're… Maybe this is all the happiness I'm going to get."

Her reasoning pierced his heart, but he wasn't fool enough to believe he could really love her. The same disgusting desperation he'd seen in hundreds of frightened, cast-off girls, he recognized in her. And in himself. He opened his mouth to disagree with her, to insist she would live to find better, but her mouth crushed his and she wound her arms around his neck. He lost his balance and they fell across the bed, her hands tangling in his hair to hold his face to hers.

As if he would let her go.

He was conscious of raising his arms, but had no control over the way they curved around her back and tightened, pulling her so hard to his chest he could barely breathe. She squirmed in his grip and he loosened his hold. He didn't want to scare her. In a crazy way, he felt if she pulled away now he would lose her forever.

Her hands splayed on his chest. Their touch burned him, but he shuddered as if she were made of ice. He moved his lips from her hungry mouth to the delicate curve of her jaw—how could he have ever thought her plain?—then to her ear. She moaned, a sound at once endearingly innocent and painfully arousing. Thrusting his fingers into the gentle waves of her hair, he gathered the softness to his face.

The feel and smell of her dredged up all the nights he'd spent in the arms of lovers, wives, wishing they would return his affection, and pretending all he desired was their bodies. They never returned his love, even when he demanded it.

Perhaps she didn't either, but he had not asked her to say the words. He'd asked her to love him. In her kiss, Cyrus had found Mouse's answer. She could, and did, love him. For whatever reason, she trusted and loved him.

Reaching for the hem of her T-shirt, he skimmed his hands up her bare legs, over the curve of her buttocks as he bunched the garment around her waist. He rolled her onto her back, covering her with his body as he did so, and her eyes flew open in shock. For a moment he imagined she would end it, but longing glazed her eyes again. He captured her mouth with his before she could have another moment of doubt. She believed he was her last chance at happiness, so he couldn't help but wonder if she was his, as well. If that was true, then he needed this.

She lifted her hips against his awkwardly, her brow creasing in frustration above her closed eyes. He leaned back, concentrating his gaze on the seam in the hem of the T-shirt. If he looked anywhere else, at the questioning on her flushed face, at the dark hair shadowing the junction of her thighs, he might think, might talk himself out of this.

Cyrus glanced across the darkened room to the stairs, but he knew no one would be watching. None of them would dare come down after the fate that had befallen their comrades.

Mouse rose on her elbows and helped him pull the shirt over her head. That moment of bravery was short-lived, fleeing once she was exposed before him. She folded her arms across her breasts. With shaking hands, he guided them away, leaving her bare to his gaze. Her chest jerked with her harsh breathing. Though the room was not cold, her skin puckered with gooseflesh and the rosy peaks of her nipples hardened.

Cyrus covered one breast with the palm of his hand and Mouse moaned, arching into his touch. He fought the temptation to compare her to the others, the ones he'd seduced into giving up their bodies and their lives. This was different. When this night was over, she would still be at his side. It was a frightening, comforting thought.

He dipped his head to her neck and kissed the hollow of her throat. When his lips strayed to the yellowing bruise where he'd bitten her that first night, she didn't tense, but he stopped cold.

She touched his back, dragging her fingertips across the skin of his shoulders. "It's okay. You didn't mean to."

"I did." He rolled off of her. "I meant to hurt you. I enjoyed it."

The gentle understanding in her eyes sent a spear of self-loathing through his heart.

She reached for her discarded shirt and held it to her chest. "I forgive you."

He closed his eyes against the tears that threatened him. Could something as simple as her absolution save him from himself? He doubted it. Maybe he would always doubt his ability to be good.

But that was, apparently, what she was there to stop him from doing. While he was content to doubt the goodness in his soul, she seemed determined to draw him back to more earthly matters. Sliding toward him, she tentatively pressed her mouth to his chest. When he didn't object, she continued to kiss him, stroking her palms in a maddening path from his ribs to the waistband of his trousers. She lay back again, and he lay beside her, bracketing her body with his hands as he slid down to rest his face against her thigh. As a vampire, he would have cut the tender, white flesh at the bend of her knee to drink her blood. It had always been his favorite moment, looking up at their faces when they'd gotten their first taste of the pain he would inflict on them. As a human, making love to a human, he had no desire to cause her pain. He bent his head and licked the warm crease there. She jerked on the bed, her eyes wide. He couldn't help his smile as he moved his mouth farther up her leg, with his hand on her firm, warm calf. The closer he drew to her sex, the faster her breathing became. When he knelt on the floor and pulled her to the edge of the bed—a little roughly, for it couldn't be all gentle—and traced the seam between her legs with the pointed tip of his tongue, she arched off the mattress and clawed at his shoulders, gasping.

The taste and smell and warmth of her intoxicated him. Her fingers tangled in his hair, pulling him closer. He groaned against her slick folds and eased one finger into her. He hadn't guessed wrong the first time he'd touched her intimately; she was a virgin. Though now she was open and willing, the thin barrier remained.

"I know it's a sin," she informed him with a moan. "But I want you to. I want you to do it."

He laved his tongue over her engorged flesh, teasing her with his teeth until her body arched again and tensed, and she pulled his hair to the point of pain. The sound of her climax started as a low moan and rose in pitch to a keening wail, and her body trembled as she peaked. Before her pleasure could subside, he rose and spread her legs. Her eyes narrowed in trepidation, then flared with panic, and she lifted her hands as if to push him away. He wondered if she would ask him to stop. He knew he would, if she did so. But her arms dropped to her sides, hands fisting as though she braced herself for what was to come.

The heat and wetness of her enticed him. His body urged him to continue, and if this was the past, he would have obliged himself. He'd taken particular delight in the cruel deflowering of many a young girl then. But he didn't want to see that pain in her eyes, the fear that she'd begun something she had no power to stop and no strength to finish. He had to work to unclench his jaw as he stroked the side of her face with his fingertips. "Are you sure?"

She hesitated a second, then wet her lips and nodded with a huge breath. Before she could think or wonder when the pain would come, he thrust into her. The barrier released with an unpleasant gush of wetness, and it was done. Beneath him, she stiffened. He expected her to scream, and she looked for a moment as though she'd expected to, as well. The sound never came.

"That wasn't so bad," she whispered with a small laugh. She lifted her hips against his, gasping when he slipped in deeper. "This isn't so bad."

They laughed together and he kissed her, his chest tight with happiness. When she moved beneath him again, the happiness was overshadowed by the urgent demands of his body. It didn't take Mouse long to overcome her inexperience. She rocked against him, panted and clutched at his shoulders, and he closed his eyes to avoid the erotic sight and maintain some self-control.

He couldn't escape her moans of pleasure, though, or the hot, wet grip of her surrounding him. He sought out her swollen bud and rubbed her with the pad of his thumb until her loud breaths and frantic, senseless pleas for release signaled the approaching culmination of her pleasure. He braced himself against the mattress and abandoned all thought of gentleness or care, driving into her so hard her breath exploded from her with every pump of his hips.

She did scream then, her nails biting into his arms where she gripped him. He let himself go, shuddering over her and inside of her. When he regained his senses, he withdrew, wincing at the friction of her grasping muscles against his painfully sensitized skin.

They lay in silence for a long time, their legs hanging off the side of the bed. Cyrus studied her with detached interest. The moonlight from the small window above them dusted her skin with silver as he watched it grow rough with gooseflesh. How she could be chilled when his heart hammered as though he'd run a marathon, and sweat still poured from him, was a mystery.

"I'm cold," she whispered sleepily, and he sat up to help her right herself on the bed. When he pulled the sheets over her, he saw her blood there, and closed his eyes. How had he ever been able to revel in the pain of others like her? How had he taken pleasure from taking life, when now he felt so guilty over a smear of virgin blood?

Those days of callous disregard were over. All that mattered now was the woman at his side, who was real and solid, and who loved him, even if she was afraid of him. Like a fool who repeatedly stuck his hand in the fire and was surprised by the burn, Cyrus once again trusted the feeble hope for happiness that grew in his soul.

This time will be different, he assured himself. It would be different, because it had to be. In his weak, human state, he wouldn't survive if it weren't.

But he was kidding himself. If he had the strength of a god, he wouldn't survive losing her.

Though sunrise loomed pink on the horizon, Max gave Dahlia the benefit of the doubt and decided to check one last cemetery. The first two had turned up only sleeping homeless people and thrill-seeking teenagers. This close to dawn, both types would have moved on.

He pulled the car to a stop at the closed iron gate and ignored the scheduled visiting hours posted beside it as he climbed the stone wall. The early morning dew made the ascent slippery and wet. When he landed, his T-shirt stuck to him and his jeans were uncomfortably chilled against his thighs. "Nathan, if you are here, I'm going to kill you."

Not that he wanted to see Nathan.

Since the day they'd spared his life, Max had made it a rule never to cross the Movement. Sure, he'd been less than diligent when tracking quarry sometimes, but there was a big difference between missing the opportunity and coming face-to-face with it, only to let it run off scot-free.

No pun intended.

Two paths curved in opposite directions around a hill dotted with leaning, broken monuments. Elaborate mausoleums lined the outside edges of the paths, marble houses that reeked of death so strongly Max couldn't believe a human couldn't smell it.

He started up one path, determined to get his patrol over with before he wound up with a terminal case of sunburn. Then he caught the whiff of something sinister on the air.

At first, he'd thought it was merely the smell of another body, probably another of Nathan's victims. Then he realized the copper scent had a warm, living edge to it, and he tore off in the direction of the blood.

The first thing he saw was her leg stretching past the end of one ivy-covered crypt. The black leather boot on her foot was muddy and torn, as though the fight had been long and rough. A rip in her pant leg showed a bloody gash from knee to ankle, laid open so wide the shocking white of bone showed through.

The sight was enough to make bile rise in his throat. When she'd attacked him outside the coffee shop, she'd seemed invincible. Now, Bella had been reduced to a broken heap of ruined parts.

Whoever had done it was still there, breathing heavily, just out of sight. Max tore around the corner of the crypt and stopped dead in his tracks.

It took him a moment to recognize the monster looming over her was Nathan. When the sick comprehension dawned, Max couldn't move to draw his weapon. The creature that used to be his best friend turned, face bloody from feeding, and snarled at him. Instead of charging, though, it looked at the lightening sky and took off, leaping to the top of a mausoleum, then disappearing behind it.

Max put his hands on the lip of the stone, preparing to chase after the beast, then heard Bella moan. If he left her where she was, someone might find her. The caretaker would probably be in to open the gate and would likely have a look around to make sure there hadn't been any shenanigans overnight. But Max didn't know anything about werewolves, and couldn't be sure she would survive that long without help.

Fuck her. She tried to kill you, he reminded himself. *If she's dead, she's one less thing to worry about.*

But he didn't work that way. He wished he did.

With sunrise just minutes away, he had no time to hunt for Nathan. To do so would probably only get them both killed. And werewolf or not, Bella was a fellow Movement assassin. He couldn't let her die.

Cursing her stupidity good and loud so she could hear it even if she'd already shrugged her mortal coil, he bent and lifted her limp body in his arms. "You better pray Nathan's got a primo fucking first aid kit back at the apartment, or you're in real trouble, lady."

It took some maneuvering to get her over the wall without breaking her neck, but the classic fireman's carry came through in the pinch. Max wrestled her into the car and positioned her head against the window so she would appear to be sleeping and not mortally wounded. "If you bleed on the seat, you're off my Christmas card list."

Somewhere in the cemetery, his assignment was escaping. He looked from the jagged stones at the top of the hill to the dying woman in the seat beside him and swore. With a final, vehement curse, he pounded the steering wheel and sped away.

14

The Past Comes Back To Haunt You

March's private rooms were at the back of the house. She led me to a huge conservatory, a glass bubble filled with verdant plant life and flowering trees. The floor, an intricate mosaic of tiny tiles, wound in paths around beds of soil. The snaking trails converged in the center of the room, where water trickled down the face of a craggy boulder that nearly reached the ceiling. In front of the impressive fixture, a striking red Shinto gate stood watch over an elaborately set tea service.

March indicated I should sit at the delicate, wrought-iron table, and despite my simmering anger, I did so. "That's an aggressively spiritual symbol you have there, considering what you are."

"What, a vampire can't be spiritual?" She looked astonished in a worldly way, a contradiction that didn't surprise me. The woman was as hard to read as a book written backward. "The Shinto tradition is concerned mainly with the spiritual affairs of the living. As I am eternally living, I don't see the harm in believing something."

"That's not what I meant," I explained as she poured blood from a Victorian-style teapot. "I thought it was an overtly spiritual thing for you to have, considering you're a vampire pimp who sneaks up on people to murder them in their sleep."

She grimaced, a smoke-roughened laugh escaping her bared teeth. "Now, why did you have to use that word? It's such a nasty label for what I do."

"What about 'kidnapping' or 'false imprisonment'? How do those suit you?" I made no attempt to hide my suspicion as I refused the blood she offered me. She'd held me hostage—granted, I couldn't have gone anywhere during the daylight, anyway—and tried to kill me. Just because she'd decided to offer me breakfast instead didn't mean I'd roll over and we'd become bestest friends.

As crazy and paranoid as it seemed—and it did seem that way to me, after I'd applied said paranoia to every person I'd seen on this trip, from tollbooth operators to truck stop waitresses—I couldn't help but suspect she knew what I was up to in the desert.

I couldn't tell from her Cheshire Cat smile if she really did know or if she'd just picked up on my discomfort. "Well, we can just put all that behind us. Your sire is the fledgling of my sire, after all. That makes us practically family."

I glared at her. "Practically. Except Cyrus isn't my sire anymore." I hesitated. "He's...dead."

"Is he now?" She poured some blood for herself and sipped it, her eyes never leaving my face. When she finished, she dabbed her lips with her linen napkin, leaving dainty spots of blood on it. "Isn't that sad? You're an orphan."

I thought of Nathan, and the word *orphan* imprinted on my brain like a searing brand. "I'm not. Even if I was, I wouldn't count the Soul Eater as my next of kin."

"You know, I've never liked that name. It's so confrontational. And it makes it sound like he's doing something wrong."

She lit up a cigarette, every movement as casual as if we were discussing the weather.

"You've got to be kidding me." I was reaching the frayed edges of my patience. "He kills vampires for food!"

"You kill people for food. What's the difference?" The practiced naiveté with which she posed the question made me stumble over my answer.

And that hesitation told her everything she needed to know: I didn't kill for blood. In her eyes, that labeled me weak. Prey.

"No matter how I feed, I still have ties to the Soul Eater," I said quickly.

"So do I." She took a long draw off her cigarette and smiled. "And I know he can't stomach your kind. Sniveling cowards who deny their true nature."

I couldn't argue with her. If the Soul Eater had his way, vampires would be more far more aggressive about their status as top of the food chain.

"Did you know who I was when I came here?" It seemed too fortuitous that Byron had led me to this place, knowing my destination.

She shrugged and flicked the ashes off her cigarette into her saucer. "A friend called and mentioned that a person of interest was going to show up."

"So, if I'm a person of interest, then you must know something of what's going on with the Soul Eater." I waved her smoke away with feigned annoyance.

"I know he's up to something. But you probably know more than I do, considering you've come all the way out here." March leaned back in her chair. "I suppose you thought I'd have all the answers? And that I'd just give them to you?"

Helplessly, I nodded. "Stupid me, I guess. I just thought your vampire daddy might be keeping you in the loop."

She chewed her lip, regarding me indecisively. Then she took a deep breath and exhaled noisily. "You're looking for the guy in the desert?"

I reached for my bag, only to remember it was still in the foyer. "I have money. I'll pay."

"Don't bring the vulgarity of money into this." She pondered a moment, a look akin to pride on her face. "I wonder what kind of kickback I'll get if I hand you over to Jacob."

"You'll get killed." I racked my brain for any detail I could use to sway her, any warning. The truth seemed the best way to go. "He's trying to become a god. I admit, I don't know the guy real well, but with a name like Soul Eater, I don't want him having cosmic power. Fledgling or not, you have to admit, if he manages to go through with this, everyone is fucked."

"It will be the end of the human race and eventually the vampire race, blah blah blah." She sighed, making a jabbering duck mouth with one hand as she rang a silver bell with the other. "He's talked about doing something like this for years. Worked on it a bit with his son, actually. But he's never going to pull it off."

"Oh, yeah?" I snapped. "Guess who's been raised from the dead?"

To her credit, her surprise didn't show as much as it could have. She ground out her cigarette with a muffled curse. After a long moment squinting at me with barely veiled resentment, she conceded defeat. "I love Jacob with all my heart. But loving isn't the same as trusting, by a long shot. What do you need from me to get your part of this done?"

"I don't have any connections here. I need a road map, at least. And old newspapers, if you have them." Where the Fangs went, chaos followed. There was no chance a sleepy area like Death Valley was going to miss marauding hordes of vampires. Something was going to end up in print.

With a long-suffering sigh, she lifted the silver bell that rested at her right hand and rang it again. The butler appeared and bent stiffly in deference to his mistress. March handed off the saucer she'd turned into an ashtray, then massaged the bridge of her nose with her fingers. "Have you taken the recycling to be done?"

Recycling? At least, March had an environmental conscience, if no other kind.

Eyeing me with distaste, the servant cleared his throat. "I believe that takes place every *other* Thursday."

"Load the newspapers in the back of her van. Just the local ones." She turned to me again and arched a brow. "Unless you think scouring the *New York Times* would help?"

"Was there anything out of the ordinary in them? Anything at all you can remember that seemed…more sensational than usual?" Of course, I supposed sensational was relative to a man who worked in a vampire whorehouse.

"I am sorry, miss, I do not read them." Turning back to March, he asked, "Will that be all, ma'am?"

She nodded. "Yeah, I think so."

With another stiff bow, he left us.

"Sorry I couldn't be of more help. We'll make sure you get the proper supplies for your trip." She grinned, looking pleased with herself.

I was still convinced she hid something. "Thanks for the hospitality." I hoped she felt the sarcasm of my words as a bite.

"Well, sweetness, I got a whole bunch of human business coming in tonight. Episcopal Women's Altar Society bus trip. Told their husbands they're going to a Bible summit on gay marriage." She stood, indicating I should do the same.

I could take a hint. She was done supplying me with information that would lead to the death of her sire. "Just one last question?"

After a moment's hesitation, she nodded. "Why not?"

"How come he didn't take your soul?" We began to walk down the path. I thought perhaps she'd decided not to answer.

Then, without a hint of deception or theatrics, she said simply, "He took someone else's."

A chill went through me at the memory of how he'd taken Cyrus's wife, Elsbeth, without a thought for his son's happiness.

March shrugged, as though the fact her soul was spared by the death of another's was par for the course. "I'm not going to say it was right. But I'm glad it wasn't me who died."

I believe there is a defining moment in everyone's life where they seal their own fate through words or actions. My parents did it when they got in their car to visit me in college and, six hours later, wound up bleeding to death on the side of the road. I'd done it when I'd gone to the morgue to view Cyrus's body, and he'd gone from being another John Doe to the creature who haunted my nightmares.

A creeping wave of icy foreboding seized me. I couldn't tell when, I couldn't know how, but I knew March had already set in motion the events that would lead to her death.

"You're not dead yet," I reminded her, my throat suddenly dry. "But you will be."

My warning didn't alarm her as much as I imagined it should have. "Well, we'll all be gone someday. No sense in fearing it."

"I've died. Fear it."

We sized each other up for a grueling minute. I would have paid several thousand dollars to know what she thought, but her mask of emotional obscurity was firmly in place. "Last town before the true desert is Louden. Drive like hell and you can get there before sunup."

I didn't see March again after she left me in the foyer. She didn't say goodbye, so much as "pleasure doing business with you," and even then I didn't truly believe it.

The supplies that had been removed from my bag were returned to me, along with some I doubted I'd have any use for: sleeping pills, chloroform, bungee cords and gauze bandages. I looked them over and raised my eyebrows at the butler.

"For 'human wrangling.' The madam's idea." He didn't sound enthused to be supporting me.

From an inside jacket pocket, he produced a map. "You'll find the most efficient route to Death Valley is highlighted."

"Why is she helping me, when she wouldn't bother giving me a straight answer before?" I took my bag, heavy with its new cargo, and tucked the map into my jeans pocket. As I trudged wearily to the door, grateful to be out of this place, the butler's voice stopped me.

"Perhaps she does not think you'll succeed. Did it occur to you she might be helping you to your death?" His imperious tone was beginning to get on my nerves. "But I believe it is more a case of 'the enemy of my enemy is my friend.'"

I didn't turn to face him, and resumed walking, pausing only to open the door. "I won't fail. This is a cakewalk compared to what I've been through."

"The madam also wishes you to know that if she sees you again, she will kill you on sight."

I stepped out into the cool Nevada evening. The stars seemed to shine brighter here, and hung so close I almost felt I could touch them. The sight grounded me in the gravity and reality of what lay ahead of me.

I had most of the puzzle pieces. Now it was just a matter of fitting them together.

"She won't see me again." I took a deep breath of the fresh desert air. "But tell her I said ditto."

When I left, I didn't look back. I think I expected to see the place had been a mirage, evaporated into heat waves in the air.

The vampires sent to fix the door woke them. Cyrus held Mouse, who clung to him in mortal terror as the two creatures respectfully retrieved the broken door and carried it up the stairs. They apologized in advance for the noise they would make.

Cyrus expected them to bow and scrape as they exited, such was their cautious demeanor. Angie had most likely put the fear of God—or, more aptly, the fear of Angie—into them.

"They're gone," he whispered to Mouse when the vampires had trudged noisily up the stairs. "You don't have to fear them."

It felt like a lie the moment he said it. Hadn't he proved himself useless in protecting her?

If she connected his words with his shameful failure before, she didn't give it away. She let go of him by increments, easing into her space on the narrow bed. They lay in the quiet darkness for a while, listening to the low voices of the vampires working at the top of the stairs. Occasionally, a mechanical whirring or rhythmic pounding shattered the calm, but Cyrus was so tired he could have slept through it.

He didn't, though. Polite or not, he wasn't stupid enough to trust the creatures. Not when they had such easy access to prey.

Mouse apparently didn't trust them, either. Though Cyrus had thought her asleep, her voice surprised him. "It's still night?"

"You haven't been asleep long." A nagging protectiveness in his head reminded him she should get her rest. But a selfish part of him was relieved she stayed awake. He liked talking with another person, something he hadn't done enough of during his former life, and he feared the changes that were about to come.

Oh, he'd probably be turned into a vampire. As much as he

wanted to stay human, if his father demanded otherwise he could do little but object. The deed would still be done. But he would make certain that Mouse never met the fate his past wives had. She would never be a vampire, and therefore would never be food for his father's insatiable craving for souls. That, he would not abide.

"What were you like, when you were one of them?" The question was startlingly familiar.

The memory brought hot shame to his face. "I told you."

"You didn't answer. You tried to scare me. I'm not scared of you now." As if to prove her words, she reached up to brush the hair from his eyes.

He didn't want to admit the truth, but he wouldn't taint their new bond with lies. "I was trying to scare you. But I told you the truth. I've done…horrible things."

Her eyes, clear and honest, searched his face in the darkness. "Why would you do those things?"

It wasn't a question he'd bothered to ask himself. The first answer that came to mind, the one most likely to be true, was monstrous, but he had no other reason to give her. "Boredom?"

The fear and disgust he expected never registered on her face. "You killed and tortured people because you were bored?"

He made an affirmative noise in his throat. "And lonely."

"That doesn't make any sense." Her frown evolved into a quirked smile. "Of course you'd be lonely, if you killed everyone around you."

"Not everyone. There were some I tried to keep." He tightened his arms around her. "Now that I have you, I don't remember why I wanted to keep them."

"I like that." She laughed quietly and nestled her head against his chest. "You have me. It's nice to belong to someone."

After a long silence, she looked up. "What were they like?"

He didn't want to talk about them now. It seemed wrong, somehow, as though he lived a double life. *In a way, you have.* It was a different life, but he couldn't forget it. If he forgot his past transgressions, he might forget how to be the man he was now. And he liked that man.

"I had a wife." He chuckled at that understatement. "I had many wives. Ten, I think. After five, it becomes hard to remember. And then there were others, ones I didn't marry."

"Did you love them?" There was an unspoken qualifier at the end of her question, punctuated by the quaver in her voice.

"I didn't love them more than you." It was a frightening truth. He'd mourned them all, but he'd come to expect losing them.

The workmen, apparently finished with their job, shut the door with a reassuring bang. Cyrus thought of locking it, but since it hadn't kept out intruders before, he didn't see the sense in leaving the comfort of the bed.

"Did you make any vampires?" Mouse fidgeted as though embarrassed by asking.

He was about to answer, "What would it matter?" Then he realized the reason for her interest, and he couldn't believe his stupidity. Of course she wondered.

"I would never make you become one of them." He sat up, dragging her with him. He knew the tight grip he had on her arms must hurt her, but he couldn't let her go. She had to understand his devotion was not dependent on his humanity. "Tell me you trust me."

"I trust you," she said hesitantly. "You wouldn't make me one of them."

"Tell me you love me." It was suddenly vitally important to hear it from her, without explanation or dissection of their motives.

"I love you." A tear rolled down her cheek. "I do."

They made love again, frantic at first, with fierce kisses as they tumbled violently across the bed. Once he was inside her, though, wrapped in the reassuring warmth of her body, the urgency melted away.

Leaning above her on his elbows, he stared into her face. "Tell me again."

She wet her swollen lips and pressed them close to his ear. "I love you."

She repeated it over and over, and he let her.

No one had ever said it to him before.

15

The Key

If not for Carrie's extensive library of medical textbooks, Bella wouldn't have survived an hour past sunrise.

And that was saying something, considering how close Max had cut it to sunup. He'd skidded sideways to the curb in front of the apartment just as morning washed down the street in a deadly wave. He'd dragged her body from the passenger seat with little care and bolted to the shelter of the recessed doorway.

Not soon enough, he thought ruefully, sponging antiseptic over his charred shoulder. His tissue had already begun to heal, and vampires were largely unaffected by germs or bacteria, but the cool liquid took some of the sting out of his burns.

With a worried glance to the unconscious werewolf on the couch, he set aside the gauze pad and bottle of solution and reached for one of the open medical books on the coffee table. He'd managed to stop the bleeding from the wounds Nathan had given her, but werewolves healed more slowly than vampires, almost at a mortal rate. Some of her injuries would need stitching, a task he didn't look forward to.

At least she was asleep. It would spare him the inevitable womanly shrieking he'd endure if she was awake when he did it.

If he was honest with himself, he'd have to admit his real fear came from the thought she might see him pass out when he first tried to jab the needle through her flesh.

Taking a swig from the flask of Scotch Nathan thought he'd hidden well, Max rose and approached Bella's unmoving form.

Asleep, she didn't look half as bitchy as she did when she was awake. But that could have been the blood loss. "Okay, we got clean towels, we got this fishing line stuff, we got a…" He swallowed a tide of nausea. "We got a needle and these steril- izing wipes. I think we're good to go." He hadn't been able to find the weird pincers thing the guy was using in the picture to hold the needle, but how hard could it be to just use fingers?

Kneeling beside the couch, Max reached for her ankle. If she'd been conscious she probably would have driven a stake through his heart for daring to touch her. She was lucky she'd decided to get mortally injured when he was in a charitable mood.

The leg of her leather pants lay open to her knee in much the same pattern her flesh did. He grabbed the bottle of Bactine and squirted it liberally into the jagged wound.

"Kill off anything that decided to move in," he said, then felt like an ass for bothering to explain himself to a half-dead werewolf.

He flipped the curling edges of the fabric back for better access to the injury, then decided the pants would just have to go. Then he felt like a pervert.

First, he tried to be civil about the process, patiently but im- potently struggling against the leather with kitchen shears. When it seemed he was more likely to slip and stab himself or her than actually cut the pants, he gripped the ruined fabric and yanked, splitting them to the waist. With another tug, her leg was bare from hip to toes.

God help him, she wore black lace panties.

He took another swallow of Scotch to fortify himself and hopefully burn the devil out of his sinful soul. There she was, practically dead and not even his own species, and all he could think about was the way her tan skin stretched over her smoothly rounded hip.

Clenching his teeth, he pulled her uninjured leg free and tossed the ruined garment aside. Bracing her foot against his chest, he peered at the book. No matter how many times he studied the illustrations, he would never be ready. So he ripped the sterile packaging off the needle and threaded it with nylon floss, took a deep breath and went to work.

His stitches started out clumsy and uneven, but he soon fell into a rhythm of pinching the flesh closed, piercing the edges and pulling the thread taut. Once wet with blood and the sweat from his hands, the needle slipped from his fingers often—the reason for the pincers in the illustrations became painfully clear—but as far as he was concerned, he wasn't doing a bad job of things. He became so absorbed in his task, a plane could have crashed into the living room and he wouldn't have noticed.

"Not bad."

He jumped at the sound of her voice, and she hissed as the needle scraped torn flesh.

"Don't startle me!" He wiped perspiration from his brow with the back of his hand and glared up at her, but he couldn't maintain his anger when he saw the state she was in.

Her usually golden skin was ashen, and sweat beaded on her forehead. Her mouth clamped in a grim line and she held her body rigidly still.

"I thought you might like some positive feedback." Her voice rasped as if she'd swallowed a mouthful of gravel, but she gave him a tight smile with pale lips.

"You don't look so good." He concentrated again on the task

at hand, trying and failing to ignore her stifled cries of pain as the steel passed through her skin.

Through uneven breaths, she gasped, "You can thank your sainted friend for that."

"Because you're injured, I'll let that slide. Along with the fact you tried to kill me earlier this evening." He jerked the thread a bit less gently than necessary to punctuate his statement, and watched from the corner of his eye as she gripped the couch until her knuckles went white. "You lost a lot of blood. When I'm done here, I'll get you set up on a transfusion."

"You know how to do that?" she asked, surprise apparent in her strange, lilting voice.

He rolled his eyes. "I'm a vampire. We're experts in getting blood into people."

"I know you knew about getting it out of people." She rubbed her neck, looking vaguely shocked to find it bandaged. "But he only bit me once."

"Maybe he didn't like the taste of dog." Max pushed the needle through her flesh again and winced at the pained sound she made in reply.

"You are making it hurt more on purpose," she accused. If she hadn't sounded so helpless, he would have shown her what it would feel like if he intentionally hurt her.

Instead, he handed her the Scotch. "Do you need a break?"

She tilted her head back to drain the flask. After she wiped her lips, she adopted a determined expression. "Get it over with."

To distract himself from the few yelps she couldn't hold in, and to distract her from the pain as much as he could, he asked questions. "So, how did this happen?"

"I took your girlfriend's tip and checked the cemeteries." Bella clenched the back of the sofa as though she was going to climb away from him.

"Relax. It'll be harder to finish this if I have to chase you around the apartment to do it." He took a deep breath and rolled his head to ease the stiffness in his neck. "And Dahlia is not my girlfriend."

"Well, it was a good tip." Belle grimaced ruefully. "In theory. I thought I had him. He seemed lucid, until I realized he was not talking to me, but to a person who was not there."

"He was talking?" That twisted Max's guts. If Nathan had simply gone insane, there was no help for him. Only one facility existed to deal with vampires who went south of reason, and the Movement probably wasn't going to welcome a marked vampire in.

She nodded, blowing out a shaky breath. "For a while. Then he completely changed."

"Into a vampire?" Max tossed his head to get his hair out of his eyes, coupling the motion with a flash of his feeding face.

Her eyes flared, a spark of anger lighting her pupils. "Do not do that. And no, he was still human looking."

Max looked doubtfully at her shredded leg. "He did this to you in regular Nathan form?"

"He managed to do the leg with the bolt I fired into him." She shrugged. "It was not my night for aiming."

"Should have quit while you were ahead." The wound was nearly closed. All that remained was to tie off the floss. "Still don't believe he's possessed?"

It took her a moment to answer. "I do not like to concede that I was incorrect—"

"Flat-out wrong."

She pursed her lips. "Incorrect. But yes, I do believe you. When he attacked me, he was not in control of himself."

Max carefully lowered her leg to the couch. "From where I stand, I think you have two options here."

"I cannot wait to hear them." She narrowed her eyes and folded her arms across her chest.

The defiance on her sweat-streaked, pale face brought a crooked grin to Max's lips. If she was well enough to be a pain in the ass, she might not be in such bad shape, after all. "The first one is you can either hook up with me and help figure out what's going on with Nathan—"

"And be renounced by the Movement."

He resisted the urge to growl at her; it might be considered foreplay to her kind. "God forbid that happen. I mean, they're only going to kill me. What will they do to you, fire you?"

"Point taken." She narrowed her eyes. "Continue."

"Or you can stay here until I can get the situation under control. It's up to you." He rose and stretched, giving his gently phrased threat a moment to sink in.

It didn't have the effect he'd hoped for, though in hindsight it had been stupid of him to think she would bend easily.

"Do you think you can keep me here against my will?" She glared at him. "You have to sleep sometime."

He reached into his back pocket and pulled out the handcuffs he'd tucked there. He'd found them in Nathan's closet while looking for the first aid kit, and while he didn't want to speculate on why they'd been there in the first place, he was glad to have found them. Her eyes widened as he dangled the shining restraints from his forefinger. "I'll even let you pick where I lock you up, baby."

"I will tear you apart," she threatened, the last of her words turning into a growl as they escaped her throat.

"Bad dog," he admonished, twirling the cuffs around his finger. "You're not doing anything of the sort. At least, not in the state you're in."

He'd expected, hell, even looked forward to, the venom she

should have spewed at him, but she only closed her eyes and rubbed her forehead with a weary sigh. "You are right. I cannot fight you. Yet."

"So, I take it we're going with option number two?" He sighed. "Remember, it was your choice."

"And remember, there is still one night of the full moon. I might forget the code of my people, just this once." Her tone was pure hatred poured into words.

He shook his head. "Sorry, honey. Max Harrison is not going out as dog food."

If looks could kill, the one she gave him would have been a wooden stake. "I would not eat you. Your flesh would taste like carrion."

"You wound, lady," he mocked, laying his hand over his heart.

She held her wrists out resolutely. "Close to the toilet, please."

Max returned the cuffs to his pocket and went to examine the shelves on the far side of the room. "I won't lock you up until I'm ready for some shut-eye."

"What are you going to do in the meantime?" She didn't seem all that interested. In fact, it sounded as if she was trying to pick a fight.

Max wouldn't give her one. "I'm going to start going through Nathan's books, and try to figure out what's happening with him. And if the possession has anything to do with what the Soul Eater has going on."

"The Soul Eater?" She spoke his name with the requisite awe all Movement assassins who hadn't tangled with the man himself displayed. "Does your friend have ties to the Soul Eater?"

Max pushed back a book on medicinal herbs. "Uh, yeah. Nathan is his fledgling. Don't you guys do research over there anymore?"

"I do not question. They gave me a kill order and the instructions to complete it immediately." She at least sounded a little ashamed at having missed that particular detail.

"Well, if you'd bothered to ask me, rather than shoot on sight, I could have filled you in. The Soul Eater is trying to become a god, and we're thinking that has something to do with the fact that his son has just returned from the dead and his fledgling has gone schizo." Max waited a minute for his words to sink in before adding, "Now don't you feel foolish for trying to kill me?"

"Does the Movement know what is happening?"

"Not that I know of. They had us on the plane before we could figure it out ourselves. The Oracle told Carrie." Another book on herbs. Either Nathan was a total pothead or he really put a lot of faith into the whole New Age thing.

"The Oracle?" Bella's voice was small, almost frightened.

Turning to her, Max hooked his thumbs in his belt loops. "I didn't mean to upset you. Here's the deal. You help me find Nathan, I'll trust you not to run. If we find him and we can figure out a way to cure him of whatever this thing is, you leave him alone. If it turns out he's past the point of no return, you can stake him and take the credit back to Breton. I'll even forfeit my pay on this one."

She considered for a moment, and Max continued. "What's the worst that could happen? You don't get to kill him. But there are plenty of other vampires out there to kill. And I'll consider it a personal favor."

She raised a hand to shut him up. "I will help you find your possessed friend and I will not kill him when we do. At least, not until we are sure there is no hope for him."

"That," Max said, a new, grim determination gripping him, "is the only smart thing you've said since we met."

* * *

I pulled into Louden just before sunrise and parked the van in the lot of a semideserted strip mall with a Laundromat and a shabby looking dollar store. I secured the doors, double-checked the ties of the canvas partition and slid into the back, where I dug into a huge pile of the *Hudson Herald* and the *Louden Times.* The butler had followed March's instructions to a tee, loading up over a week's worth of the two publications. It was tempting to just start at the date of Nathan's possession and work forward, but med school had taught me better. Cutting corners always comes back to bite you in the end.

I'd read about some fairly innocuous local occurrences: the opening of a new Wal-Mart, an eighty-six-year-old rancher caught growing marijuana in his basement. I shifted my "read" pile away from my "to be read" pile, and there, on the top of the stack, in letters as long as the palm of my hand, was the word *Fire!*

I scanned the page frantically to find the date. Three days before I lost Nathan.

"St. Anne's Catholic Church burned down early Saturday morning, and three parishioners are missing."

Unbidden, the image from my dream flashed through my brain. Two dead, covered in blood. I'd thought it a premonition, when really my stressed brain was just having a field day in-undating me with horrific imagery. The article went on to list the missing persons—a priest, a nun and a parish secretary presumed to have wandered into the desert—and an ominous warning about record temperatures making their chances of survival slim. And the missing persons had made no effort to contact authorities when the fire broke out. That struck me as a bit fishy.

I sat back on my heels, unsure what I should read into such a news item. For a sleepy town like Louden, a big fire was big news.

That there were three people wandering the desert when they should have been resting in a county morgue's cooler made it a piece of interest. If the Fangs were in town, what were the chances the victims never called the fire department because they were dead already? It would be just like the Fangs to trash a church.

I read on, searching for any other unusual news stories until I couldn't stay awake anymore, then fell asleep with my head cushioned by the local girls' volleyball scores. I don't know how long I'd been out when my phone rang.

"What the hell kind of brothel did you send me to?" I hissed after I hit the connect button. "A male prostitute tried to steal my blood yesterday!"

"Um…this is Max."

"Oh." I'd been expecting Byron to call and gloat or give me another travel tip. "How are things in Michigan?"

"Apparently not as interesting as things in— Did you say you were in a brothel?" Max's voice lacked his characteristic humor. In fact, he sounded pissed off.

"Well, technically…"

His loud curse soared above the crackle of static. "Oh, that's great. I've been sucked into a parallel universe where everyone else gets to have sex and I get to walk around with a permanent hard-on. I'm in hell."

"Let's not get graphic." I wiped a line of drool off my cheek and hoped the newsprint hadn't marked my skin.

Max was silent for a moment. When he spoke, his voice was grim. "I found Nathan."

Oh, God. My arm fell, as though it were no longer attached to my central nervous system. Had he killed Nathan? I tried desperately to connect to the tie I'd blocked before. I'd stupidly, selfishly shut myself off from Nathan, and now he was dead. I'd wasted my last moments with him.

"Carrie, are you there?"

I made a squeaky affirmative noise, not wanting to sob into the phone.

"He wounded the other assassin pretty bad. I haven't seen him since."

If I had been standing, I would have fallen down. The relief would have dissolved my knees right there. I wanted to open my mouth and shriek praises to the sky, but all I said was, "Oh?"

"Well, don't sound impressed or anything." He made one of his long-suffering-Max sounds. "I had to trail Bella forever, she kicked me in the face, she shot me but yeah, my hard work is nothing to get excited over."

I held the phone away from my face and frowned at it. "She shot you? Max, are you okay?"

"Yeah, I'll be fine. It's just a flesh wound," he assured me cheerily. "I'm going out again after sundown. Anything on your end?"

"I think so. It may be nothing." I dismissed the notion because it was too unlikely. "I don't know, this drive has been weird."

"Oh, I understand, what with the male prostitutes and all. But it's about to get weirder. I ran into Dahlia."

Though the gesture would have been lost on him, I'd been prepared to raise my middle finger at the phone. I froze at his words. "Dahlia?"

"Yeah. She had some psychic vision. I'm not sure what it was about. And I wouldn't put much stock in it before exhausting all other options, but—"

"I would." Dahlia had powers I would never underestimate. "What did she say?"

"Louden. And Hudson." He said the words as if they weren't sending electric shocks straight down my spine. "Oh, and the Virgin Mary fits in there somewhere."

"Max, I have to go." I resisted the urge to ask him to be careful one last time, and clicked the phone shut. Grabbing at the stack of papers I'd just read through, I found the bulletin about the church fire again. There was too much coincidence, too much about Dahlia's vision that supported my suspicions. Cyrus was at St. Anne's, or had been before it burned down.

I forced myself to sleep—I had no clue what I would face in the desert and I needed to be prepared for it—only to be woken just after sundown by the roaring of motorcycles.

At a strip mall in Louden, the Fangs found me. My first thought was to follow them. Then I got some sense and realized a bright orange, hulking monster of a rusted-out van was probably not the best camouflage. I was on the right track. I couldn't blow it by being impatient.

When they finally left the Laundromat—I was deeply shocked they'd make any use of that facility at all—I headed for the newspaper machine and bought a fresh copy of the *Louden Times*. A week had put some space between the story I looked for and the front page, but I eventually found a sidebar follow-up. Police hadn't been able to locate the body of Stacey Pickles, age eighteen, but they had recovered the corpses of the other two victims. The state of the remains suggested foul play, and anyone with knowledge of the whereabouts of the missing girl was instructed to call local authorities.

Using details from the articles and the map March had given me, I was fairly certain I could find the place. Whether I could find it before the Fangs did whatever they planned to do with Cyrus was another thing. Then there was the small detail of actually getting him to leave with me, but I figured negative thinking would only limit my chances of success.

Besides, I still had the chloroform.

It was time. Ready or not, it was time to face Cyrus again.

A loud bang on the passenger side of the van made me practically jump through the roof. Outside the window, Byron grinned stupidly at me. "Hello! Have a nice time?"

I lunged across the seat, forced the door open and grabbed him by the collar of the poncy, ruffled shirt he wore. He protested loudly, but had no choice but to get in. I'd caught him by surprise and had more leverage.

"Hey, this is a very expensive shirt!" he howled, grabbing the fabric from my hands.

"It's about to get dusty!" I grabbed a stake and pressed it against his chest. I hoped it tore the precious silk. "Why did you set me up?"

"Set you up?" he sputtered, his wide eyes fixed on the stake. "I never did any such thing!"

"March told me she was contacted by you. That you told her I was a person of interest!" I twisted the stake.

It was almost embarrassing the way he yelped. "I never meant any harm, I swear! I thought she might be able to help you!"

"Help me?" I released the pressure a bit. I wasn't stupid enough to believe he'd come to me without new information, and it wouldn't help me any if I accidentally killed him. "What do you mean?"

"I thought since you were looking for this fellow, she could help you. March is very well connected." He pushed away the stake, and I let him, watching with amusement as he rubbed his chest in a wincing display of pain.

"She's connected, all right. She's connected to the Soul Eater." I reached behind me to slip the stake into my back pocket. At Byron's startled gasp, I raised an eyebrow. "Oh, so you've heard of him?"

He nodded, still rubbing his imagined wound. "Heard of

him? There were rumors of him even in my time. Vampires have always been very popular. Ever read *The Picture of Dorian Gray?*"

"That wasn't about vampires," I pointed out.

With a knowing smile, he said, "Oh, wasn't it?"

I sighed. "Listen, I don't have time to talk about literature. Your friends down there are probably going to pick up Cyrus tonight, and I need to get to him before they do."

"Which is precisely why I'm here." Byron dug into the front pocket of his too-tight jeans and withdrew what looked like a glow-in-the-dark marble.

"What's that?" I wanted to add a snide comment about him not explaining why he'd told March what I was up to. But then, he couldn't have known we would be enemies.

"It's a key. The Fangs are using a cloaking spell to disguise where they're hiding your man. If you have this, you'll be able to see what no one else does." He smiled. "And what my uncouth companions will not be able to see, now that I've nicked it. But you don't have much time. They were expecting them in an hour at least half an hour ago. And they'll soon realize they're missing something."

"Wait." It was too suspicious, his risking his life to help me. "Why are you giving me this?"

"That, you see, comes at a price." He grew serious then, grasping my hands in his soft, elegant ones and pleading earnestly, "Let me write about you."

"What?" I jerked back.

"I can't get a book out of those cretins. They're vile and un-civilized. I can't spin a tale of desert heroism from *them!*"

"Oh, and you can get one out of me?" Right. Like I'd make such a great heroine.

He nodded vehemently, gesturing with his frilled sleeves as

he began to proselytize on my virtues. "You're like…a modern Corday. Striking a lonesome, yet powerful blow for your cause in a Reign of Terror you cannot abide. Readers will love it!"

I wasn't buying it. "And the fact that you just happened to be the one who sold me the knife…"

"Naturally, I—I would have to figure into it, as the narrator. Peripherally, of course," he stammered, at least having the good grace to look sheepish. "But the core of the story would be your valiant yet noble struggle for good."

"Oh, like *Blood Heat?*" I couldn't help the jab.

"Mock if you must. But you can't have the key until you give me your blessing." He held up the marble between his thumb and forefinger. It shone icy blue, as though a tiny galaxy of cold white stars existed inside.

I sighed in resignation. "You're going to write it anyway, aren't you?"

He nodded.

"Fine." I snatched the key from his hand. I'd expected it to feel magical somehow, but it was only a small, smooth weight in my palm. "Where are you going to go? They'll kill you when they find you, you know."

"I know. That's what she's for." He leaned clear of the passenger-side window so I could see the orange Volkswagen Rabbit parked beside a light post. A woman who appeared to be in her forties, with puffy, bleached-blonde hair and lipstick far too light for her orangey tan, stared back at us with worried eyes. "Her name is Penny. She's going to give me a ride to the next town."

"Don't tell me how you have to pay for the gas," I quipped as he opened the door and hopped down.

"I wish you well, dear Charlotte," he said with a sincerity I truly believed as he swept a low bow.

I smiled, in spite of myself. "It's Carrie."

He straightened and turned toward the car, where Penny waited. As he walked away, he called back, "Not in my book."

And like that, I had what I needed.

Now all I had to do was psych myself up for the job. When I'd prepared for the trip, I'd imagined actual physical combat as some far-off, never-never land probability. Now that it was a reality, I panicked. How would I fight any vampires who might give me a hard time? Nathan had taught me some simple self-defense, but these vampires served the Soul Eater, a dangerous enough task on the most mundane days. Add to that the fact most of them liked fighting and killing almost as much as they loved their bikes, and the prospect of little old inexperienced me beating one, let alone a group of them, in physical combat seemed pretty damn remote.

And if I did survive the gauntlet of hardened assassins, there was still the problem of Cyrus. If they'd turned him into a vampire again, would he be restored to his old strength? He'd crush me. Or would he still be human? Would I have to fight my own urge for revenge?

The past two months hadn't been sufficient to numb me to the memory of his cruelty. I'd felt more pity than rage for him at the end, but I was more human than most vampires would admit of themselves. After the pain of losing Nathan, the loneliness of the last weary days, would I snap and take out my aggression toward the Soul Eater on Cyrus?

Then, there was another, more terrifying possibility. When I'd been blood tied to Cyrus, I'd been drawn to him in a way I couldn't explain. It hadn't been love, but a sinister parody of it. I'd been completely enthralled. Now that our mental connection was regenerating in fits and bursts, would I fall prey to that dangerous attraction again?

No. I was a stronger person, having defeated him once. Still, the prospect of seeing him again didn't inspire a lot of confidence.

First thing first, though. I had to get to him without running into the Fangs.

The charred remains of St. Anne's Catholic Church lay like a giant, abandoned campfire in the sand. It had burned completely to the ground. How the Fangs had hidden anyone here, with no shelter from the elements, without burning up from the desert sun, was beyond me.

I drove past the ruins, aware someone might be watching, and looked for an inconspicuous place to stash the van. Unlike the Road Runner cartoons, there were no convenient outcroppings of rock for me to hide behind, Wyle E. Coyote style, while waiting to ambush, and the Fangs from town were still out there somewhere. I pulled to the side of the road and propped the hood open, praying the flashers wouldn't wear down the battery. All the stealth and cunning in the world wouldn't help me if I successfully abducted Cyrus, but had no transportation away from the scene of the crime.

I felt a little foolish as I looked over the supplies March had provided. I'd never chloroformed a person before. I'd never tied someone up—at least, not for the purpose of kidnapping. I felt like a beginner skier staring down the steep face of the advanced slope. More than anything, I wanted to go back to the bunny hill.

"Where is that damn spare?" I said a little too loudly, in case someone was around. I pulled the glowing marble thing Byron had given me from my pocket and rolled it in my palm.

Instantly, a flash of light like a heat wave shivered up from the ground. A millisecond later, the roar of an engine filled my ears.

I turned toward the source of the sound and nearly rubbed my eyes, until I remembered I wasn't supposed to be able to see the scene before me. Seemingly from nowhere, the ruined church had reassembled, the stained-glass windows illuminated from within casting weird colors on the desert sand. Bathed in the blue glow of a mercury light, a few vampires revved their motorcycles impatiently as two other figures argued animatedly in front of them.

With the sound of the engines covering their voices, I couldn't tell what they were arguing about, but they were unconcerned by my presence at the side of the road, and that was all that mattered. They thought they were invisible, and that was all right with me, as long as they didn't decide to take advantage of the element of surprise and come out to grab the tasty stranded motorist. After a few minutes of pretending to rummage for something in the back of the van, I retreated to the front and leaned under the hood, as though something might be wrong there.

From the few glimpses I could sneak of the parking lot, I saw the argument devolve into a shoving match, then a full-fledged fistfight. Now I could guess what they fought about. The Fangs from town had never shown up. Finally, the bikes grew louder, then began to roll onto the road, their riders intending to look for their friends, I presumed. The lumpy shape of an unconscious vampire remained on the pavement as the rest of the horde thundered away in the direction I'd come from. I wouldn't have much time before the two groups met up with each other.

With a distinct feeling of now or never, I slipped the chloroform in my back pocket, a stake into the opposite one, and set off.

It was just my luck the vampire came to as I entered the parking lot. He cradled his head in his hands and cursed, blinking rapidly to clear his vision. As he did, his feeding face flashed on and off, like a broken neon sign. I cleared my throat to get his attention as I approached.

"Fuck," he repeated, pinching the bridge of his bloodied nose with his thumb and index finger. The digits protruded from a fingerless black glove and were marked with bad, homemade tattoos.

"Hi. I had some car trouble. You got a phone in there?" I smiled, hoping I could squeak by before his head injury cleared up and he remembered he was supposed to be invisible.

"No, there ain't no phone," he growled, but his demeanor changed instantly as he dragged his gaze from my shoes to my legs and parts farther north. "Somebody musta forgot to pay the bill."

When he laughed, it sounded like dirty bubbles popping in his throat. He smiled—I guess I was supposed to find the expression charming—and displayed broken, rotted teeth. His dirty hair hung down beneath a ratty bandanna, but he looked as though he honestly believed I found him attractive.

"Oh, darn." I eased my hands into my back pockets, my fingers closing on the stake. I waited for the moment when he would realize something was amiss. When he was wrapped up in his confusion, I would strike.

It didn't take as long as I expected. No sooner had I spoken than his brow wrinkled and his eyes narrowed. "Wait a minute, you're not supposed to—"

I lunged forward, bringing the stake down hard so it would penetrate his sternum. The impact vibrated up my arm, shaking my bones painfully, but I'd hit my mark. He didn't have time to scream before he burned.

Good thing, too, I thought as I rubbed my elbow. I wasn't exactly in fighting shape.

It seemed too gutsy to burst through the front door. Besides, they'd spray-painted a huge, complicated mark on it, and I had the sneaking suspicion it might be another spell-type thing to keep out, or alert them to, intruders. I walked around the side of the building, where no lights indicated the presence of the Fangs.

A side door, carelessly left unlocked, opened to a dark room. I would never accuse the Fangs of being an intellectual organization. It took me a minute to recognize it was a kitchen. My gaze fell on the empty sink. If Cyrus was human, they either weren't feeding him or they were diligently doing the dishes.

I was feeling pretty confident as I crossed to the door opposite me. Then it opened, and in stepped the ugliest vampire I'd ever seen.

I think she was a woman, but I didn't have time to ask before she grabbed a butcher knife from the counter and hurled it at me. I dodged it, whirling toward the huge commercial gas stove. I grabbed one of the cast-iron burner plates and hurled it at her. She knocked it out of the air with a swipe of her huge forearm, and kept advancing.

Retrieving the stake from my pocket, I braced myself in a ready stance. But she didn't attack me the way I thought she would, with full physical contact. Instead, she lunged, grabbed a handful of my hair and jerked me upward.

Plenty of experience with battered women in the E.R. had taught me a valuable piece of combat knowledge: Never let your hair go where your body doesn't. Once the scalp was pulled free of the skull, it didn't grow back easily. I wasn't willing to chance it, so I stopped struggling, dropped the stake and clamped both my hands on my head as she hauled me over the top of the stove. With an expression of clinical disinterest, she flicked the dials and ignited the burners.

Pain exploded in my back as my flimsy T-shirt caught fire and seared my skin. Screaming, I kicked my feet, grappling for footing as I lay horizontal on the stove. I managed to hook my heels over the lip of the counter and arch upward, breaking free just long enough to get out of the range of the flames.

Though I was clear of the burners, I was still on fire. I dropped to the ground and rolled on the shockingly cold tiles, yelping in agony as my charred T-shirt separated from the skin beneath.

The vampire made another lunge for me as I rolled to my feet. I sidestepped her, and her miss proved to be my window of opportunity. I snatched the stake from the floor and caught her between the ribs as she rounded for another pass.

Her face contorted in disbelief as flames traveled up her body. She clenched my arm, my hand still locked on the stake, in a death grip, as though the simple action would be enough to drag me into hell with her. Then her hand disintegrated into ash and I tumbled backward onto my burned elbows.

With all the noise we'd made, I expected the room to flood with angry biker vampires. When it didn't seem that would happen, I climbed to my feet and shrugged off the burned remains of my T-shirt.

Of course, I couldn't have worn a decent-looking bra.

Why does it matter what you're wearing when you find him? my all too insightful brain asked accusingly. *And don't let the fact you've probably got third-degree burns bother you more than your appearance, or anything.*

Shaking my head as though I could knock the thoughts loose, I stepped cautiously through the kitchen door, into a wide hall. The floor bowed out to accommodate a curved inner wall. I'd never been a faithful churchgoer, but I knew enough to guess the room beyond the wall would be the important one. As I advanced along the curving hallway, the large, double doors of the main entrance came into view, along with the set of doors leading into the church proper. Another chalked-on sigil marked the latter. Beyond them, the muffled sound of music didn't disguise angry voices.

No wonder the vampires hadn't heard the struggle in the kitchen. I pressed my ear to the wood, avoiding the chalk marking, to eavesdrop.

"Where the hell is Angie? The glamour's not going to hold much longer if she doesn't get her ass back to the circle," an agitated male voice warned.

"She'll come back," a calmer female replied. "She's probably checking on the guy."

The guy. That could only mean Cyrus. My heart pounded wildly in my chest. That someone else acknowledged his presence made my job suddenly too real.

"If she's not back in five minutes, I'm going after her," the male vampire declared. His footsteps thundered closer to the door than I found comfortable.

I backed away, glancing around for some way to secure the doors from the outside. A row of chairs was lined up waiting-room style beside a rack of pamphlets about natural family planning and how to pray the rosary. I grabbed the nearest chair and lifted it off the floor so its legs wouldn't make a sound. With held breath, I eased the flat back beneath the door handles and slid it up until the rear legs were wedged against the carpet. It wouldn't hold them indefinitely, but it would give them some trouble, if I was lucky.

Down the hall a little way I found another door. This one was plain wood, with rough edges and a flimsy doorknob. I tried the handle and found it unlocked.

Does no one care about security these days?

A set of stairs led down into a dark basement that, at first glance, appeared to be empty. My foot was on the second step when the rhythmic creak of bedsprings stopped me.

A woman gasped and a man groaned in the darkness. The hair on the back of my neck stood up. I recognized that male sound.

I guess Angie was "checking" on him, after all. Unexpected jealousy burned in my stomach. I blamed it on the sputtering blood tie between us, and the fact I hadn't exactly planned to walk in on him mid-coitus.

I flattened myself against the wall, praying I was out of sight of the bed, wherever that was. Charging down the steps and starting a fight would only get me killed, especially considering this Angie person apparently had something to do with the spell cloaking the place. I'd had plenty of run-ins with witches—well, at least one—and I didn't feel like taking my chances with another.

It seemed like forever before they were finished, probably because of the awkwardness and embarrassment of the situation. I started to wonder how much time had passed, and if the vampires upstairs would come looking for Angie. I hadn't heard any pounding on the doors yet, but I might have mistaken it for the pounding of the bed against the floor. They were really going for it downstairs.

Finally, their ecstatic noises ceased, and the bed creaked as Angie climbed from it. "I'll be in the bathroom."

I found it strange that a vampire with the power to make an entire building vanish into ruin would speak with such timidity to Cyrus, human or vampire. Then again, mortal terror of his dear old daddy probably inspired unusual reserve in most of his followers.

I heard Cyrus's sigh of contentment over the rustle of sheets as he arranged himself on the bed. A pang of longing speared through me, the exact feeling someone would get watching the ex they dumped shopping happily for china patterns with his new love. *You can put the vampire into the human, but you can't take the human out of the vampire.*

When the bathroom door closed and I heard the sound of running water, I made my move. I came down the steps as quickly and quietly as I could, but he still heard me. My eyes adjusted easily to the darkness and I found him, staring at me in disbelief as he sat up on the bed.

He was still human. I could tell from the smell of him, and the warmth that seemed to wrap around me. He'd cut his hair.

He opened his mouth, probably to shout to Angie for help. All he managed before I covered his mouth and nose with the chloroform-soaked scrap of my burned T-shirt was "No, she's—"

Then it was done. He dropped, limp and unconscious, to the bed, and I lifted him over my shoulder. Carrying his weight this way was easier, but getting up the stairs took a bit more effort. Luckily, the woman in the bathroom seemed to be filling the tub. She never heard me struggling up the steps, into the hall and back through the kitchen.

If my departure had set off any sort of magical alarm, it was too late. I dumped Cyrus in the back of the van and drove into the desert before anyone could pursue us.

16

Unpleasant Discoveries

Despite the fact she could barely walk, the damn woman insisted she come along with him.

Max ground his teeth as he paused for the umpteenth time for Bella to catch up. "You know, this would go a lot faster if you'd just stayed at home."

"That place is not my home," she snarled—actually snarled, the vicious bitch.

"You know what I meant." He let her pass him a few steps before he started again. "You're not exactly incognito with the smell of blood all over you."

"If you would have done a better job patching me up, I would not smell like blood." She limped a few steps, then visibly forced herself to straighten her leg.

Max sighed in frustration and caught up with her easily. "Do you want me to carry you?"

Her gold eyes widened, then narrowed in anger. "Absolutely not!"

Damn. It might have been fun to let her climb on him piggyback style, her legs wrapped around his waist.

"Oh, for Christ's sake," he cursed out loud. Thinking sexually about a werewolf was practically bestiality. And if he were going to swing that way, he'd much rather do it with something that didn't talk as much as she did, like a goat or a pony.

Ally or not, she continued to grate on his nerves.

Her expression flickered for a moment, and she looked hurt and offended. Then he remembered he'd spoken aloud, and she probably thought his remark was directed at her.

He'd opened his mouth to explain when she cut him off. "Fine. Carry me, if you think it will be faster."

Recovering fast, he smiled superciliously. "I do."

She stood behind him, tentatively placing her hands on his shoulders. He stooped slightly and reached back to lift her up. The natural place to rest hands, of course, was the perfectly round curve of her ass.

Pervert. Furry. Furvert, he chastised himself as he boosted her onto his back. "Up you go."

"This is humiliating," she growled at him, her mouth so close to his ear her breath stirred his hair.

He hooked his elbows under her knees to help support her. Her arms around his neck didn't choke him. She was strong enough to hold her own weight, for the most part.

"You wouldn't have been humiliated if you'd stayed at home," he pointed out, then corrected himself. "At the apartment."

"Fine. You are right and I, a lowly female, am wrong. Is that better?" Was that a hint of playfulness he heard in her voice?

It buoyed his spirits some. "Much. Are we still going straight?"

She'd refused to let him drive the car while they searched for Nathan. She'd said she couldn't get a good scent that way.

The thought turned his stomach.

She lifted up slightly, audibly sniffing the wind. "No, turn up ahead."

Her heels dug into him and she balled the shoulders of his T-shirt in her hands and tugged. He yanked the front of his shirt flat. "Stop that, I'm not a horse."

"Sorry," she said in a way that implied she didn't care what kind of animal he was. "But turn right up ahead."

The farther she led him into the neighborhood, the more it looked familiar. Dread tightened his guts. "Are you sure we're on the right track?"

She gave a snort of disgust. "Do you have a better way of finding him that you are not sharing with me? Using it to second-guess my sense of smell? I said turn right."

In the guise of hoisting her higher on his back, he jostled her wounded leg. "Sorry, did that hurt?"

"You are a spiteful man. I will be glad when this is all over." She suddenly sounded tired and even laid her head against his shoulder as he walked.

Not for the first time that night, he wondered how much pain she was in and how she could put up such a strong front. *Idiot.* If she would just tell him she needed a rest, he would let her. Even though she didn't deserve his pity.

Maybe it was a good thing they were on the same team. If they hadn't been, he might have killed her before now.

They walked in silence for a while, her weight surprisingly heavy at his back. Though she was slender, her body was all lean muscle, firm but not hard owing to the thin layer of feminine fat that softened her curves.

She could use a little more of it, he thought, shifting her so her bony pelvis didn't bite into his back. He was not, he assured himself, *not* irritated at the fact her body being pressed so close to him would probably succeed in giving him a fatal hard-on.

He was pissed off that she didn't listen, and now he had to cart her heavy ass all over Grand Rapids.

She'd gone so long without talking, he wondered if she'd fallen asleep. But then she sat up abruptly, her body completely rigid. "He is close. That way."

"Of course he is," Max grumbled, turning in the direction indicated by her impatient shirt tugs.

The direction of Cyrus's old place.

Anger burned in Max. Of course he would have something to do with this. "I know where he's going."

"Then take us there faster," she ordered impatiently.

Max picked up the pace a little, not quite as eager to find their quarry as she seemed to be. "Why? You're in no shape to fight, and I certainly can't with you hanging on me like a diseased monkey."

She slapped him on the top of the head, a pretty ballsy thing to do to someone she was riding on, in his opinion. "I am a wolf. Please do not make me any closer to your pathetic species than I already am."

"Oh, sorry." He rolled his eyes, despite the fact she wouldn't see it. "But you seem to conveniently forget I'm not a human."

"You were, once." She said it like it was a bad thing.

He let that slide. "If I'm right—and as we've established, I'm rarely wrong—he's going to Cyrus's mansion."

"On Plymouth Street?" She sounded as surprised that he knew about the place as he was surprised she knew.

"That's the one. In cozy with him, were you?" It was a cheap shot. No self-respecting werewolf would get it on with a vampire.

That bothered him more than it should.

"I read the Movement files on him during my training. He was one of the best known outlaw vampires living in this area, so it seems impossible that he would not still have connections here," Bella insisted. "Like your girlfriend, who lives here now."

"She's not my..." Max shook his head. "Listen, this is Plymouth. If I go that way, we're going to Cyrus's house."

"Are there no other houses on that street?" She sounded so satisfied with herself, he almost dumped her on her ass.

He picked up the pace once more. "You're gonna feel pretty stupid when you're wrong."

But she wasn't wrong, at least, not right away. They walked a few blocks and got a dirty look from an elderly couple in evening clothes.

"You should have stayed home," Max whispered as he lifted a hand in friendly greeting to the woman, who screwed up her face in a sour glare and hugged her fur wrap tighter to her chest. "They're going to call the cops."

"Then I will come back and eat their housecats," Bella said close to his ear.

A completely involuntary—because he wasn't at all attracted to her—shiver went up his back at the feeling of her lips brushing his skin.

She chuckled. "Oh, I bet you hoped I did not notice that."

"It was from muscle fatigue, I assure you. Ever think of, like, Weight Watchers or Jenny Craig?" Another cheap shot. It was her fault. She reduced him to them.

The remark didn't phase her. "So, I suppose I could do that again. Or maybe..."

As her voice died away, something warm and wet and rough and unmistakably a wicked, pointed tongue traced the outside of his ear. His knees buckled and he nearly crashed to the sidewalk.

"Don't do that," he said, a little more sharply than he'd intended, as he recovered his footing.

"Why not? Do you not like it?" She was teasing him, deliberately teasing him, when they were supposed to be working.

He blew out a frustrated breath. "Because I train my dogs not to lick. It's bad manners."

Her laughter was surprisingly feminine. He'd expected something throaty and seductive, like her voice. If he'd thought about it at all, that is, which he hadn't.

She traced a fingernail down the front of his throat, then scratched beneath his chin affectionately. "You call me a dog as though you were trying to offend me. I know what I am."

"A pain in the ass? A fat, heavy pain in the ass?" God help him, he was teasing her back.

Are you high, Harrison?

No, brain. But I wish I was.

"I am not fat. I have fat, where it is needed in human form." As if to demonstrate what she meant, she pressed her breasts more firmly against his back.

Someone must have drugged her. That was the only explanation for this strange behavior. Or, dear God, did they go into heat?

"Are you coming on to me? 'Cause if you are—" He didn't have time to finish with his bad barking-up-the-wrong-tree pun. Up ahead, the mansion loomed before them.

With startling clarity, he remembered that night. Or, more accurately, the drive over. He'd never seen Nathan so shaken. Too keyed up to drive, definitely, so Max'd had to drive Ziggy's shitty old van, listening to Nathan mumble "faster" and "come on," the whole time.

"I can't lose her, Max. If I lose her, you have to do me a favor."

And then he'd pressed a stake into Max's hand.

Max wouldn't have been able to do it then, and he wouldn't be able to do it now. They'd have to take Nathan alive, and damn the consequences.

"Why did you stop?" Bella demanded, digging her heels in again as if she could spur him to movement. "He is not here!"

"Fine!" Max didn't mean to shout it. The stress was getting to him. Calmer, though his voice was still ragged from tension, he started forward. "Where am I going?"

She sniffed the air again and tugged his shirt. "That way. And straight onto that lawn."

Her directions led him to another sprawling home, past a baffled security man, who didn't try and stop them until they were nearly to the back fence. There was a gate—thank God for small miracles—and it was unlocked, so they could slip out before the guard called the cops.

"Wasteful, to have such large homes," Bella said, the flirtatious air completely disappeared from her speech.

Max thought of his own place and cleared his throat. "Well, maybe they're inherited."

"Then wasteful of their ancestors, to have such large homes." There was clearly no arguing with her.

As they crossed the next lawn, she directed him back to the street. He groaned in frustration. "We could have just gone around the block."

"The trail is fresh. Cross the street!" She sat up like a foxhunter rising in the saddle.

"You're hard to carry when you're squirming like that." He ran across the street, glad for the absence of traffic on this side of town after nine.

They were crossing another lawn when he caught sight of Nathan, naked and bleeding, sprinting through a hedge.

"Holy shit!" Max dropped Bella, though she tried her damndest to stay on him.

"Do not leave me here!" she yelped. "I thought you needed my help."

"I need to lose some ballast so I can chase him down!" Max ran toward the hedge, slipping on the grass.

"You will lose his scent!" Bella jogged beside him, her face contorted in pain.

"You're going to hurt yourself," he warned. *Let her. She'll have no one to blame but herself.*

Her breathing turned to panting, but she kept up despite the pain he knew she felt. Her stamina was amazing as they scrambled over a high brick wall and landed on a vast lawn.

"You've got to be kidding me," Max groaned as Nathan rounded the corner of a small shed.

"Wait. He has been here before. I can smell him." Bella's nostrils flared and she clamped a hand over her mouth. "And I smell death."

They crept to the huge house, a stucco monster with Spanish tiles and creeping ivy. There were no lights, save for a candle in one of the ground-floor windows. Max motioned for Bella to follow him to the back door.

The impressive oak panel wasn't locked. It led to a small, three-season room with a mosaic floor and a veritable arboretum of plants. He stumbled over something in the dark and swore quietly.

"What is that?" Bella covered her nose with her sleeve.

Max gave the bulky shape a kick, producing a sickening, dull sound. "I'd say the former owners of this place."

"How many?" She squatted beside him and lifted an arm with a frown. It came completely free of the pile and she dropped it with a gasp.

Max did a quick check. "Two heads."

"That is impossible. There are more than two bodies here. There have to be more." Her pupils dilated and her breathing sped up visibly. "We are not safe here. Let's go."

With his shoe, Max pushed aside another pile of something moist he'd rather not think about. "Why on earth would you say that?"

"It is not a time for jokes! There is so much death here I cannot breathe." She stiffened, her nostrils flaring. "Someone is coming. Run! Now!"

On the heels of her statement, he heard it: several pairs of feet clomping toward them. Max ushered Bella ahead of him through the door, but with her injured leg she was too slow. He scooped her up in his arms and ran across the lawn, boosting her over the wall. He vaulted over and dropped onto the grass beside her with a thud.

"What could have done that? And who has that kind of security?" she whispered, peering up at the top of the wall as she sank into a crouch.

"The Soul Eater's guys," Max wheezed, his fist bunching the fabric of his shirt over his chest as he struggled for breath. "Looks like someone is keeping an eye on us."

Bella shook her head. "Or on someone else."

Max's blood ran colder than it should have in a vampire. "You're right. We've got to find Nathan or he's a dead man."

It was the second time in a week Cyrus had woken cold and naked in an unfamiliar place, and he didn't like it. A foul, chemical stench stung his nose, and he swiped at it with the back of his hand. His head throbbed and his vision swam. The only thing clear was the feeling of rough carpet at his back and the unmistakable sound of asphalt passing beneath him.

"Where am I?" He sat up, the motion of whatever vehicle he was in setting him temporarily off his balance. A nagging sense that something was wrong, beyond the fact that he'd been kidnapped naked again, plagued him.

"You're in the back of Ziggy's van."

He recognized the voice in an instant of raw pain.

"Do you remember who he was?"

"Honestly, I don't." Cyrus rubbed his eyes and looked around the space for something to cover himself with. "No, wait. The boy. He was Nolen's son."

And you're my fledgling, he added silently. *Or, you were.*

"Good. Glad to see you retained your memory. I worried you had forgotten." She sounded distracted. The van lurched around a corner.

"Where are you taking me?" The feeling that he was forgetting something, something very important, crept up again.

"Back to Michigan. You're going to help us fix what's happened to Nathan."

The unmistakable sensation of motion sickness overwhelmed Cyrus. "Stop the car. I'm going to be ill."

To his surprise, the van lurched to a halt and the driver's door ground open on rusty hinges. Seconds later, the back doors opened, revealing a dark, desert highway and endless night sky.

And Carrie.

Fear, embarrassment, pain and relief cascaded in a wave over him. Disoriented, he reached for her, but she stepped back, cold and unyielding as ever. She still wore her fair hair scraped back from her face in a severe ponytail, still glared at him with her cold, blue eyes. He'd looked into those eyes once and prayed to see a bit of warmth, some sign of loving acceptance.

That memory sparked the nagging feeling of having misplaced something, and he scrambled from the van, falling to his knees on the shoulder of the road.

Mouse!

"You have to take me back," he insisted before he heaved up his dinner on the sand. He got to his feet, head still reeling from the effects of whatever she'd used to drug him. "I have to go back."

"You're not going anywhere." Carrie followed him the few steps he managed away from the van.

"They're going to kill her." Words seemed impossible. He couldn't get them in the right order, couldn't think of the ones that would convince her to take him to Mouse. "I don't know anything about Nolen, just let me go back. I love her."

"Right. Like you loved me." Carrie laughed, becoming for a moment the great, heartless creation he'd wanted her to be. He should have been careful what he'd wished for. "Listen, I'm not letting you run back to your undead girlfriend so you two can plot whatever you've got going."

Undead? "No, you don't understand." But he couldn't make her understand, either. He was drunk from…was it chloroform? A bitter trickle stung the back of his throat. "Please, I have to go back."

She stepped closer, squinting at him as though she could see into his mind and detect an ulterior motive.

Let her search. She won't find anything.

"Please." He clenched his fists at his sides. There was some vital detail that would make her bend, he knew it. But his muddled brain wouldn't seize on it. So he just repeated over and over, growing more frustrated by the minute, "Please."

Something changed in her eyes. She was much harder, almost angry. "Get back in the van."

"I won't." He realized he sounded like a petulant child, and must look ridiculous standing naked in the desert and refusing shelter. But he had to get to Mouse, before they knew he was gone. "I have to get back to her."

"Get in the van, Cyrus," Carrie repeated, pointing for emphasis. There was nothing to be done. She was stronger than him, he knew. And he was still drunk from the chemical. So he fell into the back of the van, weeping like a child. They would kill Mouse, and he would be alone again.

As they pulled onto the road, a brown bottle wrapped in a scorched rag slid to him as if pushed by a divine hand. If he'd believed in God, he would have thanked him.

The front seats were partitioned from the back by heavy canvas drapes. He wet the rag with the chloroform and thrust his arm through the opening between the curtains.

She tried to push his hand away, and the van swerved, nearly tossing him back. He clutched at the drapes and tried again, this time managing to cover her face. She had the sense to put on the brakes, and the vehicle slowed to a crawl as she went limp. Then her foot fell from the pedal and they rolled to a stop.

"We have to go back for her, because she's human," he explained as he pulled Carrie's rag doll body into the back. As he situated himself behind the wheel, he shook his head to clear it. "*Human.* That was the word I was searching for."

17

The Mouse

When I came to, I thought I was on a ship. In a storm. Then I recognized the van, and wondered who the hell was driving so badly.

And then I remembered Cyrus.

I pulled back the curtain and he shouted in surprise, swerving even worse than he'd already been, "Get back, Carrie, or I swear to God I'll stake you!"

"With what?" I demanded, reaching toward my back pocket.

He grabbed the stake he'd propped in the cup holder. "With this. Now sit down and shut up. We're going back for her."

"For who? Angie?" I laughed. "I'm sure you'll find a replacement for her."

"Angie?" He hit the accelerator hard, then let off abruptly. "No! Mouse. We have to go back for her before they figure out I'm gone. Damn it, is this the right way?"

A cold, sick feeling gripped my stomach. "Mouse?"

He glared at the road and hit the gas again. "Yes. It's what I call her. Her real name is just ridiculous. She's human."

"She was human?" I eased into the passenger seat, shock slowly numbing my body. "I didn't know she was human."

"She is. Is human," he insisted, pounding the steering wheel. "Am I even going the correct way?"

I nodded woodenly. I'd left a human being behind in that place? With those vampires? Trembling, I reached into my pocket and withdrew the key. "Take this."

He looked down for just a second, the car heading for an instant toward the shoulder as he did. "What is that, a marble?"

"It'll help you find the place. Unless…you want me to drive," I offered.

"No time," he answered tersely.

I was as eager to get the girl out of there as he appeared to be, but I wasn't willing to die in a fiery crash to do it. "Have you ever driven before?"

"No." He sounded impatient. "It looks much easier in the movies."

Ahead was the intersection just before the church. In the distance, where I should have seen the small, black shape of the burned-out ruin, the ghostly outline of the church broke the line of the horizon. Whatever spell the Fangs had cast on the place was wearing off.

"Maybe they've just gone and left her behind," I said hopefully. But I knew better. So did Cyrus.

The tires squealed as he pulled into the parking lot. If he thought the Fangs were still there, he was sure making plenty of noise.

Grabbing a stake, he kicked the door open. "They won't hurt me. They'll probably kill you, though."

"I'll take my chances." I pocketed a stake, too, just in case.

"Mouse!" he shouted as we entered the dark vestibule. But his voice fell silent at the sight of the sanctuary doors ripped from their hinges and lying like splinters of firewood on the carpet.

He seemed to freeze for a minute, his Adam's apple the only part of him moving as he swallowed. "No."

"Cyrus, wait," I begged as he ran toward the basement door. I wanted to go first, for some crazy reason intent on shielding him from seeing something terrible.

I was two steps behind him on the stairs. A single bulb hanging from the ceiling illuminated the apartment, and on the other side of the light I saw pale legs, barely distinguishable from the sheets, splayed at an unnatural angle across the bed.

The sight didn't stop him, didn't register, just as the sight of the bloody bedclothes didn't keep him from climbing onto the half-bare mattress beside her and slapping her face lightly. "Mouse? Wake up. Wake up."

"Cyrus…" I began, but he couldn't hear me. The girl's dead eyes were open. They seemed to stare accusingly at me.

"Mouse?" Grief sounded strange in his cultured, British voice. "Wake up. Please."

He buried his face close to her ruined neck, ripped from ear to ear by claws or teeth. He laid an open hand on her blood-stained hair, but his fingers curled into a fist and he lifted his head, making a sound that was a wail and a scream and a sob all in one.

My back to the cinder block wall, I slid to the floor. I'd never seen an emotion so genuine and powerful from him as this. I'd never imagined him capable of this kind of sincere feeling.

He loved her. It struck me like a cold hand slapping my face. Had I known? Had I sensed it and intentionally left her behind? The thought made me sick. If I had done such a thing, I'd abandoned a human to die a cruel and humiliating death, and I'd done it out of spite.

You didn't know. The voice of sanity in my head didn't belong to me. It was Nathan, in a moment of rare lucidity. And he was more concerned for me than for himself. That broke my heart more than it should have.

Nathan. I don't know if I can help you. I was tired, tired from my journey and tired from witnessing this carnage. I just wanted to crawl into bed and sleep for years.

Nathan's elusive clarity disappeared again, leaving me no way to escape Cyrus's raw hurt, which so closely resembled the agony in Nathan's soul.

"I'm sorry," Cyrus whispered, cradling the girl's limp body to his. "I'm so sorry."

Burdened by Nathan's pain and my own guilt over the death of this innocent girl, I closed my eyes. There was nothing I could do to fix my error, no way to comfort Cyrus or make things better. The life of this girl was snuffed out forever, and I'd caused it. Her death would hang like a noose around my neck for the rest of my life.

When Ziggy had died, I'd blamed myself for not protecting him, but I'd been able to lay most of the blame on Cyrus, who'd done the actual killing. I'd even blamed Nathan some, for overreacting to finding his son in a compromising position and driving him away. But I had no way of avoiding my guilt now, no way of reasoning it away. I'd fucked up, and now this girl was dead.

No wonder some vampires didn't enjoy the killing. How could they, with this feeling always hanging over them? For the first time, I began to understand a fraction of Nathan's pain and heartache. The agony I felt over this girl eerily mirrored the turmoil Nathan experienced now.

Something shifted in my mind, as though one of those jumbled puzzle pieces had fallen inexplicably into place. But I didn't have time to ponder it. When I looked up, Cyrus's cold, blue eyes locked on me with murderous intensity.

"You did this," he whispered. "You killed her."

"I didn't know." I rose slowly, aware the gesture betrayed

my fear of him. But what did I have to fear? He was human. I was a vampire. I had more physical strength and faster reflexes.

But he had nothing to lose, now.

"I tried to tell you." His voice was that calm one I knew so well from my days as his willing prisoner. A calm that would turn to fury without warning. "You didn't let me explain. And now she's dead."

"You will be, too, if we don't get out of here." It was an empty threat. The place was abandoned.

He shook his head with an expression of stony resolve. "I'm staying with her."

"There's nothing you can do for her now." I highly doubted there was anything that could have been done for her if we had gotten there just after they'd attacked.

"I deserted her." He kissed her bloodless forehead the way a mother would kiss her child's head. "I'm not going to do it again."

"You didn't desert her. You were kidnapped," I reminded him. Stupidly, since he'd apparently moved on from blaming me, and for a moment I'd stood a chance of not being staked while I slept. "Please, Cyrus. Let me get you out of here before your father finds you."

The words fell like a veil over him, obscuring the strangely human Cyrus before me long enough for him to assume the cold expression of the Cyrus I knew. Though it was familiar, it wasn't comforting.

"My father." He rolled the words in his mouth like a bit of food he was considering spitting out. "No, I think I'd like to see my father."

I forced away the chill that crept up my spine. "I can't let you do that. You know I can't."

"Why?" He laid her on the bed and stood. "Do you think you have the power to stop me?"

He advanced with the predatory grace I remembered. The languid movements that had made me weak-kneed with desire and terror alternately. Even without his vampire charisma, he seemed dangerous.

"You have to sleep sometime." The way he said it, as a casual comment and not a threat, made it all the more frightening. "When you do, I'll toss you out into the hot sand and watch you burn, the way you watched me burn."

I wanted to swallow, to soothe my suddenly dry throat, but I didn't want him to take it for a sign of weakness. So I spoke with a voice like a pack-a-day smoker. "And how did I watch you burn?"

"Without remorse." It didn't take him any time to answer. "With pleasure."

He turned away again, went to the dresser and pulled out clothes. The act shocked me. I'd grown so used to his nakedness, I hadn't truly seen it until now.

I waited until he had some pants on to respond. "That's not how I remember it."

He snorted. "I'm so concerned with how you remember it. Do please write it down, so I can read it should I ever find I care."

"Whether or not you care, you can't accuse me of being heartless." Shocking wetness stung my eyes, and I blinked it away. The thought that I was about to say things I wished so many times I could have said to him before lent an air of importance to the moment. It dried my words up, and I floundered to think of what I should say. "I wanted to save you so many times."

His back went rigid, and though he didn't face me, I saw his jaw tighten in profile. "Oh?"

"I wanted you to be a better person. I thought if I could see just a little of the good in you…" I shook my head. "But I never did. You never showed me an ounce of the good in you. If you had, I could have loved you."

He looked at the ceiling, his head limp on his neck as if in defeat. Then he rounded on me with frightening speed, catching me off guard and pushing my back to the wall.

His grip on my shoulders was painful, but I didn't struggle. He leaned close to my face, so close it was hard to focus on his furious eyes. "I was supposed to show you the good in me? I was supposed to make you love me?"

My breath exploded when he shoved me into the wall. He pointed to the corpse on the bed, stabbing the air forcefully as though he could wound it. "She loved me. She loved me! So maybe the problem didn't lie with me."

"She was trapped in a basement with you! You were the only other human here!" The words were cruel, but I couldn't stop them. "Of course she loved you, if you protected her from them!"

He slapped me, but his heart wasn't in it, and I barely felt the blow. "Don't say these things to me! Do you think I haven't thought them myself? She loved me. She loved me and I—"

His face crumpled and tears spilled over his eyelids. "She loved me," he repeated, grasping my shoulders, shoving me against the cinder blocks over and over.

I could have reacted with anger. I could have knocked him out and dragged him back to the van. There was still the threat of the Fangs, and the even greater threat that a passerby might notice the supposedly burned-down church had been reassembled.

Despite all this, I put my arms around him and pulled his body to mine, murmuring words of apology and comfort and true remorse. I couldn't look at the girl on the bed. She deserved better than what she'd gotten if she'd managed to crack Cyrus's cold facade.

The Fangs might have pulled him out of the afterlife, but she had made him human. It would take a lot more than few days in captivity and a bad case of Stockholm Syndrome to manage that.

I'd wanted to treat him as a thing, an ingredient in my recipe for saving Nathan. My plan had been to swoop in and snatch him up, then drive back to Grand Rapids without a care in my heart. If I had known then how naive and insensitive that plan was, an innocent girl's life could have been spared.

Cyrus wept so long, he ran out of tears, but the violent sobs that racked his body wouldn't subside. With my hands on his shoulders, I gently pushed him back. "Calm down. You'll make yourself sick."

"Calm down?" He glared at me through reddened eyes. "How can you tell me to calm down? She's dead!"

Okay, bad tactic. "I know she's dead, and it hurts you. But you're not doing her any favors if you stay here and get yourself killed."

He nodded, though I suspect he only forced himself to appear reasonable because he thought I didn't care or understand. "You're right." He rose and went to the bed. "We're not leaving her like this, though."

"Do you want to bury her?" It sounded extremely crass and earthy, but I didn't mean it that way.

It didn't bother him. I could tell by the way he looked her over, as though she were merely a fragile, valuable object and not a dead body, that he'd removed himself from the reality of her death. While the shell she'd left behind was still precious to him, he clearly didn't associate her with it.

"No. It's only sand out there. I don't want an animal finding her." His voice cracked slightly on the last words, but he didn't cry. "Get me some towels from the bathroom, so I can clean her up."

That's how we spent the rest of the night. Cyrus carefully

washed the blood from her skin and asked me to bandage her torn throat and the bite marks on the rest of her body. He combed her hair, despite the gore that matted it, and laid her head on the pillow. Using the technique I'd learned in medical school, we carefully changed the soiled sheets without moving her body from the mattress, then clothed her in the sundress that appeared to be her only article of clothing.

"The sun's almost up," Cyrus noted when we were finished, his voice strained and tired. "We should get going."

"You're coming with me?" I wondered at his motive. Grief or not, he was still the man who'd gleefully procured victims for his father's blood lust and killed innocent young girls for his own, sick pleasure. I couldn't fully trust him.

He nodded, never tearing his gaze from the girl's dead, staring eyes. Absently, he reached out and gently closed her eyelids with his thumbs. They eased slightly open again, giving her the look of a person asleep.

"I can't leave her here to—" he swallowed thickly, covering his eyes with one hand "—to rot."

"Do you think we should bury her?" I looked to the sky. The stars were beginning to fade. I didn't think we had enough time. At least I didn't. "The police are going to notice that this place has reassembled. They'll be here by morning. I'm surprised they haven't been yet. Do you really want to be burying a dead body when they arrive?"

"Oh, yes. That would be the worst thing that could happen to me, going to the electric chair." He laughed bitterly, but I don't think he really understood yet what it was to be human again. How important his life would be to him when he was close to losing it.

He covered his face with both hands, a gesture more of fatigue than grief. "We'll burn it." He fixed me with a determined stare. "We'll burn the whole place down."

Jennifer Armintrout

I left him alone with her while I searched the building for supplies we could use. The Fangs had, either in their haste to leave the place or out of sheer wastefulness, left a nearly full can of gasoline behind. I thanked God for small mercies and poured it sparingly in a line from the kitchen, around the pews in the sanctuary, and down the steps to where Cyrus knelt beside the bed, his hand covering the dead girl's stiff fingers.

"Is it done?" he asked, lifting his tear-stained face to look at me.

I had to clear my throat before I could speak. "Yes. Well, except I'm going to disconnect the gas line to the stove in the kitchen and let nature take its course. You should move the van. Get it clear."

"And what about you? How are you going to get clear?" He looked back to the girl and took a deep breath. "I don't want you to die over this."

"I thought you wanted to kill me," I said, trying to inject some humor into my voice. It fell horridly flat.

"Oh, I do. At least, I'm mad enough to kill you." His voice lowered to almost a whisper. "But I don't want you to die."

As bizarre as his logic sounded, I understood him. I'd stood over his bed once, wondering if I could kill him while he slept, so angry I probably could have done it. But I wouldn't have truly wanted him dead. "I'll be fine. But we have to hurry, before the gas evaporates."

Leaning over the girl, he gently kissed her bloodless lips and stroked her hair. Then, with a sudden violence that startled me, he reached down and tore a strip of material from her skirt. Closing the scrap in his fist, he lifted it to his nose and inhaled, pain creasing his forehead above his closed eyes. Then, just as quickly as he'd seemed to lose control again, he tucked the cloth into his pocket and turned away from the bed. "Let's go."

Arson is a bit more difficult than I expected. The stove was way too heavy to move on my own, so, after I lit a phone book on one of the burners, I held it away and turned all the dials to Light and blew out the pilot. As I hurried through the vestibule, I dropped the burning phone book on the gas trail. For a moment I worried that it wouldn't catch, and I stood, frozen in horror, as it appeared the flame would go out. Then, with a whoosh of oxygen being sucked away, flames blossomed to consume what was left of the white pages, traveling slowly down the path of saturated carpet. I turned and ran out the doors, across the cracked lot to where Cyrus waited beside the van on the other side of the road.

"Get behind the van!" I shouted, remembering too late the kind of wounds flying debris could cause. The gas in the kitchen ignited before he could move, and I dived for him, shielding him with my body until the noise of falling rubble hitting the pavement finished.

"My God," Cyrus whispered, climbing to his feet when I finally let him up.

My gaze fixed on the burning building, I nodded. "I didn't expect it to go up so fast."

We stood side by side, watching the fire. I tried not to think about the girl we'd left in the basement. When I looked at Cyrus, I knew that was all he thought of, and my chest ached with my guilt.

"Do you know where my father is?" Cyrus asked quietly, tears filling his eyes.

I didn't know if lying or telling the truth would be the best way to persuade him to leave with me, but dishonesty felt cheap after the postmortem ritual we'd just shared. "No. I know he's planning something, and I know I needed to find you."

He cocked his head, a bit of familiar Cyrus mannerism peeking through. "Really? How did you know?"

"The Oracle." I didn't bother to explain. In his vampire life, Cyrus had known the goings-on of nearly every vampire faction. I had no doubt he'd know who the Oracle was. "She told me your father is trying to become a god. But she didn't tell me what all that entails. She did say I needed to seek you out. That you would be in the land of the dead, with the toothsome ones."

Despite our grim circumstances, he chuckled. "Still speaks like Nostradamus. I never really cared for her, but she was on the mark with that prophecy."

"Cyrus, what is your father doing?" He had to know. The Oracle wouldn't have sent me all this way for nothing.

"I don't know." He looked back to the church. "But I'll do what I can to help you find out."

I blinked and turned to him. "You will?"

It seemed as if he'd never blink as he watched the flames leaping into the night sky. "If my father hadn't decided to raise me from the dead... I blame him for her death," he stated.

But I blamed myself. Because it was my fault. I could barely breathe with the knowledge of it.

The feeling of a piece falling into place nagged at me again, and I remembered my earlier observation, that the pain I felt from Nathan through the blood tie was the same as I felt over the girl's death.

And that's when I knew. Standing in the desert, watching the flames from the burning church blending in with the new day lightening the horizon, I realized the only demon possessing Nathan was his own.

I just didn't know how to save him from it.

I can't imagine my life without her, but every day it seems more likely that she'll be taken from me.

Max rubbed his eyes and reread the sentence. So far, Nathan's journal had provided insight into only one area of his life. The mopey, insecure part.

Looking up from the book, Max studied Bella. She lay on a nest of blankets and pillows she'd fashioned into a dog bed— her words, not his, tossed playfully at him when he'd asked what on earth she was doing—intently reading a tattered copy of *The Sanguinarius.* Max didn't put much stock in the book himself, but it seemed easier to let her read it than try to give her his own crash course in vampire lore.

It had surprised him when she'd said she'd never read it. Though it was at the top of the required reading list for vampire assassins, she'd told him the book had never been made available to werewolves during their Movement training. Max hoped he wasn't breaking any rules by sharing the book with her, but then remembered just how many rules they'd both broken already.

"Are you going to continue staring at me or are you going to finish invading your possessed friend's privacy?" She didn't look up as she spoke.

Max sighed. "I'm not getting anything here. Just pages and pages of how much he *loves* Carrie and how much *pain* it causes him."

"That is something." Bella sat up, the movement graceful and catlike, despite her canine heritage. "Sometimes all you need to reach the trapped soul is a piece of personal information. Perhaps if Carrie spoke to him—"

"There's other stuff, too." Max wanted to get Bella off that dangerous line of thinking. He wasn't going to be the one who fessed up to Nathan that he let Carrie read his diary. "Like his ex-wife."

"He is divorced?" She made a face. "I will never understand that human custom."

"It's not a custom, it's an exception," Max corrected. "I

don't understand it, either. If you just don't get married at all, it makes things a lot simpler."

"What I meant was, it is unnatural to be separated from your mate." She tossed a pillow at him.

He caught it and threw it back. "Nathan's not divorced. His wife died. He killed her."

"Why would he do such a thing?" The knowledge seemed to wound Bella.

Max flipped back a few pages and read, "'Every night I wish I'd done it differently. I wish I had let them starve me. If I had been strong then, I would be dead now, instead of living with this guilt.'" He snapped the book shut with one hand. "I'm guessing he ate her. Wasn't that in his file?"

"Perhaps in his sealed probation file," she snapped. "You speak of these things as though they do not matter. Because you are a creature without knowledge of death, life does not matter to you!" Her body trembled, with rage or fear or both, he couldn't tell.

Whether she was afraid or not, her accusation made him angry. He stood, fighting the urge to favor his left leg, which was engulfed in an unpleasant prickling sensation. "Listen, I know plenty about death." Marcus's face flashed through his memory, knifing pain through his chest. "I don't kill anymore."

"But you did. At one time, you did." It wasn't an indictment, just a simple statement of fact.

One he couldn't argue with. "Almost all of us have, at one time or another. And you're an assassin. You kill vampires. What's the difference?"

She sat up straighter, if that were possible, righteousness radiating around her like hellfire. "Because I kill those who prey upon the weak. I kill out of necessity for order and peace."

"Right, and indulging your animal instinct is just a perk."

This was rapidly becoming an argument. One he didn't feel like having. They'd been so peaceful for a few hours.

"I do not enjoy the killing." She said it through clenched teeth. "Those of us who appreciate the meaning of our true nature do not seek to become one of those murdering lupins."

To his amazement, she crossed herself and spit daintily after she said the name. He cleared his throat. "Yeah. Okay. Your true nature. Mind cluing me in?"

She reached for the zipper at the top of her high collar and tugged it down. Beneath her ever-present long-sleeved, black leather jacket, she wore only a bra. The horny department of his brain noted it matched the panties he'd glimpsed the day before, though she didn't wear them now. They were hanging over the shower rod in the bathroom.

He didn't have time to dwell on the thought of her naked body beneath the jeans she'd borrowed from Carrie. As Bella shrugged the jacket off her shoulders, he became more interested in the dark lines of text wrapping her upper arms.

She held one arm away from her body so he could read it. Some was Latin, some Hebrew, some a strange language he couldn't identify, and some Italian. The words all followed their native course, up and down, right to left, left to right. He picked out a single strand of Latin and translated it easily. "'A debt owing to the death of the God-Man, Yeshua, Joshua, Jesus the Christ of Nazareth, never to be repaid.'"

The sentence switched unfathomably to Italian, and he lost his ability to read it. Shaking his head, he grasped her other arm. "'The seed of Pilate will be sown on barren fields, the harvest of atonement will mock him as killer of the lamb. Let his blood be on our heads and the heads of our children.'"

"Wolves," Bella said quietly. "All of us stem from the descendants of one man. The Christ-killer."

Max released her and stood, scrubbing his hand over his face. "Pontius Pilate?"

If he'd believed in God it would have freaked him out.

"It is a curse. We seek ways of atoning, to repay the blood debt." She chuckled bitterly. "But how great is the debt of a dead God?"

"I've read the Bible. He was *supposed* to die." Great, now they were having a theological discussion. "It kind of ruined the end if he didn't."

She shrugged, a little too easy in the acceptance of her fate. "Judas Iscariot burns in hell, as well, but the story would not have been fulfilled if he had not betrayed Christ. There is no rhyme or reason to God's wrath. It is something I have come to accept."

It was a heavy thought, and it weighed down Max's mood considerably. "That seems kind of pessimistic and lazy to me."

She pulled her jacket on, momentarily drawing his attention back to her cleavage. "We hear the story of our burden every day as children. When I came of age, my father had it branded into my skin. It is a reminder that this curse is a part of me."

Max chuckled. "I suspect this has more to do with the differences between lupins and werewolves than either side lets on."

A slight smile tilted her lips. "You vampires think you know everything. But you are right. The recent division over science versus magic only served to widen the rift between our factions and drive us to align with the Movement. Lupins cling to the old Roman ways, while we werewolves have embraced the earth."

The admission seemed to close the subject. She turned back to *The Sanguinarius,* leafing through the pages as though her mind wasn't really on the material contained there.

Max cleared his throat. "I'm going to get something to eat before I try and read any more of Nathan's handwriting. Want anything?"

"Does a vampire have anything to eat, besides blood?" Some of her teasing humor was back in her voice.

It relieved a bit of the angry tension between them, even if it seemed forced. "I'm sure he's fresh out of kibble, but, yes, there's food. Contrary to popular belief, we can eat. Some of us even enjoy it."

She followed him to the kitchen, which seemed smaller than usual when she was in it. Max grabbed the teakettle from the dish strainer beside the sink and turned to set it on the burner. Bella picked that moment to try and squeeze past him, and they bumped into each other awkwardly.

Their mumbled apologies did nothing to ease the other kind of tension Max felt. He was too aware of his body, definitely too aware of her body in relation to his, and far too aware of what he wanted their bodies to be doing.

"You want me."

He opened his mouth to give her what would probably be a shocked, not witty response, but he choked on his own spit and coughed violently for a long minute before catching his breath. *Smooth, Harrison.*

"It is nothing to be ashamed of," she assured him. "I am very good looking. And to a vampire I must seem very exotic."

"I'm not attracted to you," he wheezed, pounding his chest with his fist. "If anything, I'm barely tolerating having you around. I don't like werewolves."

She laughed. Not a friendly laugh. A mocking laugh. "Right."

"Is it really that unbelievable to you that someone might not find you attractive?" He tried to sound arrogantly amused, but it didn't come off that well. He turned to the refrigerator and opened the door, searching for another bag of the premium B positive he'd found before. "Listen, I'm sure that as far as your species goes, you're a catch. But I'm not into the whole doggy-style thing."

"We would not have to do it doggy-style." She pressed against him, full body, front to his back. Her hand snaked across his shoulder, to his jaw, urging him to turn his head.

He did. His body came with it. He slipped his hands into the back pockets of her jeans and pulled her hips forward. "So, you *were* coming on to me earlier."

"I did not realize how blatant I would have to be to get your attention." She wound her arms around his neck and kissed him, not on the lips, but at the corner of his mouth. Her skin was shockingly warm, but he knew it was just because he was room temperature.

She spoke again, her voice a low, sexy whisper against his cheek. "We are not in an ideal situation. But I am attracted to you. And we are adults. What's the harm in releasing some of that…tension?"

Max couldn't argue with that logic, so he let her pull him to the linoleum, mentally rehearsing the apology he'd have to make for committing unspeakable acts of carnal pleasure on Nathan's kitchen floor.

18

Rocks and Hard Places

Cyrus had fantasized about two methods of killing Carrie as he drove through the stark, burning desert.

One way would have been to pull down the curtain and let the sunlight hit her sleeping body. But he'd dismissed it outright. She would probably live long enough to wrap herself in the canvas and chloroform him again. The trip would be unpleasant as it was. It would be worse if he had to spend every day lashed to the passenger seat with bungee cords. That was what she had threatened, and he knew she'd do it.

The other way was much more fun to fantasize about. He would pull over to the side of the road and climb in back with her, weeping and in need of comfort. When she tried to put her traitorous arms around him, he would sink the stake into her back.

But with no one to drive at night while he slept, the trip would, again, increase in difficulty. Not to mention the fact he had no money and only the clothes on his back. He wouldn't get far on those.

He gripped the steering wheel tighter. No, that wasn't the only reason. He couldn't kill her, because every time he imagined it, he remembered the tender way she'd helped him care for Mouse, and then he thought of Mouse looking down on him from the proverbial white clouds of heaven and being disappointed in him.

It was a silly thing to think of. He'd been dead before. He knew what happened. Washed-out, blue nothingness. On one hand, he hoped Mouse wasn't let down by the reality of the afterlife. On the other hand, his mortal soul dared to doubt she truly went to the same place he'd been when he'd died. Perhaps that realm was hell, reserved only for vampires and sinners. Despite her indiscretion with him, she'd possessed a pure heart.

Guilt, an emotion that proved to be a real nuisance now that he bothered to feel it, clenched his gut. Maybe what they'd done together had barred her forever from the heaven she'd believed in so deeply. Those blasted saints she'd prattled on about had certainly been prized for their chastity. He wished for a moment there were some number he could dial, someone he could phone up and explain it all to. *Listen, it wasn't really her fault. Extenuating circumstances. You'd really be making a mistake if you blamed her.*

He thought of the stories she'd told him, the ones where the pure, good-hearted maidens believed so deeply in Christ and his Blessed Mother that even something so shameful as being unwillingly defiled by a man didn't keep them from beatification. That certainly had to be the answer here. He'd been the demonic monster preying upon her flesh, never able to touch her soul.

Come now, let's not be dramatic. He pressed the brake pedal with his left foot—he didn't understand how Carrie thought he should be able to use only the right one—and rolled the van to a halt at a stop sign. There was a strange grinding noise, which he chalked up to faulty mechanics, and he rested his head for a moment on the wheel.

Of course Mouse had gone to her heaven. It was impossible that she hadn't. No man, God or not, could turn her away. In Cyrus's mind, she rivaled the Blessed Virgin in purity.

He pulled across the intersection and brought the behemoth van up to speed. How could what he and Mouse had done have been a sin, anyway? They were two consenting adults, and they'd done it out of love. Well, at least he had. She had as much as told him she was settling for the experience.

He wouldn't let himself think that. She had loved him. And someone had taken her away. He didn't solely blame Carrie for his pain. Though her actions had condemned Mouse, she would never have been looking for him in the first place if it weren't for his father. In fact, Jacob Seymour had been responsible for the death of all of Cyrus's loves. When he found him, Cyrus would make the Soul Eater pay.

"I've done everything you asked of me. How could you?"

The rustle of Carrie's nylon sleeping bag in the back brought him to the present. Her voice sought him through the thick canvas drapes. "Are you praying?"

"You were dreaming. Go back to sleep." Prayer! What a novel idea. He was a human, after all. That meant God, if he existed, had to care about him. Enough of those door-to-door missionaries had told him that. Of course, they'd recanted and cursed him as the devil right before he'd killed them, but they would be happy to know their message had sunken in.

God, Jesus, whoever I'm supposed to direct this prayer to, I'm sorry for what I did to her. Cyrus's breath froze in his chest, as if someone had stopped up his lungs and the air couldn't escape. *Please, don't hold it against her. Please, let her be okay where she is. Let her know I did—do—truly love her. It wasn't a game this time. I swear it.*

It would be the last time he admitted it, to himself or anyone else, he decided. It hurt far too much, and what purpose could the pain possibly serve? He'd keep it at the back of his mind, until he'd found his father and gotten his revenge.

It wouldn't be easy. He would probably get himself killed in the process. But he would find the man who'd been a monstrous father and a crueler sire. He would find him and Mouse would be avenged.

When Cyrus woke me at sundown, dark circles ringed his eyes. I'd heard him a few times during the day, talking to himself in a way that suggested he didn't realize he was actually speaking.

I probably looked as worn-out as he did. It was hard to sleep, to let my guard down when the person in the driver's seat seemed to be slowly losing his mind.

"Are you okay?" I asked as I eased from the back of the van into the front seat.

"I have been better. I'll survive." He slid into the passenger seat and buckled himself in. "But I need some food."

I thought of the dwindling cash supply in the back. "Will fast food do?"

Surprisingly, he didn't make a face or a snide comment, or reject the idea right out. He simply shrugged and said, "So long as it isn't the one with that insipid clown."

We rode in silence until the next town, where we found a burger joint with a drive-through. Cyrus had a voracious appetite, and he tore through his meal with uncharacteristically bad table manners.

"You're not a vampire anymore. That stuff is terrible for you," I reminded him.

"This stuff is terrible, period." He seemed to remember himself, and wiped his mouth with one of the cheap paper napkins. "It's greasy and unpleasant, but I haven't eaten in a day. I must bow to the demands of the human stomach."

"So, they kept you fed, then?" What a bizarre thing to make conversation about. *I understand the vampires who brought you back from the dead and held you hostage treated you well?*

He didn't look at me, but squinted at the starry sky through the windshield. "No. Mouse did most of the cooking. I do know how to microwave a hot dog, though."

"Well, at least you won't starve when you're on your own." It occurred to me then that I imagined a future for him beyond whatever would happen when we returned to Grand Rapids. With every passing moment, Cyrus was becoming more of a person and less of a monster to me.

He seemed suddenly uncomfortable with the subject, becoming more interested in his soda than our conversation. When he spoke again, it seemed a wall had gone up, closing off both the newly human Cyrus and the familiar, terrifying one who'd sired me. "So, the Oracle said the Soul Eater is trying to become a god. Did she say what type?"

Temporarily stunned by the fact he'd referred to Jacob Seymour by his common label and not as his adored father, I took a moment to answer. When the full import of his question sank in, it settled like a lead weight in my gut. "What do you mean, what kind?"

Cyrus sighed, clearly annoyed that I hadn't done my research. "You know. A demigod? A sacrificial god? A god of seasonal rites or fertility?"

"I have no idea. She just said a god. You'll pardon me for not inquiring further, but she was trying to twist my head off at the time." I shifted in my seat. The long nights of driving were taking their toll on my tailbone.

"It doesn't matter, anyway." Cyrus waved his hand as though apologizing by way of dismissal. "They all basically involve the same process."

"I had no idea vampires could just up and become gods." The things they didn't bother to print in *The Sanguinarius*.

"Anyone can become a god. All it takes is a collection of

souls." He paused in contemplation, his fingertips pressed together in a steeple. "They don't even have to be dead. I don't know why Father just doesn't convince some UFO religion in California that he's a messiah. It would be easier than the way he's going about it."

My brain shouted, *Could you be more cryptic?* When my mouth opened, the statement became a bit more polite. "And how is he going about it?"

With maddening slowness, Cyrus reached to fiddle with the dials on the dashboard console. He flipped the switch for the heater, then leaned his seat back. "Well, I'm here, obviously, and I wouldn't be unless Father needed me. Since there's only one ritual I know of that would need me alive, I can only assume he's out to consume the souls of the vampires he created."

I swerved the van. "What?"

Cyrus yelped in a very undignified manner as his upper body slid sideways from the seat. "What the hell are you doing?"

"You said he's trying to eat the vampires he made?" There was a strange, hysterical edge to my voice. Funny, I didn't feel hysterical, but maybe my emotions hadn't caught up to my body yet.

"Well, the ones he hasn't eaten already." Cyrus shot me an annoyed glare as he returned his seat to an upright position. "Are we going to just sit in the middle of the road all night, then?"

Grinding my teeth, I lifted my foot from the brake and pressed the accelerator.

He made a great show of checking over his body, in case a part might have flown off, I guess, then settled against the seat once more. "There's a ritual he was looking for back in the seventeenth century. Apparently, a soul eater who emerged in the prehistoric era endeavored to become a god who was eventually worshipped in ancient Greece. The ritual he used was one of the first recorded occult ceremonies."

I swallowed the acidic fear that stung my throat. "Did it work?"

"Ever hear of Hades?" Cyrus laughed and shook his head as though he were speaking of an old friend. "I can't say for certain, but Father was too obsessed with the ritual for it not to be the one he's using now. I believe it entails consuming the souls of all those he's killed. He must have been working on it for centuries."

Cyrus lapsed into thoughtful silence again. Just when I was about to speak, he came to vicious life, pounding the dashboard with both fists. I jumped, accidentally colliding with the horn.

He pounded his fists again. "He should have told me. I served him faithfully—he should have told me!"

"He couldn't tell you," I said gently. "Then you would have known he was going to kill you."

My words had no impact. "No wonder he wanted me to give asylum to those disgusting bikers all those years back…."

"Actually, it was only two months," I corrected, but again, he didn't seem to hear.

"I should have known. I should have known he was planning something like this." Cyrus shook his head, a look of pure disgust on his face. "I worshipped him. If he'd asked it of me, I would have let him take my soul."

"No, you wouldn't have." I remembered the way Cyrus had knelt beside his father's casket as though it were a holy relic. It wasn't a flattering truth I was about to give him, but it was truth at least. "You were too selfish to have done something like that."

"You're probably right." A thin smile crossed his lips. "You know, I was thinking of killing you today."

"I was pretty much counting on you trying." I'd heard him mumbling to himself shortly after he'd begun the drive at sunup. So I'd kept the chloroform handy and hidden all the stakes in the van at the bottom of my sleeping bag.

"You're not going to scream and rave at me?" He chuckled. "That's not the Carrie I remember."

"Well, the Carrie you remember has spent two months trying to get over you." I nearly choked on my tongue at my Freudian slip. "I meant, trying to get over what you did to me. You don't make me as nervous anymore."

"You're trying to get over me?"

Of course, he wouldn't let it die without comment. No matter how much had changed during the past two months, it wasn't enough to beat down his ego.

"Keep in mind when I say that, I mean everything about you." I paused and decided I wasn't quite willing to dwell on the implications of that statement. "You know, the sick, horrible things you did to me. Your total disregard for humanity, mine included. Things like that."

"I've been thinking about that, as well." His voice was suddenly husky, as though he was about to cry.

Please, please don't let him have an Oprah moment right here while I'm driving. I don't think I could handle that.

"That was, of course, until you accidentally murdered..." He turned his face away, so that when I looked at him, all I could see was his profile. "That was cheap. Of course, I can't fully blame you for what happened to her."

"How generous." I swallowed the lump of guilt that formed in my throat. "I am sorry. You know I don't like to see innocent people hurt."

"But my father does." Cyrus shook his head. "No matter. Let's talk of something else, shall we?"

"Like what? The weather?" Unbelievable. He was exactly like his old self, if he thought it was appropriate to dismiss the fact he'd laid her death on me. "You're really an asshole."

"Carrie, I'm sorry." He closed his eyes, grimacing.

He hadn't meant to apologize. And he regretted it. My breath came out with an angry, disbelieving grunt. "Well, don't kick your ass over it or anything!"

"That's a very difficult thing for me to say to you! You rejected me!" His hand clenched to a fist on the armrest.

I remembered too well his tendency toward violence, and I edged away in my seat a little. Fat lot of good it would do me, though, the centimeter shift I managed, and it only exacerbated the stiffness in my lower back. I forced my irritation—and nervousness—away. "In all fairness, you kind of killed your chances when you ripped out my heart."

"After you came into my home and betrayed me." His voice dropped to a deadly murmur. "After you willingly came to my bed, plotted behind my back every moment I was inside you."

If I could have taken my hands off the wheel, I would have slapped him. "I knew humanity wouldn't change you."

He looked startled and wounded by my comment. "You don't know a damn thing about how I've changed."

I shook my head. "Cyrus, we shared a telepathic bond once. I saw exactly how deviant your mind is. You're making an attempt, and a pretty lame one at that, to convince me everything I saw in your head was a lie?"

"No, it wasn't a lie." He covered his face with his hands, a deceptive piece of body language that made him appear less dangerous. I knew better.

Or I thought I did. He didn't lash out again, and I could only attribute his sudden defeat to sleep deprivation. "You're tired. You should climb in the back and sleep."

"No, I want to say this to you." He rubbed his forehead with the thumb and first two fingers of one hand. "I was a monster when you knew me. I can't change that. But I'm not that man anymore. I don't know how else to explain it to you, except to say that she—Mouse—she did something to me that no one else ever did, and it made me different. Ah, I sound like a complete asshole."

And he did, a little. I'd never bought into the idea that a person could be changed by something as miraculous as a bond with another person, though Cyrus had come damn close to changing me for the worse when we were blood tied. There was a genuineness in his words, though, as though he actually believed he had changed. *If he believes it, that's enough to make it so, right?*

I swallowed, my tongue suddenly dry and thick in my mouth. "What did she do to you?" *I hope it's nothing disgusting.* I couldn't shake the suspicion that this outpouring of deep emotion might be a setup, another way for him to trap me into a gruesome shock. He'd always been so good at that.

"She said she loved me." He laughed a little, but there was only sorrow in the sound.

He'd asked me once if I loved him. Well, actually, he'd demanded I say the words. But I'd refused. Guilt speared through me now. Was that really all it would have taken? If I had just kept lying to him, made him believe I'd loved him, could we have been happy together?

I pushed the thought from my mind. Of course I'd been attracted to him. He'd been an attractive man. It hadn't helped that we'd been linked through a powerful emotional, telepathic connection. But if I'd bent to his will that night, it wouldn't have changed him for the better. It would have condemned me to life as a monster.

You weren't good enough to change him. The realization brought tears dangerously close to the surface, and I cleared my throat, blinking rapidly, to chase them away.

If he noticed my distress at all, Cyrus didn't say a thing. "That was the key. No one else, not my wives, not my brothers, not even my father, ever told me they loved me. I think I must have endeavored to make myself…unlovable, for lack of a better term. I was daring someone to prove my perception of myself wrong."

"I'm glad you know yourself so well." Torn between remorse and rage, I kept my eyes on the road, not trusting myself to look at him.

"I had a lot of time to think today." The noise of his seat belt releasing indicated he was preparing to move into the back. "I'm going to go to sleep."

As he half stood, easing between the seats, he put his hand on my arm. His touched burned, just as I remembered. "I'm sorry for all the times I hurt you, Carrie. Whether or not you believe it, I needed you to hear it."

Pointedly, I removed his hand from my body. "I appreciate the sentiment." I knew it sounded sarcastic, and I wanted to take the words back, because I had truly meant them. It did mean something to me to know he was sorry.

I just couldn't trust him yet.

When I was sure Cyrus slept—I could tell by the atrocious snores only truly exhausted people produce—I took the cell phone from the glove compartment and dialed Max.

It took him forever to answer, and for a moment I grew alarmed. Nothing short of death or dismemberment could stop that man from answering a phone. Finally, he did pick up, obviously out of breath as he greeted me with a curt, "Harrison."

"What's the matter?" My first thought was that something had happened to Nathan.

Max's thin laughter did nothing to assure me. "Nothing, nothing. I'm just…you know…getting ready to go out and fight the good fight."

"You're supposed to be looking for Nathan, not fighting anyone." I was used to Max acting nonchalant in dire circumstances, but he sounded strange, even for him. "Are you sure nothing's wrong?"

He laughed again. There was a definite edge of nervousness in his tone. "Oh, yeah. I'm just, you know… So, are you there yet?"

I'd almost forgotten why I'd called him in the first place. "Actually, I'm on the way back."

"With Cyrus?"

"With Cyrus." I glanced guiltily into the rearview mirror, afraid for a second I would see him there, eavesdropping. Then he exhaled loudly in his sleep, and I almost laughed with relief. "And he snores."

"Did he have any information?"

I chewed my lip. There was so much to the story Max didn't have to know. My gaze met its guilty twin in the rearview mirror. I wouldn't be able to keep silent forever about the girl in the church, or the horrible jealousy she'd inspired in me. Today was not forever, though. I'd just give him the bare minimum he needed to keep his end of this operation afloat.

"Carrie, are you still there?" He didn't seem worried, but annoyed.

Impatient much, Maximilian? "Sorry. Keeping my eyes on traffic."

He sighed loudly into the phone. "So, what's the story?"

I filled him in on what I had learned about the Soul Eater's ritual.

When I finished, Max said, "Well, I can tell you for sure we're being watched."

"By who?" His Movement connections really came in handy.

"The Soul Eater. I found a nest of his goons last night when

I was tailing Nathan." He yelped, then muttered under his breath, "Sorry. I pinched myself."

"Max, is someone there with you?" Maybe he thought I would be angry with him for, er, entertaining while Nathan was in danger. I was a little irked, but I wasn't going to rip his head off. It was Max, after all. I wasn't entirely sure he could exist on blood alone, he was so dependant on sex.

"No, not at all." The tone of his response was a little too bright. It wasn't in sync with the question I'd asked.

An evil smile twisted my lips. "Then you won't have a problem admitting that you're gay."

"What?" He laughed. "Why would I say something like that?"

"If you don't say it, I know you're with a woman right now." Max Harrison admitting he was gay? Never going to happen, especially if an attractive female could hear.

"You're being childish."

Yes, I was. "Say it. Say 'I, Max Harrison, like dick.' Say it."

"Fine!" He let out an annoyed breath. "I found the other assassin. She's here right now."

"What?" The wheel slipped from my hand for a second and I scrambled to regain my hold before I drove us off the shoulder. "What's she doing there?"

"Calm down, she's cool. She's on our side, at least for now." He cleared his throat. "The Movement didn't fill her in entirely on her assignment, and she's reassessed her priorities."

"You should, too," I snapped. "I can't believe you're letting the enemy waltz around my house!"

"She's not the enemy. Christ, Carrie, haven't you listened to a word I've said? Now that she knows what's really going on, she's going to help us!" Max shouted, and the phone crackled with feedback.

"Yeah. She's going to help herself to Nathan's head after you lead her right to him!" I was glad miles of highway separated us, because I was mad enough to stake him.

"Nathan attacked her!" Max followed his statement with a loud curse. "She barely survived. But she remembers the attack, and she knows he's been possessed. And she knows the Soul Eater is involved."

Max wouldn't fight so hard if he had a doubt as to her loyalty to our cause. And he wouldn't let a woman sway his judgment. He might have been a womanizer, but he wasn't stupid. But I wouldn't give in to him right now. I was still too angry. "Fine. Tell me more about the Soul Eater."

"Not much more to tell. There were bodies everywhere, but no guards posted. They've been there awhile. I think they're looking for Nathan, too." He paused. "Listen, he was getting pretty close, but we chased him off. I'm thinking it's probably not a good idea for him to be loose, if his big daddy is looking for him."

"That's what I was thinking, too. But what are we going to do? I mean, we can catch him, but how are we going to keep him?" I drummed the steering wheel with my fingertips.

He snorted. "We could use the handcuffs I found in his bedroom. You perv."

"You snooped through our things, you deal with your disgust on your own time." I was just glad Max wasn't able to see my mortified blush as I thought of exactly what those handcuffs had been used for. The same kind of mortified blush I'd had the night Nathan had jokingly—but only by half—brought them home. A vampire who'd escaped police capture had been wearing them when he'd run into Nathan, who'd still been on Movement-training autopilot. After Nathan had staked the unfortunate jailbird, he'd retrieved the cuffs.

"Have some respect for the dead, Nathan."

"Come on. I bet the dead, and the GRPD, would want to see these put to good use."

And boy, did we ever put them to good use.

"Did I lose you?" Max's voice startled me out of my steaming memories.

I cleared my throat guiltily. "No, I'm here. It's not a bad idea, catching him and locking him up. Just be careful. Don't kill him. And don't let what's-her-name do it, either."

"No way I'm gonna let that happen." He sounded certain.

That was enough for me. "Okay. Just—"

"Be careful?" He wasn't mocking me. It was clear from his tone he knew exactly how much I depended on Nathan. "You know I will."

"Thank you, Max."

After we hung up and the sound of the road was the only thing to distract me from my situation, I relied on Max's words as my life raft.

It kept me from imagining Nathan's death at the hands of the monster who'd created him.

19

Rescue

To Max, it seemed the best way to find Nathan was to retrace their search of the neighborhood they'd been in last night. As fast as possible.

"Let's go this way." Without waiting for Bella's answer, because he knew it would be a contradiction of what he'd just said, Max dove into the hedges.

"Not that way!"

He heard the gentle hum of an electric fence a moment before it bit into his ankles. "Fuck!"

"It is your own fault," she admonished, laughing as he stumbled backward and fell on his ass. "I could smell it."

"You can smell electric fences?" He scowled at her. If this had happened to anyone else, even her, he would have found it funny. Especially if it had been her.

She shrugged. "Not anymore. Now I smell ozone and burned skin. Let me see."

He yanked his leg back as she knelt beside him. "It's fine."

"I am sure it is." She grasped his ankle. "Let me see."

"Fine." He rolled up his pant leg, revealing the line of pink, puffy skin where the evil wire had attacked him.

"That does not look as bad as I thought it would." She seemed impressed.

"I aim to please." He didn't realize the double meaning his words could take on until she glanced away, her olive skin tinged red.

He closed his eyes and grimaced, as though his harshly drawn breath could suck the words back in. "I didn't mean…"

Standing, she acted as if her jacket needed serious adjusting. "I have his scent, but it is old. Maybe it is from last night?"

Damn. Max thought things had gone well between them. After a good long romp on Nathan's kitchen floor, they'd spent the day researching and trading not-so-subtle innuendos. Then he'd asked a simple question, and it had all fallen apart.

"Hey, can werewolves become vampires and vice versa?" he'd asked, looking up from *A Warlock's Demon Compendium.* The book was about two miles over the Dungeons and Dragons nerd county line, and he'd needed a break.

Her face had gone pale, and she'd looked quickly down at the notebook Nathan used to keep track of local vampires. "I do not know what you mean."

"Yes, you do. You're a smart girl." Max had stood and moved to join her in her nest of blankets on the floor, and she'd scooted away nervously. "Let's pretend you bit me right now. Would I become a werewolf?"

"I would have to bite you with intent." She'd cleared her throat noisily. "That is, I would have to really want you to become a werewolf. But I do not know if it is possible to be both."

"Right. Okay. So, if I drained your blood and fed you mine, would you become a vampire?" A strand of hair had fallen into her eyes, and he'd reached to brush it back.

She'd leaped about a foot into the air and slapped his hand away. "No! No, it is not possible. Do you have nothing better to do than pester me with foolish questions?"

After that, she'd become worse than the coldhearted bitch who'd threatened to kill him a few nights previously. She'd become completely indifferent to him.

She headed off down the sidewalk now, her arms hugged tight around her middle. He didn't follow. She didn't get far before she realized she was alone.

"Are you coming, vampire?"

Vampire. A big difference from the way she'd said his name over and over the night before, when he'd had his head buried between her legs. His scalp was still sore from where she'd practically yanked his hair out.

"So, it's back to vampire now, is it?" he asked when she finally turned around.

Stalking toward him once more, her posture rigid, she narrowed her golden eyes. "What should it be?"

He folded his arms across his chest. "Well, considering the fact I spent a great deal of last night doing things to you that are illegal in most states, I thought we were on a first-name basis."

Guiltily, she eased her stance. "Max, last night meant a lot more to you than it did to me."

"What?" His voice cracked. *Smooth to the end, Harrison.*

Bella made a face and took a step back. "I am very good at reading people. You cannot disguise your feelings."

"What?" He sputtered this time. "I don't have any feelings!"

"You talk in your sleep."

If he'd been warm-blooded, Max's blood would have run cold. Her palm burned where it cupped his jaw, and he stepped away. "Don't!"

"I do not want to hurt you, Max." She lifted her hands help-lessly. "And I do not mean to embarrass you by saying these things. I thought you should know—"

He turned away. "Whatever."

"Max, please!" She grabbed his arm. "I thought it was just a fling. I would never have suggested it if I had known you had feelings for me."

"I told you, I don't have any feelings!" As far as he knew, it was true. Sure, he'd had the passing odd thought, but he hadn't dwelled on them, for Christ's sake, and he certainly hadn't consciously called them up. He wasn't interested in her or in any other woman that way.

"I do not believe that," she insisted. "Whatever it is you feel for me, your subconscious wanted me to know. And I do not want to hurt you when you realize you are not part of my life plan."

"Part of your life plan?" He rubbed his temples. What had he said? What sappy things did his big mouth blab that she'd misinterpreted to be about her? "This can't be happening. You're on the wrong side of this conversation!"

"Max," she began, her eyes growing wide.

"No, forget this. I'm out of here." He turned to leave, only to collide with a solid wall of flesh and muscle.

"Max, watch out!"

It was too late. He tumbled to the ground with his attacker and rolled into the street.

The smell of ruined blood jolted his body like the electric current of the fence. They'd been out to find Nathan, and instead, he'd found them.

"The tranquilizer!" Max shouted, kicking his friend backward. They'd decided that drugging Nathan would be the easiest way to capture him. Max had just thought Bella would be faster with her Movement-issue tranq gun.

"The tranquilizer," he repeated, then cursed as Nathan broke free and plunged through the hedge.

This time, Max made sure not to get tangled in the electric fence. By the time he fought his way clear of the branches, Nathan had already vaulted over the back wall of the yard they'd stumbled into. "Bella, hurry your ass up!"

She charged past him with speed he had no chance of matching, so he didn't bother to try. For a moment, he considered waiting for her to bring their quarry back. She'd certainly get to him first. Then Max remembered what she'd looked like after her last tangle with Nathan, and fierce protectiveness forced him into motion.

I am not worried about her because of the things she said. I am just looking out for a friend who might be in trouble. Two friends who might be in trouble. I'm doing a good thing. And I have no feelings.

He scrambled up the wall, thanking God or the devil or whoever was responsible, for his unusual ability to scale vertical obstacles. The first thing he saw on the other side was the gun, lying uselessly in the grass. He lifted his gaze and saw Bella and, looming over her, pinning her to the damp ground, Nathan.

"Shoot him!" she shouted. Battle-calm though she might be, her eyes were wide. She was terrified. "Shoot him!"

The creature masquerading as his best friend snarled, a fierce sound that raised the hair on the back of Max's neck. Nathan's face twisted for a moment into feeding mode, then back to his more recognizable features. But it wasn't the monster Max saw there. Nathan's eyes were watery and rimmed in red, his forehead creased in inhuman concentration. He opened his mouth to issue a desperate scream. "Shoot me!"

Max didn't hesitate, and pulled the trigger. He wasn't sure he would have wasted time if Bella had insisted he stake Nathan. Seeing her that way, trembling and helpless, Max had a horrible realization shoot through him: that he would have killed Nathan if it was the only way to stop him from hurting her.

The shot struck Nathan in the chest, and for a moment, Max worried that killing him was exactly what he'd done. He raced toward his fallen friend.

When their eyes met, Nathan seemed to understand his concern. "It's not in the heart. It's not in the heart." Then he closed his eyes.

Max collapsed on the grass beside him, but was back on his feet a second later. *Bella.*

She lay sprawled on the ground, taking fast and shallow breaths. When she turned her head and caught sight of him, she smiled weakly. "I am sorry, I thought I had him."

"Are you okay? Did he hurt you?" Max dropped to his knees beside her. "You shouldn't move, you know, in case anything is broken."

"I should stay here until the owners of that palace call the authorities and have me hauled away for trespassing?" She stood slowly, brushing off her clothing and shooing away his hands. "I will be all right. Besides, we have to get him back to his apartment before the drugs wear off."

"How long do we have?" Max looked reluctantly away from her, to where Nathan lay in the grass, his chest barely moving.

"Ninety minutes at the most. Only enough so I can make a clean getaway." She shrugged one shoulder as if trying to work it back into the socket. "I have never had to transport anyone before."

Max eyed his friend's body, then the woman at his side. "I think he'll be too heavy on my own, but I don't want you to help me if you're not up to it."

"I am fine. Treating me like porcelain is not going to change anything," she said firmly.

He didn't argue. There was no point, as long as she believed he was completely infatuated with her.

That's the problem, he decided. *Her wishful thinking.*

Knowing that made it much easier for him to endure the ride back to the apartment.

By the time they got Nathan up the stairs, the tranquilizer had nearly worn off. He dangled between them—Bella at his feet, Max lifting his shoulders—like a very drunk, very heavy piece of supertenderized meat.

"Take him to the bedroom," Max ordered, nodding in the direction of Nathan's room. "He's got a brass headboard. We'll be able to cuff him to that."

"You came up with that pretty easy," Nathan mumbled with a tired-sounding laugh. "Been fantasizing about me?"

"If he is lucid, perhaps it is unnecessary to restrain him," Bella suggested, her gold eyes locking with Max's for an uncomfortable moment.

He looked away. He didn't want to be accused of staring googley-eyed at her or anything.

"No!" Nathan stiffened, and Max struggled to keep hold of him.

Grunting with the strain of supporting his friend's body, Max motioned toward the bedroom with another quick jerk of his head. "I saw what he was going to do to you. No offense to either of you, but until we get this mess sorted out, we're keeping him locked up."

Bella looked as though she would argue, but closed her mouth in a tight line. "It is a good sign he is talking," she said, clearly trying to sound cheerful for Max's benefit.

"Is it?" he asked through clenched teeth. He didn't need her pity optimism.

She dropped the act at once. "I do not know. Maybe?"

"It means he's not possessed. At least, not by a demon." If he were, he'd be completely out to lunch, with no occasional popping into the office as he'd been doing. Max wasn't an exorcist or anything, but he'd seen a few cases of demonic possession in his time. Whatever had hold of Nathan wasn't controlling him full-time.

They shuffled down the hall to the bedroom. Max considered making a snide comment about this being the place where they'd first met, but he didn't want to chance giving Belle even more of a wrong impression. "Get him up here."

Nathan groaned as they lifted him onto the bed. For the first time, Max noted the dark bruises marring nearly every inch of his body. Before, when they'd first captured him, it had been dark, and they'd been more concerned with the weird symbols carved into his skin to notice the state of the rest of him.

"Jesus Christ," Max exclaimed on an exhale. It was all he could think of to say.

Bella covered her mouth, her gold eyes wide in shock. "What happened to him?"

"I have no idea. I'd put money down that the Soul Eater has something to do with it." His anger was so thick it could have choked him. He turned helplessly, his hands clutched in fists. He would have slapped the lamp from the bedside table to release some of his rage through destruction. But it wasn't his lamp to break, it wasn't his body that was ruined and it wasn't his sire to be pissed at. With a deep breath he released with a curse, he turned back to the bed.

"Where's Carrie?" Nathan's eyes, cloudy from the drugs, searched Max's face with an intensity that made his skin crawl.

How much did Nathan know? And how much should Max tell him?

Thankfully, Bella took care of it for him. "She will be here soon. Lie down. I will get something for your bruises."

"There's witch hazel. In the shop," Nathan panted. "The drugs are wearing off. Do something!"

"Give me the handcuffs." For being afraid of him before, she was awfully take-charge now. Max went to the dresser to retrieve the cuffs. She held her hands out as if to catch them. Max shouldered past her.

"Sorry, buddy," he said under his breath as he stretched Nathan's arms above his head.

"Don't let it happen again. Don't let me go back there." Nathan's fingers wrapped around Max's arm with terrifying strength.

Now I know how a life preserver feels, Max thought, carefully withdrawing from his friend's grasp. "We're going to try and help you."

For a heart-stopping moment, Nathan's face contorted into his vampire form, and he growled. Then his features returned to normal, as if they were wax melting, and he closed his eyes.

"He is unconscious again," Bella noted.

Max wanted to snap at her, to tell her he knew Nathan was unconscious, but it would have been pointless. Sure, it would make him feel better now, but later, when he had to go back to being civil, it would only make things that much more awkward. He snapped a cuff closed around one of Nathan's wrists and threaded it behind the brass bars of the headboard. Bella improvised a rope with the sheet, until they could find something more suitable, and tied Nathan's feet to the end of the bed.

"He will be uncomfortable." She stood with her arms folded across her chest, a critical, yet entirely unhelpful, look on her face.

Max bit his tongue and cuffed Nathan's other wrist. "Better him uncomfortable than us dead."

She shrugged, seeming to acquiesce to his logic, but with her it was hard to tell. In a bizarrely maternal gesture, she picked up a faded quilt from the floor and spread it over Nathan, folding the top back gently.

Max followed her into the living room, where she reached for one of the research texts they'd abandoned the night before.

"You should get some sleep before sunup," he suggested. "That way, if we need anything during the day, you'll be awake enough to go for it." Really, he just wanted her unconscious so he wouldn't have to deal with her, and having her sleep seemed like less trouble than knocking her out.

To his annoyance, she settled on the couch, not in the tangled nest of blankets she seemed to prefer to furniture. "I will be fine. I am going to go through these books and see if there is some way I can help your friend."

"I'll go down to the shop, check if there's anything I missed." Max left before she could offer to come with him, and bolted down the stairs two at a time.

Outdoors, the night was slowly becoming morning. Since the day after he'd been changed, Max had always been able to tell the subtle shift from one day to the next without looking at a watch.

It's the smell of it. Night smells like death and dirt. When the morning wakes, no matter how dark the sky might still be, everything smells new again. Even this foul city.

Max swiped at his cheek, remembering his sire's lips there. Marcus had taught him so much that night, as they'd sat on the ledge atop their building, gazing across Chicago's impressive skyline. It had been different then, of course. When Max was home, which wasn't often, and when he couldn't find someone or something to distract him from his solitude, which was even rarer, he went to the roof and wondered at the changes that had been made, even in his short lifetime. Or, after-lifetime, if he was feeling particularly sorry for himself.

I wish you were here, Marcus. I have no idea what I'm doing.

But his sire would have laughed and said something so sickly sweet and inspirational, such as "I believe in you" or "Have faith in yourself," that Max would have had to trust him. Marcus always had a way of spinning frothy sentiments to concrete.

Shaking his head at the thought, Max turned, only to find a pair of startling gold eyes studying him intently.

"Jesus Christ, make some noise when you sneak up on a person!" he shouted, trying to calm his thundering pulse.

"You should not take his name in vain." Bella moved past him, somehow still exotic and graceful in jeans and one of Carrie's T-shirts. "I came down to look through the herb pantry. There might be something I can use to calm him."

"That's a good idea," Max said, slipping a key into the lock on the shop door and holding it open for her. And it was a good idea. He'd have thought of it himself, if he'd known there was an— "Hey, how did you know there was an herb pantry?"

She shrugged one shoulder, running her fingers idly along the spines of books on the shelves as she passed them. "When I was tracking him, I broke in. It was not hard. There is only cardboard over that broken window."

Max looked to the door, where the tape he'd used to meticulously seal the empty box to the window frame hung limp and useless at one corner. "Did you take anything?"

"I am a killer, not a thief," she said, tossing him a playful smile over her shoulder.

Swearing under his breath, he followed her. He'd come down here to escape her. He was fast learning that was an impossibility. "Carrie's going to be back soon. I think it would be better for her to see him when he's not, you know, bat-shit insane."

Bella nodded absently, scanning the rows of neatly packaged herbs in their little plastic bags. "Your friend really knows what he is doing. He has everything a witch would need, and then some."

"Then you can help him?" Max realized he'd resumed his awful habit of stepping nervously from side to side, something he thought he'd had under control years ago. He commanded his feet to stay in place.

"I hope so. Some mullein leaf should keep whatever that other being is at bay. I'll give him valerian to induce sleep, and..." She traced down a column of herbs until her eyes widened at the sight of what she was looking for. "Catnip."

Max made a face. He didn't go in for most of this hippie, herbal remedy hoo-ha. "Catnip? Shall I fetch him a piece of string to play with, too?"

"You will be pleased to hear that I myself am not fond of it." She faced him, tiny plastic envelopes of herbs clutched in her hands. "But it is a calmative plant. Hopefully, these can do their jobs."

There were at least a hundred different dried herbs on the wall, not to mention whatever the bottles and vials on the shelves lining the cramped space contained. "Don't you need some more? Like this stuff—what does this do?"

She took the bottle he offered and squinted at the label. "That is oil of orris root. You could use it for a love spell, but I will not help you."

Quickly, he put the bottle back. "Very funny."

"I am only using one for each purpose. These plants, though they are dead and dried, still have a very personal energy. Imagine if I asked you to come to a party to perform magic tricks—"

"Never gonna happen."

She rolled her eyes. "Just imagine. Then I asked three other people to come and perform the same trick, because I thought you might not get the job done on your own. Would you not be insulted?"

"I suppose so. If I was some fruity magician. I might just swish my cape and go home." He laughed. It felt good to joke, to ease some of the tension of the night.

She apparently agreed, slapping him lightly on the arm. When she raised her hand to do it again, she curved her fingers around his biceps instead.

The thought of wrecking Nathan's herb closet in a fit of passion wasn't as exciting as it should have been. Probably because of her insistence that Max was in love with her. Definitely *Fatal Attraction* territory there, and he did not want to visit it.

He brushed her hand away and turned back to the herbs. "Knock it off. We have work to do."

"Yes, I do," she agreed, clearing her throat. "And you should leave me alone to do it."

His rejection bothered her, he realized as she walked away. So where was the pride that should have come with that victory?

And why did he feel like he was the one who'd lost?

20

Welcome Back, Part Two

I'd only been gone a week, but when the lights of downtown emerged from the gentle bend of I-96, it seemed I'd been away for years.

"God help me, I haven't been away from this stinking place long enough," Cyrus muttered from the passenger seat.

"You know, you could sleep. I hear it's *the* thing for humans to do at night." I myself had not gotten enough sleep on the trip. I found myself longing for my bed, only to realize it wasn't really *my* bed I wanted to be in.

A pang of homesickness brought tears to my eyes. I wanted to be lying beside Nathan, inhaling his scent, listening to his blood as it moved through my veins. For a moment, the pain was so intense I nearly screamed my longing like a child having a temper fit.

I needed Nathan. I loved Nathan. Everyone knew it but him.

"Are you all right?"

I still hadn't adjusted to the new Cyrus, so it took me a moment to realize there wasn't a hidden trap in his words. I wiped my eyes and nodded. "I'm fine. I'm just very tired."

"You could have let me drive. I would have picked up speed.

When I was more comfortable." He paused to look out the window. "My God. Nothing has changed."

"Well, the bus schedule changed. And they finished the bigger YMCA since you...died." I pointed toward the south side of town. "I'd show you, but I'd rather get home before I burn to a crisp."

He nodded. "I don't mean to sound crass, but what exactly am I going to do here?"

Signaling to change lanes, I shifted into the exit that swooped smoothly down to the heart of town. "I haven't figured that out yet. You can stay with us for a while."

"I don't think Nolen will be happy about that." Cyrus sounded almost apologetic. Probably because he didn't want to sleep in the van again.

"*Nathan* is currently indisposed to object to anything. But I'm not asking you to stay as a guest. You have to stay with us because I don't want your father getting ahold of you." I sent him a pointed glance. "And I don't want you trying to find him, either."

He gave a mock salute. "Yes, ma'am."

"I don't want to fight with you about this, Cyrus." It still stung to say his name.

He frowned. "Don't flinch. It's not like I stabbed you in *your* heart or anything. I'm human now. You have nothing to fear from me."

I opened my mouth to argue, but his deep sigh cut me off.

"I do want to find my father. But not for the reasons you suspect."

Pushing down a huge lump of fear, I tried to sound chipper. "Well, maybe I've misjudged you."

He looked at me with unwavering accusation in his eyes. "You've never done anything but."

I let his comment pass—there must have been a gas leak rendering him high and a complete amnesiac to say something so profoundly stupid—and we rode the rest of the way in silence.

But I couldn't quiet my mind as we neared the apartment. I had to forcibly remind myself that this wasn't a joyous homecoming. Our ordeal was far from over, and I had no idea what I was going to find when we arrived. By the time I pulled up to the curb in front of the building, I could barely keep the image of Linda Blair's spinning head from my mind.

I took a deep breath to fortify myself and grasped the door handle. "Here goes nothing."

"Wait." Cyrus's fingers, startlingly warm on my dead flesh, closed over my arm. He took my shocked hesitation for compliance. "It seems like it was only a few days ago you left me. My chauffer drove me here every day, and I would park at this very curb and imagine you upstairs with Nolen."

Cyrus clasped my free hand with a firm, earnest grip. "You hurt me. You think I didn't love you. I didn't. I thought I did, but now I know I was wrong. But I cared for you. I did truly care for you."

I swallowed. Maybe if I hadn't known he was dead, I would have prepared for this moment. If I had planned a confrontation, it would have been a spectacular one. But I hadn't had a reason to. I didn't know what to say now or how to react. I couldn't even tell what I was supposed to be feeling.

"You broke my heart, Carrie." His gaze locked with mine, and for the first time I saw nothing but honesty in the clear, blue depths of his eyes.

He leaned forward slowly, his catlike grace not lost to death and resurrection. Before I could think rationally—and it would have taken awhile, considering the totally bizarre circumstances of the moment—Cyrus kissed me.

The phrase "like riding a bicycle" came to mind. Though it had been two months, during most of which he'd been deceased, my body responded to him the way it had when we'd shared blood. Utter, uncontrolled desire that crashed over me like a tidal wave and stole every rational thought.

I didn't touch him, but I didn't pull away. He wrapped his arms around me. It was awkward because of the steering wheel, but he was still as good a kisser as he'd been as a vampire. My toes curled and I shifted on the seat, trying and failing to force away the tingling ache in my body.

He leaned back, his face flushed, beads of perspiration standing out on his forehead. His gaze fell to my lips, then rose to my eyes, then flitted to the windshield.

"Oh, look," he panted, pointing dismissively to something beyond the glass. "That's where I cut your heart out."

It was so matter-of-fact, so remorseless. The pain of that night—my own, coupled with Nathan's anguish, as well—sawed through me the way Cyrus's knife had. Under the weight of the stress and worry I'd been carrying, the hurt was too much to bear. Tears gushed to my eyes and I slapped him, leaving a shocking white handprint that turned quickly to angry red.

I could tell from his expression he knew what he'd done. He reached for me helplessly, but I pushed his hands away.

"How could you do that?" I wanted to wipe his kiss from my mouth, to erase the feeling of his lips from mine. "How could you…"

I couldn't finish. I didn't want to say he'd kissed me. I hated knowing that he still had that seductive power over me, that it hadn't all been because of the blood tie we'd shared. And I hated that whatever that sick attraction was, it had, for the moment, forced all thoughts of Nathan from my mind.

* * *

At the top of the stairs, the door opened to reveal a very alarmed woman with a crossbow. I recognized her long black hair and exotic features. It was Bella, the assassin from General Breton's office. The clothes she wore were familiar, as well. They were mine.

She raked an appraising glance over Cyrus and me, then flipped the bow against her shoulder in a less-intimidating stance. "You must be Carrie."

I nodded and opened my mouth to speak, but an earsplitting scream interrupted me.

The werewolf's brow creased in gentle concern. "It sounds worse than it is. I have administered a decoction of herbs to soothe him, but they have not taken effect."

I mumbled a numb "thank you." The scream had jarred me. I'd never heard it outside of my head before.

Max emerged from the hallway, wiping his hands on his jeans. "He's fed, at least." He froze at the sight of us, an indecisive smile playing tug-of-war with his lips. "You're back."

"I know." It probably seemed cruel of me not to rush immediately to Nathan's side, but I couldn't. Not after what had happened—what I had let happen—in the car.

Max frowned at me, as if he picked up on my guilty vibe. True to his damned awesome perception, he turned to Cyrus. "Hey, I'm Max."

Cyrus betrayed nothing, a skill honed to perfection over seven centuries of intrigue and manipulation. It was like a program that clicked on automatically, and I was secretly thankful for it.

He took Max's hand and shook it firmly. "We've met before. When you and your friends broke into my house and murdered me."

Max's good-natured smile never wavered, but I saw Cyrus's knuckles turn white in his grasp. When he released him, Cyrus surreptitiously wiggled his fingers.

Max cleared his throat. "Nathan's been asking for you."

"Then he's…" I didn't know how to phrase the question, so I looked helplessly to Bella, who seemed, strangely, more compassionate than Max.

"No, he's still possessed. He just got a whole lot more lucid when we shot him with the tranq dart," Max said, throwing the bloody towel over his shoulder. "He's messed up, physically. He's just a mass of bruises. And he's terrified. Maybe you could help calm him down."

As if on cue, another scream rent the air.

"Yeah." I wiped my sweating palms on my jeans and threw a quick glance to Cyrus. "Stay here. Max will play nice."

I expected some comment as I walked down the hall, something to either buoy my spirits or knock me down a peg for being such a lousy fledgling. But I should have known better. Max would scold me privately, after the hard part of all this was finished.

The room was dark, probably to lessen the stimulation for Nathan. When I stepped through the door, he shouted and twisted against whatever restraints Max had come up with. His big body stressed the bedsprings and made the frame groan. The sound immediately conjured up memories of all the times I'd heard it under much more pleasurable circumstances. Then I felt suddenly guilty and perverse.

I wondered if he knew I was there. *I could escape now. I don't have to stand here with him knowing what I've done.*

Then I remembered the blood tie, and I wanted to smack myself in the head. I hadn't been consciously blocking him from my thoughts. Could he have heard them?

Would he understand if I spoke? The last time I'd seen him, he'd been a mindless, blood-soaked animal. We'd communicated through the blood tie, but only briefly, before whatever was wreaking havoc with his mind had taken hold of him again.

I couldn't speak, anyway. I opened my mouth, but what would I say? I leaned against the cool, painted wood of the closed door, my breath far too loud in the tortured silence.

Finally, Nathan spoke. His voice was raw and exhausted, but it was Nathan, not the monster who'd attacked me. "Carrie?"

"It's me." I took a careful step forward. Though I knew he was restrained, though I knew he was my sire and I had nothing to fear from him, all I could remember was the blood splashing onto me from his torn skin. Morbid as it seemed, Nathan's blood had always smelled like home to me. The memory of the putrid stench of it the night he'd attacked me kept my feet rooted stubbornly to the ground.

"They've tied me up, *dotaír.*" His slurred endearment, Gaelic for *doctor,* brought a sad smile to my mouth. After a drunken sigh, he added, "And drugged me."

"I've missed you." I had to force the words past a lump that felt dangerously like impending tears. "How do you feel?"

"Drugged," he repeated with an inebriated chuckle. "I've missed you, too."

"You sound a lot better than you did the last time I saw you, at any rate." I tried to inject some humor into the statement, but it fell flat.

Only silence greeted me. For a moment, I wondered if Nathan had fallen asleep. Then, very quietly, he said, "Did I hurt you? I don't remember."

With sudden violence, he strained against his bonds and shouted in the frightening language he'd used the night he'd been possessed. He finished his angry tirade with a growling, "Let me up!"

"I can't do that, Nathan." I tried to be firm, but my voice shook. So did my hands, as I stepped closer to the bed and laid just my fingertips on his chest.

He sank back onto the mattress almost immediately. "Carrie?"

After all I'd been through in my life, the death of my parents, the heartbreak of failed relationships, the physical pain of having my heart literally ripped out, nothing had ever hurt as bad as watching my sire struggle against this unseen enemy.

His helplessness evaporated the last of my fear. "It's me."

"Don't leave me alone," he begged, clawing frantically at the cuff around his wrists.

"I won't." I climbed onto the bed, into the slim space between his body and the edge of the mattress. "I'm not going to leave you, Nathan."

He relaxed more when I pressed myself flush against him and draped my arm over his chest. Despite the darkness, I saw something change in his eyes. They were still glazed from whatever herbal concoction the werewolf had given him, but now I recognized him there.

His foot found its way from under the blankets and he hooked it around my ankle. "I've made a mess of things, haven't I?"

"No," I assured him, reaching to smooth a stray lock of hair from his forehead. "We're going to fix this."

He shook his head. "I meant with you."

I couldn't hold back my tears anymore, but I refused to let him see them. I buried my face against his side. "I'm not afraid of you, Nathan. You haven't done anything to hurt me."

"You were my second chance," he said sleepily. "And I screwed it up."

I stayed with him, partly because I'd promised, partly because I needed to touch him to assure myself of his presence, physical if not mental. Being there seemed to keep the beast at bay, and if nothing else, I could assure him some rest.

Still, his words echoed in my brain. *"You were my second chance."*

I didn't want to apply any hidden meaning to them, but as in most things, what I wanted and what I got were two different creatures.

Was I his second chance at love? That sounded incredibly corny, like the title of a movie you'd see on the women's channel. His second chance to have a relationship with someone he didn't end up killing? I should certainly hope so.

Or did the words even apply to me? He was drugged and possessed, drifting in and out of lucidity. What were the chances he was talking to some demon creature in another dimension?

Or this one? I cast a fearful glance around the shadowy room, then dismissed that notion. I was too old to be afraid of the dark, especially since the other half of me was consumed by fear of the light.

Well, maybe not half. There had to be room for guilt. I'd banished that useless emotion for two months. Why was it leaking into me now at every available chance, like water into a sinking ship? I didn't like the feeling. I wondered how Nathan could live with it.

Then it hit me, as obvious and absurd as a fish falling from the clear, blue sky.

He couldn't live with it. And that was what kept him in this state. His guilt kept him prisoner.

* * *

As soon as Carrie had left the room, Cyrus found himself descended upon by the two assassins that remained.

"Make yourself useful," Max growled, and the woman handed Cyrus a thick book with yellowing pages. As she leaned over him, he caught a whiff of what could only be described as "wet dog" smell.

He brightened instantly. "You're lupin?"

He should have realized his mistake before he made it, he noted as she lunged for him. Her fingernails sank into his shoulders and her teeth snapped inches from his throat before the vampire hauled her off.

"Filthy, murdering beast!" She spat at him, kicking out with such vehemence that she left the floor, the vampire's grip the only thing keeping her upright.

"Whoa, calm down, it's an easy mistake," Max said, turning her away.

Poor bastard's going to get it now, Cyrus thought with an inward chuckle. If the most demeaning insult to a lupin was being called a werewolf, it was ten times worse the other way around. "I apologize, deeply. I meant no offense. In the past, my only experience has been with your estranged brethren."

"They are not our brothers, murdering coward!" Her voice still held an edge of hysteria, but she was controlled enough to brush the vampire's hands aside without seeking to do more damage immediately after. "I know who you are!"

"Have we met?" It was an intentionally cruel remark. He folded his arms across his chest and waited for what she would inevitably say.

"I read the files! I know of your cruelty to my kind. The hunts you arranged for the pleasure of the lupins. Only you called them dogfights when you joked with your friends!" Her golden eyes widened. Would she weep?

The vampire put his arm around her in a proprietary, protective gesture. *Very interesting.*

"He's done a lot of things." Max glared at Cyrus. "But we need him, for the time being."

Sighing deeply and theatrically, Cyrus spread his hands. "Look, I'm very sorry for any wrong I've committed, intentionally or accidentally, against any member of your pack or kennel or whatnot. I mean that truly and sincerely, from the very core of my being. But I'm tired. Please imagine what it's like to be raised from the dead by a deranged vampire-motorcycle-gang-religious cult, only to be dragged across the country in a van driven by your ex-lover and fledgling who hates you and no longer sympathizes with the human need for waste elimination. I have neither the energy nor the inclination to write a ten page statement officially apologizing for the evils of my past, and if you expect me to, kindly throw yourself beneath the wheels of a moving train."

When he'd begun to speak, the words didn't sound so bad. They weren't tactful, but they didn't seem confrontational in his mind. Apparently, the vampire had a different perception of things. This time, he lunged forward, only to be held back by his woman. "Don't talk to her that way!"

"I'll talk any way I please." Cyrus's patience, worn thin by grief and too many hours without sleep, had reached its limits. "I'm not here by choice. If I had it my way, I'd walk out that door and never see any of you again."

Except Carrie. He'd already lost her once. Since being with her again, he felt too keenly the heartbreak that had still been with him when he'd died. But if she'd have let him, he would have stayed with Mouse, in the desert, until death came to him again.

It seemed death was the only time he had a moment's peace.

"No one's stopping you," the vampire growled, his face

shifting to take on the fearsome snout and snarling teeth that marked his true identity.

For a moment, the werewolf stepped back. As if feeling her horror himself, Max shook his features back to a more human visage. Then, apparently aware she'd hurt his feelings, she laid her hand on his arm. "We need him to help us, Max. He is tired and he has been through much. We cannot expect him to react any differently. He is only human."

The words were intended to wound him, but Cyrus was glad he no longer fit into the bizarre, parallel reality they inhabited. He picked up the book and dropped into an armchair, flipping the pages without really seeing them.

It was strange and uncomfortable to be here, in Nolen's personal home. Here and there, photographs in cheap frames cluttered the bookshelves and end tables. Some of them depicted Ziggy, the young man Nolen had called son.

Cyrus remembered the boy with fondness. He'd been bright and pleasant, and very talented in the bedroom. And Cyrus had repaid him with cruelty, drawing the youth to him and pushing him away by turns.

Shame burned in him at the memory. *"You do know your father and I have a history, don't you? Of course, he wasn't nearly as responsive as you are. Does that excite you? To know you're a better lay than he was? God, what would he think of you if he saw you, on your hands and knees, begging me to fuck you?"*

And he had begged. Cyrus had made sure of that.

Absently, he reached out and flipped down the nearest picture, so he wouldn't have to see the smiling faces of father and son staring back at him.

Max immediately stepped forward and righted the frame.

Ah, so that's how it would be then. It made sense. In his life, Cyrus had done abominable things, and worse. Now, he was receiving retribution. But if this puffed up child-masquerading-as-tough vampire thought he could dole out the worst of the punishment, he was sadly mistaken. Some vampires in the desert had already claimed that particular prize.

Morbidly, Cyrus's mind made its way back to the church basement. Did the fire still smoke? Had anyone found her? Had her body burned away? It seemed wrong that he'd left her there, helpless in her death. His logical mind recognized the fact she felt no pain, but his emotions played havoc with his brain, showing pictures of her serene face contorted with terror as she woke to find herself abandoned to the flames.

He should have made Carrie leave him with her, so he could have said goodbye in private. Oh, he wouldn't have used her the way he had done the girls he'd killed himself. The thought was disgusting when applied to a person he cared about, a person whose life he'd valued. But it had seemed rushed. He'd wanted to hold her, to lie beside her, close his eyes and pretend she lived, despite the stiffness creeping into her limbs and the coldness of her skin. Maybe he would have stayed a few days, never moving. Maybe he would have died of a broken heart.

It was a possibility that eluded him now. His grief, left untended, had subsided some. He didn't want to survive losing her, but circumstance had forced him to heal to a cruel plateau. He ached for her, but he could not bring that ache to drive him to the madness required to harm himself.

The werewolf—Bella, Max had been calling her—walked in a few lazy circles around a pile of blankets before lying down. She pillowed her chin on her arms, stretched in front of her like a dog's paws, her eyes scanning a book.

Max stretched on the couch, trying valiantly to read something handwritten. His eyes flitted occasionally from the pages to the woman on the floor.

Cyrus wanted to urge caution. Love was fleeting, and it could be taken so easily. But he didn't care enough about either of them to impart this knowledge, and if they were smart, they would have known it on their own.

Instead, he gestured to the book in Max's hands. "What is that?"

"The Big Book of None of Your Business." He frowned at the lines as if he'd been concentrating on the words and not the object of his obvious desire.

The rejection rolled off Cyrus like water. "It looks like a journal. A book of shadows?"

Max didn't look up. "It is a journal, and you can stop talking at any time."

"I'd like to know what I'm supposed to be looking for. Unless you'd just like a comprehensive report on the entire text?" Cyrus closed the book with a loud snap that sent up a puff of dust. Emblazoned in cheap, gold ink across the cover were the words *Vou Dou Spells of Possession and Control.*

Lovely.

Max finally deigned to glance up, cold fury etched in every line of his face. "You'd know better than we do what he's up to."

"He?" Cyrus shrugged innocently. "If by that you mean my father, you are mistaken. I haven't heard from him since before I died, and he wasn't happy with me then."

"Right, and we're supposed to believe that. I suppose you have no idea why he brought you back from the dead?" Like a shark circling a reef in search of dying fish, Max stood and paced around the room.

It wasn't quite intimidating enough. In fact, the absurdity of the situation brought a bubble of laughter from Cyrus's throat, which he quickly suppressed. "No, I do know that. Carrie told me. He's trying to become a god. But you're not going to find anything in here to stop him."

"Where would we find it?" Her attention finally captured by the conversation, Bella sat up. Cyrus would have found her attractive, if not for the fact she was a dog, but he didn't believe it would be wise to make a pass in front of her boyfriend, especially when he was so obviously besotted with her.

Instead, Cyrus gave her an answer simple enough even the caveman vampire could understand. "I don't know. As I discussed with Carrie, my father was obsessed at one time with the quest for an ancient spell that would help him achieve such status. But I have no idea if he found that spell in particular, or if he did, where. And I would certainly have no idea how to stop it. If it's anything like most of these ancient rituals, it will require some impossible undertaking to stop it once he's begun. Which he must have, if I'm here. Father sticks to a very rigid schedule when it comes to any occult business. Things run more smoothly that way."

"We are trying to find a way to help Nathan. We think your father may have done something to him," Bella volunteered, ignoring Max's glare.

"Oh, he's absolutely done something to him," Cyrus agreed. Turning to Max, he admonished, "Isn't it amazing what you find out when you ask civilly?"

"Shut up and tell us what you know, asshole." Max leaned against the frame of the doorway that led, presumably, to the kitchen.

Cyrus's stomach rumbled. "I'm hungry. Does Nolen have anything to eat that isn't blood?"

"Get him something," Bella ordered Max. The vampire gaped at her in rage, but turned to do her bidding.

Oh, yes. God save us all from a vampire in love. Only when Max had left the room did Cyrus begin to speak. It was an intentional slight, to put Max in his place.

"If my father is using the ritual I believe he is using, he'll need to purify the souls of all those he's turned. The only way to do that is to consume them, at which point he'll perform another part of the ritual. I'm not sure what exactly that entails. But after it's done and all the souls are destroyed—"

"Destroyed?" Bella's eyes widened in shock.

It took Cyrus a moment to remember how barbaric that should sound. A soul was all a mortal creature had—did he have one now?—and humans prized theirs very highly.

"Yes. Once the impurity has been obliterated, he'll be able to finish the ritual as written." Cyrus laughed, shrugging. "That will be the best way to stop him. Keep him from collecting the souls he needs."

"That's what we plan to do." Max returned from the kitchen, a crumpled bag of some snack food in his hands. "Here. Kitchen's closed."

Though they were stale and horrid tasting, Cyrus pretended to enjoy the "cheese puffs," as the bag proclaimed, with gusto. "Well, I'm assuming Father has simply used his blood tie to Nathan to call him back."

"Blood tie?" Max smirked. "I'm pretty damn familiar with that, and it couldn't make me carve myself up and go on a killing rampage."

Cyrus shook his head. "No, but perhaps you'd go a little mad if you spent most of your time trying to block it out. I know my father. He used to torment me day and night with visions of—"

No. He wouldn't share those horrors with these strangers. "With visions of unpleasant things. He'd do that until I gave him what he wanted."

"Whatever he's doing, it's a lot worse than a scary picture show." Max shook his head. "If we could just figure it out…"

"We will keep looking," Bella said, lifting another book. "Nathan has an impressive collection. We will find something."

As the hours ticked by, Max on the couch glancing furtively at the werewolf while she pretended not to notice, Cyrus feigning interest in the dusty text cradled on his lap, he felt a bizarre peace. Though his companions didn't accept him, he felt involved in their single-minded task and the hope that fueled them. He might not die this week, or the next. He might live a whole year, maybe even two. As long as he had this optimism afforded only to the good guys.

I'm a good guy now, Mouse, he thought, believing with all his heart she could hear him. *I think I might stay this way.*

21

The Dark Night of the Soul

I woke before sundown. Drugged into oblivion by whatever potion he'd been given, Nathan didn't stir when I eased from his side. It hadn't been a restful day. Every time I'd dozed off, I'd come dangerously close to falling off the bed. I'd jerk awake, disturbing Nathan in the process, and have to assure him I was not leaving him. I made a mental note to ask Bella to double his dose tomorrow, so I could get some sleep.

In the living room, Max lay sprawled on the couch, an old-looking book over his face. I sincerely hoped the thing didn't have paper lice. Bella lay in a pile of blankets on the floor, whimpering like a dog having a nightmare. There was no sign of Cyrus, but my bedroom door was open a crack.

I leaned against the frame and gently eased the door open, hoping to avoid the creak of the sticky hinge. Inside, everything was as I had left it, with one notable exception.

Cyrus lay curled in the fetal position on my bed, the blankets twisted artistically across his nude body.

He was too bizarre, too out of place there. My stomach pitched as though I'd just gone over a particularly nasty hill on a roller coaster. I grabbed the doorjamb for balance.

There had always been a neat division between my current and former lives. The apartment I'd lived in as a human had burned down, so there was no tie left to that time. My only encounters with Cyrus had taken place at the hospital, where I no longer worked; at his home, which I assumed now belonged to Dahlia and therefore I was in no danger of visiting; and in the alley outside the bookshop, where he'd cut my heart out, a place I strenuously avoided. In my mind there were Cyrus Spaces and Nathan Spaces, and they rarely overlapped. To have the two collide so violently and under such stressful circumstances was…well, it was just plain creepy.

"What are you doing?"

I jumped at the sound of Max's voice and turned to see him stretch sleepily and scratch his stomach.

I nodded to the open door. "Visiting the scene of my nightmares."

Max chuckled. "Aw, the little asshole's all tuckered out."

"You were supposed to be nice to him," I admonished. Though I shouldn't care how they treated Cyrus, so long as they left him alive, every time I tried to make myself indifferent to him I remembered the dead girl in the desert and the pain her death had caused him.

Max didn't have that problem. "Well, he was supposed to be dead. If he can't return common courtesy, why should I?"

"He's different now." I wondered if he really slept, or if he was just faking it, and listening to every word we said.

With a deep, pained sigh, Max shook his head. "What is it with you and this guy, Carrie? I mean, I know he's your—was your—sire, but he's not anymore. And after the stuff he did to you, and what he's doing to Nathan now…why can't you just let him go?"

Whatever hackles are, mine were raised by that comment. I

knew I was being overly defensive, but I couldn't help it. My feelings for Cyrus, no matter how convoluted, were something I protected like a cherished family heirloom. I closed the door as quietly as I could and faced Max. "You wouldn't understand."

"Explain it to me in a way I would. We've got nothing but time." He leaned against the wall and folded his arms across his chest, daring me in his cocky, silent way to defy him.

I could have brushed him off with a simple refusal, but that would have closed off a part of me to him, and that was something I was unwilling to do. Max was a friend, and it wasn't as if I had those in spades these days.

"When I lived with him, Cyrus played so many mind games I had a hard time sorting out what feelings were mine and what ones he manipulated me into feeling." I took a deep breath. I didn't like talking about personal matters to anyone, even Nathan. At least with him, he knew what I was feeling before I did, and our "conversations" were little more than telepathic exchanges of emotion. "I didn't get it quite sorted out before he died, and now that he's back, some of those feelings are back, too."

"Do you love him?" The question was so blunt and naked, it sounded perverse.

"No. I don't love him. Not in a romantic sense." At least I could deny that much.

"What about other senses?" Max's tone implied his bullshit detector was reading off the charts.

That was one of the main problems with men. They couldn't accept the concept of love unless it applied to sex.

"I don't love him. But I see the potential in him to become a good person, and I have a lot of admiration and yes, affection, for the man he is when he lets his guard down. But that doesn't mean I'm going to run off with him or anything." I thought of

Nathan lying in the other room, and what might happen if we couldn't save him. Was I ready to live a lifetime alone?

"But I didn't ask you to go easy on him because of any feelings I might have for him." It seemed almost cruel to betray such private information about my old sire, but Max needed to understand my pleas for sensitivity where Cyrus was concerned. "Something happened in the desert. Not between him and me, but it was my fault. He wasn't the only human being held by the Fangs. There was a girl—I guess they were keeping her alive to watch him or care for him. But they were... intimate. And I made a stupid mistake and got her killed. Max, I think he really loved her. She managed to reach some place inside of him I knew existed but had no clue how to unlock. Now that she's gone, I'm afraid he's closed that part of himself off again, and that's going to make him susceptible to anything the Soul Eater might offer. I don't want him to be a monster again."

Max didn't speak. What could he have possibly said? Of course, before we could say any more, my bedroom door opened and Cyrus, clad only in the black slacks he'd worn on the trip, stepped out. "Whispering sweet nothings in the hallway? How romantic."

Max straightened instantly, looking a little disturbed by the implication. "No."

Cyrus laughed, and I flinched at the sound. It was too much like the monster who'd sired me. "I was joking. I know you've got your eye on the werewolf," he stated.

Now it was my turn to laugh. "Of course he does. He's Max, and she's female."

A patient smile formed on Cyrus's mouth, and Max looked away, rubbing his neck in a classic gesture of social discomfort.

"Oh." I cleared my throat. "Well, I'm impressed, Max. I was

beginning to think you were always going to be the love 'em and leave 'em type."

He let out an exasperated breath. "Hey, I am the love 'em and leave 'em type. And I don't love her. It was just... boredom fucking."

I exchanged an uncomfortable glance with Cyrus, the ocular communication equivalent of "thanks but no thanks for the details."

"I'm going to take a shower," Cyrus announced, striding purposefully toward the bathroom. "I'll leave you to your awkward moment."

I followed Max into the kitchen, where he rooted in the fridge for blood. When he reached for the teakettle, I offered, "I can do that."

He shook his head. "Nah. I need something to keep myself busy, or I'll be in there waking Nathan up by worrying over him. How'd he do?"

"Fine." I sat at the table, apologizing for the loud scrape the chair made against the floor.

"Don't worry about waking her up, she sleeps like the dead. At least, like the dead who aren't currently possessed." Max winked at me as he set the kettle on the burner. "Did you get any sleep?"

"None at all. So, what's going on with you and Bella?" At his pointed look, I raised my hands helplessly. "I'm sorry, I'm a doctor. We're supposed to ask questions."

"About people's personal life?" He raised an eyebrow.

Squirming under his knowing gaze, I shrugged. "Sometimes."

"You're not that kind of doctor."

"And what kind of doctor is that?" For a second I thought he'd respond with a smart-assed answer about venereal disease.

Instead, he took the other chair and rested his big forearms on the cracked Formica tabletop. "A head doctor. A shrink. Just admit you have a case of nosy frienditis."

"Fine. I have a case of nosy frienditis. Now answer the question." It wasn't a command, but gentle urging.

Something was warring inside Max. I could see it in his boyish, blue eyes. He sighed and leaned back in his chair. "I have no idea. One minute we hated each other, the next I'm finding her split open like an overcooked hot dog. I bring her back here and bam, we're all involved."

"That must have hurt for her," I observed sagely.

He gave me a look that suggested I keep my mouth shut lest I enrage him further. "It wasn't like that. I had to finished stitching up her wounds first. Thank God you have so many boring medical books."

"I live to serve." I drew patterns on the table with my fingertip, trying to figure out a way to delicately phrase my next question. "So…does this mean you're…her mate or something?"

"Well, we did 'mate,' so to speak. And I owe you guys for some broken dishes—"

"Yikes."

"Yeah." He shook his head. "The thing is, she thinks I'm in love with her."

"I take it you're not?" I chuckled. "Max, you could save yourself a lot of trouble if you just kept your pants zipped."

"It's not like that, this time. She thinks I love her, and she doesn't love me, so she thinks she's hurting my feelings or something." The teakettle's whistle sputtered, and Max jumped up to turn off the burner. Once blood boils, it burns, making for an unpleasant, scorched-pot-roast taste.

"Well, you've really got no problem then, right?" I moved past him to snag a couple mugs. "If neither of you love each other, then you're free and clear."

"And she walks away thinking she dumped me?" He swore, though I couldn't tell if it was at the idea of being rejected by another sentient being, or if he'd made contact with a hot part of the kettle.

"Is that the worst thing in the world?" I knew Max had a major pride problem, but I hadn't realized it went so deep.

He poured the blood into the mugs and set the remainder on the back burner. I assumed he left that portion for Nathan, and his thoughtfulness brought unexpected tears to my eyes. I quickly shooed them away, blaming my overemotional state on the fact I hadn't had any sleep.

"It's not the worst," Max conceded as he returned to the table with our breakfast. "But it's not good. I got a rep to uphold."

I reached across the table to slap him lightly on the shoulder. He laughed, but the levity was brief. "Besides, I couldn't be with her permanently. I think of that, then I think about Marcus—"

"Your old sire?" I asked for clarity.

He gave an affirmative nod. "I think about the fact that he's gone, and all I've been carrying around is this yearning for him, wanting to feel what I felt with him. You know, in a totally not gay way. But then I think, wow, love. That's a thing I have no power over, and it might feel good to know I'm not alone, and it's like I'm betraying him."

"You're not betraying him by moving on." I spoke so vehemently the sound of my own voice startled me. Embarrassed, I cleared my throat and continued more softly. "What is it with you men, you think you have to hang on to everything."

"What do you mean?" He took a swallow of blood, his eyes meeting mine in a silent question over the rim of the mug.

"You know exactly what I mean." And if not all the details, well, it wasn't my place to spill Nathan's personal beans. "Nathan thinks he has to carry around a sack load of guilt over

Marianne, and because of that, he can't just get over it. You're doing the same thing. Your guilt over the way your sire died is so precious to you, you refuse to give it up for even a second in case you might actually get over it and move on."

"You should have been a head doctor," Max said in a way that didn't quite sound like a compliment.

We sat in silence, sipping our breakfast and doing our best to ignore the conversation we'd just had. Occasionally, Max would look up at some imagined sound from the living room, but when Bella didn't appear he settled down in a disappointed funk.

I thought he was imagining things again when he swore and shot up from the table, nearly toppling it as he tore from the kitchen. "What are you doing?"

Despite the fact Bella still slept, he raced through the living room, turning on lights and lifting books, swearing repeatedly.

Bella sat up sleepily, a crease on the side of her face from the blankets she'd slept on. "What's going on?"

"Where's the book you were reading last night?" Max tossed aside an expensive-looking volume with gilt-edged pages.

Rubbing her eyes, Bella frowned. "Which one?"

"Max, what are you doing?" I saved a particularly prized text from knocking over a glass of water on the coffee table.

"You said Nathan is carrying around loads of guilt over killing Marianne. Who, besides you and me, know about that?" He grabbed the book Bella held out to him and began flipping through the pages with such force I worried he would rip them from the binding. A lock of golden hair fell across his forehead, accentuating the madness that seemed to have gripped him.

"Well, Cyrus knows. He was there. And so was the Soul Eater."

"Max, you don't think that has something to do with…" My stomach roiled. I had a feeling the blood I'd drunk would soon be wasted.

Strong hands closed over my shoulders, and I realized belatedly I no longer heard the water running in the shower.

"Has something to do with what?" Cyrus's breath stirred the hair at the back of my neck.

Max coughed and I stepped out of Cyrus's proprietary embrace.

"Do you remember the name of the spell Bella told us about last night?" Max asked, the proverbial look that could kill on his face.

Cyrus and Bella answered at the same time, in two different languages. Cyrus's words were the ones I could understand. "Dark Night of the Soul."

Fully awake now, Bella stood beside Max and tried to take the book. "You are going the wrong way, it is in the back!"

I turned to Cyrus, dismayed to see he wore only a towel draped low across his hips. "We think we know what your father is doing to Nathan."

"I told them exactly what he's doing. They didn't believe me, until she ran across it in that blasted book." He rolled his eyes. "Apparently, my word is only good if I can back it up with written proof."

"What is he doing?" I took his hands in mine, not caring what Max would think. "Please, Cyrus. I have to have him back."

"Do you love him?" The words sucked the air out of the room. Even Max and Bella stilled.

I swallowed what felt like a ball of razor blades. "Does it matter?"

We stared at each other a long moment. In Cyrus's eyes, I saw the hurt he felt at losing the girl in the desert, and the hurt he would feel if he thought there was no chance I'd ever return to him.

I felt the word leave my lips before I thought to say it. "Yes." The admission sliced something open inside me, and I felt the poison that had festered there for the past two months spill free and evaporate. "Yes, I do love him."

Whatever had opened in me corresponded to something closing off in Cyrus. He shrugged as though indifferent to the entire conversation, and looked away. "Dark Night of the Soul goes way back. It started out as a spell to test the faith of a shaman or mystic. Basically, it forces them to live the most troubling, painful moments of their life over and over. The only thing that keeps them from going mad is the strength of their mind and their belief in the training they've received. For example, a very religious person might call on the Judeo-Christian God for strength when enduring such a trial, and their very faith would break the spell." He stopped, a hard set to his jaw, but the emotion in his eyes was unreadable.

"But if you used it on someone who had no hope to begin with…" I knew instantly what Nathan's Dark Night entailed. "He's killing her."

"Over and over again," Cyrus agreed grimly. "Father wouldn't let him off too easily."

"But why?" Bella asked, looking up for a moment from the book. "What purpose does it serve to make him insane?"

"He's not insane," Cyrus explained. "He's sane enough to know what he's doing, but he can't control the memory. It's already happened, so he's helpless to repeat his actions. He knows who is responsible, at least who is responsible for making him kill his wife in the first place. Father needs to gather to him the souls he's corrupted. What better way than enrage and torture them until they seek him out to end it?"

"If we kill the Soul Eater, will the spell stop?" Good old Max, always ready to hack and slash his way out of any problem. Not that I blamed him. At this point, I wanted to kill Jacob Seymour myself.

Cyrus shook his head. "That's the beauty part. Even after the caster is dead, the spell continues."

"The sigils," Bella interjected. "They are the anchors."

Cyrus nodded, looking a bit too impressed with his father's cleverness. I turned away, disgusted. "Well, then what, he's just screwed?"

"No." Bella's golden eyes scanned the pages. "It will not be easy, but there has to be a way to fix this."

"Does there?" Max laughed, a weary sound despite the fact he'd just gotten up. "Well, that's a relief."

"Everything has an opposite. No spell exists that cannot be broken." She sniffed derisively and snatched the book from his hand. "I will be downstairs. I assume I have the supplies there at my disposal?"

"Of course." I was fairly certain Nathan would have given away his entire inventory to escape the hell he was in.

Bella closed the book and slipped it under her arm as she walked toward me with unnerving grace. "Do I have you at my disposal?"

"Of course," I repeated, though this time I sounded less certain. "What will I have to do?"

She tossed her hair and gave a thoroughly European shrug. "Maybe nothing."

As she passed Cyrus she paused to give his near nakedness an appreciative once-over. Then she took the keys from the hook on the wall and left.

"Don't you have any clothes?" Max growled.

An antagonistic grin twisted Cyrus's mouth. "They are, unfortunately, the same ones I've been wearing for nearly a week now."

"I'll loan you some of mine. And keep them on." Max shoved past us and went to the foot of the couch, where his duffel bag lay open. He pulled out a pair of jeans and a T-shirt and tossed them to Cyrus. With an angry glare my way he added, "I'm going to go feed Nathan."

"Stay away from my girl," Cyrus muttered in an exaggerated American accent when Max emerged from the kitchen and stalked down the hall.

"Leave him alone. He's kind of having a rough time." I turned my back as Cyrus let the towel drop. He'd been naked in the desert, but those were extenuating circumstances. I didn't need to see it every chance I got.

"Having a rough time? Is that emblazoned on some twisted family crest you people wear?" His words were muffled, indicating the shirt was going over his head.

I turned in time to see him hitch the jeans up his hips. They were at least an inch too big around the waist.

"The way you people are intermittently feeding me, my weight won't be a problem," he quipped.

"I'm sorry. Help yourself to anything in the kitchen." If there was anything in the kitchen. I hadn't even looked since returning home. Funny, that when I was a human woman food had seemed to dominate every facet of my life. Was I eating too much? How many calories were in that slice of pizza? Were eggs good or bad that particular week? Now that I was a vampire, the necessity for food had completely slipped my mind.

Not the enjoyment of it, though. Nathan kept a huge stock of junk food. I looked forward to the nights the supply seemed to be waning, as it often resulted in a manic trip to the twenty-four-hour grocery store. We'd load up on all the bad-for-humans treats we could find, from Doritos to birthday cake, head back to the apartment, snack ourselves into a sugar coma and fall asleep watching videos. Nathan preferred war movies and intense psychological dramas. I always voted for romantic comedies or historical movies with sumptuous costumes.

Inevitably, our disagreement would be settled with a screwball comedy like *Young Frankenstein* or *Half Baked*.

"He's going to be all right, you know," Cyrus said, interrupting my reverie. With an apologetic smile, he added, "You had that look."

"What look?" It seemed too intimate, too soon for him to be able to read my thoughts from my facial expression. Part of me didn't want to give him that power. The same part worried that if Cyrus knew how important Nathan was to me, it would give him ammunition to hurt me. In my logical mind I recognized the changes in him, but my emotions still lived in a place where Cyrus was my manipulative sire.

"You have a look when you're thinking of him. It used to drive me crazy." What began as a smile on his face faded to a tight grimace of regret. As if he could still read my thoughts—maybe he could—Cyrus said quietly, "What would yours be? If the spell had been cast on you? That's all I could think of, when I realized what had happened. What if my father had put that spell on me?"

"My parents?" I laughed at how absurdly human that seemed now, compared to all the hell I'd faced since. "Or you. I don't know."

"Me?" He didn't sound at all surprised. "When I first turned you, I suppose? It wasn't an ideal circumstance."

"No. When I killed you." The tear that slid down my face surprised me, and I swiped it away. Not before Cyrus saw, though, and came to my side.

An emotion that would have been sadness if it hadn't held so much relief clouded his face. "I heard what you said to your friend this morning. About me."

I'd suspected as much, but I hadn't wanted to discuss it. "I didn't intend for you to hear—"

"You don't have to worry about making me a monster. You weren't the one making me a monster when you lived with me. I chose to behave the way I did. Yes, there were times you hurt me. Particularly when you stabbed a knife through my heart and sent me to some bizarre purgatory. But you were not so devastating as to destroy my humanity with your rejection. There wasn't any left to destroy, by the time I met you."

Unexpected tears sprang to my eyes. I wiped them on the back of my hand. "I'm not so egotistical that I thought… Well, I don't know what I thought."

Nathan screamed, the sound ripping down the hallway and pushing me over the edge. A loud, hiccuping sob tore from my throat.

Cyrus held out his arms, but didn't embrace me, clearly waiting for me to make the first move. I walked into his embrace, for the first time not doubting his motives or his humanity, because he was human, he saw my pain and he wanted to help.

His arms were strong around my back, his face warm where he buried it against my shoulder. If he'd been this honest when he was my sire, I could have fallen in love with him.

He drew back, smoothing a tendril of hair from my face. "May I ask you a question?"

I nodded, feeling a bit foolish for my breakdown. "As long as it's not 'Will you marry me.'"

We laughed liked old friends reunited after a long time apart, not an easy laughter, but one that suggested we were at least working up to that comfortable place.

His expression turned serious. "Let me kill my father?"

The easy moment dissipated like vapor into the air. "Absolutely not!"

"Why? Afraid I'll turn to the dark side?" He scoffed. "You'll never believe I've changed."

I swallowed the lump of tears that formed in my throat. "I believe you're changed. I do. But I'm not willing to take that kind of risk."

Nathan screamed again, the headboard thumping the wall and echoing through the house. This time, I ignored the way it unsettled me, and concentrated on Cyrus.

"The risk that I'll return to my father? That I'll become the monster you remember?" He shook his head. "That's not going to happen."

I didn't respond, trying to block out the sounds of Nathan's frantic, pleading voice coming from the bedroom.

"Right. I'm just a weak-minded human who'll succumb to the Soul Eater at the first promise of power and wealth." Cyrus twisted angrily away, marching down the hallway to my room. I followed.

The way he paced inside the small room alarmed me. I worried he would snap and do something violent or break something. Instead, he grabbed the framed picture of Ziggy off of my desk and thrust it at me. His face twisted with remorse. "I killed this boy. I killed him, because that's what I was told to do."

Ziggy's face smiled at me from the photo. The glass of the frame caught the light in a glare, and I could only make out his mouth and eyes, giving him the faded appearance of an accusing ghost. My chest tightened.

"My father taught me to kill for fun and pleasure. He asked me to do terrible things for him, and I did them. How did he repay me? By taking away everyone I loved, until I couldn't feel love anymore. I could only feel this burning, selfish want. I desired to possess them, that was all." He sounded as though he would break down and sob. I didn't know how I would handle it if he did.

On the other side of the wall, Nathan had become more restless. I closed my eyes and pressed my hands to my temples. Cyrus was there in an instant, this time wrapping his arms around me without looking for permission. He kissed my hair, whispering, "If my father is dead... As long as he's alive there is always a chance I'll turn to him, return to the way I was. I never want to become that man again! Do you understand? I want to kill my father."

Another pained howl rent the air, and I gasped, shocked by the violence of the sound and the hurt that had caused it. "I have to go. I can't stand this."

I ran out of the room, to the front door, ignoring Cyrus's call of, "Carrie, wait!" I took the steps two at a time, burst through the door at the bottom before I took a breath. I dragged the chilled night air into my lungs, wanting to drown in it. From here, I couldn't hear Nathan crying out, but the memory haunted me. It was worse now that I knew what caused it. The thought of Nathan forced to kill his wife every second, the wife he still loved so much he could not let her go, was too much for me to fathom. I stumbled to the van parked at the curb and leaned my forehead against the side, not bothering to stop the shuddering sobs that racked my body.

Behind me the door opened and closed, and I knew it was Cyrus just from the sound of his footsteps. He put one hand on my shoulder, and I spun at his touch, startling him.

"I don't think you'll become a monster," I blurted, a bit too loudly, but I didn't care who heard. I just needed to get some of the crushing, confusing emotion off my chest. "I don't want you going to him because I don't want you to die! I don't know what I'd do if—" I choked on the rest of my words, but they echoed in my head. *If I lost you again.*

Though I hadn't spoken them, Cyrus heard them. He stared at me, hard, his blue eyes, which had always looked so cold boring into me with an intensity he could have been pretending.

I thought of Nathan upstairs, struggling and in pain. I thought of the agony Cyrus must be going through, over what his father had done to him and the girl in the desert. I wanted the pain to be somehow deeper in me, fearing I wasn't feeling it enough to truly understand. And then I realized that was all I had been doing—feeling all that horror and guilt until it felt normal, numb.

When Cyrus kissed me this time, it wasn't passion and anger overcoming him. His hands tangled in my hair, his mouth crushed against mine as if through touching me he could erase my pain. He did care that he had hurt me in the past, and now he sought to make up for that.

I didn't resist him. I still loved Nathan. He was my sire; it was impossible not to feel something for him. But too much lay unresolved between Cyrus and me. It wasn't betrayal, it was closure.

Cyrus fumbled beside me for an instant, and I heard the back door of the van swing open. He never let me go, never moved his mouth from mine as he shifted me toward it and laid me back on the horrible gold carpet inside. Maybe he thought if he broke contact and gave me a second to think, I would tell him to stop. I wouldn't have. I hurt. I wanted for just a moment to feel something that didn't.

I scooted back as he climbed in beside me and pulled the door shut. There was a second of hesitation on his part where I saw the thought, *We shouldn't be doing this,* flicker across his face. I pulled my shirt over my head and grabbed him, smashing my lips across his. He straightened with shock, then relaxed again, laying me back and covering my body with his.

When he shrugged out of his borrowed T-shirt, I forced every thought from my mind, for better or worse. We didn't speak, but moved in a strangely easy dance of pulled clothing and hurried kisses on reachable skin. It wasn't romantic and it wasn't tender. It was fucking, in the most disconnected sense of the word.

He slipped inside me easily and I gasped involuntarily at how warm and alive he felt. Vampires were cold, room temperature. He was human. When his hands closed over my hips to pull me harder, faster against him, they were human hands, not the twisted talons of a monster.

I clutched at his back and shoulders, shocked all the more by the warmth of him. When he spilled into me I shuddered, but I didn't come. He withdrew immediately, not looking at me.

"That was a mistake," he said, his voice hoarse.

I nodded, trying to find my voice. "Let's forget it, then."

We dressed silently, feeling dirty and used without really blaming each other. Only when he pushed open the door to the van and the clean, night air spilled in did I speak.

"You asked me what I would see, if the Soul Eater had put me under that spell. What if it had been you?" I asked, and he looked at me, his face grim. "What would you be living, if it were you under the spell?"

"Fire," he said without hesitation, and my heart twisted at the thought of the girl in the desert. "I would remember fire."

22

Do-Over

A good, long walk always helped Max clear his head, but for some reason, wandering the streets with the Soul Eater's goons in town seemed like a bad idea. He'd headed downstairs to the shop, remembering belatedly that Bella was there. So he sat on the steps in the misting rain, paralyzed by the maelstrom of thoughts whirling around his head.

How could she? He'd just finished drugging Nathan for the night when Carrie and Cyrus had stumbled in, clothes disarrayed, post-sex guilt written over both their faces. It was bad enough that Carrie had brought that bastard into Nathan's house, but sleeping with him? After what he'd done? The very thought of it made Max feel used. Betrayed.

Oh, other words were hot on the heels of that one. Words like *conned* and *slut* and *bitch*. Then, more forgiving words. *Stressed. Hurting. Confused.* He forced those resolutely away. He didn't want to rationalize her behavior. The cold, hard fact of it was Carrie had fucked her old sire while the new one lay practically dying in their bed, trapped in his nightmares.

Fine, it wasn't their bed, per se. Nathan and Carrie hadn't

really committed to each other, aside from the blood tie. But in Max's opinion, that was commitment enough.

Even if he wasn't practically dying—that had been an exaggeration, and Max hated to exaggerate—Nathan was still out of commission. Every second, Nathan relived the worst night of his life, a night whose horror Cyrus had taken part in.

Max was a smart man. He could fool himself with anger for only so long before it would inevitably desert him. When it did, he would have to face the real reason her betrayal bothered him so much.

It mirrored his own.

A light drizzle made the pavement wet. He ducked his head and brushed his palms over his hair, slicking it back from his face with the rain. It would be morning way too soon. He should be seeking shelter. But if he went upstairs, Carrie was there, either waiting for Nathan to get better so she could dump him, or waiting for him to die so she wouldn't have to, and downstairs was Bella.

And temptation. God forbid Max forget that one.

Whether from a natural attraction or the revulsion between them, Bella made him painfully aware of his body. She made his blood vibrate in his veins just by speaking. His cock got hard at the sight of her. The memory of her taste and smell tormented him. Even her weird, canine habits seemed sexy in a disturbing way. He hadn't slept the last two days because she was too damn there.

In that time, he'd barely thought of Marcus.

He had no right to forget. Hell, he had no right to have to remind himself that his own stupid actions had gotten his sire killed. The image of the girl with the sweet smile and cold eyes flashed through his brain. As always, the parade of what-ifs followed. What if he'd resisted the ridiculous urge to meet her again? What if he'd told Marcus about her before things had gotten out of hand?

No, he knew why he hadn't. Marcus would have told him to end it, whether he'd known the girl's true identity or not. Marcus had loved Max fiercely and far too protectively.

If only Max had realized she'd been an assassin. The signs should have been obvious, if he hadn't been so horny and stupid and young and in love. But now he knew better. Love didn't get you anything, and it was more trouble than it was worth. Not that he loved Bella, or the bitch that had killed his sire. It just seemed better to nip the notion in the bud before things went any further.

With the air growing warm despite the drifting rain, he chose Bella, and stepped into the bookshop.

She'd taken to the place the way only a truly strange person could. It had good "energy," she'd claimed. Max had explained that the pipes had broken earlier in the year; the good energy was probably the lingering mildew smell. Yet another example of how different they were. He could squirrel it away in the back of his mind, with the others he'd been squirreling away for days now as ammunition against his attraction to her.

When he opened the door, the bells announced his intrusion, and she looked up. Her eyes narrowed and her body tensed in the split second before she recognized him and smiled.

Her smile was amazing, but then, nothing about Bella was less than incredible. The way she moved, as though she were aware of every muscle in her body at every moment. The way she kept her expression maddeningly neutral, so there was no hope of discerning what was going on in her mind.

She's too good for you, anyway, he decided. Then, firmly, to soothe his reality-bruised ego, *No, not too good. Too complicated.*

"You are all wet." How did she manage to make such a simple statement sound like a proposition?

The accent, probably. "I was taking a walk," he lied, hating himself for lying to her. "Thinking."

"Oh?" She turned back to the counter, where an odd assortment of candles, bottles and herbs lay in neat piles. She lifted a notebook and frowned at the page. "No. You were outside the door. I could smell you."

"I don't love you," he blurted. *Very smooth, Harrison.*

She looked up, clearly startled, and it gave him some satisfaction to see that he could shake her cool demeanor. "Good."

"Oh, whatever. I just broke your heart, lady. You know, and I know it." He tossed his hands up in a gesture of total defeat. "Otherwise you wouldn't be pulling all this 'I don't want a relationship' bullshit."

Slowly, as though he were a rabid dog about to attack—great analogy, Harrison—she set her notebook aside. "I meant all of that. And although you repeatedly assure me I am wrong, I am still afraid you do not understand."

"A lot of women have said a lot of things, trying to tie me down, babe. You're not the first to play hard to get." The moment the words left his mouth, he had the distinct feeling he'd made a complete ass of himself. "You're not playing, are you?"

"And yet you did not believe me the first one hundred times I said it." She laughed softly. "I am not trying to trick you or trap you. I like you. You are funny and good in bed. But there honestly is not room in my life for a relationship."

"Mine, either," he agreed emphatically. If this was the outcome he wanted, why did it feel as if he was losing a very important game in the final quarter?

With a roll of her eyes, she went back to her inventory. "No, you are tied up in your own obligations."

"Why did you say it like that?" He went to the counter and pulled himself up to sit on the end.

"Count these," she instructed, handing him a neatly tied bundle of candles. "There should be seven."

He didn't bother to look at them before tossing them aside. "You think I'm not too busy with other things for a relationship?"

With a heavy sigh, she braced her arms against the counter and hung her head. "Do you forget I have animal instincts? Do you think I cannot sense what you are feeling when you are inside of me?"

Her blunt words drew graphic pictures in his brain. "I know that when we're… I know I feel nothing from you."

"You are holding on to guilt I cannot fathom. Whoever you lost, you cared for them very much. But the only thing standing between you and another love is your unwillingness to let the past die." She didn't answer his accusation.

He rarely let himself get angry. It seemed the last few days he'd found compelling reasons to allow that part of him to slide. "Why don't I feel anything from you?"

"Because there is nothing to feel." The words came quickly, as though they were rehearsed.

Or used often.

Cold fury coiled in his gut. He jumped down and faced her, his hands balled to fists in his sides. As long as his nails bit into his palms, as long as that pain kept him aware of his body, he wouldn't be tempted to take his anger out on her physically. "Was this all a trick?"

"What?" Confusion crossed her face.

"You know what!" His disgust and pain overwhelmed him, forcing bitter laughter from his chest. "You're playing with me, trying to get me to fall for you so you can get some sick pleasure from rejecting me. How many men have you done this to?"

"None!"

Were those tears in her eyes? They were a nice touch. "Right. This isn't some sick game you play to get your kicks. You came on to me on a whim. I can't believe I fell for it."

"It was not a trick!" She folded her arms across her chest. No, not folded, wrapped, as though hugging herself for support or comfort. "You were the only one."

The air in the shop felt tight, as though the oxygen had been sucked out of it. Max swallowed. "What?"

"You were the only one. Ever." She looked away. "I have been so stupid."

There must have been a gas leak somewhere in the shop that was making him dizzy. "That's impossible. You said—"

"Before I was a liar. Now everything I have ever said is true?" She cried openly now, a sight he'd never imagined he would see. "Decide for me which it is, because it is not fair to change the rules!"

"Why didn't you tell me? I would have…" He wouldn't have. That's what he would have done. Virgins weren't for him. He liked an experienced girl, a girl who didn't need to be coddled, a girl he could—

God, he was going to hell.

"The rules are different for my people. We must pretend to be human in a world where our culture is constantly attacked as being old-fashioned. This, casual sex, it is not the kind of thing a werewolf does. But I am to pretend I am a normal human female? Perhaps, if I were, things would be less complicated." She smiled sadly, a tear sliding down her face. "Werewolves mate for life. I could not…experience what I did with you with another of my kind without grave commitment. I wanted to pretend, for just a minute, with you, that I am a normal human female. I do not know why I chose you. It was not a trick. I thought, from your reputation at the Movement, that you were a man who would go to bed with a woman and think nothing of it. We would both be safe. But I do like you, even if there is no chance we could be anything more than a happy memory in a month's time."

Women's tears were a weakness Max couldn't stand. He reached out and pulled her in, reveling in the warmth and life of her.

She was the sensible one. Of course they had no future. He was little more than a glorified corpse. She was a cursed dog person. What kind of life could they have, besides one of complications?

It was all a pretty fantasy. How could he be offended, when she'd used him to build something so beautiful in her mind?

He touched his lips to her forehead, intending only comfort. His body, dead though it might be, wasn't satisfied with a tender moment, and soon he was kissing her without any idea how he'd gotten to that point.

"The ritual," she mumbled against his lips, turning her face slightly away from his.

"We've got time," he promised. The clock on the wall chimed 6:00 a.m. "It's probably too late for me to make it back upstairs, anyway."

"So I should take pity and have sex with you?" Her smile curved against his.

"No." He lifted his head and gazed down at her. Had there ever been any clue to her innocence in her face? Something hidden there he might have noticed if he hadn't let her looks and hard demeanor fool him? "Let's pretend we've never done this before."

She seemed hesitant. "What do you mean?"

He brushed a wisp of sleek, black hair from her face. "Let me do this right. If I'd had any idea I wouldn't have been so…"

"Advanced?"

He didn't want her to think he was laughing at her, but he couldn't hold his amusement back, either. "That's one way of putting it." He felt the smile die on his lips as he stroked the side of her face with his thumb. "I could have made it better for you."

"It was good. Not great." The Bella he remembered was back, her mysterious expression teasing him. "We will try it your way. I will do anything once. Or twice."

Max wanted to believe he'd found some peace of mind by confronting her, but as he sank into her on their makeshift bed of discarded clothes, he knew he'd only lost himself more.

23

Fear and Loathing

I was waiting in the living room with Cyrus when the sun went down and Max and Bella returned from the bookshop. I hadn't gotten much sleep. I'm sure I didn't look any better than they did, though I hoped my expression wasn't quite so grim as theirs were when they came through the door. I noted the way they gripped each other's hands, and for a terrifying moment, I thought the worst had come to pass.

"Oh my God," Cyrus whispered beside me. "There's no hope then, is there?"

Max frowned. "Why the hell would you say something like that?"

I found my voice, buried under layers of potential grief. "Because you look like something horrible has happened."

"Nothing horrible has happened. In fact, I came up with a way to cure Nathan." Bella gently pulled her hands from Max's grasp. "But it is not ideal."

"By not ideal, she means it will definitely work, but it's crazy. And you'll probably go along with it. At least, if you're any kind of fledgling you will." Max stood and paced behind the couch, but offered no further comment.

"Does someone want to tell me what I'm supposed to be going along with?" I stood and moved away from Cyrus, too aware of his nearness. I knew Max and Bella had noticed it, as well.

So did Cyrus, apparently. He went to the other side of the room entirely, leaning on a bookcase to put as much space between us as he could.

"The Dark Night of the Soul only works if someone has a shameful memory or a regret," Bella began, looking to Max as though inviting him to jump in anytime. "Max told me you knew better than any of us what that memory would be."

Cyrus scrubbed a hand over his face, appearing wearier than I'd ever seen him. But I wouldn't excuse him from hearing what I had to say.

"I got a fly-on-the-wall view of the night Nathan was turned." I focused on Bella's clear, unprejudiced eyes. If I looked at Cyrus and saw his remorse, or at Max and saw his anger, I wouldn't be able to continue. "Cyrus showed me, by combining his blood and Nathan's. Nathan had taken his wife, Marianne, to see the Soul Eater, thinking he was some kind of faith healer."

I recounted the whole tale in the graphic details I'd seen, and the back story I'd heard from Nathan himself. Marianne had been young and beautiful once, until cancer had ravaged her body and left Nathan with precious few options to save her. He'd taken his weak and emaciated wife to Brazil on the word of a doctor who'd recommended Jacob Seymour as a faith healer. Nathan couldn't have known, but the Soul Eater had set a trap for them on the night of the Vampire New Year, a trap Cyrus had helped plan. When they'd arrived, Marianne and Nathan had learned too late the kind of monsters they'd fallen in with. Cyrus had brutally used Nathan in front of his dying wife. I shut my eyes as I recounted his horrified screams and the way he'd pleaded with Cyrus, not to stop for his sake, but to do whatever he wished and only leave Marianne alive.

As I spoke, Cyrus slid to the floor, sobbing openly, and Max glared down at him with hate-filled eyes.

"His father made him do it," I said quietly when it seemed Max would stalk across the room and tear Cyrus limb from limb. "Leave him be."

Still, I held nothing back for Cyrus's sake as I explained to Bella how he had drained Nathan's blood and left him weak for the Soul Eater. "After Jacob turned him, he tormented Nathan. The Soul Eater's blood was already diluted from a year of not feeding, and it wasn't enough for Nathan. But he didn't offer him any hope of relief, and Nathan was helpless. He killed Marianne and fed from her because of the hunger."

Cyrus sat with his arms wrapped around his bent knees, his face down. When he looked up, his eyes were rimmed with red.

He opened his mouth as if to speak, but Max cut him off. "If you talk now, I swear to God I'll rip your fucking head off."

"Max—" I began, but Bella interrupted.

Her voice was stern yet kind, like a mother admonishing her child. "You cannot change the past by killing him."

To my utter astonishment, Max returned to her side, still shooting murderous looks at Cyrus, but seemingly pacified.

Bella looped her arm through his. "Has he confronted Cyrus about this?"

I nodded. "They didn't have a big, tearful reconciliation or anything, but they exchanged angry words."

"And the Soul Eater is controlling him now, so they have an open link." Bella nodded decisively. "It will work."

"That's wonderful," I said, dabbing my moist eyes with

the sleeve of my shirt. "But do you mind cluing me in on what 'it' is?"

"Bella thinks that if Nathan has made peace with himself, the Soul Eater can't use the memory to control him," Max said, the muscles of his jaw ticking as he clenched his teeth.

"He has faced two of the parties involved, but it is the third he really desires closure with," Bella explained patiently. She hesitated, clearly waiting for my light bulb moment before she continued.

"Marianne," I breathed. Of course, Marianne. "But she's dead."

"So was I," Cyrus interjected, his voice thick with recently spent tears. "But here I am."

"You can bring Marianne back?" My stomach clenched in anticipation of her answer. If Marianne lived again, where would that leave me?

I scolded myself silently for my selfishness. What did it matter where my path lay in the scheme of things? I should just be happy Nathan could be with his wife and be happy again. If I could give him happiness, even through my own misery, I should want to. He was my sire. It would be the right thing to do. It wouldn't make up for betraying him with Cyrus. But I'd do it, gladly. He deserved that, at least.

"Not exactly," Bella said, glancing uncertainly to Max. I should have been somewhat grateful for her admission, but what she said next destroyed my relief. "I am not as advanced as some members of my race, but I did have an opportunity to study necromancy during my training with the Movement. I can call Marianne's soul forth from the astral plane for a short time."

"The astral plane, is that where I was when I died?" I asked, a cold chill running up my spine at the thought of the shadowy figures that were probably gliding unseen through the very room we sat in.

She shook her head. "Not unless you died human. The astral plane, or heaven, or the Summerland—whatever you call it—is only for uncorrupted souls. Vampires, anyone who is cursed, goes to an in-between world. Hell, for those who believe in the Judeo-Christian God. Those spirits still exist on this physical plane, but they are separated from the living."

"Limbo?" Max asked, lines creasing his forehead. "I thought the Catholic Church did away with that teaching years ago."

I gave a soft laugh. "Well, the universe must have missed that memo, because I've been there."

The room fell so silent all I could hear was the ticking of the clock in the kitchen. It worried me, that Nathan was so quiet. "What did you give him?"

"He's getting worse. The herbs didn't help him at all. I had to shoot him again with the tranquilizer to keep him from gnawing off his hands to escape." Max winced at his phrasing. "I probably could have spared you that detail and just said I took care of it."

I couldn't stand the thought of Nathan panicking like a trapped animal. He was usually the one who calmed me down, the one who kept things under control. "We've got a stash of drugs in the emergency first aid kit, morphine and merepidine, some Valium, I think. When the tranquilizer wears off, I'll try a pharmaceutical cocktail before you go shooting him again." I chewed my thumbnail and stared at a spot on the carpet as my brain worked furiously over the details of the night.

Marianne. My undeclared rival for Nathan's affection. So far, she was winning, and she didn't even have a pulse. I had no doubt if we used Marianne's soul as bait to pull him back from whatever dark place he'd gone to, it would be for nothing when we had to return her.

"I don't know. Let's say it works, for just a minute or so, and when we send her back to the astral plane, he flips out again. Then what? We'd be back to where we are now. Is this the only way?" I didn't want to sound confrontational, but the tension in the air made me jumpy. I hated having the decision rest solely on me, to the point I almost resented being involved at all. If we'd returned from our lapse in judgement to find they'd already done it— "Sorry we didn't wait for you, but we raised Nathan's dead wife and fixed his possession problem" —I wouldn't have necessarily minded.

"As long as he breaks free, even for a second, the spell is over. The Soul Eater would have to recast it." Bella looked at Cyrus as though expecting him to speak, but he was lost in his own shame, staring blankly ahead through swollen eyelids. "And ultimately, it would be impossible for him to do so, if we can get Nathan to stop feeling guilt over her death."

"That's not going to happen," Max said with a tired sounding laugh. "We guys, we like to hang on to stuff."

I hated that he would use our private conversation to mock me. "Shut up."

"What, I'm just telling it like it is," Max said, but the tone of his voice implied anything but innocence. "Your little friend there raped your sire and forced him to murder his wife, and now he's messed up in the head over it. And you're afraid to fix it because you're afraid that once Nathan has seen Marianne again, he's not going to want you anymore!"

"Shut up," I repeated, the words a hurt whisper.

"Max, you're not helping," Bella snapped.

"Oh, I'm sorry. I didn't realize I was supposed to be a pillar of goddamn strength here while everyone else starts making bad choices!" Max jabbed his finger at his chest so hard it made a thumping noise. "I'm sorry, but it's my turn to fall apart. That's my friend in there, and I've been caring for him, feeding him, cleaning up his puke and his blood and sitting at his side while he freaks out, while she runs around with the bad guy! Only he's not a bad guy anymore, because now he's human. It's bullshit!"

"Max!" Bella shouted, rising to her feet.

He didn't look at her, but glared directly at me. "It's bullshit and you know it, Carrie! Why aren't you jumping at the chance to save Nathan?"

"Because I'm afraid of losing him!" The words tore from my throat in an agonized wail. "You're right, I am afraid of what will happen when he sees Marianne again! I'm afraid of the pain he'll feel when she's taken once more, because I honestly think it will destroy him. And I'm not strong enough to live without him!"

I dropped my head to my hands, and in the next instant, strong arms enfolded me. I knew from the cold radiating from his skin that it was Max.

Another set of hands rested on me, one on my head, the other rubbing my back gently. Bella leaned close to my ear to whisper soothing words in her native tongue. Then, softly, she said, "I need you to be strong for this. What I will ask you to do will be very hard."

I looked up to meet her guileless, golden eyes. I don't remember what I said through my tears, but it must have been something that convinced her of my strength, because she responded, "I need you to be a host for the soul."

Fear knifed through me at the thought of the in-between world and the possibility of being lost forever. "What do you mean, be a host?"

"You will remain in your body," she said quickly, as if she could read my thoughts. "But you will not control it. Most of you will belong to Marianne, for as long as I can keep the spell going. Through you, she can speak to Nathan and hopefully forgive him for what he did to her."

"Hopefully?" Max asked quietly, lifting his face from my hair.

"I will not lie. If Marianne's spirit is angry, if she does not forgive him, I cannot make her. But perhaps just the confrontation will be enough." Bella tried to sound hopeful, but it was clear she had as much doubt as she did optimism.

"I'll do it," I said firmly.

From his corner, Cyrus almost whimpered, "No."

"I have to." I looked to Cyrus, then to Max, and then to Bella, beseeching them silently to understand. "If we don't do this, Nathan is already gone forever. Even if things don't work, I'd rather be able to say we tried everything we could."

There was a moment of silence before Cyrus spoke again. "But my father is still alive. This will never be over. He'll never let it be as long as he needs Nathan's soul to complete his ritual."

Max rubbed a hand over his chin, working the flesh of his face out of shape in a gesture that betrayed his exhaustion. "After we get Nathan tip-top, I'll call the Movement and get a strike team assembled. We'll take the bastard out once and for all. No offense."

Cyrus shook his head. "None taken. I would most definitely like to see someone 'take the bastard out.'"

"So, when do we do this ritual?" Although I was truly supportive of whatever Bella had planned, a part of me prayed for more time. To do what, I wasn't sure. But I wanted to stave off the inevitable.

She rose and retrieved a notebook from the coffee table, flipping pages as she paced before the couch. "I need to gather supplies and do more research, but the spell must be performed by midnight. It is the last night of the waning moon."

She'd said the words as if I'd know what they meant. I stared back at her, clueless. "Which means?"

"The waning phase of the moon is the best time for banishing magic. Minor banishing can be performed at any time, but this..."

"Is not minor," I finished for her. "And if we don't do the ritual tonight?"

"It will be another month before we could successfully perform it." She let the statement hang in the air for a moment before saying, "I will go and make preparations. Please be ready at midnight."

Midnight. Before I could think about it too much, I nodded. "Sounds great."

Damn the consequences, at midnight, Nathan would be reunited with his wife, and I would abandon myself to an uncertain future.

24

First Impressions, Reconciled

Though I was exhausted mentally, I wasn't physically ready for sleep. It was too early in the night. Bella went to the shop to further prepare for the ritual. Max mumbled something about needing time to himself, and left. I don't know where he went, but I hoped it wasn't far. Cyrus remained where he was on the floor. He refused all my attempts to comfort him.

"I just need some time to think, Carrie," he said, brushing my hand away when I laid it on his arm. "It's nothing personal."

I told him I understood, and I did. Still, I didn't want to be alone. If I was alone, I could think, and the only thoughts my mind was particularly interested in were frightening ones of what would happen at midnight.

I showered, letting the water wash away some of my tension, but more importantly the feeling of Cyrus's hands on my body, the smell of him that still clung to me.

What a stupid thing to have done. What misfiring synapse in my brain had convinced me having sex with Cyrus, even just as a "one last time" thing, was a good idea? Had it ever been a good idea before?

I stepped from the shower and toweled off, strenuously

avoiding my reflection in the mirror. Sex should just be off-limits for me. I never made good choices where it was concerned.

All of my clean clothes were still in Nathan's room, but I didn't want to disturb him. At least my duffel bag was still packed from the trip. I went to my bedroom to retrieve some of the more gently used clothes in it.

Cyrus had seemed pretty safely comatose when I'd left him in the living room, so it was a shock to find him in my room, sitting motionless in the dark on my bed.

I pulled my towel tighter around my body, not that it would cover much more. "I didn't know you were in here, I'll—"

"I wish we hadn't done that." When he looked at me, his eyes were filled with tears.

I sat beside him and awkwardly maneuvered my arm around his shoulders while trying not to expose myself. "Yeah, I know what you mean."

He wiped his nose on the back of his hand—a very un-Cyrus thing to do—and shook his head. "No. You have no idea what I mean."

He stood, but there was no place to go in the closet-size space. It was a miracle I'd fitted a bed and a desk in there, let alone two people and a duffel bag. He unzipped the bag and pulled out a shirt and jeans, making a face—I assumed at the smell and not the style. "Put something on."

"You've seen me naked before," I said softly as I pulled the shirt over my head, while he stared resolutely at the wall. "And I do know what you're thinking about."

"Really?" His laugh was short and harsh. "Then tell me, oh wise one, why exactly do I regret our ill-advised tryst?"

"You can turn around now." I shimmied the jeans over my hips as he did. "You're feeling bad because of the girl."

"She has a name." Until he pointed it out, I hadn't noticed my reluctance to use it.

"Because of Mouse." That crazy, jealous part of me that had reared its head in the desert wondered why he'd given her that nickname. "You think you betrayed her."

"Did I?" He leaned over my computer and parted the dusty, never-opened blinds. The window faced the narrow alley behind the building, where he'd left me for dead. It took a moment for the recognition to settle in. When it did, he let the thin, metal blinds snap decisively closed. "I can't betray her. She's dead."

My door stood open a few inches. He moved to it and closed it the rest of the way, then leaned his back against it. "I'm never going to be rid of you."

"Excuse me?" I put my hands on my hips. "What the hell is that supposed to mean?"

His beautiful lips bent in a sad smile. "Don't take it personally. There was a time I would have done anything to keep you. But I'm human now."

"And the people around you aren't," I finished for him.

"I'm never going to get away from this life. The blood and sex and horror. I knew what was going to happen between us. It was just a matter of time. And I knew what it would mean when we did it. I was willingly giving in to that part of me I should be fighting against." He paced the tiny area in front of the bed, no more than three steps, his forefingers pressed in a steeple at his lips. "I could have just killed you in the desert and disappeared."

"There's a cheery thought." I eyed the nail file on the edge of my desk, thinking I could use it as a weapon if he tried to attack me. *You could use yourself. You are a vampire.*

He cleared his throat, actually looking remorseful. "I'm sorry, it's not meant to be insulting, it just is what it is. I could have started over, completely new, and had all the things I wanted the first time I was a man."

"What did you want?" I imagined the Soul Eater's corruption had begun early. The thought Cyrus had, at one time, had wishes and needs of his own seemed impossible.

He knew exactly what I was thinking. "He didn't become so hungry for power until he fell in with his own sire."

"What did you want?" I repeated quietly.

There was a long pause. He was no longer with me, in my room. The faraway look in his eyes suggested he'd removed himself from me by seven centuries. "A peasant knows better than to want more than a reasonable life and an easy death. In my wildest fantasies, I had a home of my own and a real bed. As it was, my first wife had to spend her wedding night on the hard-packed dirt of my family's cottage, with my brothers and father and their wives not a foot from us."

He gave a grim chuckle. "That was how it always was then, there was no help for it. But I was a shiftless dreamer, like my father. That's probably why we managed to tolerate each other for so many long years."

"Did you have any children?" When I'd been his fledgling, he'd dispensed information on a need-to-know basis—namely, what he thought I needed to know. The subject of his family had never come up.

"No. I wanted them. And it wasn't as if I didn't do my husbandly duty by her. I just never got a child on her." The corners of his eyes lifted at the mention of his wife, then fell when he seemed to remember how long ago and unalterable the past was. "She killed herself, after I turned her.

"That's why I didn't want to fall back into this life. This was supposed to be my second chance."

The similarity between his words and Nathan's was jarring.

"It still can be," I insisted, but I wasn't speaking only to him. "You can have anything you want. You just have to get through this."

"The ritual Bella mentioned, it made me think…" His words died on his lips. "It was a foolish thought."

"Tell me." I liked the human Cyrus, and I wanted to encourage him. Maybe it was a comparison exercise. If he could survive all this, I could survive what lay ahead of me. Stranger things had happened.

"If making peace is all Nathan has to do to be well, maybe I should look into it myself." Cyrus laughed. "But, no. I have too much to atone for."

"It wouldn't hurt to try." If anything, it would steer him away from another fall. Despite his pretty words of apology and lament, he was still dangerously unstable. He might want to make amends, but he'd likely fall to evil again like an alcoholic falling off the wagon. As long as he was making a conscious effort to avoid his old ways, I would sleep easier during the day.

"I suppose you're right." He smiled, an expression meant more for himself than for me, and ran a hand through his hair. "Or maybe I'm agreeing out of exhaustion."

I rose and made a sweeping gesture of invitation toward the bed. "Please, make yourself at home. I'm going to sit up with Nathan."

As I turned to leave the room, Cyrus caught my wrist. I let him pull me in. Hooking his normal, human fingers, which seemed so out of place on him under my chin, he tilted my face up. "I wasn't using you."

"I know." I rose on tiptoe and kissed him chastely on the side of the mouth, the way an old friend would.

It wouldn't hurt to let him believe that of himself, that he hadn't merely used me to satisfy some need. But as I sat beside Nathan's sleeping form through the long night, I knew why Cyrus and I had done what we'd done.

We were lonely, and we were punishing ourselves for it.

25

The Heart's Filthy Lesson

I don't know when I fell asleep, but I woke to the gentle touch of Bella's hand on my shoulder. I lifted my head and saw Nathan. He was awake, but clearly drugged. I'd pulled a chair to his bedside just hours before. When I'd finally collapsed from exhaustion, I'd rested my head on the bed next to him. Now, my back ached and a cold sheen of drool coated my cheek. "Good morning."

"We must talk," she said humorlessly. "About the ritual."

I didn't think we'd talk about the weather, but now wasn't the time for sarcastic quips. "Just tell me what I need to do."

She led me to the kitchen, where Max and Cyrus waited. The former handed me a mug of blood and the latter rose to offer me his chair. I waved for him to sit, and turned to Bella. "Okay, give me the gory details."

The basic form of the ritual sounded simple enough. Despite his unreliable state, Bella insisted Nathan not be given another sedative. It would ensure he could become conscious during the ritual and reap the full benefits. But since he was still crazed, Max would stand in for him, a proxy or a magical power of attorney, I supposed, as Nathan wasn't truly able to give his consent. The whole thing seemed oddly democratic for a magic ritual. Of course, my notion of "magic" came from various sensational news reports about witches, and David Copperfield specials. The combination created a strange picture in my mind of Max wearing a hooded robe and waving burning herbs while Bella sawed me in half.

I shook the scene away and tried to concentrate on Bella's instructions. Thankfully, she didn't seem to notice I'd drifted. "You will be fully conscious of what is happening around you, but you will not be able to control your physical or astral bodies. Once you get there, it will be important that you do not panic."

"Get where? Where am I going?" I hadn't realized bilocation or astral travel or any of the other mind-numbingly boring topics that interested Nathan would be involved, and I certainly wasn't prepared to actually *do* any of those things.

Bella hesitated, looking at Max and Cyrus before saying, "You will be going to the night Marianne died."

I waved a dismissive hand in the air and made a plosive sound like a slow leak. "No problem. I've been there before."

"But you didn't see it through her eyes," Cyrus interjected quietly. "Are you sure you can do this? Are you ready to know what it's like to have Nolen kill you?"

Though Cyrus's words sent a shock of horror down my spine, I forced myself to project an illusion of bravery. "Will everyone stop looking like you're preparing for my funeral? I can handle it."

Max looked at Bella, one hand over his mouth as if trying to hold in the words he couldn't help but say. "I think we should slow down and think about this a little more."

"No!" I stamped my foot. "Would everyone stop treating me like I'm so damn fragile? If it's going to fix Nathan, let's get it over with!"

I don't know why it took a total, public hissy fit to kick my compatriots into gear every time a monumental task was ahead of us, but it was starting to get on my nerves. Of course, that wasn't fair of me. They probably weren't as used to harrowing escapes and heart-pounding adventures as I was. It made me feel worldly and a little proud when I looked at it that way, though I would gladly trade it for a few consecutive years of boredom.

Bella explained the rest of the process to me without sensitivity or second-guessing my ability to participate, and for that I was very grateful. The more she talked, the more I doubted, and the last thing I needed was for them to offer me another out clause.

At midnight, Max, Bella and I filed down the hall to the bedroom.

Cyrus hung back, and when I asked him what he would do during the ritual, he shrugged and said, "Take a nap?"

"I did not think it would be wise to include him, considering he was involved in...well." Bella cleared her throat and smoothed her shirtfront, then placed her palm flat against the door. "Are we all ready?"

"Ready as I'll ever be," Max said, rolling his head to one side and cracking his neck. "How about you, Carrie?"

I took a deep breath. I was about to surrender my body completely to a long dead and possibly pissed off ghost-woman, whose husband I had been sleeping with for the past two years. "Let's do it."

Bella pushed open the door and motioned for us to be quiet. Nathan still slept soundly, and I prayed he would continue. We couldn't afford to have anything go wrong.

As she had instructed us to do earlier, Max and I took our places: him at Nathan's bedside, myself kneeling on the floor at the foot of the bed. She walked the perimeter of an irregular circle from one side of the bed to the other, pouring white sand from a clay jug as she did so. The circle broke where it intersected the bed, so she poured the line right over the pillows, as though it were perfectly normal to dump two good handfuls of dirt into someone's bed.

Between the four corners of the room she placed four candles. In the little space left within the circle she paced, fanning the smoke from a burning bushel of herbs with a long, brown feather. Then, in a quiet voice that was much less impressive than the mighty shouts of the wizards in the movies, she said simply, "I consecrate this space, seeking only to do good within it."

Max's skeptical gaze met mine, and I pushed back a twinge of unease. This felt too much like a twee game, something a young hippie girl with a guitar would do to invoke a muse. *She's the only one who's come up with a solution,* I reminded myself sternly.

At each of the candles, she mumbled an incantation asking the spirits of each direction to lend their power to our "circle." When the candles were lit and the circle consecrated, she handed a thick, white candle to Max and another to me.

"Hold his hand," she instructed Max. Then she drew a single quartz point from her pocket and held it over her head. "Badb, Anubis, Hades, Lucifer, Kephas, and all the keepers of the underworld and afterlife in your many names, join us now in this circle."

She brought her arm down in a fast arc, kneeling so the crystal connected with the ground. The candle flames flickered, throwing eerie shadows on the walls. It must have been a trick of the light, but I could have sworn I saw the shape of a jackal's head grow into the shadows of the corner, a raven flicker across the ceiling. My throat went dry. While I'd been busy reassuring everyone I was up to the task at hand, I suppose I hadn't really thought about how serious things were.

This is for Nathan, I reminded myself, looking away from the shadowy shapes that seemed to grow and multiply as we stood helplessly beneath them.

"Bella…" Max's voice was a hoarse whisper in the silence of the room.

But it wasn't silence. A strange, humming tension filled the air, dousing the circle with loud, soundless noise.

Bella raised a hand to motion for quiet, then began to murmur words of thanks to each entity she'd called forth. Badb, a crone goddess. Anubis, a death god. Hades, lord of the dead. Lucifer, God's fallen. Satan, if I remembered my Catholic upbringing correctly. I couldn't see how he would be on our side, if the stories were true. The hair stood up on the back of my neck. I tried to reason with myself that I shouldn't fear the beings she'd invited in. For all intents and purposes, I was dead myself. Still, I couldn't ignore the malevolent cloud that seemed to surround me. I imagined a million fingers of darkness closing around my throat, crushing my windpipe, severing arteries. I imagined Cyrus's claws slitting my throat in the hospital morgue six months earlier. And I wanted to run.

Max appeared uncomfortable, as well. He clenched his shoulders as if he wanted to rub the back of his neck, but couldn't, as both his hands were occupied. Nathan began to stir, one long leg sliding from beneath the sheets to drape over the side of the bed. He mumbled something, his voice gaining volume as his struggles continued. Only when he was thrashing and shouting did I recognize what he said. It was the prayer to the Archangel Michael.

"How are they gonna like that?" Max whispered, as though the deities surrounding us wouldn't be able to hear him.

"He is crazed," Bella reminded Max, or maybe the spirits.

"He does not mean to offend." She raised her voice over Nathan's fervent prayer. "We humbly beg the release of the soul of Marianne Galbraith, soul-bound through the sacrament of marriage to this man."

A chill knife went through my heart at her words. Soul bound. It seemed so much stronger than blood tied. If my heart was destroyed, there would be nothing left binding me to Nathan. Marianne had been gone for years, but her bond with him was still strong enough to control his mind. Strong enough to call her back from the dead.

When it came down to it, my bond with Nathan could decompose. A human soul…that was eternal. I wanted to vomit.

"I need Nathan's consent now," Bella reminded Max.

He sputtered and looked at me, then at his friend writhing in panic on the bed. "Bella, I don't know about this. Carrie doesn't look so good—"

"You are here to give consent on his behalf. That is your only function in this circle. If you cannot do this, you should leave!" Bella snapped. Her eyes were hard and furious, but her hands trembled. She was afraid.

Her fear intensified my own.

Max swallowed and looked to me. I wanted to communicate with him somehow, but I didn't know whether I wanted him to stop this or continue. Something paralyzed me. I wondered if Marianne was already inside of me, if that's why I couldn't think clearly or even move my limbs, or if it was just crippling fear and sadness.

Like a judge's gavel falling after the pronouncement of a sentence, Max cleared his throat and whispered, "Yes."

With a warning noise and a flinty look, Bella stepped forward and lit Max's candle. Then, turning to me, she asked for my permission, as well.

Only now could I find my voice. But when I opened my mouth, I didn't tell them I'd changed my mind, that this wasn't the way. I opened my mouth and issued a calm, "Yes."

And then it was out of my hands. Bella lit my candle, but instead of stepping back to her place, she gripped my wrist and raised the crystal point above her head again. "Keepers of the afterworld, return now the soul of Marianne Galbraith to this circle."

Bella's eyes closed. Her hand burned where it gripped my wrist. Her entire body seemed to vibrate power.

I kept inhaling huge quantities of air, like a drowning person anticipating being claimed by the waves. It would have helped if I could have known what was happening, but this was, conveniently, the part Bella had left out. The air buzzed with even more tension, if that were possible. As Nathan fervently shouted the Lord's Prayer, I sent up one of my own.

When the wait seemed interminable, when it looked as though we had failed, Marianne's soul entered the circle. I could pinpoint the exact moment her spirit arrived. Nathan's madness subsided for a moment, then returned as a fierce panic. His body arched from the bed like the string of a drawn bow, and he screamed, the most pitiable sound of pain and fear I'd ever heard. He was terrified he'd hurt her. I couldn't help but remember the way he'd pinned me to the floor in the shop, threatened me with a chunk of broken glass. He hadn't been afraid to hurt me.

Max was visibly shaken. He clasped Nathan's wrist and turned wide, frightened eyes to Bella. "We have to stop this!"

"Marianne Galbraith," Bella shouted over Nathan's voice. "Take this empty vessel and do with her what you will!"

Before I could wrench away, she pulled me forward and pressed the crystal to my forehead. The splitting pain couldn't have been worse if she'd used an ax. The cool, smooth surface of the stone focused the pain into a thread that wound down my spine, into my torso, branching into my limbs. The thread widened, opening like a telescope until I was filled to bursting. There was no room left for me in my body, and the thing kept growing, crowding me farther and farther back.

My eyes rolled back in my head. The last thing I saw was Max's face as he screamed, but a tremendous roar filled my ears, thundering over him. Then my vision flared silver and I was falling. It was nothing like the gentle, backward suction I'd experienced when my sires had shared their memories with me. That had been mildly disconcerting. This was nothing but pain and horror. And then, I was gone.

Standing before the big, oak double doors, Marianne didn't bother to disguise her observation of the man at her side. *My husband is so handsome. I'm nearly a corpse.*

Nolen gave her a smile and squeezed her hand. She knew the smile. It was not the one that had charmed her when she'd been young and pretty and not aching with every step. Not the one that had made her give into him in the stock room of her father's shop. She hadn't seen that smile for a year now. Not since the last baby wasn't born. Not since she'd begun to fall apart.

No, this was the pity. He would never look at her the way he used to, not even if this "faith healer" did help her.

"Do I really look all right?" Marianne toyed with the heavy chain around her neck. *How many more times will you drag me across the world on my father's money? How many more cures will I be forced to endure before you let me die?*

"You're a vision." He smiled and touched the heavy pendant hanging at her throat. His fingers never touched her flesh. He'd become so good at withholding all but the most sterile of touches. "Although I don't think this suits you. It's a decent sign, though. No one would give away a bauble like this on a whim."

"Unless it's meant to be a rejection gift." The thing was too heavy. Her shoulders ached. What would he do if she collapsed right now and ruined the good impression he hoped to make?

A faith healer. I'd have to have some first. She hadn't told him, but she'd given up believing in God. Every night, when he held her hands and they said their prayers, she recited empty words. She was too angry to speak with the Lord or the Virgin Mother. It was considered holy to share Christ's pain, but on the worst days, when the cancer seemed to be dissolving her very bones with acid claws, she envied him. Christ had only suffered for two days. And it was too cruel to venerate the Blessed Mary. What praise did she deserve? She may have endured the pain of losing a child, but Marianne had lived through that hell five times, and she'd never been able to hold her children. They'd gone to their Golgotha inside of her and ascended into heaven on a rush of blood. The fruit of her own womb was less than holy, the disease that now destroyed her from the inside out.

Nolen believed, though, that God would send them a miracle, that the future hadn't been denied, only delayed. To ease his mind, she acted the part of the pious wretch.

The doors before them opened. Marianne had assumed they'd be meeting with Jacob, Simon and Simon's beautiful young wife, Elsbeth, as they had the two times they'd both been invited to dine at the mansion. Oh, Nolen had been invited far more often than she. Jacob had taken an almost fatherly interest in him, sending invitations that called Nolen away in the evenings, entreating him to leave his diseased wife at home to rest. She did not know what had transpired those nights, but the group assembled around the table now, bored-looking and beautiful, surprised her. Their gazes all held a strange hunger as every pair of eyes examined her. With a sudden, crashing clarity, she realized something was terribly wrong.

There wasn't enough time to bend her intuition into action. Those guests who'd seemed so impressive and imposing a moment before transformed into demons before her eyes. They moved faster than Nolen could and tore her away from him as he tried to shield her.

Marianne's world narrowed to a void of claws and fangs. They cut and tore her flesh, but she welcomed the pain. It felt different than the slow burn of the disease devouring her body. Faster. It would be better this way.

And then she was dying. The thing she'd not been above praying for, even after she'd shunned God, was finally upon her. Vision dimmed, then returned like a tide teasing the shore, but it wasn't disorienting. In fact, it was disappointing when clarity returned, because she wanted to see what was on the other side of the darkness. Wanted to see if she was damned for her lack of faith, or if she'd be proved correct. The prize at the end of the race seemed so very close when it was cruelly yanked from her grasp. Pain exploded in her head as she connected with the floor. The groping hands had dropped her.

They were alone with the one she knew as Simon. Nolen was praying, invoking the aid of Mary and the archangel against the demon that embraced him. Simon's hands caressed her husband like a lover's hands. *Give in to him,* she urged wordlessly. *It will be finished sooner. He will grow bored and kill you.*

But Simon didn't intend to rape Nolen. His violation was more sinister. He was gentle and tender, aiming to seduce his unwilling partner into consent, forcing Nolen's body to betray him, making him take pleasure from unforgivable sin.

This is my fault. The sadness and regret gripped her then. A fine time to get her heart back, when she lay dying a world away from home.

Simon took his time with Nolen, and Marianne, too weak to turn away, watched her husband weep as he came, trembling, beneath Simon's mouth and hands, even as the monster penetrated him.

"Your husband did this to you, Marianne." Simon groaned, hissing in pleasure as his hips pumped against Nolen's body. "Tell him how you hate him for it."

She found her voice then, to whisper a weak, "No." For all she resented him, she loved him. She would not have him die thinking she'd scorned him. Her gaze lingered for a moment on Nolen's fingers clutching futilely at the slick marble floor. Then her eyes slipped closed.

As life continued to slowly ebb from her, Marianne wished for the strength to cry for joy. They would both be gone soon, abused to death at the hands of these monsters. And then she would be free of a worse pain, the pain of walking the earth in a faltering shell, watching her husband transform her from an object of desire to an untouchable martyr in his eyes.

I have to tell Nathan. The thought startled me, namely because it had rung through my mind so clearly. I remembered instantly where I was, what was happening, but where had I been? I'd seen it all, but it hadn't been me. Marianne had truly taken me over. Now, as she died in the past, her control slipped.

Concentrating hard, I felt myself detach a little from her flickering soul. Silvery threads of pain webbed around my mind, but I fought past them. It was like running through knee-deep water, but the struggle was worth it. I heard sounds from my own time, namely, Bella commanding me to stop fighting.

"It's important." I didn't recognize my own voice. Was it

Marianne's voice, or was I Marianne, not recognizing Carrie's voice? Where did she end? Where did I begin?

"I want to die." I felt the carpet beneath my knees now, at the same time the marble cooled my back. I shook my head. No, I shook Marianne's head, and she shook mine. I stood on weak legs, while she delighted in my strong ones. "Nolen, I want to die."

We were alone in the Soul Eater's dining room. Nathan's bed was here, now, with him handcuffed to it, but there was no sign of the madness that had tormented him.

I touched him with Marianne's hand and felt his skin beneath my own in another time and place. His throat convulsed as he swallowed, and a tear slid from his eye. "I don't want to kill you again. I kill you every time I close my eyes."

"You can't keep me here any longer. It hurts to be in this body." Was I talking, or was she? Did she speak of the past or what she lived through now? "It hurt, Nolen. You answered my prayers. You blessed me with death. Now let me go."

In the past, a phantom hand closed over Marianne's wrist as she reached to unlock her husband. In the present, Max restrained my arm as I tried to release Nathan.

"Let her," Bella urged, and then Nathan was free.

He fought it at first, trying to hold back the madness. "I can't. I want to stay with you."

"You can't have me." I heard my voice speaking in a gentle Scottish lilt. Marianne's voice. "Kill me. For the last time. Set us both free."

When his arms closed around her body, they crushed the air from my lungs. When his fangs pierced my neck, she cried his name.

Tears poured down his face as he drank my blood. That was a part of me I couldn't mistake. Though Marianne's soul was in my body and I was crowded into her mind, my blood was his. It mocked him as he tasted it, but in it he saw the truth and acceptance. No matter how many times he replayed this night, he couldn't change what he'd done to her, and now he knew he shouldn't wish to.

As I died, so did Marianne, but I had a much farther distance to fall. Her eyes closed on Cyrus's ballroom, her second death as much a relief as the first one, and this time she died with her husband's name on her lips.

When her soul left my body I came jarringly awake, shivering uncontrollably from the blood Nathan had consumed from me. His mouth was still fastened to my neck, but he no longer drank. He kissed my wounded flesh and sobbed, crushing me to the rock-hard wall of his chest.

"She is gone," I heard Bella say, and for a terrifying minute I thought she meant me.

Nathan lifted his head. His eyes met mine and went cold. My heart froze with them. It wasn't me he wanted. For a moment, he'd held his wife in his arms again. Now that she was gone, only I remained.

To his credit, he masked his grief quickly, trying to smile for me as though his tears were joyous at being reunited with me. "Did I hurt you?"

More than you know. I didn't trust myself to answer him. Instead, I eased from his grip and tried to stand.

When I collapsed, Max caught me. Instead of easy encouragement, he whispered, "I'm sorry I let you do this."

He'd seen it, I realized. He'd seen Nathan's disappointment when he'd found it was me in his arms.

"I will tend to Nathan. You make sure she is all right," Bella instructed.

I wanted to lash out at her, to slap her or scream at her, but

I didn't have the strength and it wasn't her fault, anyway. All she had promised was to cure Nathan of his possession, and her ritual had done just that. She'd never guaranteed I wouldn't be left empty and hurt in the process.

Max scooped me up in his arms and carried me to the living room, to lay me on the couch. "We'll get some blood into you."

"You could let the rest out of me." I tried to make it sound like a joke, but the horror of the suggestion was evident on his face.

"Don't say that. You're just upheaved by this whole ordeal." He squeezed my hand. "I can't imagine what you went through."

"Hell." The word bubbled from my throat and I coughed, spilling wetness onto my lips. When I wiped it away, I saw it was blood.

Max went to the kitchen and made a horrible racket. He hurried as if my life depended on it, and in a way, I guess I was in danger. But it would take a lot more to kill me.

The floorboards in the hall creaked, and Nathan emerged from the shadows. His hair was still matted, his skin marred by the sigils he'd carved there in a time that seemed ages ago. But he was at least half-dressed, in a pair of jeans, and the feral anger was gone from his eyes.

The tenderness on his face broke my heart as he stroked my hair back from my forehead with the palm of his hand. "Thank you."

"It was no problem. It's still not the worst dinner party I've been to." I smiled weakly, but inside I fell apart. I loved him enough to sacrifice myself, at least symbolically, on the altar of his pain. While he clearly appreciated my devotion, it was impossible for me to forget who he really wanted. I could never be Marianne. And he wasn't ready to give her up.

And he knew that I knew. He lifted my hand in his and kissed my palm. "Don't hate me."

"I can't hate you. I love you too much." I didn't fight my tears any longer. He held me, but it was a bittersweet comfort. Touching him, smelling him, feeling the pull of the blood tie between us wasn't enough. It would never be enough.

At least now we were acknowledging it.

The floorboards in the hall creaked again as Bella joined us. Max stepped out of the kitchen and Nathan reluctantly let me go.

I wiped my eyes as I watched Bella ease open the door to my bedroom. After what I'd seen and been through, I didn't have the strength to explain why Cyrus was in our apartment. "Maybe now isn't a good time to—"

"Where is he?" Bella stepped into my room. The light clicked on and she swore.

"Who is she talking about?" Nathan asked as I used his shoulder for support to stand.

Before she returned with the folded paper in her hand, I knew where he'd gone. There was no time to shield Nathan's feelings. "She's talking about Cyrus. And I know where he's heading."

26

Desperation

"How could you have let him into my house?" Nathan raged for the third time since our conversation had started.

I took another hurried swig of blood as Max wrenched open the weapons closet. Inside, axes and crossbows and sharpened stakes were stockpiled, as though we were planning a return trip to the dark ages. Not that I'd be good for much. I was still weak from blood loss, but I was quickly recovering. Whatever strength I had to contribute, I would.

"I've already explained. He's human now, and we needed to keep him away from the Soul Eater." Nathan was never one to see the big picture if it didn't suit him. I added that to the list of reasons I should be glad we would never have a relationship other than the blood we shared.

Max lifted an ax and handed it to me. My arm fell under the weight and the mug in my other hand tipped, sloshing blood onto the floor. Max steadied me and took the ax back. "You're not going, you're still too weak. Bella and I will handle this."

"Nobody is going," Nathan growled, pulling the weapon from Max.

I was of the opinion somebody was going to get killed if they didn't stop recklessly tossing axes around, but I didn't inter-ject that into the conversation.

"You've been off the scene for the duration of this mess, so maybe you don't understand what will happen if the Soul Eater gets ahold of Cyrus." Max got right in Nathan's face, so they were almost nose-to-nose. "We don't have a lot of time to go over it in detail again, so I'll give you a brief summary. Bad things will go down if the Soul Eater eats tonight!"

Nathan dropped the ax to the floor with a clatter. "I don't care, you're not going to go save him!"

"No one is going to be eaten tonight," Bella pointed out, not helping our cause at all. "We do not know that the Soul Eater is here in this town. His minions are, though, and I agree with Max and Carrie that we should not let Cyrus fall into their hands."

"Cyrus is reformed," I said, hating the way I sounded—as if I was defending his past actions. "But his father is persua-sive. If he turns him—"

"I'll kill him and I'll make damn sure he stays dead this time." Nathan spun away. "This isn't a discussion. I'm telling you, we are not going to save him."

"Fine. I won't save him. I'll go kill the Soul Eater's guys." Max grabbed a larger ax from the closet and hefted it over his shoulder as if daring Nathan to make a wrong move.

"Are you nuts?" Macho posturing was one thing, but the Soul Eater had a seemingly endless retinue of guards. Even Max, Bella and I together couldn't take out all of them. "We'll get killed."

"It is not a bad idea," Bella said, shocking us all into silence. "If you kill them, it might draw the Soul Eater out of hiding. Then we can exterminate him."

Nathan stood in front of the door. "I'm not going to let you risk it. Any of you."

"I don't want Cyrus to die!" I blurted, unthinking. The loss of blood had made me stupid with fatigue. *Choose your words carefully,* a cautious inner voice urged. *You might not think things could get worse between the two of you, but you proved tonight that they always can.*

I looked at Nathan, but offered no apology. "I don't want Cyrus to die. He doesn't deserve it. You killed Marianne! He didn't. And as for the other crimes he's committed, he's served his penance!" It felt good to vent some of my hurt on him, though I knew I should feel ashamed for taking such a low road.

"Every time I go to sleep in the morning I remember holding your dead body in the alley." Nathan pounded his chest with his fist. "Every time I close my eyes, I see Marianne's face—"

"That's your fault, not his!" I laughed at the ridiculousness of it, a bitter, explosive sound. "Didn't you learn anything tonight? Marianne was dead long before you walked into that trap. It's not Cyrus you hate, or even the Soul Eater. It's you! You hate yourself because you couldn't save her, not from the cancer, not from yourself. And you hate that she wanted to leave you! But it's over, Nathan. It's over!"

He nodded, his expression tight and pained. "You're right, Carrie. It is over."

Brushing past me, he growled at Max, "Do whatever the hell you want. I'm not one of your Movement flunkies anymore. Look to someone else for help."

The bedroom door slammed so loudly I thought it would break off the hinges. It was so final, so jarring, I couldn't even feel sadness.

With grim resolve, I turned to Max and Bella. "Let's go find Cyrus."

"We can't just leave Nathan here. If the Soul Eater's guys came, he'd be alone," Max began.

I cut him off. "Nathan has lived in the same building for fifteen years now, worked the same business for just as long. If the Soul Eater really wanted him, really wanted any of us, he would have sent someone by now. Don't you see? He's just playing with us, waiting to drive us out! And I, for one, am sick of being toyed with!"

"She is right," Bella said softly. "The Soul Eater knows where we all are, every moment. Why else did he have men here in town?"

"So, what, he's not really all that into becoming a god? Have you all lost your damn minds?" Max punched the wall with the side of his fist and the plaster crumbled beneath his hand. "You're not thinking straight!"

"And you are not listening!" Bella placed a palm on his shoulder and it actually appeared to calm him some. "Whatever the Soul Eater's plans are, he is not finished with your friend. He will not come for him tonight."

"You sound so sure of that," Max said bitterly. He shrugged off her hand and headed through the door, slamming it behind him.

But she was sure of it, I realized as we stood silently staring at each other. Whatever the Soul Eater wanted with Nathan, it wasn't to kill him, yet.

And that terrified me more than anything we'd encountered so far.

Bella was able to locate Cyrus with stunning speed. I couldn't help but find it comical that she did so with her head stuck out the window, sniffing the air as we drove around the neighborhood where they'd first found evidence of the Soul Eater's minions.

"Left!" she shouted, and Max jerked the steering wheel, nearly pulling the car onto two wheels as we careened down the street.

"This is a one-way!" I shrieked, grabbing at the dashboard.

"I'll honk the horn so they hear me coming," Max said through clenched teeth. "It's not like anyone's going to be out jogging at this—"

"Watch out!" Bella screamed as a figure stumbled into the road.

Max hit the brake and we spun sideways, skidding to a halt just feet from the man, who stared at us from blackened, swollen eyes.

Thick, bloody trails dripped from a wound at his hairline. His garments were torn, not so much clothing him as draping over him.

"It's Cyrus." I pushed open the door and raced to his side.

He looked at me with a dazed expression, as if he didn't recognize me.

I took his hand in mine, careful not to startle him. He was warm, thank God. I took it as a sign he had not been turned again.

"Cyrus, it's me. Carrie. Do you know who I am?" I tried to lead him to the car as I spoke, but he resisted.

"He wants me dead. He sent them…. He really wants me dead." His words sounded as though they came from an empty room. I'd heard the phrase "I was beside myself" before, but I'd never actually seen someone in the literal state. Wherever he was, Cyrus was not in his mind at the moment.

"Come on, let's get someplace safe." I looked in the direction he'd come from. The Soul Eater's men would be searching for him any second now.

Max had exited the car, but stayed safely behind it, watching us from a distance. When I called for his aid, he sprinted to my side.

"The vampires you two found. Do you remember which place it was?" I asked Max quietly. The huge houses looked sinister in the early morning darkness, like horror movie sets crammed onto one lot.

"Not far from here. They could be anywhere." At an imploring look from me, Max nodded, his face grim. "I'll check it out."

"Be careful," Bella called after him as he jogged down the street. She approached us as though Cyrus were a wild animal I'd tamed, and she didn't want him to run away.

"He needs medical attention. Can you get him to the hospital? I'd take him, but there aren't many more hours until sunup and I don't want to get trapped in the ER." Or spotted by anyone I knew. It would make an awkward reunion with my former co-workers if I shambled in with a confused, bleeding man.

"Can you not care for him?" Bella wasn't challenging me, but I could tell she didn't want to be left alone with Cyrus. After what I'd seen in the circle, I wouldn't have wanted to, either.

"I can't take him back to the apartment. Nathan." I shrugged helplessly. Cyrus had been through enough tonight, and he wasn't likely to live through much more.

Neither could I. The entire business of the ritual and its aftermath had been too confusing. I needed time to myself, to think. Another cruel irony, as days ago I'd been going mad from the isolation of living on the road.

Max reappeared, brushing dried leaves from his hair. He'd apparently jumped—or tumbled through—a few hedges.

"Did you find them?" I called, jogging toward him.

"The vampires? Gone. I saw a couple combing a park over that way, but I don't think they saw me. So I went back to the house, tripped the burglar alarm. The cops will be here soon, and that'll hopefully set them running."

As if on cue, the distant, tinny sound of approaching sirens wafted to us on the breeze. I sighed heavily. "Damn."

"Let's go," Max urged. We ran back to the car, where, with Bella's help, I coaxed Cyrus into the backseat. We all piled in and Max drove the few short blocks to the nearest emergency room. He stopped to let Bella and Cyrus out at the ambulance bay, and I gave her strict instructions not to let them admit him to the psychiatric ward.

I didn't know if Bella would bring him back to the apartment, or if he'd just wander off on his own. My throat stuck shut at the thought of Cyrus, homeless and with no money, trying to survive in the mortal world.

Or worse, going back to Dahlia.

Still, he wasn't coherent enough for a tender goodbye and there wasn't time for Max and I to waste. The sun would rise soon and we had to get back.

It was a short drive, but somehow we managed to hit every red light on the way. Max and I sat in uncomfortable silence for a long while, until he turned down the radio and said, "You could come back to Chicago with me."

"What do you mean?" I asked nonchalantly, as though he hadn't just witnessed a perfectly awful non-breakup between Nathan and I.

He shrugged. "You've been through a lot. Hell, if I'd done what you just did for somebody, and they treated me the way Nathan acted toward you, I'd need some cool-off time."

"Cool-off time. Sounds like a good idea." I tried to force a smile. "Chicago, huh?"

"Yeah. I have a pretty sweet condo overlooking Grant Park." He chuckled. "Not my style, but it was a gift. I don't spend much time there. The place probably needs a good airing out."

I chewed my lip as I rolled the thought around in my mind. Chicago wasn't far. I could make it in a night's drive if I desperately wanted to get back to Nathan. And it would get me out of town, so I could have a clearer perspective on things. Max wouldn't hover over me the way Nathan would. But then again...

"I don't know. I have to think about it." I worried what

Nathan would do alone, if the Soul Eater tried another spell. I also had no clue where Nathan would go. It wasn't as if he could stay in town, whether the Soul Eater was just toying with him or not. Plus, I didn't want to screw up any romantic plans Bella and Max might have. "And you'll want to ask Bella, of course."

"I don't think Bella is going to be a problem. We're probably not going to see each other again after this." His tone was light, but I could tell from the way his smile faltered he would be bothered by losing her.

"I'm sorry." I didn't have enough energy to come up with a better comfort for him. "Maybe it will be fun, then. Two rejected vampires, living it up in the big city."

"There are some awesome blues clubs," he said, gently wheedling.

"I don't want to leave Nathan behind. I'm worried about him." I paused, the stupid hope swelling up beneath my ribs. "Let me talk to him. See if we can't work it all out."

"It's an open invitation," Max said, turning his eyes back to the road. "It's a big place. I'm always glad to have company. Makes it seem less empty."

"That's not why you don't go back often." I studied the way his expression changed from friendly to defensive. "You lived there with your sire."

He nodded. "It's a funny thing, when you've got a blood tie with someone and it suddenly goes away. Things you'd never thought would bother you really…hurt."

"I know." I laughed bitterly. "Believe me. I know."

Bella returned to the apartment later that morning. Nathan was asleep, so when she asked if she should let Cyrus come up, I told her it would be all right.

We sat across from each other at the kitchen table while he

stared bleakly at the peanut butter and jelly sandwich I'd made for him. His eyes were still ringed with ugly, purple bruises, but the blood had been washed from his face. Small lines of stitches stood out against his pale skin at his hairline and chin. His lips were swollen and split, and he winced when he tried to drink the soda I offered him.

"What were you thinking?" I didn't mean to sound so angry, but he'd frightened me. I remembered all the times my mother, upon reclaiming me from a department store security guard or the yard of a playmate she wasn't acquainted with, would grip my arms and sternly admonish that I'd scared her to death. When we'd discovered Cyrus missing, I finally understood what she'd been feeling.

He didn't look up. "I don't know. I wanted to die. But when I got there, and my father's guards… When they were beating me, I realized I didn't want to die. I fought them so hard. But when I got away, it was back. This pain. I don't know what it is, Carrie. It makes me want to die. But when I get close… Why does this hurt so much?"

"It's guilt. It's supposed to hurt."

I looked up sharply. Nathan stood at the kitchen door, his eyes hard and his face lined with fatigue. Below the sleeves of his T-shirt I saw the dark lines of scabbed-over sigils.

I didn't know what to do. If Nathan went after Cyrus now, there was no way I'd be able to intervene. Nathan was too strong and a way better fighter than me. Besides, I hadn't been able to make myself fight him when he'd been pinning me to the floor in the bookshop.

Cyrus's posture straightened a little, but no discernable emotions crossed his face. "Nolen."

Nathan's gaze met mine, but there was no clue in his eyes as to what he would do. "Run into your father?"

Shaking his head, Cyrus lifted the soda can to his mouth. "His goons."

"I can't say I'm not sorry you didn't get killed." Nathan leaned against the doorframe, frowning down at him.

Cyrus swallowed and wiped his mouth. "I can understand that."

Nathan pushed off the wall and came to stand in front of us. "What, no snide comment? You're not going to lord your intellectual superiority over me?"

"Stop it," I warned.

"Let him." Cyrus sighed, weary and resigned. Nathan opened his mouth, but no words came out. Looking up at him, Cyrus smiled sadly. "It's my gift to you, Nolen. Spew whatever bile you need to."

"Why? So you can feel better about what you did to Marianne?" His voice choked with emotion and tears, I could barely understand Nathan's words. "What you did to me?"

"I was sick." Cyrus wasn't apologizing, but he wasn't justifying, either. "I did far worse to many others."

"Like Ziggy?" Nathan laughed bitterly. "I could rip you to pieces right now."

"I wish you would. It would be much easier for me." Cyrus rested his forehead on the table and covered the back of his head with his hands.

Nathan's own hands clenched to fists at his sides. He looked at me, his eyes rimmed red and teary, then back at Cyrus. He cleared his throat and scrubbed a hand over his face. "I'm not here to make things easier for you. And I'm not going to forgive you. I want you to remember all the fucked up things you've done. I want them to torment you at night. But do me a favor."

Lifting his head, Cyrus met Nathan's eyes. "What?"

"If you ever feel like committing suicide again, let me do

the honors." Nathan turned around and left the kitchen without a word to me.

Cyrus and I sat in stunned silence for a long time. Nathan hadn't forgiven him, but he'd made some sort of progress by not simply tearing him to shreds right there.

"What will you do now?" I asked when Cyrus finally moved.

He picked up the sandwich and took a bite, chewing thoughtfully before he answered. "No one has notified Mouse's next of kin yet, I assume."

"The police are bound to have found her..." I trailed off. It seemed dirty to refer to someone he'd loved as "remains."

He nodded. "I know. But they wouldn't be able to find her family. She was very much like me in the respect she didn't have many earthly ties."

When he finished his sandwich, he stood, wordlessly moving toward the door. Sadness, more keen than I'd felt when I'd stood before him and plunged a knife through his heart, gripped me. I clenched my hands into fists to stop them from trembling, and felt the wetness of blood where my nails bit into my skin.

"If you ever need anything, money or—" I began, but he cut me off.

"I'm not going to ask you for anything. You've done enough." He laid his palm against my cheek and cupped my jaw, his gaze moving over my face as though he was committing my features to memory.

I put my arms around him and buried my face against his shoulder. "I don't want you to disappear."

He smoothed my hair and kissed my forehead, but he didn't promise anything. The funny thing about a broken heart, you don't remember how it feels until it happens again. Even if it happens twice in one day.

"Goodbye, Carrie." He kissed my cheek and stepped away, then turned and walked out the door.

Despite all he'd put me through over the course of our acquaintance, I sat on the floor and cried for him.

27

Loose Ends

Max had nearly loaded the Trans-Am with his meager luggage when Bella came to say goodbye. She stood on the sidewalk and watched him pretend to be busy with something in the open hatchback.

"When does your plane leave?" he asked without looking at her.

"The charter is in Africa. I will be here for two more days." She stepped closer to him. "Your friend has graciously offered me his living room couch."

The thought of Bella staying with Nathan alone twisted his guts. Not that he thought Nathan would try anything. In his logical mind, he knew his friend was too busted up over what had happened to him to even think about romance. But the caveman part of Max wanted to challenge Nathan to some sort of wrestling match to protect his woman.

"If you are ever in Spain, you know where to find me," she said, clearly attempting humor.

Against his better judgment, and the litany of "Max Harrison does not beg" that had been chanting through his brain through the long, sleepless day, he said, "Stay with me."

"You know I cannot." Her response came easily, as if she'd known the question would come and it had only been a matter of time.

That made Max hate himself even more for asking. "I don't know that. We have something together, Bella."

She flinched at the sound of her own name. "You are confusing sex with love."

"Really?" He laughed angrily. "I'm glad you know what I'm feeling. Can I get a number to your direct line, in case I'm ever stuck in a rut and can't decide if I'm angry or just need to take a shit?"

"Do not be crude! Just because you have let yourself believe some fantasy that I would, what, melt into your arms? Forsake my life as I know it to be with you?" She folded her arms across her chest. "I told you from the beginning what this was. It was purely physical."

"That's a lie!" He slammed the hatch and stalked toward the apartment. If they didn't get on the road soon, they might not make it before sunup. But he couldn't leave Bella like this. If she was going to walk out of his life forever, she was going to damn well listen to what he had to say.

When he turned back to her, she still stared at him with her expressionless gold eyes. It was as if she stayed merely to pacify him. As if she would indulge him by taking whatever verbal abuse he wanted to dish out so she could walk away guilt free.

He wouldn't give her the satisfaction. "I like you, Bella. Not because of the sex, not because of the circumstances we were thrown into. I like you. Just you, without all that other shit cluttering things up."

Tears rose in her eyes, but she didn't display any other outward show of emotion.

"And you know we could have something together, if you were willing to try." His voice was hoarse, and he swallowed, trying to force away the ragged sound.

She closed her eyes. "I am sorry I hurt you."

"That makes two of us." He walked away from her, not wanting this to be the memory of her he carried, but his pain had tainted the good memories with a bitter edge.

So he left her standing on the sidewalk and went inside. He just hoped she would stay away until he left. No sense in ruining a perfectly angry goodbye with social awkwardness.

"You'll call?" Nathan stood by as I packed, trying to seem worried and supportive, but radiating anger and relief. His emotions were too strong. There was no sense in him trying to hide them from me; I would have felt them anyway.

I'd expected him to argue with me when I proposed the idea of leaving and letting us take a break from each other. The speed with which he'd agreed stung me to the core.

I grabbed another handful of underwear—probably more than I needed, but it gave my hands something to do—and jammed it into my bag. On the road again. "As soon as I get in. Are you sure you'll be all right?"

"I'll be fine. I just need time." He grabbed my watch off the nightstand and handed it to me.

Snatching it from him, I turned back to my packing. "Time away from me."

"You need time away from me, too." He fell silent then, and I bit my lip to keep from picking up the thread of the argument. I zipped the bag closed. Whatever I might have forgotten, I could pick up in Chicago. Right now, I just wanted to get away. "You should leave," I tried for the last time. He hadn't been swayed before, so I don't know why I bothered. "It's not safe for you here. Max says Dahlia is still in town. The Soul Eater had men here. You've got to get out."

"No," he said quietly, shaking his head. "He's taken everything else away from me. He's not driving me out of my home."

"You're so stubborn." He'd be willing to get himself killed just to prove to his sire he wasn't afraid? We definitely had different ideas of winning.

"I know you don't understand." His expression softened. "I've been here fifteen years, Carric. It's the first thing I've ever truly owned. This apartment has everything I've ever cared about. This is where Ziggy grew up. This is where I met you. This is our home."

A small sob escaped my throat, and I covered my mouth.

His hand closed over my wrist. "You're still my fledgling. Don't forget that."

"How could I?" The tide of hurt in me surged, spilling cold tears onto my cheeks. He tried to take me into his arms, but I shook my head vehemently and jerked the strap of my bag over my shoulder. "I'm your fledgling. But that's not enough for me, Nathan."

I didn't kiss him goodbye. That would have confused things in my heart, the traitorous organ that frequently won over my mind. If I kissed him, I would tell him that I wanted to stay. I'd convince myself it was worth the pain of staying by his side, knowing he would never choose me over the woman he could never have again. And I was afraid of believing that.

Max waited for me at the car. He pasted on his stock, carefree face for me. "Ready?"

I nodded. "As I'll ever be."

Tossing my bag into the back, I climbed into the passenger seat. Low-riding cars made me motion sick. This was going to be a long five hours.

"You think he's going to be okay? I mean, what about the Soul Eater's guys? They could still—" he began.

I shook my head decisively. "He wants to stay. To stand his ground. And he wants me to go."

"He'll come to his senses," Max said with forced certainty. "You wait and see."

Wait and see. The question was, for how much longer?

How long should Nathan wait for his sire to call him back home? The Soul Eater wouldn't give up after just one setback. No, he would regroup and come back stronger than before. And the Movement wouldn't give up looking for Nathan. And he would be waiting for them both, too brave to leave, too weak to protect himself against the threat.

How long would I wait before my sire was dead, my heart broken all over again? How long until the next calamity would come to test me?

Wait and see. We could start now, stay on guard, be ready for whatever came at us. Or we could lie down and wait and see.

From where I sat, we didn't have that kind of time.

Prologue

"Hey, Baker! You give her the seven o'clock meds yet?"

Don swung his legs from where they'd been propped on his desk, knocking the tower of empty soda cans from the corner. "Yes. I did. At seven o'clock. Check the sheet."

Leave it to Sanjay to ask a stupid question. Don shook his head and watched the new guy retrieve the clipboard from the hook beside the door and frown at the words. How he'd managed to live a hundred years was a mystery. Hell, Don had had close scrapes in his own twenty years as a vampire, more in his thirty years previous. How someone with double the lifespan could wander around in a state of constant confusion—

"Then this doesn't make any sense." Sanjay flipped the pages on the clipboard, but it was clear from the rapidity of his movements that he couldn't possibly be reading the charts. "It doesn't make any sense!"

"What doesn't make sense?" Always with the drama, these Movement scientists. "I gave her the meds."

Sanjay's worried brown eyes flicked up to meet Don's

gaze. "I know you did. I see it on the chart. But her brain activity is...too active. It's like she hasn't been sedated at all."

"Chill out, chill out. There's a reasonable explanation for this." The newly assigned guys tended to flip out over every little thing, but he'd seen what had happened the last time the Oracle had shrugged her meds. "I'll feed her another tranquilizer, keep her as down as I can until morning report. Dr. Jacobson will take it from there."

The meds for the Oracle were fed to her hourly, through a tube that first dissolved the sedative in warm blood, then injected the whole solution through intravenous lines. It was so simple. And Don hated it.

It wasn't as if he wanted glory, like the big guys got. Or danger, like the assassins. He just wanted a job that a trained ape couldn't pull off.

Hell, at least he could watch TV between doses. And the faster he got things under control, the faster he could get back to *Will and Grace* reruns.

Slipping the key to the tank room from his pocket, he slid it through the card reader. The door popped open with a hiss, and he stepped inside. It was ten degrees colder than the rest of the facility—the monitoring equipment and various pumps and containment machinery would overheat if it wasn't—and the rest of the facility was damn cold. Don rubbed his hands together and blew into them. It smelled like blood in this room, but it always did.

"Honey, I'm home," he called to the slumped figure of the lab assistant asleep at his workstation. Couldn't handle the day shift.

The blinding white of the room was interrupted on one

side by the huge, dark wall of glass. Inside, floating suspended in gallons and gallons of blood, was the Oracle. Sleeping, if the tranquillizer had worked. He popped two tablets out of the meds cabinet and strolled to the access tube, whistling while he did so, hoping to annoy the lab tech enough that he'd wake up. "I hope they check the security tape in the morning. Because you will be so busted."

The meds pump was attached to the wall just below where the glass ended. He knelt down and pulled the drawer open. The tablets would be inserted into a clear, glass chamber inside and dissolved. The whole process was a pain in the ass, but she'd built up a resistance to nearly all the sedatives that came in liquid form. Don didn't know why it worked, but he was glad it did. The bitch could get downright nasty when she woke up.

He blinked in disbelief at what he saw in the drawer. The glass chamber, which should have been empty to receive the next dose, was still filled with blood. Hands trembling, he followed the intravenous line to where it disappeared into the wall. A chunk of a pill that hadn't dissolved was stuck in the thin plastic tube, forcing the flow of the blood to a trickle.

The Oracle had never gotten her sedative.

The rest happened too fast. He looked up, saw the face of the Oracle, pale and inquisitive, touching the glass. Her eyes were open. He staggered back, screaming, tripped over his own feet and landed at those of the sleeping lab assistant. Blood pooled around the guy's sneakers. He wasn't just sleeping.

Don opened his mouth to scream, but the sound never made it out.

ENDLESS LIFE. ETERNAL STRUGGLE. JUST ANOTHER DAY IN THE AFTERLIFE.

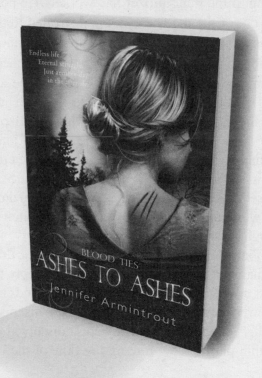

The Voluntary Vampire Extinction Movement headquarters are destroyed. Now the Oracle wants to turn the world into a vampire's paradise, even if it means helping the Soul Eater become a god.

An ancient vampire, a blood-sucking near deity and my currently human former sire Cyrus thrown into the mix. I say bring it on. May the best monster win.

www.mirabooks.co.uk